RECLAMATION

R. COLLINS

Copyright © 2024 by R. Collins

All rights reserved.

No part of this publication may be reproduced, distributed, or transmitted in any form or by any means, including photocopying, recording, or other electronic or mechanical methods, without the prior written permission of the publisher, except as permitted by U.S. copyright law. For permission requests, contact: rcollinsauthorofficial@gmail.com.

The story, all names, characters, and incidents portrayed in this production are fictitious. No identification with actual persons (living or deceased), places, buildings, and products is intended or should be inferred.

Designations used by companies to distinguish their products are often claimed as trademarks. All brand names and product names used in this book and on its cover are trade names, service marks, trademarks and registered trademarks of their respective owners. The publishers and the book are not associated with any product or vendor mentioned in this book. None of the companies referenced within the book have endorsed the book.

First edition 2024

To James and Genevieve for bringing my romance writing journey to life. XX

CONTENT WARNING

Book includes mature content not suitable for all audiences. Please see my website if you would like the content warning. If you have triggers or concerns, please view before proceeding.

My website: rcollinsauthor.com

Also by R. Collins

*Scan this code to view my
book titles in order.*

PROLOGUE

Jude Jackson James Barlow - 1933

I hope to God no one can see or smell the blood all over my jacket. When I told Wyatt and Frank my ideas for the Council Entry Ceremony, they assured me that they understood my vision. I should've known not to trust them with something so serious. Things only get done correctly when I do them myself.

When my brothers, cousins, and I formed our society last year and made our blood pact, we decided that once our first son turned eighteen, we'd have our first Council Entry Ceremony. My little Maxwell is only two, so it'll be a while before that happens, but I don't like to procrastinate, and as the Head Father of this society, I want to establish a solid system early.

I run my hands through my messy black hair while I wait for the last person to arrive. Normally, Rebecca helps me style it in the mornings, but she refused me help today because she's angry with me. It's her twenty-first birthday today, and it also happens to be mine. I was supposed to take her to her favorite spot for breakfast, but I had to cancel last minute for this meeting.

Things are going well in our society. Our perfume business is growing exponentially, which was the main reason for this meeting today. However, we also need assistance with our meat distribution as well as our home products, and we also want to bring in someone to help with societal operations. Currently, I manage everything, but with Max's high energy and another little one on the way, I'm burning the candle at both ends.

I met with a manufacturer a few days ago at our flagship perfume location in Newburgh, and he offered to collaborate with me and take on our brand with the goal to open fifty new locations within the next year. I agreed, and he introduced me to two other men. One will be working on our home products with the goal to eventually create food products as well, and the other will take over our meat manufacturing. The last man is the only one I haven't met yet, and he's fifteen minutes late which means the blood on my suit jacket should be dry at this point.

I didn't plan on showing up to this meeting with blood on my clothing. It happened completely by accident.

While describing my vision to Wyatt and Frank, I explained to them how I wanted all new council members baptized in animal blood. If they made it through the Council Entry Ceremony, they'd be cleansed at the end with water. We agreed that we should run through the ceremony a few times with a few of us to test out the ritual, and we decided on my home being the testing location. Little did I know it would result in me having a shit start to my morning.

In addition to this meeting today, I promised the guys we'd perform our trial Council Entry Ceremony afterward which is another reason I had to cancel breakfast with Rebecca.

If my wife wasn't addicted to my irresistible body, I'm pretty sure she'd try and leave me. But I'd never let that happen, and I'm working on a provision right now to ensure that if any of our wives ever try and leave us, they'll go through hell first. And I'm setting the provision in place for our son's wives too.

I woke up on time and was ready for the day, but things went downhill when I went out to my garage to get in my car. It was dark, and I couldn't see very well. As I neared my vehicle handle, my foot slipped on something slick, and I fell on my ass. Fortunately, my pants didn't get wet, but my hands did. And what I had on them was not what I expected.

Without thinking, I dragged my hands over my coat, and then my nose was hit with the most overwhelming smell. Once I opened the garage, I saw the disaster of what had happened. Wyatt and Frank placed a tub of blood beside my car, and before they sat it on the ground, they managed to splatter it everywhere. The worst part was that there wasn't nearly enough blood for what I had planned, and I was frustrated that they didn't follow my instructions. Not to mention, my clothes were soiled, and I didn't have enough time to wash and change, so I got in my car reeking of pig guts to come to this meeting today.

After twenty minutes, the door opens and the final man walks through. He's tall and muscular like me, but he's got a silly mustache and glasses that are too big for his face. He sits down at the table across from me, and Bill, the first one I met, stands and begins the meeting.

"Thank you, Jude, for meeting with us on such short notice. As you can imagine, it's hard to get all of us in the same room at once, and today worked best for all of us." He takes off his burgundy blazer and looks toward the other men. "I met Jude here recently at his perfume shop. We got to talking, and as I let you all know previously, he is the leader of his society known as The Wild White Orchids.

"The Wild White Orchids are a group of men interested in maintaining a sense of... order within their family while contributing to our economy. As we're all aware, right now is not a good time for our economy, but Jude and his family have been surviving the storm, and things are only going to get better from here." He looks toward me and I stand.

Glancing down at my blazer, the blood isn't visible on my dark jacket under the lighting in this room, and that gives me all the confidence I need.

"Thank you all for meeting with me today. As Bill stated, my family and I are doing quite well right now, and we're looking to expand and improve things for everyone. You men helping us means more jobs for more people and that means more food on the table for our friends and families. Each of you will be overseeing operations for our businesses apart from you." I gesture to the man across from me. "What's your name, sir?"

"Shane."

"Nice to meet you, Shane. You'll be overseeing our societal operations. Currently, that's what I do, but I need a little help right now. You'll all report to me, but when I'm no longer Head Father, the next Head Father will report to all of you or your successors, that is. You'll be a private group that only the Head Father and potentially his right hand will know about. You all will be known as The Caledonia Council."

Caledonia orchids are Rebecca's favorite. I came up with the name on the way over here.

Shane nods his head. "That sounds excellent. I'm looking forward to working with you, Jude. I'll also make sure all of our operations remain private. No one needs to know about the society unless they're in it or are a friend of it."

"I agree."

He leans back in his chair. "What all will I be overseeing?"

I sit down in my seat. "To start, you'll help me keep track of budgeting and spending. Make sure no one's going over their limit, and report all expenses to me. I want to know where every single penny goes. I want all men employed, and you'll make sure they're working and that they are working one of the pre-approved jobs I've chosen. You'll help me keep an eye on everyone and make sure that the tenets are being followed, and if you notice anyone breaking any rules, you'll report the infraction to me immediately. You're my eyes and ears, Shane."

"Absolutely, Father."

Bill smiles. "Jude is the Head Father, and I am right under him. Jim, you'll manage the home products and food expansion, and you'll be under me. Derek, you're over meat, and you'll be under Jim. And Shane will report directly to Jude, but when Jude is unavailable, he'll report to Jim."

I clear my throat. "That's fine with me. But I don't see myself being unavailable. I need to always know what's going on."

Bill winks. "Of course. We won't let you down, Jude."

"Good. I'm counting on all of you. You'll lead your sectors quietly and privately, and I'll follow up on who your direct reports are later today."

Bill stands. "We're looking forward to it, Father. May The Wild White Orchids always prosper."

Chapter One

JAMES

May The Wild White Orchids always prosper. God, I hate that fucking phrase. It's at the bottom of nearly every page in my Head Father's Text, and every time I see it, I want to slam my head against my desk.

I'm sitting in my new office downstairs while Gen is upstairs sleeping, and my mother is in her guest room with my baby.

My little girl was born a week ago, and I'm fucking miserable. I should be happy. Happier than I've ever been. And I want to be, but I can't. And I can't because I'm scared shitless about meeting with The Caledonia Council, and I'm worried out of my mind about my Gen.

After Zahara was born, Gen was fine. At least I thought she was. I placed our baby girl in her arms, and she held her while I looked over my cryptic note from The Caledonia Council. I had to tell her what was on it right away, and once I made sure no one was lurking outside the hospital, we agreed that we'd worry about the note later.

I stayed glued to my girl's side day and night. She was tired after giving birth, and when she tried to breastfeed, Zahara wouldn't latch, and she got really upset and cried for nearly an hour. At first, I thought Gen was just overwhelmed after her traumatic experience, but when I got my girls home, I knew something was wrong.

Genevieve has been home from the hospital for four days, and she's cried every single day. She wakes up crying, and she goes to bed crying. And I don't know what the fuck to do.

When I called Meredith and told her what was going on, she told me the one thing I never expected her to say. Something I never even considered and something I wouldn't wish on anyone. My wife has postpartum depression. I don't know shit about postpartum depression. Or at least I didn't an hour ago. But when I got off the phone with Meredith half an hour ago, I decided that I was going to learn everything there is to know about it and help my wife feel like herself again.

I want Gen to feel like herself again because I love her. And I'm terrified. I've never seen her so distraught. I know she's dealt with depression before, but this is my first time being aware of her depression as it's happening. I don't think her depression has ever been quite like this.

When Zahara didn't latch at first, Gen tried again a few times, but by the third time, we decided it'd be best for her to start pumping. I help her pump every few hours, and apart from that, she won't let me anywhere near her. My own wife won't even let me shower with her. I try to hold her at night in bed, and she won't even let me touch her. And she hardly touches our baby.

As much as my mother's overbearing nature annoys me, I asked her to stay with Gen and me for the foreseeable future. I'm hoping I can send her home soon, but I know I need help. I have to take care of Gen and Zahara, and I can't take care of them both on my own right now. I could if I had to, but it's easier with my mom's help. And since Gen won't let me help her dress and shower, my mother helps her.

I know my mother and my wife are close, but being shut out hurts. I hate that Gen won't let me be there for her. It makes me feel like I did when she first moved in, but worse. Not only is she distant with me, but she treats me like a stranger. Since our baby was born, I've kissed Gen a total of three times. Three. She won't let me close enough to her for more.

How did this happen? How did I end up here? Everything in my life was good. Really good. And now it feels like I'm losing everything. The only thing I've gained is a baby who I can hardly stand to see without wondering if I've made a mistake. I feel so horrible for feeling that way, but I've wondered what it would be like if we didn't have a baby. I know my wife wouldn't be depressed right now.

I love my daughter. Deep down I know I do. I love her smile and her eyes and how she looks like the perfect blend of me and the love of my life. But right now, my favorite person in the universe is sadder than she's ever been, and my entire world is gray as a result.

Chapter Two
GENEVIEVE

I sit in bed staring out the window. Zahara was born eight days ago, and I feel . . . nothing. I mean, I feel something, but it's not overwhelming love for my baby.

I wipe the tears from under my eyes that I shed fifteen minutes ago. Or was it twenty? I don't know when my crying ends or when it begins. All I know is that it happens on and off all day long, and I can't believe I have any tears left.

I remember the day I woke up at the hospital. I heard James come into the room when I was getting ready to open my eyes. And I heard our baby. I was nervous about James becoming a father due to his aversion to kids. But

I had nothing to be worried about. He's incredible at it. James is way better at being a dad than I am at being a mom.

Fuck. I wish I would stop fucking crying.

When I first held Zahara, I swear I was happy. I thanked God that I survived and that my baby was okay. And I couldn't believe how much she looked like me and James.

I can't remember when I first started feeling this way, but I started feeling sad pretty quickly. I thought the sadness would pass. That I'd feel better within a day or so. But I've been home for days, and I'm miserable.

Zahara is in her crib sleeping. It's next to my side of the bed on the right, a few feet away. James sleeps on the left side of the bed by the door. He swears Zahara sleeps better when she's closer to me, but I think he's just trying to be nice. I know he wants me to hold her more than I do, but I can't. I want to hold her, but I'm scared. Scared that I might drop her or hurt her.

James got up early this morning to feed her, and he went downstairs to the office afterward. He was there for hours yesterday, and he's been there a few hours so far today. And we've barely spoken to each other the past few days.

I don't know what to say to James. I want to talk to him and spend time with him like everything's alright, but everything isn't alright, and I can't pretend to be happy when I'm upset. I want to tell him how I feel, but when I open my mouth to speak, nothing comes out. I freeze up and can't find the words to say. I can't figure out how to tell him how broken I feel. How empty I am inside.

How do I tell my husband that I don't feel connected to our baby? I don't want anything bad to happen to her, but I don't feel attached to her like I'm supposed to. How do I tell him that I look in the mirror and hate what I see? All I see are my stretch marks and my swollen belly and the scar beneath it. None of my clothes fit like they used to, and I'm most comfortable wearing a blanket wrapped around myself to cover up everything.

How do I explain that I feel damaged? Like something is terribly wrong with me. I've been depressed before and dealt with anxiety, but I've never felt like this. I'm sad every second of every day. I don't want to eat or move or do anything. But I have to eat and I have to move and I have to pump because I'm no longer living for myself anymore. I'm a mother whether I want to be or not.

James sits on the bed bottle feeding Zahara. I remember when I first tried to feed her, and she wouldn't latch. I felt like a failure. I still do. But I'm honestly glad she prefers bottle feeding. I guess I'm not a complete failure if she still wants my milk at all. And bottles allow James to feed her which helps me sleep. And as natural as breastfeeding is, I don't know if I can handle connecting with Zahara that way right now. I feel like a stranger in my own body and don't want anyone interacting with it, including my husband.

He glances at me watching him and takes a breath. "There's something I want to talk to you about. Something that I think might help you feel better."

The past few times James and I have talked since I've been back home, he's hinted at me getting help. He hasn't elaborated on what help I should get, but I'm figuring he's going to be more direct now.

I pull the hood of my sweatshirt over my head and lean up against my large black pillow. "And what's that?"

He sighs and cradles Zahara tighter against his navy blue T-shirt. "I think—maybe it would be helpful for you to talk to someone."

Therapy. He wants me to go to therapy. He's the one who needs fucking therapy.

"I don't want to go to therapy, James."

"Would you at least consider it?"

"Will *you* consider it?"

He puts the half-empty bottle on his nightstand and wraps Zahara's favorite pink blanket around her. "At the very least, I think you should at least try and take something. There are . . . medications for things like this."

"Medications for things like what, James?"

"Postpartum depression. I called Meredith and she already wrote you a prescription."

I've been home for barely a week, and James has already diagnosed me. I know he's not wrong, but it doesn't feel good being analyzed and knowing he's discussing things behind my back. I can't explain how I really feel to James. I don't know how to form the words. But what would be the point anyway? He's already decided he knows what's best for me, and he got me a prescription for medication without even speaking to me first.

"I'm not taking it."

He places Zahara on her nursing pillow on the bed. "You're taking the medication, Genevieve."

"You are not my boss, James."

He covers his face and groans. "You're right, Gen. I'm not. But I'm your husband, and you're going to do what I tell you to do."

I stand up off the bed and stare down at him. "Like hell I am."

"Gen, sit—"

"No. You don't get to barge in here and boss me around like I'm a child. You have a child, and her name's Zahara. If you want me to do something, you can ask me, but don't ever order me to do anything."

Silence fills the room as he glares at me. He looks at me like he can't stand to be around me. It makes my eyes burn with tears that threaten to fall.

As if he can read my mind, his gaze softens. "Genevieve, I love you. I love you, and I'm freaked out right now. I just want you to feel better. That's all I'm trying to do. I just want to help you feel better."

He holds out his hand, and I sit on the bed next to him. I can't hold his hand. I want to, but I don't want to at the same time. I don't want him to coddle me. I just want him to stop treating me like there's something wrong with me. I already know there is, and having him walk on eggshells around me isn't helping me feel like myself.

"I don't want to take the medication or go to therapy, James. I can't."

He pulls Zahara into his lap and rubs her back. She giggles and spits up a little milk on his gray sweatpants.

"I understand that you don't want to do those things, baby. But you—we need to try something. We need to actively work on helping you feel better."

"I pull my knees to my chest and close my eyes. "Give me a few weeks. Five more weeks. If I'm not better by then, I'll try the medication and go to therapy."

He nods his head and plays with Zahara's black curls. "Okay. Deal. And what do you plan on doing in the meantime to get better?"

"I don't know."

Zahara laughs while James scoops her up and walks her back to her crib, making his way over to my side of the bed. He kisses her cheeks and places her in gingerly. Seeing him with her makes me jealous. I'm not jealous of her but jealous of how easy things are for him. He acts as if he's been a father for years. I thought I'd be teaching him. But I feel like he needs to teach me.

I slide to the center of the bed to sit, and he sits down beside me, taking my seat and sitting between me and Zahara.

He pulls my right hand into his, and I let him. Without warning, the tears I've been holding back rush over. I feel his lips on my forehead.

"You're not going to feel like this forever, Gen. I promise."

I choke out my words. "I don't know what to do."

He grips my hand tighter and sits for nearly a minute before responding. "If I come up with another suggestion, will you promise to give it a try?"

I don't want to make a promise to something without knowing what it is, but I don't want to fight with James right now. I don't have it in me, and I know it wouldn't make either of us feel good.

I wipe my face with the sleeve of my oversized hoodie. "I promise I'll give it a try."

He lets out a breath. "Good." When his hand slips away from mine, he stands up, and I think he's headed back downstairs. But he stands at the edge of the bed staring down at me.

"What?"

He bites his lip. "I want to kiss you, Gen. Will you let me do that?"

James and I have only kissed three times since Zahara was born. We kissed at the hospital shortly after Zahara was born, we kissed the day I got home, and we kissed the day after that. He's tried to kiss me in the mornings and before bed, but I haven't let him. And I feel like shit for it.

It's not that I don't want James. He's the only man I want and I love him more than anything. But I don't feel like I love myself right now, and it's hard to imagine him loving me in the state that I'm in.

However, I do miss his kisses, and I don't want him to think that I don't love him.

"You can kiss me."

His chocolate-brown eyes sparkle, and he holds out his hands for me to take. I place mine in his, and he helps me off the bed to stand in front of him.

One of my favorite things about James is that it's so easy for him to lead. He cups my cheeks with his soft hands and brings his forehead to mine. Another thing about James is that he's a romantic. He can't just give me a peck and move on. He has to draw out every moment.

My heart rate quickens when he brushes his thumbs against my neck. I close my eyes and let him hold me while he softly presses his lips against mine. Our past three kisses have been quick, but this one is a step further.

I part my lips and let him slide his tongue into my mouth. I forgot how much I missed this. He wraps his arms around my waist and I brush my nose up against his. I go to pull away, but he squeezes me tightly and bites my bottom lip before letting me go. I want to give him more, but I can't. Literally and figuratively. I won't be cleared for sex for at least another five weeks, and I'm too upset to do anything more than what we're doing right now. When he senses I've reached my limit, he takes my hands in his and kisses my knuckles.

"I love you with all my heart, Gen."

I squeeze his hands tightly and fight off the new wave of tears threatening to flow. "I love you too."

Chapter Three

JAMES

I sit downstairs in the office with a sleepy Zahara swaddled against my chest in a long blue cloth. While I was down here earlier, I watched some video on baby-wearing and learned how to wrap her up like a burrito and attach her to me like an accessory. Although I want Gen to spend more time with her, I don't want her to feel like I'm pressuring her to be around Zahara if she can't, so I try and keep her with me as much as possible. However, I'm very busy, and I can't tuck her under my arm like a football, so this'll have to do.

She makes little noises here and there while she sleeps, but for the most part, she stays quiet and sleeps for hours.

I thank the Lord daily that I was blessed with a good baby because if Zahara was a terror, I don't know how I'd survive.

I hear a knock on the door, and there's only one person I want to see behind it. I try to put on a smile when I open it and it's not my favorite person in the world. It's my mother.

"Hey."

She gives me a half-smile, but her eyes are puffy and red and there are bags under them. "Hey, baby. Can I come in?"

I gesture to the large brown leather couch in the middle of the room. "Sure. Go ahead."

The office at our new house is smaller than our old one, but it's still exceptionally grand. The floors match the ones in the hall and throughout the house apart from the bedrooms which all have carpet.

There's a large Persian rug in the center of the room, and on top of it is the couch. The office is positioned in the layout of the home where there's a window with a view of the front of the house as well as a window with a view of the back. My old study had floor-to-ceiling bookshelves, but we have a separate small library in this house right next to our small home gym, so there's only one shelf and it's practically empty right now.

The walls are deep mahogany like the floors, and my desk is made of black granite while Gen's is made of white marble. She hasn't used it yet, but I'm looking forward to us spending time together down here. My favorite part of the room is the forest green curtains that I installed for Gen. She loves little pops of green around the house, and anytime I see a way to add it somewhere, I do.

My mother looks out one of the windows and a single tear streams down her face. In addition to having a sad wife, I also have a sad mother. The one person I know who always seems to be holding it together is falling apart because she's lost the love of her life. Or at least she thinks she has. And I think he's gone too.

I don't want my mother to be upset, but I can't deal with her emotions right now. I have to be strong for everyone, and usually, I can be, but right now, I'm exhausted.

"Was there something you needed?"

She wipes her face and stares at me with her bright green eyes. "I wanted to ask if you've heard anything else from the council."

Since I received the note requesting a meeting from The Caledonia Council, I've been on edge. I didn't know if they'd show up at the hospital while we were there or follow us home, but I figured they'd want to meet rather soon. However, I haven't heard from them since Zahara's birth, so I have no idea when or where this meeting will be taking place.

I take off my reading glasses and rub my newborn's back while she snores. "I haven't. When I do, I'll let you know."

She sighs and closes her eyes. "Do not provoke them, James."

"We're way past that. I've already provoked them."

Her low chuckle reverberates around the room. "I mean, don't fuck things up more than you have already."

I feel a pang in my chest at her sharp words. My mother has been upset with me before, but she's never cursed at me.

I fight the urge to raise my voice. "Don't worry, Mother. I'll be the good little society boy you raised me to be and follow all of the idiotic rules that are in place."

She shakes her head and scoffs. "Do you plan on meeting with them?"

"Do I have a choice in the matter?"

She plants her feet on the ground and smooths out her white sweater dress. "Not really. But you've proven that you'll do whatever you want, James."

I wonder who I learned that from.

"Yes. I will meet with them. As soon as I get the time and place, I'll get it done and get it over with."

She leans back against a green pillow, and I think she's done with the conversation, but she stands up and starts pacing around the room.

"Let them lead the meeting. Don't offer anything, and don't agree to anything there."

As old as I am, my mother still feels the need to tell me what to do.

"Why shouldn't I?"

She walks up to stand in front of my desk with her arms crossed. "Because you're not prepared to make a deal, James. Not on your own. After the meeting, come back home, tell me what they say, and we'll figure this out together. Maybe everything can be brushed under the rug and we can continue as normal."

I stand up and tower over her. "Nothing has ever been normal. Do you think our life is normal? Because if you do, you're mistaken. And if you're referring to me staying in this society as Head Father and raising my daughter in it, you can take that shit and shove it."

She lets out an exasperated sigh and waves her arms around her. "You can't just get everything you want, James! I'll admit—you haven't had the easiest life, but you were spoiled."

I roll my eyes and she shakes her head.

"I'm serious, James. You grew up in a mansion, had access to whatever you wanted, and you still do. You're richer than anyone you've known outside of this family, and you can't just be happy and grateful and stay out of trouble."

I wrap my arms around my baby and go to stand in front of one of the windows. "You're right. I can't be happy because I have everything I could ever want or need, but I can't enjoy it. I'm a prisoner in this society. We all are. And I don't want this lifestyle. I never did. I don't want this for me, for Genevieve, or Zahara. I want our goddamn freedom, and I'll do anything to get it."

Her shoulders drop, and she starts to really cry. "That's what I'm most afraid of."

I'm headed out to my car wearing my favorite black suit and silk shirt. Instead of wearing a pair of black dress shoes, I'm wearing my burgundy wingtip oxfords which are Gen's favorite. Whenever I look at these shoes, I think of her, and I need a piece of her with me for what I'm doing tonight.

We should've had our weekly council meeting already, but I postponed it since my wife just gave birth. With no right-hand man, there was no one to dispute me, so we're all meeting tonight.

It's nearly the end of August, but it's still hot out, so I'm not wearing my cloak. I'm not wearing my cloak because of the temperature but also because the very sight of it reminds me of the most grim and beautiful day of my life. Zahara's birthday.

There was a private funeral for Jace and Hades yesterday. Closed caskets for them both. Damion and Simon set up the arrangements, and I didn't attend. I wanted to, but when Angel and Drake reached out and told me how upset Gabriella and Ella were, I knew going would be a terrible idea. I'm wary about seeing everyone at the council meeting tonight, but I have both of my guns on me and my knife, and I have Obsidian and Orion prepared to take out anyone who tries to harm me.

My mother thinks I'm so independent and unrestrained, but I'm still just a fucking cog in this society. I bend the rules, but at the end of the day, I still do what I'm told. That's why I'm headed out on a Wednesday night to conduct a meeting for this godforsaken secret society when I should be upstairs holding my girls and winding down before bed. But when I go to grab my car door handle and see a white note tucked under it, I know my night is about to change.

I grab the white envelope and tear it open while my heart pounds. My eyes roam quickly over the red cursive ink.

Postpone all council and community meetings until further notice. We'll see you one week from today. Come to the gray office building across from the Italian restaurant four blocks away from the Orchid Oblivion flagship store. Be there at noon—not a minute sooner or a minute late. You can even bring Genevieve and Zahara if you'd like. We'd love to meet them too.

-Your friends from The Caledonia Council

Chapter Four
GENEVIEVE

At eight p.m., James comes upstairs and jolts me out of my sleep.

"Are you awake, Gen?"

I rub my eyes and drag my hand over my nightstand until I find my glasses. My chest hurts from crying so much and my eyes are heavy and swollen. I look to my right and Zahara is still sleeping. I left the curtains open, so the moonlight illuminates our forest-green room and reflects off of the pristine white carpet.

"Barely. What's going on, James? I thought you were headed to the council meeting." I brush my curls out of my face. I haven't bothered with purchasing a new bonnet since I sleep on silk sheets every night. I'm grateful for the silk sheets because putting on a bonnet at night is one less thing I have to do daily, and I barely do anything lately. I've been slacking on my self-care this week, and it's been too long since I've washed my hair. However, I don't have enough energy to do anything about it.

He slips off his blazer and takes off his shirt, showing off his chiseled chest and abs. "I was getting ready to head to the meeting, but I had to cancel. I don't know when the next council meeting will take place."

Cancel? The meeting has already been pushed back a few days because of Zahara's birth. It doesn't make sense to push it back further.

I turn on my bedside lamp. The sight of the pale green lampshade makes me smile. James came home with green lampshades one day when we lived at our old house, and we've had them since.

"Why did you cancel the meeting?"

He strips off the rest of his clothes apart from his black boxer briefs and turns on his bedside lamp. "Do you want to come take a shower with me?"

The thought of showering with James makes my cheeks heat like they did the first time we showered together. I remember it like it was yesterday. The night the heat went out at our old house, he asked me to shower with him after we had sex three times. I remember getting nervous about doing something so intimate together, then I looked between my legs and saw his cum leaking out of me and laughed at how silly I was being.

I haven't showered with James all week, and I haven't let him see me naked either. I've showered by myself with Odette sitting outside the bathroom in case I needed anything, and she's helped me with whatever I've been unable to do alone. I'm just now feeling comfortable on my own, and I know James is eager for us to start behaving like we did before our baby was born.

But I can't handle James seeing my body right now. *I* can barely stand to look at my body right now. I had stretch marks before I got pregnant, but everything seems so much more visible now. And loose and saggy. My breasts are twice the size they were before giving birth, and they leak at the most inconvenient times. And I don't know if I'll ever get over my scar. Not to mention, my swollen belly makes me look like I'm a few months pregnant again.

I wear sweatpants and sweatshirts every day because they're comfortable but also because I hate my body and don't want James to look at it. I don't even know how he'd react if he saw it. Would he be shocked at how much I've changed? What if he doesn't see me the same way anymore?

I snuggle against my pillow. "No. Thanks. I already showered today."

He smirks. "I know you did. I did too. But I didn't get to take one with you."

I turn out my bedside lamp, trying to end the conversation. "I'm really tired. I don't think I can tonight."

His smile drops. "What about tomorrow?"

"Maybe."

He sighs and slips off his underwear, showing off his large, hard cock.

My body warms up, remembering what that thing is capable of. "Are you taking another shower?"

He turns out his lamp and pulls back his side of the covers. "No. I just feel like sleeping naked tonight. Is that okay with you?"

Before we had Zahara, James and I slept naked most nights. Since I moved into our old room on my birthday last year, we've rarely kept on clothes in bed. But he's stayed dressed all this week.

"It's fine with me. This is your bed too, James. You don't have to ask me for permission."

"I'll never stop asking for your permission, Genevieve."

I take off my glasses and bury my head into my pillow and feel his strong hands graze my hips.

"Can I hold you?"

Another thing I miss is James' arms wrapped around me. I haven't let him hold me because holding me means he can feel my body. He can feel how different it is and how it's changed. But I don't know how much longer I can go without his touch. Having his arms wrapped around me makes me feel better than anything else. But having his arms wrapped around me means that he'll bury his head in my neck or my hair. And if he does that, he'll start kissing me. And if he starts kissing me, things will escalate from there.

"James—"

"I'm not going to try and fuck you, Gen. I just want to hold my wife. I'm just asking for this one thing."

As much as I want to say no, I want to say yes more.

"Okay."

"Are you sure?"

"Yes. I'm sure."

He breathes deeply and slides closer to me, wrapping his arms around me and burying his head in my hair.

I feel his hardness against my ass, but I don't care. I breathe in his familiar scent and am overwhelmed by my emotions. My body shakes softly while tears stream down my face.

James kisses my hair and holds me tighter. "What's wrong, sweetheart?"

I open my mouth to speak, but it feels like a boulder is sitting on my chest. My voice feels like it's been stolen from me and locked in a box. The words won't come out no matter how hard I try. I croak and suck in air, but nothing comes of it. I cry for God knows how long while James stays wrapped around me until I have no tears left. When I finally come up for air, I piece together the only thing I can manage.

"I just want to feel like myself again."

He kisses my neck and wipes my cheeks with his thumbs. I start to doze off when he rubs my back and whispers in my ear. "I want that too."

Chapter Five

GENEVIEVE

I wake up at ten a.m. exhausted. James helped me pump a few times in the night and I never fully got back to sleep. I take a peek in Zahara's crib, and she's not there. That means she's either downstairs in Odette's room, or she's with James.

The past few days, our routine has been mostly the same. James gets up and feeds Zahara. He thinks I sleep while he does, but I'm usually awake and listen while he sings to her or tells her jokes or whatever random facts he knows. It's really sweet, and reassuring knowing that they have such a strong bond.

After he feeds Zahara, he leaves her with Odette while he checks on our farmhand and sometimes works with him. Once he's done with that, he grabs Zahara and spends time with her in the office downstairs or somewhere else around the house. Then he comes upstairs to put her in her crib for a nap while he exercises, and then he showers before we have dinner and then gets ready for bed.

Usually what I do during all that time is pump, and when I'm not pumping I sleep, cry, and eat when James makes me.

I slide out of bed, grabbing my scrunchie on my nightstand to put my hair in a bun and put on my glasses. I keep on my light gray sweatpants and matching hoodie, slide on my pink slippers, and head to the bathroom.

To save me time from walking back and forth getting dressed, Odette moved my postpartum underwear in here into one of my drawers under my sink. The seamless solid-colored panties aren't the most stylish, but they fit the pads I need to wear and are very comfortable, so that's all that matters. Yesterday I was able to start wearing smaller pads, and that makes me happier than anything else has this week. I'm looking forward to wearing my favorite bras and undies again.

I slide out of my pants and underwear and grab a fresh pair with a new pad. I nearly cry when I slide them up and put my pants back on. A pad is still a pad and a pad is never comfortable, but this smaller one is way better than what I had to wear for days.

The biggest shocker about childbirth to me was the amount of blood there was. Not necessarily during the delivery because I was out cold for that, but afterward. I didn't realize with a C-section that I'd need a sanitary napkin the size of a diaper, but I did. I wish someone would've told me how much blood there'd be.

Once I've cleaned everything up, I head to the hall to go downstairs. Although we have two staircases, I'm still a little sore and my incision can bother me going up and down two flights of stairs, so I prefer to take the elevator.

Pressing the button to go down, I take a look down the hall at all of the empty rooms on this floor. The rooms that are going to be for our future babies.

I don't know if I can handle giving birth again. If you'd asked me five years ago if I wanted a bunch of kids, I would've said yes without a doubt. But right now, in this moment, I don't think I'd answer the same way.

I can barely connect with my current baby. How would I be able to connect with any others? If I get pregnant again and again, will I be in a perpetual state of depression for years? That could literally kill me.

Do I even want to be here anymore?

Jesus. What the fuck is wrong with me? I shouldn't have thoughts like that. But they've been popping in and out of my head randomly. Sometimes I don't want to be here, but I'd never say it. Saying something like that would make me look crazy, and the last thing I need right now is to be committed. That would make me more depressed than I already am and I'm sure I'd die just from the stress of it all.

I shake myself out of my nightmare and step into the glass box to see my family.

One of my favorite places to be lately is inside the elevator. It's ironic because it's a place where so many people are uncomfortable and don't feel safe. Most people hate elevators and have a horrible fear of getting stuck in them or having their heads chopped off. But our elevator is one of the few places where I feel most secure. It's a place with no mirrors, so I don't have to see myself. And it's small and compact and makes me feel grounded. There's no noise or distractions. It's a place where I can just escape. I also enjoy the glass exterior which gives me the perfect view of our backyard that leads to our farm—another one of my favorite places. The ride up and down floors is short, but it's scenic and relaxing nonetheless.

When I get to the bottom, I step out and smell the most savory scent waft over me.

What is going on?

For the past few days, my breakfast has been very simple. Mundane healthy things like oatmeal, fruit, and smoothies. The first few days, James brought up breakfast to me, but then I told him I wanted to have it downstairs, and he reluctantly agreed. I'm not sure what I'm having today, but I know it'll be something new and exciting.

I make my way into the kitchen, and my jaw drops at what I see. There are plates all over the countertop, and they're stacked with a myriad of things. There are pancakes, waffles, bacon, eggs, grits, sausage, toast, cinnamon rolls, and more.

I stutter over my words, trying to gather my thoughts. "James—what—how—what's all this for?"

His back muscles flex as he pulls a pitcher of juice from the fridge and turns to face me. He's wearing nothing but a pair of sweats hanging off his hips and our baby swaddled up in a black cloth that wraps around his front and back.

His fair skin glistens with sweat and his cheeks are flushed. "Hi, Gen."

I sit on a barstool at the island. "Hi, James." I point at all of the food in front of me. "What is all of this for?"

He pours me a cup of what I know to be homemade orange juice. "Zahara and I wanted to do something special for Mommy."

My core heats at his use of *Mommy*, and I get a cramp that makes me wince silently. James doesn't call me Mommy all the time, but whenever he does, it rolls off his tongue in the most delicious way.

I must be making a face because he comes up to me and strokes my cheek with his warm fingers. My eyes fall closed when they slide down my neck and dust my collarbone.

He licks his lips and purrs. "Is Mommy going to be a good girl and eat all of the food that Daddy made for her?"

I let out a noise that makes him chuckle, and I smile at the sight of his. All bright and white and wide. I haven't seen him smile in days, and forgot how beautiful his smile looks on him.

"I cross my legs and refrain from biting my lip. "I'll try my best."

He kisses my forehead. "That's all I need you to do."

Before I know it, he's walking away, grabbing a plate, and loading it with food. My mouth waters and my stomach grumbles at the beautiful sight before me. As excited as I am to eat, I suddenly remember something that I need to address before I do anything else.

I take a sip of the juice James places in front of me. "You never did tell me why you canceled the council meeting last night."

He freezes in his tracks and sets the plate down on the counter beside him. "I was ordered to."

Ordered to? That could only mean one thing.

"The Caledonia Council?"

He nods his head. "Yes."

"Did they call?"

He rubs Zahara's back and she coos against his bare chest while he averts his gaze. "They left a note."

My heart plunges to my stomach. "They know where we live?"

He picks back up the plate of food and continues loading it. "Yeah. But nothing is going to happen. Everything's going to be alright." He sets my breakfast in front of me but I push it to the side, unable to stomach anything.

"What did the note say?"

"Eat your breakfast and I'll tell you afterward."

"You'll tell me right now, James."

He straightens his spine and pushes my breakfast back in front of me. "I'll tell you when you've finished your food."

"James—"

"Genevieve, you will finish everything on your plate right now, or so help me God, I will fucking make you."

He stares me down, but the look in his eyes isn't playful. I look down at my overflowing pile of food and groan.

"Every single bite?"

He makes a plate for himself with less food than mine and licks his plush lips. "That's right."

I start to get anxious. "I'm not going to be able to eat all of this food, James. This is torture."

He unwraps Zahara from his chest and places her in the bassinet beside the bar. "Genevieve, there are far worse things I could do to you if you want to be tortured. And I'll do them gladly if that's what it takes to get you to eat a complete meal. You've barely had anything the past few days. Eat. Now. Quit complaining when I've been working hard in here all morning to get this prepared for you."

I hate when James tells me what to do, but I love it too. I know I shouldn't argue with him and egg him on, but battling for power with him does something to me. It makes me feel alive, and I need that to keep me going right now.

When I go to push my plate away again, he gives me a look I've never seen before, and I decide to back off. My mouth starts to water when I pick up a piece of sausage from my plate and take a bite. It has the perfect amount of crispiness on the outside, and the inside is juicy and tender. Within a few minutes, I've finished all of the links on my plate.

James winks at me and puts more food on my plate from his. "That's my girl. Eat the rest of this, and I'll tell you what I know."

I finish the rest of my juice and pace myself while I eat the single pancake and waffle slices on my plate, the two poached eggs, the slices of avocado, and the small cinnamon roll. After thirty minutes, my plate is cleared, and my stomach aches from fullness. But I feel the most awake I have in days.

James clears our plates and moves his chair closer to mine. "The note said to cancel all council and community meetings until further notice."

I rub my sore stomach. "That's probably for the best. It's not like anyone's talking to us right now. We're safer away from everyone."

I'm not sure if everyone hates us right now, but I know some people do. James tried to call Ella, and she's rejected his calls. I haven't tried to call her, but I miss her. Half of the council members are still on our side while the other half still despise us. And like usual, we don't know what everyone else in the society thinks. We should meet with everyone eventually, but it'll probably be better to show our faces once things have calmed down and I can stand to be around people without crying sporadically.

James scratches his chin. "That's true. It's probably not a great time to see everyone right now. But that's not all the note said."

"What else is there?"

He faces me and takes my hands in his. We haven't kissed since early yesterday. I haven't initiated anything and he hasn't either. I know he's unsure of what I'm okay with and what I'm not right now. I'm unsure too. But I let him lace his fingers through mine to show him that this is okay. Holding my hand is okay.

His dark eyelashes flutter. "I have to meet with them in a week. Next Wednesday at noon."

A meeting is set. After all this time of stressing and wondering, we're finally going to see who's behind this damn council.

"Where are we meeting them?"

He shakes his head. "I'm meeting with them. In the city. You're going to stay here with Mom and Zee."

"Zee? You're calling our daughter Zee?"

He smiles and rubs the back of my palms. "It's a good nickname for her. It fits her. All of our kids are going to have nicknames, Gen. If you don't like it, we can pick something else."

All of our kids. James is always talking about multiple kids. I know he's eager to have a big family. I hope I'm capable of giving him what he wants.

"Zee works. Do they not want to meet me then?"

"They want to meet you. They want to meet you both. But the meeting is at a place I've never been to, and I need to scope things out first. I don't even know what they're going to say or what's planned. I can look out for myself but I'll be stressed trying to watch out for all three of us in an unknown environment."

My mind races while I try to process everything. Meeting with The Caledonia Council members is exactly what we wanted and what we've been seeking for months. We're that much closer to getting what we want. But now that we're right there, everything is suddenly more real and frightening.

"How do you know the location is secure? How do you know that they won't ambush you? That this isn't some trap?"

He stands up and pours us each a glass of water. "I don't know that it's secure right now, but I'll make sure it's secure before I meet with them. The meeting will take place a few blocks away from the Orchid Oblivion flagship store. The building they've requested to meet me at is a few blocks away from an office building I know of. The person at the nearby office building has connections and will look into things for me."

I sip my ice-cold water, enjoying the refreshing feeling it gives me after my sweet and savory meal. "And who would that person be?"

He rolls his eyes and groans. "Cousin Draco."

Chapter Six

JAMES

I sit in my room working on the Head Father's Text while Rebecca sleeps. I canceled my meeting with Wyatt and Frank since nothing was set up the way I needed it to be anyway. Once I got the blood cleaned up and took a shower, I went upstairs to find my wife and take her to lunch. She must be really upset with me today as she was in bed pretending to sleep. I know she's pretending because our phone has been ringing off the hook, and she never sleeps through the telephone ringing. If I were in a worse mood, I'd make her get up by pouring a bucket of ice water over her head and tan her hide for embarrassing me, but today's meeting went so well that I'll refrain. And it's our birthday. And she's pregnant.

Plus, as much as I adore my Rebecca, I like it when she sleeps. Sometimes she talks too damn much, and it gets on my nerves. She thinks she knows more than she does, and her nonsense irritates me like nothing else. And when she sleeps, I can work.

When I'm not at the perfume store, I'm laying down the foundation of this society. I created our tenets early on, but as the eldest founder and first Head Father, I have to put all of the rules in place. The only problem is I can't get any work done because Wyatt and Frank keep calling. They knew that I had a meeting earlier, but they didn't know what it was about, and they're eager to find out. Deep down, I know I should tell them, but I can't. It would spoil the entire purpose of The Caledonia Council. They need to remain discreet. Incognito. And that means I can't tell my idiot little brother Wyatt and our equally dumb cousin Frank.

-From the Diary of Jude Barlow, 1933

I sit on the porch in the front of the house to take a call. Genevieve is feeling more energetic today, but she's still not herself. She's spending time on the farm with

Olive, her favorite cow. At first, I was really disturbed when Genevieve told me she got attached to one of the cows and named her, but in hindsight, I'm really glad she did. Genevieve has gone to see Olive a few times this week, and every time she does, she comes back with a little smile on her face. Not her normal bright smile that pulled me into her orbit when we first met, but a smile nonetheless. I'll do whatever it takes to make my girl smile like she used to again.

Fuck. I miss her. She's still here and she's still Gen, but she's so different. I know it's only been nine days since Zee's birth, but nine days feels like years when each day is filled with tears. I hate that Gen cries every day. It makes me so fucking sad to see her sad. I miss her laughter and sassiness. I miss her cuddles and kisses that she used to give me all day long. I miss the feel of our baby in her belly. I miss having my cock buried in her warm cunt.

Not being able to see my wife naked has been agony. And I wish she would quit wearing those sweatpants and that hoodie every day. She's so beautiful. If I'm not allowed to touch her, it would be nice if I got to at least enjoy her beauty. I don't even want her in lingerie. Just an oversized tee. Something to let me see her hard nipples poking through her shirt. A glimpse of her ass when she bends over. An unlimited view of those soft and strong thighs I love being between.

God. I've got to stop myself. I don't know how I'm going to make it another five weeks without combusting.

What if she doesn't want to fuck me after five weeks?

No. She'll want to. Right? God, I hope so.

But what if she doesn't?

I need to do something to distract myself. Maybe I should do what I came out here to do in the first place. Mom will be home from her walk soon with Zahara, and then I'll need to feed her, so I should get this over with now.

I pick up my phone to make a call.

After three rings, the other line picks up.

"James?"

"Hey, Draco."

He lets out a loud breath. "What's going on, man? How are Genevieve and the baby? How are you? Why did the council meeting get canceled? You weren't at the funeral—can you catch me up?"

One of the hardest parts about this Head Father shit is having to keep things to yourself. There are things that everyone knows about, and there are things that I can't talk to anyone about. Anyone except Genevieve. And some of the things we're dealing with would be easier with a little help.

And with my lack of faith in Damion and Simon, the unreliability of the twins, and the youthfulness of Orion and Obsidian, I'm taking a chance on a new ally. Someone a little more seasoned, trustworthy, and reliable. Draco.

Draco and I have our differences, but he's the only person I can go to right now for help. With Hades gone, I have no one. I didn't realize how much of a help he was until he was no longer around. I'm devastated that he's gone. But I can't shed a tear about it because that's not what I do.

I lean back in my rocking chair and close my eyes.

"I need your help with something."

"Anything. What is it?"

I empty my lungs and give him a surface-level explanation of The Caledonia Council, my altercation with Jace, what went down on the Exit Ceremony field on Zahara's birthday, and the meeting I have next Wednesday.

I'm met with silence and wait for nearly two minutes before he speaks.

"There's a secret council that rules over us?"

I hope I don't end up regretting this.

"Yes. There is a secret council. And it needs to remain a secret. It's not even something you should know. And, I don't want you getting hung up on that detail. What's most important is getting as much information as we can."

He groans. "Yeah. Don't worry—I'll figure out who the building belongs to—maybe I can get access to the security cameras and see who works there. My buddy from work—"

I shoot out of my chair. "No. No buddies from work. No one can know about what we're doing. This is a job for you and you alone."

"James, I don't have access—"

"You can get access to whatever you need."

He pauses. "Do you realize what you're asking me?"

"I'm aware."

"James—you're asking me to lie and to steal. To cross lines and boundaries. That's what I'm going to have to do if you want me to help you."

I feel myself starting to get pissed the fuck off. "Isn't that what you do for a living?"

He lets out a half-laugh. "Yeah. But I'm getting paid for my job. I'm not getting paid for this."

I take a walk around the back to see if I can spot Genevieve. From this distance, I can't make her out very well, but she's sitting on the grass wearing the outfit she wore to breakfast this morning. The past few days she's showered before lunch, but I know for a fact she hasn't yet today which means she's waiting for tonight. That's perfect, because I prefer to take my showers in the evening, and I'm going to try and convince her to bathe with me later today. Showers and baths are very special to me and my wife, and they're always better when we do them together. I'm hoping some quality time under some warm water and a little candlelight will help us get back on track.

I snap myself out of my daze to tell Draco how this is going to go down. "You're right. You're not getting paid to help me. But if you don't help me, you'll be the one who ends up paying. And you'll pay with your life."

He groans. "My apologies, Father."

I take a seat on the back of the porch and watch my wife lay her head on Olive's back who is sitting on the grass beside her.

"Do you want me to go to the meeting with you, James?"

"No. You can't come with me. I'm going alone."

"What about Gen and—"

"Genevieve."

I hear him make a noise and I know the fucker is smirking. "What about *Genevieve* and the baby?"

"They'll be waiting at home for me."

"Will they be alone? Shouldn't you have someone looking after them while you're out? I could come over and sit with the girls while—"

"My girls do not need you. You will stay the fuck away from my girls, and you will help me with what I've asked you to help me with. Nothing more. Do you understand?"

He gulps. "I understand."

"Good. Before I let you go, there's something else I want to ask of you."

He answers nervously. "Sure, Father. What can I help you with?"

Although all society meetings and functions are postponed for now, I know at some point I'm going to have to convene with everyone again, and I'd like to do it with someone I trust by my side. My wife will be on my side of course, but Hades was my go-to on the council, and I need a guy like him again. I thought Damion could be that for me, but I can't trust him. Especially when he's so carelessly breaking tenets and screwing his brother's wife. His dead brother's wife.

"Will you step into Hades' place and be my second?"

He answers me with his laugh before he does with his words.

"Are you kidding? Fuck yeah, man."

After I get off the phone with Draco, I head to the field where Gen is. We had a pleasant enough breakfast together, and I'm hoping she'll spend a little more time with me today. I'm so lonely without her. I feel like a lovesick teenager.

When I get within six feet of her, I hear her sniffle.

She's crying. My baby is crying again.

"Gen—"

"I'll be back inside in a little while, James."

I know I shouldn't pressure her, but she's got me worried sick. I literally feel sick worrying about her. I'm more stressed right now than I was when she was giving birth.

"Baby—"

She chokes back a sob. "I'm fine, James. Please—I'll come back in soon."

I hate this. I hate this more than anything in the world. This depression. This barrier blocking me from my Gen. It's like we've got the goddamn Berlin Wall between us. And it's my mission to tear it the fuck down.

I want to tell her there's no way I'm leaving her out here to sit for hours. I want to toss her over my shoulder and tell her her ass is coming back in the house whether she wants to or not, and she's going to sit on my lap while I play with her hair and kiss her neck, and we're going to order takeout and watch movies like we used to. But as much as I want to do that, I've got a gut feeling that it's a terrible idea. If there's anything I've learned about my girl in the four-plus years we've known each other, it's that she moves when she wants to. She can't be forced or rushed. She does things when *she's* ready. It's one of my favorite things about her.

My heart tells me to scoop her up in my arms and kiss her until she can't breathe. But my brain tells me to give her space.

"Okay. I'm heading back to the house."

She nods her head but doesn't look at me.

I turn to walk away, but something stops me. I don't think Gen would ever hurt herself. I pray to God she wouldn't. If she ever did anything like that, I would die. My heart couldn't take it. It would stop beating in my chest. Just the thought of anything like that makes me want to vomit.

There's nothing nearby that she could hurt herself with as the nearby shed is locked and there's a key with our farmhand and I have the other one in the house. But I wouldn't be doing my duties as a husband if I didn't check in on her one more time.

"Are you sure you're going to be alright out here? You don't need me to stay with you, do you? I can get Mom if you want."

She shakes her head and sniffles again. "I'm fine. I promise. I'll be back inside in less than an hour, and if I'm not, you can come back and get me."

She'll be back in an hour, and if she's not, I can come and get her. I repeat it over and over to myself.

"Okay. I love you, sweetheart."

She sobs softly. "I love you too."

As soon as I get back inside the house, I run upstairs to our bedroom and open the window curtains to make sure Gen is still where I left her. When I look out and see that she is, I let out the breath I was holding on the entire way back to the house.

This is why I never wanted to get married or be in love. This shit is fucking crippling. I am addicted to this woman. She's my obsession. My light. My entire fucking life. We have literally created life together. My happiness is rooted in hers. I feel like I have to win her over all over again, and I need to figure out how to do that as soon as possible.

The door downstairs opens, and I hear a stroller rolling across the floor—my mother is back with my baby.

I head to the bathroom to splash water on my face, but before I do, I look out the bathroom window to make sure

I can still see Gen. She stretches out and lies on her back. That's good. Connecting with nature is good, and it's got to help her feel better. At least a little bit.

I turn on my sink and cup my hands together before I toss the water on my face and let the cool chill calm me down. When I look in the mirror, something catches my eye.

What the fuck?

I lean forward and grab at the thing sticking out above my right ear.

A gray hair?

I'm thirty-three, and this is my first gray hair. I have gray hair. I'm going gray. I'm so stressed from being a father and worrying about my wife that I'm going gray.

What is happening to me?

I slide the strand behind my ear and decide that I'll deal with it later. Right now, I need to grab my baby for her feeding and then head to my office to do some research.

Chapter Seven

GENEVIEVE

After sitting outside for fifty-five minutes, I went back to the house to pump and fell asleep on the couch for a long nap. I'm woken up at six p.m. by Odette. Her hair is in her signature ponytail, and she smiles softly, but I can see sadness in her eyes.

"Hi, baby."

"Hi." I sit up on the couch and crawl into her outstretched arms. Her black sweater dress smells like jasmine and lavender, and the combination makes me want to go back to sleep.

Her soft hands rub slow circles on my back, and I start to cry softly into her shoulder. She squeezes me tighter and rocks me back and forth while I fall apart for the millionth time this week. My entire body aches. I wish I could just shed my skin and escape myself for a day. A few hours even. I just don't want to be . . . me.

I'm suddenly hit by a fear I never imagined which makes me cry harder.

Zahara is going to hate me.

My daughter is going to hate me because I'm a bad mom. She's going to have her earliest memories permanently etched into her psyche, and she's going to remember how I neglected her. How I barely held her and wouldn't look at her. I'm ruining her life, and it's only just begun.

Odette cups my face in her hands and sniffles. "Look at me, Genevieve."

I blink away my tears and look into her glistening green eyes.

She huffs. "Whatever guilt you are feeling right now, I need you to let it go."

My chest is so sore and I feel like I can hardly breathe. "I can't."

Her fingers brush the tears from under my eyes. "Yes, you can." She takes my hands in hers. "I'm going to tell you something that I should've told you months ago."

I feel myself start to panic. "Please don't tell me you have more secrets. I don't think I can handle any more secrets right now."

She chuckles and shakes her head. "No. This isn't a secret, but it's still something you should know. Can I tell you?"

"Sure."

She frowns. "Being a mom is hard, baby."

"Yeah. And I don't think I'm going to be any good at it."

She squeezes my hands tighter. "Not true. You're going to be amazing at it. You already are."

I feel my eyes roll. "How? Look at me." My eyes water again, and I fight back my emotions threatening to flood over.

Her ponytail sways when she nods her head. "Yes—look at you. You get up every single day, every few hours to make sure your baby gets enough nourishment. You eat daily so that your body can have enough fuel for you and Zahara. You grace all of us with your beauty and sweet nature each day, and you bring those farm animals joy and you've extended a few of their lives."

When she words it like that, it does feel like I'm doing something important each day. The only part I'm confused about is the animals.

"How have I extended their lives?"

She rolls her eyes. "Are you serious? The only reason that tan and white cow is still around is because of you."

"Olive?"

"Yes—Olive. James planned to have that cow slaughtered but when he saw how attached you were to her, he knew he couldn't do that to either one of you. More chickens are on the way too so that you can keep those ones that follow you around whenever you're out there." Her laughter makes my heart hurt less.

I lean up against the pillow tucked under my side. "At least I can be good for something."

She pops my leg. "You are good for a lot of things, Genevieve. James thinks he couldn't survive without you, and that's true, but I'd die too. You're my daughter. My baby. I would not make it without you, girl."

I don't know what I'd do without Odette either. James is my other half, and I need him just as much as he needs me, but I need Odette too. I can't even imagine what our lives would be like if she wasn't around.

She squeezes my thigh. "But even though being a mom is hard, you're not doing it alone. You have James, me, Mai, and Ella too once she starts to feel better. We all love you so much, and Zahara is the luckiest girl in the world with you as her momma."

Her words cleanse my muddy thoughts and make me feel the slightest bit lighter. Happier, almost. "Thank you."

She pulls me in for a quick hug and then leans back. "And speaking of James, he asked me to wake you up and send you upstairs, and I know if you're not up there within the next five minutes, he's going to come down here and wonder why I'm keeping you. So get going."

I take a look around the room, suddenly wondering where my baby is.

Odette gives me a knowing smile. "She's in my room sleeping. I'll have her back to you kids before you go to bed."

I stand up and stretch my legs. "Okay. If you need me, let me know."

"I will. I love you, baby girl."

A smile tugs at my lips before I turn to head to the elevator. "I love you too."

I lean back against the glass frame of the elevator, enjoying the solace as I head up to my bedroom. Usually, James drags me downstairs around this time, so I have no idea what he's got planned. I step out of my oasis when I get to our floor and head into the master suite.

I'm completely unprepared for what I see when I open the door. All the lights are out, and the curtains are drawn, allowing the sunset glow to filter into the room. There are a few candles lit, and James pours two glasses of sparkling water.

When my eyes wander the bed, my stomach growls at the sight before me. There's a giant pizza on top of the comforter. The pizza is coated in our favorite toppings—black olives and mushrooms.

I go to my side of our bed and hop onto our deep green blanket. "I can't live off of pizza, cinnamon rolls, and pancakes, James."

He smiles and prepares a plate for me. "I know. But we don't do this every day, so you'll be alright."

I take a whiff of the warm bread and toasted cheese, and before I know it, I've finished half a slice.

"What did I do to earn a pizza party in bed?"

He chugs his water. "You had my baby."

I explode with laughter which makes him grin from ear to ear.

He winks at me. "I just thought it would be something fun for us to do."

I finish my slice and lean against my pillows, staring into his chestnut eyes. "A breakfast buffet and junk food for dinner. I feel like you're trying to butter me up. What do you want from me?"

He blushes. "I'm not trying to butter you up. But I was hoping we could try something after dinner."

The flush to his cheeks has me worried that whatever he wants to *try* is something that I am certainly not cleared for.

"And what would that be?"

He licks his lips. "First, I want that shower with you that you promised me yesterday."

My stomach drops. Did I agree to that? The thought of James seeing me naked tonight has me going into a panic.

I replay the conversation back in my mind. "I said I'd think about it, love."

He smirks, and I know it's because I called him love. He loves it when I do.

"We will shower together, like you previously agreed to, and then I want to try something that I think will help you feel better. Remember when you agreed to try whatever I suggest?"

I tense up and fidget, trying to get comfortable. "Yes. But I was in a vulnerable state."

His jaw clenches. "I'm not a predator, Gen. You don't have to be scared of me."

I sit up straight. "I'm not scared of you."

He relaxes. "Good. So does that mean you'll have a good evening with me and let me take care of you?"

Normally I like being doted on, but I don't know if I can handle it at this moment. I feel like I'm supposed to be taking care of everyone else right now. Not the other way around.

I don't know what *taking care* of me entails, but I know if I resist, he's just going to get upset and we'll get into an argument, and I don't have the energy for it tonight.

"Yes. I'll have a good evening with you."

He smiles softly, and we sit in silence while we finish our meals.

Once we've had our fill of pizza and the cookies he had stashed in the spare room, he cleans everything up and starts undressing.

His eyes meet mine, waiting for me to take off my clothes, and anxiety takes over me.

"What's wrong, Gen?"

What do I say?

"I—I—"

He slides his hand down his face and groans. "Am I not allowed to see you undress? I'll close my eyes if that'll make you feel better."

My cheeks heat with embarrassment. "You don't have to be rude."

"I'm not trying to be. I just want to know what the issue is. It's nothing I haven't seen before."

I look down, and a tear falls. I hear James curse under his breath.

"That came out wrong. What I meant is that if you're worried about your body, don't be. I know what you look like, and you're stunning. You don't have anything to be nervous about."

"But you haven't seen me like *this* James. You haven't seen what I look like after birth. I think you'll be surprised."

He sighs. "Genevieve, do you see me right now?" His eyes fall to his thick, hard dick. "This is what you do to me, Gen. It has been nearly impossible not to touch you every damn day. I'm fucking exhausted because I barely get any sleep at night. I barely get any sleep because when I'm not waking up to feed our baby, I'm waking up to go to the bathroom and jack off to the thought of being balls-deep in your sweet little cunt."

I gasp and he goes on.

"I am so fucking hot for you I can barely stand it. When I wake up before you each day and look at those pouty lips, all I want to do is shove my cock between them until you gag and choke. If you think I'm going to have a problem with your body now that you've given birth, you're mistaken. Now take off your goddamn clothes right now or you're going to see a side of me you never have before."

My hard and sensitive nipples chafe against my bra, and I let out a shaky breath.

I look at the soft white carpet under my feet, and I remember that I still have a pad on. "I need to go to the bathroom to change."

He rubs his head and groans. "Go ahead. Let me know when I can come in."

My heart thuds against my chest while my lips move faster than my brain. "You can come now. You can watch."

His eyes light up and the corner of his mouth lifts.

I head to our bathroom and he follows behind me. I start to sweat when I grab the hem of my sweatshirt. James stands on the marble floor behind me, watching me in our massive mirror. I pull the fabric over my head slowly, finding comfort in the cool air as it hits my chest. Once I've pulled the fabric over my head, I stand in front of the mirror with my fists clenched at my sides in just my bra, panties, and sweatpants and my eyes glued shut.

James' heavy breathing fills the room. "Look at yourself, Gen."

I force my eyes open and look at him through the reflected glass.

He licks his lips. "Don't look at me. Look at yourself."

I tear my eyes away from him and look at what I see. My curly hair that is desperate for a wash. My blue eyes that are puffy and red from crying nonstop. My tits that bulge out of my pink nursing bra. My soft stomach that still has a slight curve to it. The stretch marks on my hips that stand out on my dark brown skin. I'm a lot different than I used to be.

James steps a little closer to me, his voice coming out as a low whisper. "Fucking beautiful."

My nerves start to settle slowly. "Thank you." I don't feel beautiful. Far from it actually. But I'll take the compliment.

His hungry eyes rake over my exposed skin. "You don't have to thank me for anything, Gen. Go ahead and take your bra off."

I drag the soft fabric up and over my head, and I instinctively grab my breasts when they start to leak softly.

James grunts. "Move your hands."

My mind becomes a blur of desire and embarrassment. "I need to pump, babe."

He shakes his head. "No. We'll shower first, and I'll let you after. Does that work for you?"

I bite my bottom lip and debate with myself internally. I really do need to relieve myself, but Zahara does have enough milk for now. I guess I can wait. "Yes—that works." Before I can chicken out, I move my hands away and clasp them in front of me, letting my milk run down.

James runs his hands through his tousled, shiny jet-black hair while he ogles my leaking tits. "Jesus Christ, Gen. I can't believe you've been denying me this all week. Take your hair down."

I reach for my bun and remove my scrunchie, letting my curls fall loose and fall past my shoulder blades and over my nipples.

He smirks when I glance at him. "Take your panties off. I want to see all of you."

My shyness returns as I go to pull down my pants. I'm still wearing my postpartum underwear, and I'll only need pads for a few more days, but James hasn't seen me with one on, and I don't think he's prepared.

I kick my pants to the side and grab the granite countertop in front of me. "I should probably take these off privately."

His voice comes out low and sharp. "No. You can do this in front of me."

I bask in the comfort of my hair that covers my nipples which are still dripping.

A concerned expression spreads across his face. "Do you want me to step out? I will if that'll make you more comfortable."

I shake my head. "No. You can stay. But don't get freaked out."

He smiles, and it gives me the slightest bit of courage needed to pull my panties down. I wince when I step out of them and tear at the pad to throw it away. Not out of pain but at the sheer absurdity of me doing this in front of him. He stares at our reflections, following every move I make, and his eyes wander down to my incision.

"Are you in pain, Gen?"

I chuck my empty panties to the side and cross my arms in front of me. It has the opposite effect of what I intended, and my heavy swollen breasts stand out even more.

"No—I'm not in pain right now."

He breathes deeply. "Good."

Before I get another word out, he starts stroking himself while he watches me in the mirror.

I can't believe he's turned on right now. It makes me feel . . . good.

"Turn around and face me."

Grateful for the break from staring at myself, I turn around to face him.

His brown eyes darken. "Move your hair out of the way, Darling."

I take a breath and grab my thick hair, moving it away from my breasts and behind my back, leaving me fully exposed.

A growl escapes his chest. "Genevieve, you have no idea the unholy things I am dying to do to you right now." His eyes focus on my nipples and he bites his tongue like he's holding himself back from attacking me.

My milk trails down my stomach and legs while I watch him get off. My thighs heat in response.

I keep my eyes trained on his cock, afraid to look into his burning ones that draw me in like gravity.

"I'm not ready to have sex yet, James. And even if I was, it's too soon."

He squeezes his cock harder, moving his hand up and down while he fucks his fist. "I know. I just want you to know that you drive me crazy, baby, and as soon as you're ready, I'm going to make up for lost time and show you just how perfect I think your sexy little body is."

I let out a whimper, and he shudders. His groaning fills the room as he gets closer to his release.

"Sit on the sink and spread your legs open."

"Did you hear what I just said, James?"

He pants. "I'm not going to stick it in. I promise."

I obey his command and spread my legs wide on the countertop. Light blood stains the top of my inner thighs, and his eyes go wide when they fall to my crotch, making him moan with his mouth open.

"Close your eyes, sweetheart."

I shut my lids and lean back on my hands to brace myself. Heat pools in my core as I wait, already knowing what he's about to do. There's only one reason he asked me to close my eyes.

In an instant, I feel his hot cum on my neck, chest, and abdomen. I shift my legs and I feel some of it drip down onto my clit. My body vibrates in response, and all I want is for him to pin me against the mirror and fuck me brutally.

My legs start to shake and I tense up before I can even process what's happening. I open my mouth and let out a scream while my orgasm rips through me making my stomach tighten and cramp as a result.

Did I really just orgasm?

I feel euphoric and slightly embarrassed as I come down from my high.

I can't believe I came and he didn't even touch me. My body must really miss him because I've never experienced anything like that in my life. Just the sight of him touching himself in front of me made my pussy ache with need. So much so that it apparently had a mind of its own and behaved as if he was inside me.

When I open my eyes, I stare into James' sated ones. He comes up to me and cups my cheeks while he plants a kiss on my lips.

"You're beautiful, Gen." He moves his hands down to my stomach, and his fingertips trail over my scar. "I still can't believe I got so lucky."

#

After James and I cleaned up outside of the shower, we got in the shower where he washed my hair. He wanted to clean my body too, but I did that step myself, still slightly embarrassed about my milk flowing out of me and the blood between my legs. He's only seen blood between my legs two times before, so I'm still a little embarrassed about it. And although he's helped me pump many times, he's never seen me like *that*. With everything out in the open and spilling everywhere.

And he liked the sight of everything way more than I anticipated.

I sit in the bed waiting for him to come back upstairs. Once we dried off, he blowdried my hair and we went back to the bedroom where we filled up more bottles for Zahara. He then got dressed to go get her from Odette, and he's going to bring something back up with him too, but I don't know what.

I smooth my hair into a ponytail and snuggle up under the blankets, starting to fall asleep. When my mind starts to drift, James returns, and I hear our baby's soft giggles. He always knows how to make her smile.

He places something on my nightstand, and I open my eyes to watch him place Zahara in her crib. She kicks her feet in her pink onesie and her brown and blue eyes glow. He kisses her head, her nose, and her cheeks before he lays her down. He plays with her black curly hair before he whispers to her, telling her to go to sleep.

I close my eyes to resume my slumber, but he pulls the blanket off me and plays with the hem of my cream-colored cotton camisole.

"Take this off."

I slide out of his grasp and shiver from the chill on my bare legs. All I have on is my tank top and a pair of turquoise postpartum underwear.

"What for?"

He opens a jar of something on the nightstand and takes off his black T-shirt and shorts, standing in just his matching underwear. "You'll see. I will warm you up in just a second. Take off your top and lie down on your stomach if you can."

I reluctantly pull my cozy shirt off and twitch when the cool air hits my bare chest. Once I've gotten into a comfortable position with my arms crossed under my head with my head face down on my pillow, James climbs on top of me.

He messes with the jar on the nightstand and rubs something on his hands. "I've been doing some research, and I learned that massages may help you feel better. Physically and your mood. So I'm going to start massaging you at night before we go to sleep."

James has rubbed my feet often, but a full-body massage is rare. It's something I haven't thought about recently, but hearing that I'm going to get one daily makes me perk up.

"I think I'd be okay with that."

He places his warm, large hands on my shoulders and starts to rub me softly. "I thought you would be. I'm just rubbing some warm almond oil on you. I added a little lavender, so you'll probably smell that too."

The fragrant scent fills my nostrils, and I instantly start to relax. Today has been a pretty decent day compared to the first few days after Zahara's birth, and I'm hoping I'll feel even better tomorrow. When I'm alone with my thoughts and my feelings, it can be suffocating, but little distractions here and there have been nice.

I moan as he moves his hands slowly down my back, massaging the warm oil into my skin while he presses down on me with his thumbs. He caresses my sides and rubs me softly and tenderly. "Does this feel good, Darling?"

I smirk at the mention of my classic nickname that makes me melt into a puddle. It's the second time he's called me Darling tonight. It's the second time he's called me Darling all week. I'm glad to hear it again. "Yeah. It feels really good."

He continues to work my body while I breathe in and out slowly. "I'm glad. Have you missed having my hands on your body?"

One of his hands trails up and down my spine softly while the other massages the dimples above my ass.

I turn my head to the side on my pillow and close my eyes. "Yeah. I have."

"Good. I've missed that too." He grabs my hips with both hands and squeezes my tender flesh. "I can't get over how pretty you are, Gen."

I snort and he freezes.

"What was that for?"

My breath catches. "I don't look like I used to."

He leans over me, placing his hands on either side of my pillow, and whispers in my ear. "I don't want you to look like you used to. I like the way you look now."

Tears prick my eyes while my insecurities cloud my mind. "I thought I was perfect to you before."

A tear falls when he presses a butterfly kiss on my neck. "You were. So imagine what I see when I say you look even better now."

I tuck my bottom lip between my teeth and squeeze my eyes shut, hoping I can force my emotions back down. He smoothes my ponytail out of the way, not pulling it like he normally would in the past, and kisses my cheek before moving down and planting his lips across my back and shoulders.

The tenderness he shows me makes me come undone, and I let everything out into my pillow. He stops kissing me and hovers over my back, lacing his fingers through mine under my head and burying his face in my neck. His body cocoons mine, making me feel like I'm locked away in my own little shelter. I squeeze his hands tightly until I stop shaking, and when the tears stop falling, my head aches.

I let out a broken laugh. "My head is killing me."

He presses a kiss up against my temple before sitting up straight and letting my hair loose. "Does that feel better?"

I sniffle. "Yeah."

He gets some more of the warm oil on his hands and slides his fingers through my strands until he reaches my scalp. He works his way around my head softly, and the soft pressure eases my mind and forces me to calm down. I don't know how long he rubs my head, but it must be a while because I feel him wake me up and tell me to flip over on my back.

I switch positions, and my body feels way warmer than it did before we got started. He clears his throat while he straddles me and rubs my abdomen with soft strokes.

His eyes stay trained on two large things, and I feel the need to lighten the mood.

"My eyes are up here, love."

His big brown eyes lock on mine and his cheeks turn scarlet. "I'm sorry. I'm not trying to make this weird."

A smile tugs at my lips. "I'm teasing. You're not making things weird."

He smiles softly and moves his hands below my scar, rubbing me with the lightest touch. "Good."

Heat pools in my core with his hands so close to my private place. I grip the silk sheets under me. "You can touch them if you want."

His eyes go wide. "Are you sure?"

"Yes. Just don't touch my nipples. Not right now at least."

A light flush tinges his neck. "If I do anything you don't like, stop me."

I nod my head, and he slides his hands up to my breasts slowly. When his hands cup them, we moan simultaneously which makes us both break out in laughter.

He squeezes and rubs me softly. "I can't believe you're mine, Gen. I'll never get over that fact."

I cross my legs which are positioned in between his. "I wouldn't want to be anyone else's."

His eyes sparkle and he blinks a few times, not allowing himself to get upset. "That means more to me than anything."

His hard cock bulges in his underwear and he slides his hands down to mine, hooking his fingers in the sides.

I grab his wrists and hold him steady. "I'm not ready for anything more tonight."

He releases my panties and grips my hips. "Okay. That's okay."

I slide from under him to sit up and put my top back on, and he cleans everything up and climbs into the bed next to me. His strong arms wrap around my waist, and I let him pull me against his chest, loving the way his naked skin keeps me warm.

His soft lips brush up against my ear. "I adore you."

I turn to face him and tuck my head under his chin with his arms still wrapped around me. "I love you too." He squeezes me tighter than he has all week, and I close my eyes to drift off to sleep.

Chapter Eight

JAMES

I wake up at seven a.m. and groan. I forgot to shut the curtains last night, and the light pouring through our bedroom makes my eyes burn.

The past few days have been pretty shit. My new cows and chickens are delayed, one of our trucks filled with cow's milk crashed and spilled everywhere, two of the sheep are sick, and Zahara has been waking up more in the night. On top of all of that, my phone has been ringing off the hook with calls from Simon, Damion, the twins, and other council members wanting to know what the fuck I'm doing and why we haven't met. I had Draco send out notices to everyone that meetings would resume shortly, and although I'm grateful for his help, I'm frustrated with him too.

He hasn't found out shit about the gray building in the city, and I'm stressed out of my mind because I'm meeting with The Caledonia Council today. I've had plenty of time to prepare for this meeting, and I don't feel the least bit ready.

What the fuck am I doing? Why did I want to have this meeting? My mother was right—I am spoiled. I should've just kept my damn mouth shut.

No. I don't mean that. Fuck this place. I want to be a regular person so fucking bad. I want to raise my daughter in a normal environment. I don't want her to ever know her daddy was a cult leader. I want my wife to wake up each day with a smile on her face because she loves her life. But I have to earn those things.

As concerned as I am about this meeting with the council going smoothly today, I'm even more concerned about Gen. The other night, we had an amazing time together. She let me look at her for the first time in days, and I was overcome with emotion by how stunning she is. My girl has always been gorgeous, but her beauty has truly multiplied since giving birth.

Her skin seems to glow even more, her hair is longer and thicker and glossier, her hips are a tad wider, her ass is a little more plump, and her tits are insane. I love her soft tummy and I can't wait to put another baby in it. Her natural petite hourglass makes me fucking feral. I can't believe she can't see what I can.

I had every intention to have a simple shower with her where we washed and I gave her a quick back rub before bed. But when she got undressed in front of me, I lost the ability to think clearly. I've been pleasuring myself at night while looking at her naked photos, but seeing her in the flesh is so much better. When she stood before me, I couldn't help myself. I was so hard that I think I would've died if I didn't come. I had to touch myself, and when she spread her legs for me like the good girl that she is, I came harder than I had all week.

I had her close her eyes so nothing got in them, but seeing my cum all over her body after made me want to paint her lips with it. Her tits were begging to be sucked, but I know she's not ready for that yet. But she will be soon, and I know it's going to be a beautiful experience for both of us that brings us even closer than we already are.

After I gave her a massage and went to sleep with her delicate body wrapped in my arms, I thought we'd wake up the next day like our old selves. But she woke up in tears again, and she's still down and depressed, even with the addition of nightly massages.

It's the end of August, and the weather will be cooling down soon as we transition into fall. That concerns me because with the transition to fall and winter comes seasonal depression. I need for Gen to get better. Not worse. If she's not better in four weeks, I'm making her take that medication. Or she'll go to therapy. Maybe both. I just don't know how much longer this will be good for her.

I try to give my mom as much quality time as I can with Zahara. Not only because it helps me and Gen, but because when my mom is away from my baby, she gets down in the dumps too. She hasn't brought up Shane, but I know she wants to know what happened to him. My priority for today is doing whatever it takes to get my family out of this society, but if I can find out what they did to my mother's ex-lover, I'll try to so that I can hopefully bring her some peace, and she can move on.

Once I drag myself out of bed, I feed my baby while my wife sleeps. Once I get her fed, I take her downstairs to my mother and go back upstairs to get dressed to meet with The Caledonia Council. I try to keep quiet to not wake Gen. I know sleep is important to her recovery, and she wakes up in the night nearly every time I do. I want to make sure she gets as much rest as she needs, and if I can keep her asleep until I get back, then I won't have to worry about her being stressed while I'm out.

After slipping into my white dress shirt, I slide on my black blazer and slacks with my white wingtip oxfords. When I grab my keys and wallet, Gen shuffles in bed and turns to face me.

"Where are you going, James?"

I curse myself silently for waking her. "I'm heading to the meeting. Go back to sleep. I'll wake you up when I get home."

She sits up in bed and puts her glasses on. Her eyes wander over to the clock on my nightstand. "It's not even ten a.m., James. The meeting is at noon."

I sit next to her on the bed and pull her into my arms. "I know. I'm going to see Draco beforehand at his office. I want to keep trying to find out whatever we can until it's time for the meeting."

Her soft yawn makes my body ache with the need to crawl back into bed. "Please be careful."

I kiss her pouty lips. "I always am. Don't worry. It won't be long."

She frowns. "You don't know that."

"I'm sure they're all very busy. I doubt it'll take all day. Please don't start stressing. This is what we wanted. This meeting is bringing us closer to a normal life, Gen. That's what we asked for."

She buries herself against my chest. "Promise me you'll come back home, James."

I kiss the top of her head and hold her close. "I promise. I'm always coming home."

#

After getting Gen settled back in bed, I kissed her and my baby before heading to the city for my tasks of the day. The drive to New York City was long and stressful. It took less than an hour to get to Draco's office, but like usual, there were a million idiots on the road who definitely should not have received their driver's licenses. I hit every single traffic light, bought coffee on the way that I nearly spilled all over my pants, and I had to park two blocks away from the building which was the icing on the shitshow cake.

By the time I enter my cousin's building, I'm sweating like a whore in church and angrier than I should be for this early in the day. I give my name to the front desk and head to the silver elevator that takes me to the very top.

Once I'm twelve floors up, I find my calm, and the cool air inside the building helps dry out my pits. I check my hair in a mirror on the wall, pull my black reading glasses out of my pocket and slide them on, and head to the large office at the end of the hall with large oak doors.

I don't even have to knock before the doors open, and my cousin greets me with open arms and a smile on his face.

"James—it's great to see you again."

I pat his back and step inside the large room. "It's great to see you again too. How's Raven?"

He heads toward his desk and I follow behind him. "She's wonderful. Sweet, loving, and obedient. Just like she should be." He winks, and I have to clench my fists to refrain from smacking him.

I sit across from him in a wine-leather tufted chair. The sunlight shining through the floor-to-ceiling windows warms the room, making me heat up again.

"I'm glad you two are happy. I never thought you would settle down."

He leans back in his black leather chair and laughs loudly. "You know me, man. I never had any intention to. But this damn society is an albatross around my fucking neck. It was easier to pick a wife than to die. Plus, Raven and I have an understanding."

It's already nearly eleven a.m., so I only have around thirty good minutes to spend with Draco before I need to head out. I should be focused on finding out whatever I can about the gray office building, but my curiosity about his relationship intrigues me more.

"What kind of understanding?"

He smirks and reaches under his desk, pulling out two lowball whiskey glasses and a bottle of bourbon.

I sit up in my chair. "I'm good."

He pours two glasses. "Don't make me drink alone, cuz."

As much as I'd love a drink right now, I'd rather not show up to the most important meeting of my life hammered. And from all of my past experiences with my slightly younger cousin, I know one drink will turn into two, and two into three, and I'll end up passed out on the floor within an hour.

I open up the fresh bottle of water beside his computer. "This is enough for me."

He rolls his eyes. "Suit yourself. More for me." Not to my surprise, he tosses back both glasses of booze. "Raven does whatever I tell her to when I tell her to. But I let her have a little fun here and there, and I have mine."

His voice lowers and he takes off his burgundy blazer, leaving his white dress shirt and gold tie underneath before he leans across his desk and whispers. "Raven has . . . friends that I allow her to see. One man, once a week, and she has to see him at the house in one of the guest rooms. And in return, I have my friends—one girl, once a week, and I get to see her in one of the guest rooms. Sometimes we invite a couple over for a little group fun, and we fuck our respective partners in the same bed. Or switch."

I could say I'm surprised, but I'm not. My cousin has never been one to limit himself. I've been with a lot of women too, but never with more than one at a time. It ruins the intimacy to me.

As messy as his marital arrangement is to me, it's not really any of my business. Remaining faithful to your wife is one of our tenets, but if Raven and him have an understanding that they both have agreed to, it doesn't count as infidelity in the way that Damion is cheating on Theresa by screwing Jessamine behind her back.

I finish the rest of my water, desperate for it to cool me down from the hot sun shining on me. "Well, I hope things continue to work out for you two. And I hope you both are looking out for yourselves."

He pours another drink and chuckles so loudly that I'm afraid someone in a nearby office will hear. "Don't worry—we're both clear, and we get everyone tested before we let them in."

I'm completely caught off guard by what he asks next.

His jade eyes glaze over, and he tucks his bottom lip between his teeth. "That being said, I'm always in the mood to make new friends, and I was wondering if your sweet Genevieve would be interested in getting to know me. Maybe she could come over in a few weeks once she's feeling better?"

My blood boils. "Excuse me?"

He sips his third drink slowly. "I've been thinking about her nonstop since my wedding day. And my Raven needs friends too. I'm sure she'd be interested in spending some time with you if you wanted."

Oh *hell* no.

He licks his lips and winks. "And I know how possessive you are of Genevieve, so if you wanted to be in the room while we, you know, I'd let you watch. We could even please her together. Has she ever tried anything like that before?"

I lean forward in my chair and grip the knife in my waistband. "Draco, I need you to listen very closely, because I will not be repeating myself."

He smiles. "Go on."

"Genevieve is not cattle. She is not for sale. She does not need new friends. Or a new cock. My wife gets everything she needs from me, and that's how it will remain. She's mine to love and fuck and use however I want, and no other man will ever have the pleasure of knowing what that's like. And as for Raven, I'm not interested. My wife is it for me. You might need a new cunt to come in every week, but the thought of any woman outside of my wife touching me makes me sick to my stomach, and I'd rather die than join the sick twisted fuckery you've created."

His cheeks go red, and he opens his mouth, but I continue.

"And if you *ever* suggest anything like this ever again, if you ever make a pass at my wife, look at my wife for too long, or even think about fucking my wife, I will skin your dick before I chop it off and feed it to one of the pigs on my fucking farm."

He tosses back the rest of his drink while sweat stains his pits. "Cool." I lean back in my chair until he smirks and flashes his white teeth. "But if you ever change your mind, let me know."

My body moves on its own as I shoot out of my chair and grip him by his shirt collar. Before I know it, my knife is at his neck, and he's breathing his boozy breath in my face.

I whisper into his ear with the most rage I've ever felt. "Tell me you understand, or I will slit your throat right here and leave you bleeding all over your desk."

He blinks and sucks in a few breaths. "I understand."

I press my knife in and nick his skin. His eyes go wide, and he breathes erratically. "I fucking understand, man. Please. I swear to God I understand."

I release him and he falls back into his seat, coughing and spitting on his desk.

Looking at my watch, I see I don't have much time left, and I'm pissed that I've wasted all this time here finding out nothing.

I snap my fingers to try and get my cousin out of his drunken haze. "As you know, I came here for information. I'd like for the last fifteen minutes of our meeting to be productive. I know you haven't found out anything about the building, so can you open your computer and let me take a look?" A lot of the buildings around here are owned by the same people, and I'm certain there's a file or something on his computer that can give me a lead or a starting point.

He sits up straight and runs his hands through his messy black hair. "I actually did find out something. Shortly before you got here."

My heart slams against my rib cage. "We should've started with that. What did you find out?"

He boots up his computer. "The building has four people on the lease. Some woman named Annabelle, a guy named Jack, one named Eric, and someone else. Unlisted."

I turn the screen toward me and look over the document he has. "Unlisted? No. That's not a thing."

He scoffs. "They're unlisted, James. If I had their name, I'd tell you. Rest assured." He points to the screen. "Look. It literally says unlisted."

I groan and lean back in my chair. "That is not how leases work. Their name has to be on it. Somewhere. This must not be a real document."

"It's real. Trust me—I am not bullshitting you. Whoever the last person is wants to remain private. These individuals own the building, and that's all I could find out."

I check my watch and see time is running out. "No photos?"

He frowns. "Nope. I couldn't find photos of anyone. I might be able to get addresses though. But it's no guarantee."

"And Shane? Did you find anything on him?"

He clicks his tongue. "No. I couldn't find anything on this Shane guy. He's a ghost too. Has to be dead."

I sigh at the confirmation that Shane is gone. I'm going to have to tell my mother that he's not coming back, and I don't know how she's going to take it. Zahara has been keeping a smile on her face, but my mother cannot live with us forever. And going home to an empty house with the knowledge that her one true love is gone might destroy her.

I stand up and walk around the room. "Okay. Shane's gone, so the other four on the lease must be the remainder of The Caledonia Council."

He stands up too. "That's my guess. See what they want, and keep me in the loop. I'll do whatever I can to help. Everyone has calmed down, but I know the guys are looking forward to meetings resuming soon. We'll have to give the council something or they might start to riot."

Our smaller and more insignificant council is the least of my worries right now. I'm sure everyone in the society wants to know what's going on, and I'll try to catch everyone up as soon as I can. But deep down, I'm hoping I get my family away from all of this shit before I have to.

"I'll find out what I can at the meeting, and I'll fill you in later. They're the ones who wanted the meetings postponed, so I'm sure they'll have a plan."

His brow creases, and it's the first time I've ever seen concern on his face. "This is way over all of our heads, James. I've never heard anyone mention anything about this council. Not my parents, not your father, not anyone."

"I know."

His jaw clenches. "I'm not going to lie—this meeting has me worried. Please be careful. And whatever you do, don't get yourself killed. Because if this council is as good as they seem to be, there's not going to be anything I can do to expose them."

A bead of sweat drips down my spine sending a chill throughout my body. "I know. Don't worry. I've got it covered."

I turn away to head toward the door, but he calls out to me, and I stop in my tracks.

"James?"

"Yes?"

He leans against his desk and sighs. "Don't leave us, James. The Wild White Orchids would be lost without you."

I never told Draco that I wanted to leave. Never hinted at it. But out of everyone in my family, my cousin Draco has been the one to understand me the most. To know what I'm thinking without even saying it.

But I don't know how to respond to his vulnerable confession, and even if I did, whatever response that I could think of would be something he wouldn't want to hear. So instead, I say nothing and head out the door.

###

I get back to my car and process the news I just learned.

Four people are on the lease. Four people I have to request my freedom from. Four people I may have to kill. But I hope it won't come to that. I'll meet with these two men, a woman, and a mystery person, we'll have a civilized chat as adults, and I'll get what I want. It will be that simple.

My stomach gurgles as I drive down the road and head to my location. Before I know it, I've arrived at the chrome gray building, leave my car with the valet, and head inside.

My body shakes as soon as I step into the building. It's got to be only fifty degrees Fahrenheit in here. There's no lobby or front desk. Only a black elevator. The walls around me are black, and there are no windows. The floor is white marble. I check my phone and see that I suddenly have no signal. I sent Gen a quick message before I got out of the car, and I hope she'll be alright while I'm here. I know my mother is with her, but I hate the thought of her not being able to reach me whenever she needs me. I need to wrap things up quickly so I can get home to my family and let them know what I've found out.

My brain tells me to run for the fucking hills, but my heart knows that I need to see this through. I want to make my wife and daughter the happiest girls in the world, and reaching that goal starts here.

God, be with me.

I run my hands through my hair a few times, straighten out my blazer, and press the black button on the wall to head to my salvation.

I take deep breaths to calm myself when I step into the elevator. There are no numbers. Just one fucking button. I feel like I'm a dumbass in a horror film heading straight to the murderer. After I press the button, the doors close slowly, and the metal box moves up.

I check my phone, and it takes four minutes to reach the top. When the doors open, I step out into a secluded hallway. The floors and walls are identical to how they are on the first floor. It's a little warmer up here, but not nearly enough.

Seeing a glow at the end of the hall, I take that as a sign, and I head toward it with my asshole clenched in fear.

I take long strides and hold my chest high, hoping the actions will give me the confidence I need when I face the individuals at the end of the hall. I leave my reading glasses on not because I need them at this moment but because they make me look even more put together, and I don't want anyone to think for a second that they can play me.

Once I reach the end, I pat my knife to make sure it's still there, open the door, and walk inside.

The office I step into is similar to Draco's—floor-to-ceiling windows, but a little smaller. The temperature in this room is also better. The carpet is beige, the walls are white, and there's a small oak desk in the center of the room with a bookshelf behind it. Standing in front of the bookshelf is a short woman, about the same height as my wife and mother, who looks a little like my mother. Maybe five years younger.

She puts her hands on her hips wearing a light pink sleeveless sheath dress, and her black hair sways behind her back.

She swipes her tongue against the top of her red lips, widens her hazel eyes, and gives me a bright and superficial smile. "Hi, James. Have a seat."

I look around the room with my peripheral, wondering what the hell is going on. "Where's everyone else?"

She frowns. "Who's everyone else?"

Gaslighting. She's starting this meeting by gaslighting me. "The rest of The Caledonia Council. I got your note—where is everyone else?"

She grits her teeth and draws her eyebrows together.

Does she even know what I'm talking about? Is she just a secretary? A hired assassin? I keep my eyes trained on her, prepared for any move she could make.

"James, have a seat, and I'll tell you what's going on."

My eye twitches. "Tell me who you are, and then I'll have a seat."

She squeezes her eyes shut and then glares at me. "Fine. I'm Annabelle. I'm one of the sector leaders, and my main project is Orchid Oblivion."

Annabelle, sector leader, and Orchid Oblivion. She must be legit. Unless she's masquerading as the real Annabelle.

I take my seat across from her as she sits. "Hello, Annabelle. When will everyone else arrive?"

She beams. "No one else is coming today, James. You're only meeting me—for now at least."

There are five total people in this council, four excluding Shane, and I'm only meeting with one. I was under the impression everyone would be in attendance. This is already turning out in a different way than I expected, and I don't like where it's going.

As much as I want to tell her off and make my demands, I can already tell that's not the best approach. So I calm the devil inside of me and try to remain peaceful.

"Okay. What can I do for you, Annabelle?"

She leans back in her chair and dusts her hair off her fair shoulders. "There's something you're going to do for me, for the council that is, but before we get there, I want us to get to know each other a little better. Of course, I already know everything about you," she chuckles and taps a white file on her desk. "But you don't know me."

I nod my head for her to go on, deciding not to tell her that she doesn't know shit about me.

Her cool breath sends a chill down my spine when she leans closer, making me instinctively push my chair further back. "I'm the newest member of The Caledonia Council. I came in a few years after Orchid Oblivion was created. I'm celebrating fifteen years with The Wild White Orchids today."

"What made you join us?"

She grins. "I was approached by your father. I was on a business trip in Los Angeles, and he approached me at a bar."

My stomach churns and she chuckles.

"Don't worry—I didn't sleep with your father. But I can't say I didn't want to." She sighs. "Anyways, he told me he had friends in high places who could help me get out of the shithole I was in with better pay, better benefits, and the opportunity to do something really meaningful with my life, so I took a chance."

My mind races, wondering what other secrets my father hid from me. "And what do you do exactly?"

"This and that. Mainly, I manage suppliers, triple-check the budget for the brand, and keep everything important about Orchid Oblivion and its ties to the society concealed from the media. Speaking of which, I admire Genevieve for standing up to Georgia, but we did lose a lot of money when she gave away all of those shoes. Regardless, I like a strong woman, and I can't wait to meet with her soon."

My skin crawls at her mention of Genevieve. And I could care less about those goddamn shoes that are ugly and overpriced. "You won't be meeting with Genevieve."

She bites her lip. "Yes, I will."

I clench my fists in my lap in order to not grab my knife and gut Annabelle right here. "How do you have access to any of this information? The budget, the suppliers—"

"Shane."

Shane? "He's not around anymore."

Her eyes sparkle and she laughs. "I like you, James. I can tell you're going to be good at following directions. You're catching on already."

"Look. It's been great meeting you. But I'm sure neither of us wants to be here right now. So let's get to the point of this meeting."

She grits her teeth. "You're right. I'd rather be somewhere else. You're here James because you've broken too many rules. And when a Head Father breaks too many rules, he has to be punished."

It's nice to know that all of my rule-breaking is finally being acknowledged. "I'm not here for punishment."

Her smile returns. "I figured. But regardless, we still need to discuss your infractions, James. I need you to understand the severity of our situation here."

"Go ahead."

"Good. First, you helped Deacon escape. Well, almost. As I'm sure you're aware, that's a big no-no. We should've stepped in then, but we didn't. You can thank Shane for that."

Thank you dead man who used to screw my married mother on the weekends.

"Nice. What else?"

"Well, there's the unlawful murder of Dave and Jace. And you failed to punish Damion for his infidelity. So, you killed two people you shouldn't have, and two people you should have, you didn't."

I feel myself smile. "What can I say? I like to keep people on their toes."

She lets out a genuine laugh. "You're so funny, James. And charming. It doesn't surprise me that you won Genevieve over so quickly. And I'm glad you did—I didn't want you to die, and you really did make her life better even if you feel like you didn't at times."

My jaw clenches. "You don't know the first thing there is to know about me or my wife, and I'd appreciate you keeping her name out of your mouth."

She blushes. "I actually know more than you think, but I'll offer you that courtesy as I don't want to cause problems."

She doesn't want to cause problems? Her entire existence is a problem.

"Thank you."

"That being said, I know you've looked through your Head Father's Text, and that means you know your punishment is beheading. Had you just committed the unjust murders, you would've been granted a trial. But you blatantly disregarded your duty to enforce the first tenet allowing Deacon to run as well as tenet six with Damion cheating on his wife. Those are the reasons you are supposed to die."

I grip my knife under my jacket. "Fun. So where's the guillotine?"

She winks. "At one of the other office buildings. Like Shane, I like you so much, James. Jack does too. So we had a little vote as a group, and we're offering you an alternative."

Here we go. "And what would that be?"

"Apologize for your wrongdoings, swear to never do them again, and we can all move past this."

She can't be serious.

I stand up. "I'm not interested. There's something else I want."

Her eyebrows dance. "We figured you'd say that. Now's your chance. Make your demands. But make them carefully—you only get one chance."

Sweat drips down my spine from anxiety. One chance. I need to speak with my wife. I need—I need time.

"When do you need my demands by?"

"Sixty-seconds. Starting now."

Fuck.

Fuck fuck fuck.

Sixty seconds? Sixty seconds to make one of the most important decisions of my life? Shit. Gen's going to be so mad if I fuck this up. I look down at my watch and I have less than thirty. God. Good God. God.

I'm terrified to say anything. I'm sure it'll get twisted somehow. How do I know they'll honor a deal? Do we sign a contract? I feel like I need a lawyer, but what good would it do me? No good at all.

Fuck it. "I want the freedom of myself, my wife, child, future children, and mother from this society—I want to cut all ties to us from the society. And I want all of my earnings I've made through teaching and what I'm giving you through my farm paid back to me in full."

Annabelle claps her hands and squeals. "Mmmm. I love that those are your demands, James. Simple and to the point." She picks up a pen off her desk and twiddles it between her fingers. "This means we get to play a little game. I know how much you love games."

My throat tightens with nervous anticipation, waiting for whatever horrible revelation is coming next.

She stands up and clears her throat. "In exchange for your demands, you will complete a series of tasks. Instead of a standard trial for your wrongdoings, you will participate in a trial of sorts—The Caledonia Trials." She steps from behind the desk and walks around the room while I keep her in my line of sight. "There are five levels. Once you complete a level, you will have the privilege of advancing to the next and so on. Once you complete the final level, you will receive what you desire."

A test. Of course, this would involve a test. "And what will I be required to do?"

She twists her hair around her finger like a middle schooler. "You of all people should know I can't tell you ahead of time, James."

I take off my glasses and shove them in my pocket, feeling like an idiot for thinking they'd make me seem more sophisticated. "And what if I decline?"

She shakes her head. "There's no declining, James. If you decline this chance at freedom that you're willing to risk everything for, you'll never receive another opportunity like this. You and your family will forever belong to the society, your little Zahara will join the council and be subject to a set of rules that we will come up with, and you'll remain Head Father until you die. Or until you're killed. You don't seem to be very good at making friends."

My head starts to hurt trying to come to terms with everything. Do whatever I'm told, no questions asked, or be a prisoner forever.

But how can I trust Annabelle? Was she the woman Jace was meeting with? She fits the description. If so, that makes her my enemy.

I tuck my hands into my pockets. "Didn't you try to have me killed?"

She frowns. "Why would I do that, James?"

I stare into her eyes looking for any hint that she's as oblivious as she seems to be. The look on her face is genuine, but my gut tells me it isn't.

"Because you wanted someone else to take my place. Jace. Remember?"

She scratches her chin and makes a face like she's focusing on something. "Hmmm. Jace. Like I said, James, I rule over the fashion sector. Shane was over societal operations and knew who everyone was. I knew of Jace, and I know you shouldn't have killed him, but I didn't know him well enough to want him to take your place."

More gaslighting. Very original.

I scratch my chin and match her expression. "No—I think you know Jace quite well. Or knew him pretty well, before he died. He mentioned you, you know?"

Her eyes light up. "Is that so?"

"Yeah. He said you were really into him, but that he wasn't into cougars."

Her cheeks burn red and she clenches her jaw. "Look, James. Jace is dead and gone. Like Tiberius and your father and every other man you're responsible for killing. Whatever he told you certainly isn't true, and even if it was, you couldn't prove it could you?"

I glare at her and she smiles.

"So why don't we just cut the bullshit. As of right now, I'm your only true friend. The only one who can help you. You will take this deal, you will succeed, and you will leave the society with your demands and never speak a word about anything you've endured for the rest of your life. That means no contact with anyone else in the society either. Or friends of it. You and your wife and children can live in your cute little brick house with your farm animals and never have to worry about hearing from us ever again, as long as you keep your mouth shut."

Easy. That's how this sounds. Easy. But I know it's going to be hard. If I accept, whatever I have to do will certainly be harder than I could ever imagine. Nothing comes easy with The Wild White Orchids.

I take a breath before I make my next move. "If I accept and go through this challenge . . . what happens if I fail?"

Her hazel eyes darken and the corner of her mouth lifts. "If you fail, your wife, mother, and daughter will be slaughtered in front of you. Sacrificed. The same way that all daughters were meant to be before you got enough power to change things. And you? You'll owe us not only for this grand opportunity that you've been given but for all of your transgressions too. You'll remain a servant of the society forever in captivity under The Caledonia Council."

My heart drops to my stomach. What kind of fucking offer is this? "I'd like to negotiate—"

She throws her head back and laughs. "There is no negotiating, James. You will decide, and you will decide now. Ten. Nine—"

Jesus Christ.

I will not fail my family. I will not lose my family. I will not fail.

"I'll do it."

She licks her lips and grins like a Cheshire cat. "Oh, James. There hasn't been a Head Father like you since Jude. Or so I've heard. So bold. With a bias for action. And enviable confidence. I don't know—maybe we should forget about the whole thing and we can start over fresh. What do you say?"

"Annabelle—"

"I'm kidding, James." She sighs. "Unfortunately, it's not up to me. You've made your deal. Let's conclude." She walks back behind her desk, pulls out a glass jar, and unscrews it. I tense when she draws a knife out of her drawer and holds it out to me. "Your blood."

I ignore her offer and pull out my own knife. The knife I used to cut my bride's dress over a year ago, and the same knife that I used for my first kill. I slice my hand with the sharp blade, embracing the thrill of this moment, and drip my crimson blood into the jar.

She slices her hand and does the same. "By this blood, you are bound by your oath to complete The Caledonia Trials. Your failure to deliver on your promise or failure of any challenge will result in death."

She seals the jar, tucks it back in her desk drawer, and pulls out a white envelope with an embossed orchid. "Level one. Be here in four days at nine a.m., and don't be late."

I grab the letter from her clenched fist, tuck it in my pocket, and head out the door.

Chapter Nine

GENEVIEVE

I sit in bed wearing an oversized gray tee with my hair in a bun. I am tired of wearing my hair in a bun, but it's all I can manage to do lately. Odette offered to do my hair for me, but she's never done hair like mine before, and I'd rather her not start now. James washed it for me, and I love it when he washes my hair, but I'm not sure he's up for the task of styling it either.

Standing up, I put on my glasses and head to the spare room connected to our master bedroom. It's big enough to be a baby's room with plenty of space for a crib and more, but Zahara still sleeps beside me every night. She rustles in her crib when I walk past, and I know she knows what I'm up to. Once I'm in the other room, I get some of her milk out of the fridge that I pumped an hour ago, heat it, and put it in a bottle for her.

I'm still a little heartbroken that she wouldn't nurse from me. I could try again, but I don't know if I can handle it if I fail again. In addition, I'm still not used to my new body and am a little insecure about how different everything looks, so maybe it's for the best that I keep bottle feeding when I'm not even comfortable in my own skin.

My baby chirps and drools on herself, and I grab her soft pink baby blanket that James keeps in my bottom nightstand drawer. Normally James feeds her, or if I feed her, I only do it when he's around. Or Odette feeds her. But it's half past noon, and James is still out, so I don't have his help right now. And as much as I love Odette, it's embarrassing being so dependent on her, and I want to try and do this myself.

You can do this.

I take a breath and lift Zahara out of her crib. She's barely been alive, and she already has so much hair. The color is identical to James', and I think about him every time I look at her.

Tears cloud my eyes as I crawl into the bed with her in my arms. I still can't believe I have a baby. A baby I made with my best friend. My husband gave me exactly what I wanted in life—why can't I just be happy?

I know I love my daughter. I didn't know if I loved her at first. Her birth was so traumatizing and I was in a lot of pain afterward. Then the stress of what James did at the Exit Ceremony field overwhelmed me. Everything felt like it was too much to handle. I'm not sure when I realized that I love my baby, but I know my life is better with her in it, even if it doesn't feel like it at times.

It's comforting knowing that she's beside me at night. Hearing her soft breathing eases my mind knowing that she's alright.

One of my highlights of the day is when James gets up with her in the mornings and feeds her. She rewards everything he says with a little giggle, chirp, or gasp, and it's like the two of them are having a real conversation. In their own way, they are. She loves him so much, and I can already tell she's going to be such a daddy's girl.

My heart warms whenever I see her wrapped up in his chest. He's so strong, loving, and nurturing. I'm so lucky that my daughter has a father who loves her more than anything. I didn't have that, and I'd never wish it on anyone. I hope they'll always be this close.

I'm affected by her most when I stare into her little blue and brown eyes. She's the cutest little baby in the world.

Her skin is more tan now, and her complexion is like Jace's was. I should be relieved that he's gone, but it just is an added factor to my depression. I know Ella is devastated, and it crushes me that she may never speak to me again. How can I look her in the eyes ever again?

No one has met Zahara yet, and I'm glad about it. I know a lot of people are probably eager to meet her, but I want to keep her away from everyone as long as possible.

She grins at me, and I smile without trying and wipe away a tear from my eyes. When she huffs, I know she's ready for me to stop dilly-dallying, and I pick up the bottle and feed her.

I can't believe how tiny she is. A pang of guilt stabs me in the chest for neglecting her for so long. She's so pure and innocent. She didn't ask for any of this. She didn't ask to be here. How could I be so cruel?

My tears start to spill on their own, and I rock her gently while she eats to distract myself. Once she finishes, I put her on the bed near me and lie down. I want to hold her more, but I can't. And I feel so bad every time I put her in her crib, especially when she's awake and active. So this gives me the best of both worlds. I'm not strong enough to give her more right now, but I don't want either of us to be alone. Before I know it, she's drifted off to sleep.

I'm woken up at one p.m. by Odette who sits on the bed beside Zahara.

"Hey, sleepy girl." She smiles and reaches over to rub my cheek.

"Hi." I look at Zahara between us and panic.

I didn't mean to fall asleep. I was supposed to be watching her. What if I had rolled on top of her? My cheeks heat with embarrassment.

I sit up and bring my knees to my chest. "I didn't mean to fall asleep."

She crosses her legs under her green shirt-dress. "It's okay. You need rest."

A sob catches in my throat. "I know. But Zahara—"

"Is fine." She picks up Zahara and stands up. "I wish I took naps with James when he was a baby. Believe it or not, I was way more distant with him than you are with her." She looks down at Zahara and kisses her soft curls.

"Really?"

She blushes. "Yeah. Really. You're already warming up to her. Before you know it, you won't be able to be away from her for five minutes."

I sniffle. "Do you think so?"

"I know so, baby." She picks up Zahara's pink blanket and holds her close. "Why don't I take her for a bit, and you go have something to eat? You've missed breakfast, and it's past lunch. You need food just as much as Zee does."

A wave of nausea hits me and I can't tell if it's because I'm starving or need to throw up.

"Okay. I'll be down in a bit."

She winks and heads toward the door. "See you in a little while."

Once she's left, I take a few deep breaths and head to the closet to get dressed. I don't want to change, but I plan on going to the farm after I eat, and I know if I go out there half-dressed, James will have a fit when he finds me.

I miss him and can't wait for him to get home.

He hasn't been gone that long, but being anywhere near him makes me feel better. Even just having him in the house makes me feel lighter. But I instantly feel worse when he's not around.

I wish I would quit pushing him away. I want him close and I crave his affection, but it's hard to be intimate when I feel so fucking strange and depressed right now. He's still the sexiest man I've ever laid eyes on, but sexy is not a word that I would use to describe myself right now, so it's difficult to accept his advances when I feel way less confident than I used to.

Rummaging through the silk-covered hangers in our walk-in closet, I pull out a pair of teal leggings with a matching maternity bra.

This should be good enough.

It'll be fall soon, and I won't be able to go out in just a sports bra and leggings, so I'm taking advantage of that luxury now. Though I don't like having my body super exposed, I like to lie on the grass outside sometimes as it helps me feel better, and I feel more connected with nature when I don't have as many layers. James doesn't know this, but since we have complete privacy where we live, if Odette is out of the house and our farmhand isn't here, I'll take off my hoodie and lie on my back, letting the sun hit my bare chest. It might seem bizarre, but it makes me feel better.

After I finish getting dressed, I take the elevator down and grab a protein bar from the pantry and a bottle of water from the refrigerator. I should be having something more substantial, but this is better than nothing. I finish my snack quickly, grab my sunglasses off the kitchen island, slide into my white sneakers, and head out back.

I instantly feel relief stepping outside. Not necessarily joy, but like a crane is lifting the boulder off of my chest allowing me to breathe again. I walk slowly across our backyard and I eventually arrive at the farm.

It's crazy seeing how much land, produce, and space we have when we just used to have a tiny garden. It wasn't tiny, but it was small compared to what we have now.

I go over to our horses and lean up against the fence. Faith, our gray Arabian, comes up to me. Our other horses are a little more independent, but Faith is my girl. I wrap my arms around her neck and nuzzle my head into her mane. Her warm heavy breathing feels like a blanket over me, and I never want to let her go.

I call out to our Clydesdale, Sam, and he ignores me. He's a bit moody, but I'm sympathetic because I am too. Sometimes he's friendlier than others, but I'd never wrap my arms around him like I do Faith at the risk of being knocked in the head. Regardless, he has such a fun personality, and I love how different all of the animals are.

After grabbing some blueberries and rinsing them off, I head to my favorite spot to meet with Olive. Like always, she comes up to me as soon as I enter the fence, and she follows me to our own little patch of grass to sit.

I cross my legs on the ground, and she lies down beside me. I eat my fill of the blueberries and give her the rest. James gets frustrated when I do as he doesn't want her getting spoiled, but she's the sweetest companion and deserves a little treat here and there. I scratch her ears and my heart starts to hammer in my chest.

I hope James is alright.

I haven't heard from him in a few hours, and when I messaged him that I would be out here for a while, my text didn't go through, and I'm worried he doesn't have a signal.

What if they try and kill him?

What I want more than anything is for us to have a normal life. I don't want to raise our daughter in this cult, and the sooner we get away from everything, the better. But I have this terrible fear that that'll never happen or that the society will try and do something to us beforehand.

I wish that James brought me with him. I hate being out of the loop, and I don't want him to be alone. He probably thinks I'm so weak and fragile right now which is probably why he left me at home.

Here I fucking go again.

My cheeks are wet with my tears. I don't want James to think I'm weak. I want to be strong for him. For him and Zahara. I feel like I'm failing my daughter and my husband. I rely on him for so much. He should be able to rely on me too, and he probably feels like he can't right now.

I go to bring my knees to my chest to curl up in a ball, but before I do, Olive puts her soft white and brown head in my lap. I rest my hands on her and sob while she lets me.

She understands me so well and always comforts me when I need her. Maybe it's because she's a mother too.

Depression fucking sucks. I was so depressed for years of my life after my mother died. There were so many times when I just felt hopeless. Like I had nothing to live for or to offer back to the world. I tried to pursue dancing because it was the one thing that made me feel alive. When I turned eighteen and started seeing Antonio, I was distracted from my depression. But it resurfaced when he called things off.

Eventually, I got over him and discovered that I wanted to travel and learn as many languages as possible and found my passion in teaching and being around kids. Shortly after, I got with Tyler thinking I'd find happiness, but I got nothing but heartache. That being said, I still had a lot of joy toward the end of my relationship with Tyler, and all of that joy came from seeing James at work every day.

But the depression hit again when I got dumped by Tyler and moved in with James. Not because of James but because of my fucked up life. Then James and I started to get closer, and I thought my depression would disappear forever. While getting to know James more, I began to find myself for the first time in my life. And I truly fell in love for the first time in my life with him. I fall in love with him more and more every day.

However, I've fallen back down, and I have no idea when I'll get back up. And the most frustrating part is that my life is better than it's ever been before.

I find my breath again, but the tears still flow while I sit on the grass with my little pal.

At least I'm not alone.

I cry more often than I knew was possible. I'm struggling to eat enough each day. I keep the people I love most at arm's length, and most of the time it feels like a boulder is crushing my sternum. I'm sleep-deprived and feel like I'm barely functioning. But at the end of the day, I don't have to do this alone. I'm *not* going through this alone.

I wouldn't survive if I had to do this alone.

Chapter Ten

JAMES

It's been a month since The Caledonia Council has become a part of the society, and things are going ... well. Business is booming, and ten new perfume stores will open in a few weeks. The council is just as covert as I need them to be, being within reach but staying hidden so that none of my brothers or cousins are aware of their existence.

My Head Father's Text is coming along well, and the Council Entry Ceremony rules have been written. My only concern is that we may need to induct multiple members at once if any of our sons have birthdays that overlap, so I'm working on a few alternatives to make the process go quicker for those instances.

The Wedding Ceremony is straightforward, so there wasn't too much to write on that. I've got an idea for a New Birth Ceremony as well as an Exit Ceremony, but we won't practice those in advance and will save them for when they take place for real. The last ceremony I have in mind is a Vows of Submission Ceremony. It's the one that'll be the most flexible. The vows will remain the same, but I'll allow each man to perform it in his own way, so long as the bride submits and agrees to the vows. This one will certainly be the most entertaining, and Rebecca isn't aware yet, but she and I will practice it in our home later tonight.

I'm headed to pick her up from her hair appointment, and I'm dreading it. She has been hysterical with her pregnancy recently, and I don't know how much more of her nonsense I can take. Bill is helping me create an elixir for the perfumes, a drug if you will, to benefit the customer, and I'm hoping he can concoct something for me to use on my Rebecca also.

I hate paying for her overpriced hair appointments, but I sent her out for one today just to get some space. She's always up under me, and with her constant needs, I can hardly think straight. I love the girl to death, but I like her best when she's tied down to our bed with a pair of panties in her mouth. Unfortunately, the way I like her best has led to two pregnancies, and I was planning to stop at one.

RECLAMATION

When I get to the salon, I park out front and wait for her to come out to the car, hoping she'll take longer than needed. As soon as she gets in, she'll talk my ear off all the way home, and I'll have to refrain from pulling the bottle of whiskey from under my driver's seat just to cope.

-Jude Barlow, 1933

###

I sit in my car in front of my house after my first meeting with The Caledonia Council. It's nearly two p.m., and I'm desperate to get back to my girl. Being away from her is excruciating, and I've been so worried about her lately that I hate having her out of my sight. And I love being around her because I love her voice and her laugh and her smile, even though I haven't got to enjoy those things very much lately.

What am I going to say to her?

I have to tell her what happened at the meeting, but I'm terrified to tell her. I'm terrified because I made a life-changing decision without her, and I'm regretting it already. I don't regret having a chance at freedom, but making a choice without my wife feels like I'm breaking a vow. And I don't ever want my wife's faith in me to waiver. And I'm shitting myself because she's already upset, and telling her about the meeting and what I've done is only going to make her feel worse.

After taking my blazer off and leaving it in the passenger's seat, I step out of the car to talk to Gen. I got a text from her that came in late saying she was headed to the farm, and I'd bet my bottom dollar she's still there now.

When I make it around the house, I see her out in the distance, and my heart stops. She's sprawled out on Olive like a rag doll, and panic courses through my body.

I sprint at full speed to her and slow down when I see her rustle and sit up straight.

She was sleeping.

I need to calm down. I need a drink. No—what I need more than anything is Gen in my arms. As I get closer, I see her wipe her face with her hands, and I can already tell she's crying.

She's probably been crying out here for the past hour. Why did my mother let her stay out here by herself for so long without me home?

I stand behind her, a few feet away, and call out to her. "Gen."

She slumps over, weeping, and my heart hurts like someone beat it with a sledgehammer.

I can't tell her what happened right now. I need to make her feel better. I have to. It's my duty as her husband. As her lover. As her best friend. I sit down behind her on the grass, not caring how dirty my clothes get, and pull her small body up against me. She squeezes her eyes shut and shakes, and I wrap my arms around her tightly, squeezing her like she might fly away if I don't.

Every shiver of her body pulsates through me, and I feel myself shutting down with her. I want to scream and cry, but I can't let those emotions out. Tucking her head under my chin, I rub my hands up and down her arms and rock her softly, trying to soothe her like I soothe our baby. I don't know how long it takes, but eventually, she starts to breathe normally again.

I kiss her neck, feeling a wave of nostalgia wash over me when her white orchid perfume fills my nostrils, and take her hair out of her bun, burying my face in her soft curls. Once I've calmed down, I move her hair to the side and whisper in her ear while she leans against me. "I swear to you, Gen—you will be happy again. I vow that I will make you the happiest you've ever been in your entire life. Happier than you ever knew was possible."

#

After I got Gen back inside from the farm, I put her down for a nap and retrieved Zee from her grandmother. My mother didn't want to let her go, but my wife needs rest, and I don't have a support animal, so I need my baby to comfort me.

When I scoop Zahara up in my arms, she squeals and I laugh automatically. It's amazing to me that as fucked up as everything is around her, my baby girl is always full of so much unbridled joy. I don't deserve her. Someone as fucked up and evil as me doesn't deserve anything good.

I carry my baby to my office and shut the door behind me, hoping that my mother will take that as a cue to leave me alone. Whenever I leave the door open, she walks right in and plops down on the couch, talking my ear off. Right now I want to be undisturbed and left alone. I place Zahara in her crib by my desk and lie down on the couch, facing her.

It pains me so much that Gen hasn't fully connected with her yet. If Zahara is as happy as she is already, I know her joy will only quadruple with Gen's affection. I know because Gen's affection quadrupled my happiness. And without her energy source, I feel dead inside. Like I did before I met her.

Rolling onto my back, I look up at the light beige ceiling. It reminds me of my grandfather's cabin that Genevieve and I stayed at before Zahara was born.

The cabin where we made Zahara.

I want to go back there now. With both of my girls. But there's too much going on. And I have something I have to do in four days. Something I can't prepare for.

I'm a procrastinator, but that doesn't mean I like to be unprepared in every scenario. If I can scope out a situation beforehand and get an advantage, I will. But The Caledonia Council holds all the fucking cards, so I'm left with just my imagination.

My weapons will be on me when I arrive at the address, but who knows if I'll need them. I wonder what they'll have me do. Deliver a package? They've certainly got more secrets that I don't know about. Maybe they want to use me as a messenger. An errand boy. Whatever it is, I'm going to have to do it if I want to pass. Failing is not an option. The consequences of not fulfilling my mission are too devastating.

Turning my head back over to my baby, I notice a bottle of vodka on the corner of my desk. My stomach tingles for a sip. Just a taste of that smooth and refreshing tonic.

Who am I kidding?

I want more than a taste. Three or four shots should be enough to take the edge off. But I won't touch it. I'm saying no to booze right now because it's irresponsible with my daughter in the room. Not only is it my responsibility to look after her, but her little mind is developing so rapidly that I know she's watching every single thing I do, and I don't want her to develop bad habits someday because somewhere down in her psyche is a memory of her daddy getting toasted next to her playpen. No. My kids will be better than me. They will be sober, well-adjusted individuals who focus on their goals and dreams—not money and drugs and sex.

And the next time I drink, I would like to do it with my wife. She hasn't had alcohol in nearly a year, and I'm sure that when she's feeling better, she'll want to have a big glass of wine, and I'm going to have one with her. I've never intentionally taken a break from alcohol, but having the goal to stay away from it until Gen is better is exactly what I need. Something motivating to look forward to. And it'll probably be good for my health. I've never gone more than two months without a drink, but if my wife can do it for over nine, I'm sure I can manage.

I hate how hard Gen is on herself. It's not lost on me that she feels guilty for her emotions right now. She had this picture in her head of what motherhood would be like, and so far, it's not living up to her expectations. I've learned more and more about postpartum depression, and I've found relief in knowing that it's way more common than a lot of people know. What she's going through is normal. She's not broken. And it won't be like this forever, even though right now it's really hard.

I just wish she could see how incredible she is. I'm so proud of her. I always have been proud of her and her accomplishments have always been impressive to me, but she just keeps getting better.

Not only does she have all of her professional accolades, but she had my baby. This woman gave me a child that she grew in her womb. I'm still mind-blown every day that the little baby I get to cuddle came from her. That this baby is half of my favorite person in the world. She's done something that I could never fathom doing. I'd rather cut out my heart and eat it than have to deliver a child. She's a goddamn rockstar.

And her beauty. I'll never get over it. Never get used to it. I'd write a song about her if I had the fucking talent to do so. I wish I could come up with a poem to describe how stunning and perfect she is. She should be painted and framed above my desk. But I don't have a talent for any of those things. I don't know how yet, but I *will* find a way to show her just how much she means to me.

#

I wake Gen up at nine a.m. to help me feed Zahara and get ready for brunch. She was out of it for the remainder of the day yesterday, and I couldn't find a good time to tell her what happened at the meeting. However, she's had a good night's sleep, and I'll have my first task in three days, so I need to go ahead and catch her up to speed. Plus, I haven't taken her out since she gave birth, and brunch is our first step back to going on dates.

Gen showers in our bathroom while I rummage through the closet for something to wear. I thought we'd have a shower together, but I think I stared at her too hungrily and freaked her out, so she asked if she could have one privately. I put my desires to the side to allow her some privacy, and I showered in one of the spare rooms down the hall to speed things up.

Sweat slides down my back as I try to put together my outfit. Dressing usually comes easy to me, but for my first time back out with Gen, I want to impress her. I want to look put together, but not overdone, and I want to wear something that she'll remember and be pleased with.

It's a cool day, nearly September, so I grab a caramel knit sweater and a pair of dark blue straight-leg jeans. I've been wearing a lot of black lately as it's the color worn by the Head Father, and I'm worried that it's affecting Gen's mood. Black is timeless and sexy, but I want to catch my wife off-guard and surprise her, and I'm hoping this look will do the trick.

Once I put on my clothing, I grab a pair of black socks and wine-leather combat boots, a wine-colored scarf, and my black sunglasses. After double-checking that everything is in place, I grab my things and head downstairs to wait for Gen.

I'm not ready to leave my baby with anyone without Gen nearby, so my mother will have the house to herself while Zahara comes with us to breakfast.

It doesn't take me long to pack Zee's baby bag, and before I know it, Gen is coming out of the elevator ready to go.

My heart beats twice as fast as she approaches me. She's wearing a knee-length, long-sleeve, baby pink sweater dress that flares out. My eyes are instantly drawn to the V that shows off her cleavage. She fidgets uncomfortably and I silently chastise myself for staring, moving my eyes up to her face. Her pretty curls are fluffed out around her face and shoulders in a half-up, half-down style, and she has on a pink velvet choker that I wish was the red leather one I got her earlier this year instead. I get a peek at her bare legs before my view gets blocked by her matching knee-high suede boots.

I hold our daughter in my arms and extend a hand for Gen to take. "You look beautiful. Are you ready to go?"

She places her soft hand in mine. "Ready."

#

I drive us thirty minutes out of town to a place that I know Genevieve will love. They serve avocado toast, poached eggs, and a whole bunch of other fancy shit I know she adores.

Zahara sleeps quietly in the back while we ride, and Gen looks outside the window the entire time.

When we get to our destination, I help Gen out of the car, grab Zahara, and head inside.

The walls of the quaint cafe are covered in teal wallpaper with light green flowers. There are plenty of windows, and the white tablecloth on the tables matches the white chairs. The floor is made up of colorful tiles, and I can't tell if I'm impressed or overwhelmed by the combination of everything.

We're quickly greeted, seated, and handed menus. Gen peruses hers while we wait for our waters, and Zahara stays in her slumber.

I try to remain focused while I stare at her glossy lips. "I need to talk to you about yesterday."

She puts her menu down and looks up at me. "Go ahead."

I take a breath and let it all out, telling her the offer and what's at stake, hoping that the waiter will take his time before he returns.

Her pale blue eyes water while she processes the news. "You agreed to that, James? Knowing that we might die as a result?"

My throat tightens. "You know me well enough to know that I would never let that happen, Gen. I swear to God that nothing will happen to you or Zahara."

She clenches her jaw. "Or Odette."

"Or Odette."

Guilt consumes me when she shakes her head. "I still can't believe you, James. Why couldn't you have just mended things? Or stalled or something? You're gambling with our lives! Why didn't you agree to keep things as they are?"

"Because I know that's not what you really want. If I agreed to that, you'd never forgive me, and you know it. I'm taking a risk, but it's going to work out. I'm doing this for us, Gen. Please don't be angry with me."

The waiter returns with our waters. "Are we ready to order?"

I shake my head and stare at my wife whose head is about to explode. "Give us a few more minutes, please."

"Absolutely, sir." He turns on his heel, oblivious to Gen's attitude, and walks away.

She sighs frustratedly. "What are they making you do?"

I clasp my hands together to prevent them from shaking. "I don't know."

Her eyes go wide. "This can't be happening. What if they ask you to steal? Commit murder?"

I grip my jeans and talk low. "You say those things like I haven't done them before."

She lowers her head, and her voice softens. "I didn't think you'd keep doing those things forever."

I hate how she's looking away from me. It makes me feel disgusting. I don't want to disappoint her. I don't want her to be ashamed of me.

"I don't plan on doing those things forever, baby. But I might have to do them for a while."

Her tears start to spill, and my head throbs. She already cries so much, and I'm ruining the start of her day by making her cry more.

"Gen, please look at me."

She stands up and covers her face. I know her well enough to know that she's planning to walk away from me.

She's either after the bathroom or the car. Anywhere to get away from this situation. But I won't allow it.

The restaurant is nearly empty, but I keep my voice low. "Genevieve Barlow, sit back down. Now."

I'm taking a risk by speaking to Gen this way. She doesn't like being told what to do, but she likes being bossed around in the right circumstances. Right now is definitely the wrong circumstance, but I'm hoping my sternness still has the same effect on her.

She looks up at me and bites her lip, standing in place.

I feel my confidence grow an ounce when she doesn't turn to walk away. "Genevieve, I will not ask you again. Sit down, right now, or I will grab you by your hair and make you."

Jesus Christ—am I really trying this right now? I say my words seductively, but she's definitely not in the mood to be seduced.

I say a silent prayer, hoping I didn't piss her off more. But when her heavy tits rise and fall rapidly, I know I've got her. She sits back down and glares at me.

I reach across the table and pull her hands in mine. "Look, Gen. You don't have to like me right now, but I know without a doubt that you love me, and you know I'm doing this for us whether you want to admit it or not."

She frowns, but her eyes sparkle. "I do love you. Yes. But you're right—I don't like you right now. You're doing something that I don't know if I agree with, and you didn't consult me first. I should've been there with you. And you didn't bring me. I'm pissed."

I squeeze her hands tightly, grateful that she's stopped crying and is talking to me instead. "I know you're mad. I want you to be mad because I want you to *feel*, Gen. You've been so down lately, and I want you to feel something other than sadness. Even if it's rage."

She pouts and tries to pull her hands away, but I keep them tucked in mine. "And I want you to hold onto that anger as long as you need, Gen. Let it radiate throughout your body and stay angry with me as long as you can. Because in a few weeks, I'm going to fuck you, and I'm going to fuck you *hard*. Brutally. Ruthlessly. And we're going to let out all of our anger together and have hate sex like you've never dreamed of."

She gasps. "Oh, really?"

There's that sass I love.

"Yes, really. You're going to thank me for pissing you off in this moment when you come harder than you ever have in your life, you dirty little slut."

She scrunches her eyebrows and huffs, but I catch the smallest smirk before she tightens her lips. "I don't know. I'll probably still be too angry to let you fuck me, James."

I shake my head. "False. You will not deny me."

She gasps. "Are you saying you're going to take it from me?"

Fuck. Is that what she thinks I meant? I would never—shit. My wife thinks I just threatened to force her to have sex with me.

My palms start to sweat. "Gen, I would never—"

She smirks for real this time.

Is she flirting with me? My lips move faster than my brain. I lean in closer and whisper to her. "Do you *want* me to take it from you, Gen?"

She bats her eyelashes before she brushes her lips against my ear. "I don't know if you could. But I'd like to see you try."

My cock twitches and my neck heats. I lean back in my chair away from her delicious scent to try and calm myself down. "Gen, if you want me to do what I *think* you're asking me to do, I'm down. But we have to have a serious discussion about it first to make sure we're on the same page."

She leans back in her chair and wets her lips. "Okay."

The waiter returns, and I grab my napkin to toss over my throbbing crotch.

"What can I get started for you today?"

Gen nibbles her lip and glances at the menu. Her voice comes out low and sultry, not enough for the waiter to notice, but in the same tone she uses with me when we're in bed. "I'll have the spotted dick with poached eggs and smashed avocado on the side. And sausage." She pokes out her lips. "And a coffee. With lots of cream." She locks her eyes on mine and I swear I feel precum drip from my tip.

He smiles. "Sounds *delicious*. And for you, sir?"

I open my mouth to speak and freeze, flustered. There's nothing I want to eat more right now than my wife's cunt, but that's not on the menu. Unable to get a clear fucking thought in my head, I go with the only words I can gather. "I'll take what she's having."

Chapter Eleven

GENEVIEVE

I have no idea what got into me at breakfast this morning. I had a really rough day with my emotions yesterday, and although I wanted to hear the details of James' meeting as soon as he got home, I couldn't stop crying, and I slept a lot. He told me before bed that we'd discuss everything today over brunch, and I'm glad we waited.

When I woke up, I wasn't in the mood to go out. But after having a warm shower and putting on something cute for the first time in a while, I did feel a lot better.

And James.

I was taken aback when I saw him in jeans and a sweater, but I loved it. His hair was perfectly messy, and my ovaries felt like they were going to explode watching him hold our baby. *He's such a good daddy.*

I got so upset with him at the restaurant, but something awakened in me when he told me to sit down. Even though I was angry, I was suddenly turned on. And what really did it for me was him telling me he was going to hate fuck me. It made me want to stay mad at him and had me hoping that he'll get angry too just to see what that's like.

I don't know who was possessing me when I asked him if he was going to take it from me. As soon as I said it, I thought I might've gone too far, but when he told me he was down, I felt like I was going to come from clenching my thighs together so hard.

There are things about me that will never change, but I've also evolved in so many ways since being with James. Before we got together, all I had was vanilla sex, and I thought that's all I could ever want or need, but he's awakened this side of me that wants him to try whatever he wants with me. Even if we just do it one time.

I lie on my stomach in bed, waiting while James gets the massage oil ready. He's kept up with his promise of nightly massages before bed, and I'm hoping he never stops.

My head raises off of my crossed arms on my pillow when he pulls it back by my hair, making me let out an involuntary moan. I still don't have the energy to do my hair and the only person I trust with it is Ella.

I hope we patch things up with her soon.

However, James has been having fun with my curls out by burying his face in them constantly, and he's already back to his favorite hair activity: pulling.

His warm hands glide across my strands, and he yanks on my hair a little more while he twists it to tuck in a bun.

Once he's done, I hear him open the jar of oil. "I'm going to start rubbing you now."

"Okay." I rest my head back down before I feel his soft fingers coated in oil glide across my back. He rubs them in circles with medium pressure, making me feel instant relief.

"That feels so good, love."

He leans over me, pressing his lips to my neck. "I love it when you call me that, Gen."

I feel myself smile. "Well good. I came up with it just for you."

The crotch of his underwear brushes against my ass while he rubs me. "Really? You didn't call your past boyfriends *love*?"

"Nope. Just you. Did you call any of your past girlfriends *Darling*?"

He gets quiet, and I don't even have to look at him to know he's blushing. "First of all, they weren't my girlfriends. Just sex partners. You already know that. And no. That name is only for you, Gen. I had a lot of firsts with you."

I chuckle into my pillow. "You? No way. You didn't have any *firsts* left when you got with me."

He pops my ass and my pussy twitches. "Yes, I did, smart ass."

I turn my head to the side and peek at him over my shoulder. "Like what?"

He massages my hips. "I'd never been called Daddy before you."

Really? I thought every girl James fucked would've called him Daddy. It fits him so well.

"Oh. Very interesting." I wink at him. "Is that it?"

He really blushes now. "I always used condoms before you."

No way. "You're kidding."

He turns my face back down and massages my neck. "No. I'm not."

My voice comes out muffled, trying to talk over my pillow. "So, I'm the first woman that you ever came inside of?"

He presses his erection against my ass cheeks. "Yes. I vowed to never come inside a woman I wasn't prepared to impregnate."

I feel a pang of something in my chest, remembering the time I told James I couldn't have kids. "But you thought I was infertile."

What he says next surprises me more than anything. "Yeah. I thought you were, most likely. But I still really wanted to get you pregnant."

My pussy throbs and my body warms up even more thinking about the first time we had sex. "Really? You wanted to get me pregnant that early?"

He sighs. "Yeah. I knew you wanted a baby so badly, and I wanted to give you everything you wanted. I still do. I wanted to be the first man to impregnate you. The *only* man."

My heart swells in my chest, and I turn over on my back to face him with him still hovering over me. "You *are* the only man, James. I want to give you everything too."

His eyes sparkle, and he blinks them a few times before regaining his composure. "You already do give me everything."

He spreads my legs and wraps them around his waist, sliding on top of me. The only thing separating his hardness from my heat is the thin fabric of his underwear.

I suck in a breath when he rests his elbows on either side of my face, his lips inches from mine. The starving wanton in me takes over to speak, feeling his balls pressed against the seam of my ass. "I still have *firsts* to give you."

He bites my neck and whispers in my ear. "I know you do. And I want them all."

Chapter Twelve

JAMES

Today's the motherfucking day.

I get up at six a.m. to feed Zahara before I get ready for "level one" of The Caledonia Trials. I woke Gen up at four to pump, and she's back asleep. I'm hoping I can sneak out without waking her.

I'm feeling so many emotions right now, and none of them are good. Gen and I had such a lovely sexually charged brunch the other day, and for a brief moment, I thought I had my girl back. I nearly came in my pants at the table with the way she was flirting with me. I'm super excited to talk through her latest fantasy with her.

And later that night, she basically insinuated that she wanted me to fuck her ass. I would definitely confirm before attempting to, but it shocked me that she'd even want to try.

Though I'm not very big on anal, the thought of doing something with Gen that she's never done with anyone else makes me feel possessive and crazed. I will gladly make love to her sexy little ass if that's what my girl desires. Just the thought of it makes me rock solid. I want to claim her in every way possible.

But all of those potential activities will have to wait. She's been crying a lot the past couple of days, and I know she's still not feeling like herself. On top of that, she's still recovering physically, and I don't know how long it'll take for her to be one hundred percent again.

What shocks me the most is how shy she still is about me seeing her new mommy tits despite everything we've already done together and what she wants to try. When I have her riled up and in the moment with me, it's like she forgets that she's changed and can just enjoy what's going on whether I'm massaging her or we're taking a shower together. But in regular moments like pumping, she gets nervous around me like I've never seen her body before. I wish I could say it didn't bother me, but it does, and I've got half a mind to burn all of her tops and bras so she's forced to expose herself to me at all times. But I won't do that because I'm not a dick.

I scoop our baby out of her crib and rock her softly to keep her sleepy. She gets hyper so quickly, and I don't want her adorable little giggles and squeaks waking her mommy. After I've gotten her bottle ready, I carry her tiny little body out into the hall while her tiny hands reach for her bottle.

My emotions surge through me in an overwhelming way, and I almost feel tears forming. Gen and my mother are going through things, but I am too. I feel so much pressure right now, and I feel like I'm about to break. But I can't. Instead, I take a few deep breaths and push back my threatening tears while I feed my oblivious baby.

My mother is in her guest room on the floor below us, but I'm not worried about disturbing her pacing back in forth down the hall as she's an unnaturally heavy sleeper. She always has been. When she wasn't busy doing something I wasn't aware of (like screwing her secret lover), she was asleep. I think it was her safe place from my father's rage.

I kiss Zahara's forehead while she guzzles her milk. Sometimes I like to talk to her while I feed her. She hasn't responded yet, but that hasn't deterred me from keeping our morning conversations going.

I look into her eyes to get her attention. "Do you want a little sibling?"

Her mismatched eyes sparkle, and I take that as a yes. The last thing I should be thinking about right now is more kids. If I'm honest, I can barely handle the one I have.

But as I walk around the hall with my newborn, I can't help but wonder what it would be like to have all of these rooms filled with our babies. And as soon as that thought pops up in my head, it shatters like broken glass.

What if Gen doesn't want any more kids?

I can't believe this is an actual fear I'm having. I'm not supposed to want children. That's never been my desire. But it became something I wanted when I got with Genevieve. I'd be completely content with just this little one, but I would be ecstatic with more.

I remember after we brought Zee home, I was so worried that we made a mistake. I feared that I wouldn't be a good father. That I wouldn't love her.

But I adore this little girl.

She's so much like her mom, and I couldn't be happier about that. She's got such a big personality already, and I can't wait to see all that she does and accomplishes. I know Gen hasn't bonded with her yet like she thought she would, but she'll get there. I know it.

I just hope my Gen won't be more obsessed with our baby than she is with me.

Once Zahara finishes her bottle, I get her put back in her crib, take a quick shower, put on my black suit and matching shoes, grab my weapons, and my phone, and head downstairs.

I leave the house at seven a.m., to head to the address I'm scheduled to be at. It's a little under a two-hour drive give or take a few minutes for traffic, and I should be there right at nine a.m. when I'm supposed to be.

I have no idea what the location I'm going to looks like or what I have to do when I get there. What if I do have to kill someone? I've killed before, but all of my kills have been on my own accord. No one held a gun to my head or made me.

Am I prepared to do something against my own free will?

Another concern I have with committing murder is the effect it has on me. I handle violence differently than mentally stable individuals, and I'm worried that I may get too comfortable with killing. I may get hooked and crave to do it again and again just to let off some steam.

Is that a bad thing?

If I'm killing bad people, it's not that bad, is it? Like, what if I'm killing rapists and murderers? That would definitely be a positive.

But I am a murderer.

I push the thought away and try to think of other alternatives. Who knows—I could be getting ready to do something *good*. Maybe my mission has something to do with philanthropy. I could be going to a soup kitchen or an orphanage to volunteer my time. I smile to myself, trying to remain positive.

Who the fuck am I kidding?

There's no way they're going to ask me to do something good. Whatever they have planned will be something horrible that'll keep me up at night.

What if they ask me to do something really horrible? What if I have to hurt more animals? I guess I already do hurt animals. I send my cows to slaughter and eat my chicken's eggs.

What if it's worse than that? Maybe I'll have to burn down someone's house. Or steal from a government building. I have no fucking clue what they've set me up to do, and I've agreed to it already like a goddamn idiot.

My heart starts to fucking pound, and I roll down the windows to catch my breath. My head hurts and I regret not eating breakfast before I left the house. My palms sweat, and my throat closes. *I cannot have a panic attack right now.* It would do me no good.

I count to ten a few times and keep breathing until I feel like I'm no longer suffocating. Once I settle back down, I roll back up the windows, and the sun slowly starts to rise. The gentle glow comforts me, and my mind instantly goes to my girls. I wonder if Zahara and Gen are still sleeping.

I love that Gen's okay with the crib by her side of the bed. I know they both sleep better because of it. My mother told me Gen took a nap with her the other day, and my heart nearly burst. I can't wait for them to get closer to each other.

I haven't even been gone that long and I miss them already. My heart has truly expanded since becoming a father. I had no idea I had so much love to give. And I can't wait to pour that love back into my wife and children.

Reality slaps me in the face when my GPS brings me to a one-lane road that leads through tall trees. There's no more wondering and waiting—it's finally time to do what I have to do whether I'm ready or not. I drive slowly down the road, taking note of every strange thing I see. For one, there's a camera about every six feet on either side of the road. I drive for nearly ten minutes, and there aren't any animals. No squirrels running around or birds. There's so much nature and it all feels . . . dead.

When I finally make it to the end of the path, I'm surprised by what I see.

What the fuck?

At the end of the path is a nearly empty open lot. There are no buildings, and I don't see anyone around. There's just a semi with an open trailer, and inside is a black car with a white envelope on it.

No. Am I supposed to get in there? That's crazy.

But this is exactly where I'm supposed to be.

I feel myself starting to get stressed, and I suddenly have the urge to pee. Though I'd prefer not to pull my dick out and piss on the ground, I don't want to leave here to find a bathroom and be considered late for my first mission. However, I clearly am going somewhere, and since I don't know how long the journey will take, it's best that I relieve myself now.

Stepping out of my SUV, I take another look around before doing what I need to do. Once I've gotten myself situated, I curse myself for not having hand sanitizer, send my beautiful wife a text letting her know what's going on, climb into the truck, and stand by the car inside it.

I pick up the embossed envelope, instantly tensing as I tear it open. Of course, the red ink says what I'm dreading.

Get in on the driver's side, and get comfortable.

Great.

I hope this doesn't take long. It already took me a while to get here, and it'll take me a while to get home. My mind instantly goes to my girls.

Will they be alright while I'm away?

I know my mother is home with them, and they're safe, but I'm not normally away from them for this long.

I pick up my phone and send Draco a quick message. While Gen was taking a nap the day I got home from meeting with The Caledonia Council, I caught him up on how the meeting went so he knew I made it in and out alright. My fingers move quickly across my touchscreen, not wanting to delay things longer than I already have.

> Hi. It's me.

> Everything alright?

> Yeah. I'm just getting ready to do that thing I told you about.

> Don't die James.

How fucking encouraging.

> I won't. Can you stop by the house and make sure everything looks alright? Just keep an eye on things in the neighborhood while I'm away.

> Of course. When will you be back?

> I don't know. But keep me posted if you see anything strange.

> Of course. Godspeed Father.

I roll my eyes, shut my phone, and get seated inside the vehicle. Though I don't want everyone to know where my family resides, having someone who can be a second set of eyes to keep an eye on things helps with my stress levels. Draco isn't my first choice, but my first choice is dead, so he'll have to do. And Draco having my address can't be any worse than The Caledonia Council. After a moment of sitting in my seat waiting for what happens next, the trailer closes, and I'm left in darkness.

Chapter Thirteen
GENEVIEVE

I sit in the bed trying to journal while Zahara sleeps in her crib next to me. James has been gone for nearly four hours, and I'm antsy as fuck waiting for him to return.

I haven't been able to get back to sleep since he got out of bed. And about thirty minutes after he left, I needed to get up anyway to change Zahara's diaper, and she was hungry again. Once I got her put back down, I put my hair in a bun, grabbed an oversized tee, and scrolled on my phone for way too long. Now I'm trying to do something productive.

Everything is a distraction. The A/C cuts on, and it rustles our black bedroom curtains. I stare at the green walls, and my mind wanders thinking of all sorts of things like how paint was made and if I'd like the walls if they were painted blue instead. Looking up at the ceiling, I wonder if we should replace the chandelier. I think I'm trying to distract myself so I can avoid doing what I set out to do when I got up: reflect on my feelings and try to process them.

James has been doing a lot of research lately, and he thought I might be able to process my emotions better by getting them out on paper. So he bought me this journal with prompts, lists, and activities, and I'm trying to use it now.

My eyes stare at the gratitude section, and I have to take a few deep breaths to stave off my tears. I've been so upset lately, but I have so much to be grateful for.

First, I'm grateful for James. Our lives have changed so much since getting together, but he's still my best friend and my true love. He takes care of me like no one else, and sometimes I question if he's real. I don't know how I'd function without him by my side. He just gets me. Like, *really* gets me. He understands me and my quirks, and he likes the things about me that Tyler found annoying. And he knows what I need even when I can't vocalize it.

Next, I'm grateful for Zahara. My hand shakes when I write down her name in my journal. I can't believe this little baby was given to me. This soul to take care of and raise. I do sleep better having her beside me at night. And when I'm away from her, I feel more anxious. And I know she makes James so happy. She's so small and fragile, but she's a big part of our lives already. I can't imagine being without her either.

I close my notebook and stand beside her crib. She breathes softly, and it's amazing to me how content she is. One of my biggest concerns about having a baby was that my child would cry and scream for hours, unable to get comfortable enough to go to sleep. But my baby is so quiet and calm. Zahara barely cries, and she loves to sleep. She's amazing.

I want to pick her up and hold her, but I can't. I feel like a phony. Like a piece of shit for treating her the way that I have been for the past three weeks. I want to be the mom she deserves so badly. She should be tucked in my arms all day. I should be breathing in her sweet baby smell. Cuddling her and rocking her to sleep. But all of those things feel so foreign to me right now. Like if I try, I might hurt her or she might reject me. I just want to stop feeling so fucking horrible.

I turn away from her and slump down against her crib, shutting my eyes to pretend I'm not crying again.

Something tugs at my head, and I look over my shoulder to see Zahara playing with a loose lock of my hair. She smiles, gripping it tightly while she stares at me.

My chest tightens and I turn to face her, letting her keep the strands in her hands. She squeaks and giggles, and I watch my curls touch hers which look nearly identical to mine. The only difference is hers are black and mine are dark brown.

She's gorgeous. I can't believe how cute my baby is. Has she always been this adorable?

Her blue eye has more color to it than the day she was born, and it looks so much like mine do. Her brown eye is identical to James' eyes, and her curls are getting longer each day. That caramel skin is yummy enough to eat. Her long dark lashes flutter, and she starts to doze off while her hands slowly release me. I don't know where I find the strength, but eventually, I manage to stand up, and when I do, I reach into her crib and stroke her curls softly.

She likes me. I think my baby actually likes me. Maybe she'll forgive me for how I've treated her. Maybe deep down she understands.

My baby's sweet affection gives me the boost I need to make it through the day. Surprising myself, I lean down to give her a kiss, and she grins from ear to ear.

I love you, Zahara. Mommy will get better soon. I promise.

Chapter Fourteen

JAMES

The minute the truck starts moving, I lose my cell signal. I look around with my phone light and don't see keys in the car, so I don't have the radio to keep me entertained during my journey. Staring at my phone nearly the entire time, I see the drive takes forty-five minutes, and eventually, we get to our destination.

The trailer opens, and outside of it is a ramp that I assume I'm supposed to drive down, but there's no key.

I'm an idiot.

I feel something under the heel of my shoe, and I pick up the key to start the car. When I drive down the ramp, I take in my surroundings. I'm behind a house. In the backyard of some old abandoned mansion in the woods. Of course, it would be in the woods.

On the back porch steps is another note. I waste no time tearing it open.

Open the trunk.

I suddenly get a bad feeling out of nowhere. When I was on my way to my mission, the sun was rising. But now, the sky is cloudy and gray. The truck drives off, and I kick myself for not getting a look at the driver. Now I'm left here all alone.

I'm on high alert, whipping my eyes all around, making sure no one's about to sneak up on me. My heart sinks when I head to the back of the car and hear movement in the trunk. I've seen enough movies to know where this is going.

Killing. The mission is clearly killing.

But who the fuck am I killing?

Damion instantly pops up into my mind. It's because of Jessamine. Damion has been cheating on Theresa with Jessamine, and I should've killed him but didn't. They must be making me do it now.

I don't want to kill Damion. I won't. If that's what this is, I'm not fucking doing it.

Gen.

They might try and hurt Gen or Zahara if I don't kill him. I don't have a choice. I have to kill him.

What if it's not him at all?

I pop open the trunk and keep my eyes wide open, prepared for a wild animal to jump out. Instead, I just see a man with bloodshot eyes who I don't recognize with tape over his mouth and his hands bound with rope behind his back.

He's got cuts all over his face, and blood is dripping from his salt-and-pepper hairline. His eyes meet mine, and he starts freaking out, convulsing and making noises.

Is this some random civilian? I reach for the tape covering his mouth, and my phone pings in my pocket.

> Stop right there.

> There's a weapon in his left boot. Take it out and kill him. Bury him out back. There's a shovel on the porch.

The man makes noises under his tape, and I glance at the porch, noticing the shovel I missed when I arrived.

My eyes trail down his dirty and torn black shirt and bloody jeans, wondering what happened to this man before we met. Digging into his black cowboy boots, I pull out something long, cold, and sharp.

An ice pick?

His eyes go wide and he shakes his head while I hold the nine-inch titanium spear in my hand. I'm supposed to kill this man, and I'm supposed to kill him with this ice pick. Right here, right now. I don't know what I thought would happen during this mission exactly, but I thought I'd at least get to speak to someone beforehand.

I grip the tool tightly and start to panic.

Who is this man? What if he has a family? Is he evil or is he innocent? I can't kill him without knowing. I'd never sleep again.

I reach for the tape again, and my phone stops me with another chime.

> Whatever you do, do not remove the tape. Kill, bury, get back in the car, and drive back to your SUV. This is only level one. Don't fail.

Just like my wife, I hate being told what to do. Will I kill this man? Probably. But there's no way in fuck I'm doing it without getting information first. Level one is killing him, and I will do that. However, I'm going to start by doing what I want.

I reach for the tape for the third time, tearing it off in one tug. He spits out a bloody sock, and tears stream down his face. "Don't do it, James. Please, don't do it."

James? "How do you know who I am?"

He looks around frantically. "Get out of here. Now. Take Genevieve, the baby, and Etty somewhere far away from here. Take as much money as you can, and hide."

Etty? Etty. Ett—

Odette.

My palms sweat, staring into the man's pale blue eyes. "Who are you?"

He clenches his eyes shut. "I'm Shane. My dad and grandfather were also Shane, but I'm probably the only one you've heard about."

Shane. The sector leader. My mother's lover.

He's still alive? "Shane, what's going on? I need you to tell me what's going on."

My phone makes me jolt, pinging again.

> Thirty-seconds, James. Or we take a life.

Shane's eyes go wide. "James, no."

Fuck. I'm on a countdown again. What do I do? I can't walk away from this. But how do I kill him? My mother is in love with this man. And what did he ever do wrong to me? I like justified violence. This isn't justified.

I grip my weapon, staring at him with my mouth open.

His voice shakes. "James, listen to me, son—"

My head pounds. "Shane—stop talking. I can't—"

> Ten...nine...

"James! Please for the love of God, don't do it. They'll never let you go."

The wind picks up, and I see lightning in the distance even though there's no rain. It's cool out, but my body feels like it's being doused in fire. I feel adrenaline, rage, and fear, and I can't decipher which feeling has the strongest pull.

This was never supposed to happen. I was supposed to die, and Genevieve was supposed to live a happy life without me in it. But nothing is like I thought it would be.

Will they ever forgive me? If I do this, I don't know if my wife and mother will forgive me.

The adrenaline surges throughout my body, and I bask in it, letting the thrill take over me. My blood pumps in my ears, and my mind travels to that place I seldom let it go.

I clutch the ice pick in my left hand and send a prayer to heaven, praying that God will accept my wife and daughter when I go to hell.

"Shane, I'm sorry."

"James!"

Gripping the wooden handle with both hands, I position the tip of the pick at Shane's ear, bite my lip, and ignore his cries while I drive it in.

Chapter Fifteen

GENEVIEVE

Four hours after James has left, I hear a knock at the door. Instinctively I tense up, wondering who it could be.

I hope nothing happened to James.

He's okay. You need to calm down. I'm downstairs in the kitchen having a smoothie while Odette is upstairs in her room with Zahara. I had her three weeks ago, and I feel like I'm slowly returning back to myself. I'm still worlds different than I was before giving birth, but I no longer need postpartum pads, I haven't gotten a random cramp the past few days, and I'm getting my appetite back.

Whoever knocked at the door might go away if I ignore them. As soon as I have that thought, it's shot down by more knocking. I hear a muffled voice come through the door.

"Genevieve? Are you there? It's Draco. Are you alright?"

Draco? What is he doing here?

Running up to the door, I peek out the peephole and confirm it's him. "Hi, Draco. I'm fine—give me a moment. I'll be right back."

He smiles. "Take your time."

I know James asked his cousin to step up beside him in the society, so I'm not scared about him showing up at random, but I'm still confused by it. I try to call James three times, but I get sent straight to voicemail.

Fuck.

I can't just leave him standing outside. And it feels wrong to send him away without finding out what he needs. I'm still a little too fatigued to be walking up and down the stairs, so I take the elevator up to the second floor to Odette's room. Her door is open, and I walk in and have a seat on her queen-sized bed.

She rocks Zahara in a pink blanket that matches her pink sweater and pajama pants. Her black hair is loose around her shoulders. "Who is downstairs?"

"Draco."

She sighs. "Oh, okay. Wait, what is he doing here?"

I bite my lip. "I don't know. He was asking if I'm alright."

Her eyes dart around the room. "If he has this address, it must be because James gave it to him. Do you want me to go talk to him?"

I stand up and pull my oversized tee down. "No—it's alright. I'll talk to him and see what he wants. I still haven't heard back from James."

She stands up and nods her head. "Okay—yeah. See what he wants, and if you need me, I'm here. Bring your gun downstairs with you."

My mouth flies open. "Odette!"

Her eyes go wide. "What?! You know James would want you to."

I can't argue with that. "You're right. I'm going to hurry up and get changed. I've already kept him waiting a while."

"Okay. Go on."

I exit her room and take the stairs to the third floor, trying to get a little bit of movement in.

What do I wear?

I don't want to look unkempt, but I don't want to look too fancy either. He's just family. But this is my first time seeing anyone outside of my husband and mother-in-law since giving birth, and I want to look somewhat put together.

Rummaging through the closet, I pull out a pair of black leather leggings. I had a video call with Meredith yesterday, and I'm cleared to start wearing my belly binder, so I grab that too. I grab my favorite black silk camisole, a strapless nude bra with matching panties, and a white cardigan. After a few minutes, I toss everything on with a pair of black suede pointed pumps.

Where do I put my gun? I lift my top and make a makeshift holster, attaching my weapon to my corset. It's secure and easy to reach while still being concealed. It gives me an idea for a new design. I've been so removed from Orchid Oblivion the past few weeks, and Odette has been doing everything on her own. I'm looking forward to getting back on the horse and working on things that inspire me.

I focus my attention back on getting ready. Taking my hair out of my bun, I shake out my thick, heavy curls and fluff them out. Once I spritz my perfume and peek in the mirror to make sure everything's in place, I take the elevator downstairs to get the door.

"Hi, Draco. What can I do for you?"

He smiles brightly and looks me up and down. "Hi, Genevieve. James asked me to stop by and check on the house while he was gone. I should've called first. Sorry to show up unannounced."

Yeah. You should've called first, but you didn't. "Did he?"

"Yes. Let me show you his messages."

Draco hands me his phone, and I scroll through, seeing James did in fact text him. I hand him his phone back and rest my hands on my hips. "Yeah. He's very protective, so I'm not surprised." I look at my phone to check the time. "He'll probably be back home in a little while. Do you want to have a cup of coffee or tea until he gets back?"

He beams and his green eyes sparkle. "I'd love that, Genevieve. Tea would be perfect."

Letting him step inside, I close and lock the door behind him. We walk side by side to the kitchen, and he takes a seat at the island while I prepare a cup of tea for him.

His eyes follow me around the room, and the slightest shade of red tinges his cheeks. "Genevieve, you're absolutely stunning. I can see why you took over our clothing label. You're such a fashionista."

I feel my cheeks warm at his compliment. "Thank you. Yeah, I've always been into fashion, but James really helped me discover my passion for it by encouraging me to step up."

He takes off his crimson blazer that matches his pants, leaving him in a white button-down, and runs a hand through his midnight hair. "You and James are the cutest. I can't believe my dorky cousin got a girl as cool as you."

My eyes go wide and he chuckles.

"Don't get upset. I'm just teasing. I know James is a great guy."

I finish preparing his beverage and sit it in front of him. "You better be teasing. James really is a great guy."

He sips his chamomile tea. "I know. I'm jealous of him."

I grab a stool and sit at the bar across from him. "Why? Don't you have everything he has?"

He rolls his eyes. "No. I've got a wife who chastises me for every little thing I do, a house that's too small, and a job I hate."

I laugh against my will. "I'm sure Raven doesn't chastise you. And if she does, there's probably a reason for it. You should try and see things her way."

He rolls his eyes but smirks while I go on. "And I've seen your house. It's massive. You should be grateful."

"It's not as big as your house."

I ignore him. "And for your job, you can change professions. You don't have to be a lawyer forever."

He sighs. "Yeah. All of that's true. But James has this beautiful home where he's made a family. He has a career he likes and a smart, pretty wife who adores him. And a sweet little baby too. Speaking of which, where is she?"

My heartbeat quickens at his mention of Zahara. I don't think he'd do anything to hurt her, but I feel a possessiveness over her, not wanting to let him meet my baby.

"She's upstairs, sleeping."

He quirks a brow. "By herself?"

"No. She's with Odette."

He grins. "Of course. She's with her overprotective grandmother. So I guess the chances of me meeting her right now are slim to none."

I smile. "Yeah. Maybe another time."

He sips his beverage slowly and glances around the room before catching me off guard. "Genevieve, how are you really?"

I sit up straight. "I'm fine!"

He frowns. "You can be honest with me, Genevieve. I'm family. Tell me the truth. How are you really? You were nearly killed by multiple men in my family, you were thrusted into this Guiding Mother role faster than you probably thought you would be, and you just gave birth. Just tell me how you really feel. Let it out."

Tears prick my eyes, and I take a few deep breaths to avoid crying.

No one has asked me that.

No one has asked me how I feel about all of this. Not even James. He's the most incredible husband, and I wouldn't change a thing about him, but he's been so caught up with everything that I don't know if he's truly considered how I feel about everything.

A tear streams down my face, and I feel shitty for even expecting James to ask me how I feel. He does so much for me, and I should be grateful. I shouldn't expect more of him when he already gives me everything. But my chest tightens and my throat burns when I think about all of the emotions I've been bottling up and keeping down.

The tears and words flow on their own accord. "I'm overwhelmed. More than you can imagine. I'm scared. I'm depressed. I feel like a shitty mother. Like a shitty wife. And sometimes, I want to die." I chuckle softly and he frowns.

I stand up, embarrassed. "God, Draco. I'm so sorry. I shouldn't be unburdening on you. This is my own shit to deal with. I should be discussing this with James."

He stands up and his brows draw together. "Genevieve, please don't apologize. You're not any of those things. You're an incredible wife. An amazing mother. And the world is so much better with you in it. Just being in your presence has made my day better."

I wipe my eyes and cover my face. "You don't have to lie to me."

He shakes his head and comes around the counter to put his hands on my shoulders. "I'm not lying to you. I mean everything I said. And yes, talk to James. If he doesn't already know how you feel, make sure he does. I know he would fall apart if he knew you were feeling like this and he was unaware. And I'm James' cousin, but I'm yours too. Please don't ever feel like you're alone."

I look up at him and stare into his bright green eyes. "Okay."

He smiles softly, giving my shoulders a light squeeze. "And if you ever want to talk to someone outside of family, we can make that happen."

I sniffle and look down. "I know. You're not the only one who wants me to go talk to someone."

He laughs. "I don't like shrinks either, Genevieve. I just want you to know that whatever you need, it's available to you. You can have anything you want."

Chapter Sixteen

JAMES

I stare at Shane's lifeless body while I catch my breath. Blood leaks out of his head, and my hands are covered in it.

What have I done? What the actual *fuck* have I done?

I'm overcome with immense guilt while I stare into the trunk of the car. Another life. First, Tiberius, then Deacon, Dave, Hades, and Jace. I didn't directly kill them all, but I still have all of their blood on my hands.

If I had any chance at redemption, it's gone now. Who does something like this? I killed this man. This man who was a husband. This man who had a family. I killed him for no good reason, and I can't undo the damage I've done.

But I justified it for myself. I told myself that it was okay because he was an adulterer. He cheated on his wife with my married mother for years. He was a piece of shit. He deserved it.

Then I remembered how he looked out for me. For my wife and family. How he kept an eye on us and protected us. I spit in his face by taking his life.

However, he stalked me and my family. He tracked my spending and kept tabs on me. He probably had so many secrets including horrible things that I had no idea about. My mother herself said he wasn't a good man.

And my family. Letting him go meant I would've failed my first mission. I couldn't do that. Letting him go meant sacrificing not only my wife but my daughter and mother in the way that all daughters born are sacrificed. Letting him go meant three lives would be taken instead. And I know he wouldn't have wanted me to sacrifice my family if he knew their lives were at stake. So I let his bad outweigh his good, and I did what I had to do.

Now I'm at a crossroads. I hate that I killed this man. I hate that I keep murdering, and I hate that I'm going to have to break my mother's heart all over again.

But I feel invincible. My heart is still racing, and I'm ready for more action. I'm ready to climb to the top of the ladder of freedom. I don't want to wait any longer, and I'm willing to do whatever I have to.

Shane helped me. He's fueling the dark fire within me. He's made me want more. And I don't have to hold onto this darkness forever. I just need to harness this feeling long enough to get to the other side. To free my family.

I feel more energetic than I ever have in my life. Wasting no time, I go up to the porch and grab the shovel. I don't know how long I dig for, but eventually, I have a hole deep enough for Shane's body in the backyard.

Hoisting his bloody corpse out of the car, I carry him to the hole and place him inside. I've already mutilated him with the way I killed him. Although I've got a thing for violence, it feels disrespectful to toss him in the hole like he's trash.

Once I've got him in position, I cover him with dirt quickly, scared that if I look at him for too long, I might realize the gravity of what I've done and cry until I pass out.

What did I do? It's too late. I'm in too deep. It's too late.

My jacket is covered in grime, and I feel disgusting. I take off my jacket and bury it too, scared that if I leave it on, Gen will know what horrible thing I've done as soon as I get home.

The back of my eyes burn, but I keep pushing, keep moving to ignore the overwhelming guilt I feel. My emotions battle with each other, making it hard to decipher what I actually think of everything. Once I've buried my mistakes, I head back to the car and hop on the driver's side. When I buckle my seatbelt, my phone pings.

> You've completed level one. Only four more to go. We'll be in touch soon.

#

As soon as I get back on the road, my cell signal goes out. It's once I get back to my car that I notice I have three missed calls from Genevieve.

I try to call her back immediately, but the phone rings until I'm sent to her sweet voicemail message. I try to call my mother, and her phone rings until I'm sent to the automatic voicemail.

God. Oh, God.

I pick up my phone and call the one person who was supposed to have my back today. Draco. He picks up on the third ring, and I hear a woman laughing in the background. My woman.

"James! Where are you, man?"

I let out a breath and bite my tongue to avoid clenching my teeth. "I'm on my way right now. What are you doing with my wife and why isn't she answering her phone?"

He chuckles. "Relax—she's just having fun. And she missed your calls because she was in the bathroom and her phone was out here."

My blood boils. "So you saw me call her, and you didn't pick up the phone?"

"No—why would I? It's her phone, man. I figured she'd call you back when she got out. Relax."

He's right. I definitely don't want him touching my wife's phone. But I'm still pissed that he's with her. I keep a hand on the wheel while I check her location.

"Draco, what are you doing at my house?"

He sighs. "You told me to check on the house, remember?"

Fucking idiot. "Yes, I told you to check on my house. I didn't tell you to go inside."

He whistles. "Well, I misunderstood. Anyways, Gen is—"

"Genevieve."

He laughs. "Genevieve is such a good hostess that she invited me in for a cup of tea. And she got pretty upset earlier so I comforted her. Hold on—she's saying something to me." I hear him whisper over the line. "What did you say, hon?"

Hon? Did he just address *my wife* as hon?"

He whispers softer. "Sorry—I just know he's worried about you. I just wanted to tell him how you were doing."

I floor it and run two red lights. "I'll be home in about an hour and a half."

He clears his throat. "Great! Then maybe we can all have dinner together. Genevieve said she was cooking something really delicious tonight. I can't wait to taste it."

I hang up and squeeze my phone tightly so I don't throw it out the window and speed home.

When I arrive a little after three p.m., I am equal parts shocked and annoyed that my cousin is still at the house. I thought my obvious rage would make him take a hint and leave, but his flashy sports car is parked in my driveway. In my spot.

I pull a wet wipe out of my glovebox to clean my hands before running them through my hair. I'm a little unkempt, but I don't look like I committed murder which is what I'm going for. Once I smooth out my shirt and lint roll my pants, I get out of the car and head inside.

My heart stops at what I see before me. Draco is kneeling before my wife with his hand on her shoe, gripping it like he has some claim on her.

Her baby blue eyes meet mine, and she smiles at me. "Hi, baby."

I break my gaze away from her and walk up to my cousin who sits at the floor of my world. When he looks up at me, I kick him in his chin and hold him down on the ground.

Genevieve grabs at my shoulders but I shake her off. "JAMES! What are you doing?!"

I lift my fist and Draco yells. "Hey! Hey! Easy man—what the fuck?"

I hold my hand in place, deciding not to let it connect with his jaw. "What the fuck are you doing to my wife?"

He breathes rapidly. "I was just looking at her shoes. We were talking about Orchid Oblivion and I know she designed them—I just wanted a look up close. I'm considering getting some for Raven. That's all."

Of course, he would want to get my wife's shoes for Raven. That way he can create a version of my wife for himself since he can't have her. I look into my wife's terrified eyes and stand up.

"Get out of my house."

He frowns. "I can't stay for dinner?"

I give him a look that makes him get up off the ground and grab his things.

"Alright, James. See you later. Call me. See you later, Genevieve."

She waves at him with a frown and then glowers at me. As soon as the door shuts, she lets me have it.

"What the hell is wrong with you?"

I stand in front of her, staring down. She's wearing the sexiest black silk top with a cardigan hanging off her shoulders, and I want to tear it off her.

I can't believe she wore this sexy little outfit in front of him.

"What's wrong with me? What's wrong with you? I have barely been allowed to *touch* this body for *weeks*, let alone look at it. And I get home and find you in these pants that drive me fucking feral with your tits nearly hanging out for someone else?"

She huffs and her eyelashes flutter. "I didn't wear this for *him*, James. I wore it for me. In case you haven't noticed, I've felt like shit the past few weeks, and I wanted to feel good about myself before seeing guests. Is that so fucking wrong?"

God. I'm a bastard. I take pride in my own appearance, so I know exactly what Genevieve means about wanting to feel good and dress for herself. I don't care whether she dresses up or down, but she hasn't been interested in fashion since giving birth. I should be excited that she's getting her old clothes out again. And she looks freaking gorgeous in them.

I reach out for her hands, but she pulls them away, making me want her even more. "I'm sorry, baby. I'm a jerk. You look amazing."

She crosses her arms, pushing up her pretty tits. "Then why are you treating me like I'm some slut?"

I can't lie to my wife no matter how hard I try. "Because I'm jealous, Gen."

Her eyes widen. "Jealous? Of what?"

I corner her up against the wall, and her breathing picks up. "Jealous of any man that tries to look at you. Or speak to you. I hate the way that he looks at you, and I know you see it too."

She tucks her bottom lip between her teeth. "Yeah. But I don't care, James. I married you. You're the only one for me. Don't you know that?"

"Yeah. But that doesn't change the fact that he wants to sleep with you."

She frowns. "What are you talking about?"

I tell her about my conversation with him at the office and what he offered.

She laughs loudly. "James, I want nothing to do with any of that. You're the only man I want. I swear."

"Good. And I'm going to keep treating you like a slut because you are a slut."

Her lips curl into a frown. "Excuse me?"

I shove my hands in her hair. "You're *my* slut."

She grins and bats her eyelashes. "I know I am. And I'll never be anyone else's."

My heart pounds in my chest as I look into her adoring eyes. I know she's telling the truth. But I'm just so possessive that I want more. "Tell me you belong to me."

She gasps. "Excuse me?"

My cock throbs. "If you want me to stop, use your safe word. Do you remember it?"

Her chest rises and falls rapidly. "Yes."

"Tell it to me."

"Zahara." She looks up toward the stairs. "What if Odette comes down?"

"She won't." I grab her by her hips and pull her closer, breathing in her vanilla scent mixed with her perfume. "Tell me you belong to me."

She licks her lips. "I belong to you, James."

My pants tighten. "Wrong name."

Her voice comes out lower and softer. "I belong to you, Daddy."

I kiss her neck and she moans. I wrap my arms around her while I whisper in her ear. "That's my good girl. Don't you ever forget that you belong to me because if you do, I'll tie you down and slap your dripping wet cunt until you remember."

She pants and grips my hands that hold onto the waistband of her pants. "James, it's too soon."

Three weeks. I have been fucking my fist for three weeks. I hold her close and brush my lips against her ear. "Genevieve, I need you so fucking bad, you don't even understand."

She buries her head against my chest and wraps her arms around my neck. "I know. But you'll wait until I'm ready. Won't you?"

I pull away and kiss her soft hands. "Of course. Absolutely."

She smiles. "Why did you ask me about my safe word? We're not doing anything that crazy."

I brush my thumb across her pretty lips. "Because I took things too far with you once before. I vow to never do it again. So whether we're doing the most vanilla shit or I'm degrading you like never before, I want you to know you can always use your safe word with me in any situation if you want to stop."

Her eyes sparkle and she winks at me. "You're the love of my life, James Barlow. Do you know that?"

I scoop her up and carry her to the den. "You're mine as well."

She cozies up against my chest and I sit on the couch with her wrapped in my arms.

"How did Draco comfort you?"

She sighs. "He made it seem more serious than it was over the phone. I was crying and he talked with me and hugged me. It was a non-sexual hug, I swear."

"I know. I believe you. But why were you crying?"

Her next words make my heart break. "He asked me how I was. Like how I *really* was. And I just broke down. About how hard things have been lately. How I feel like a bad mom. A lousy wife." She looks down, and I tilt her chin up.

"Don't *ever* call yourself a lousy wife. Or mother. You're incredible, Gen."

Her eyes water. "And I also told him that—sometimes I want to . . . die."

My stomach does a backflip and my palms sweat.

She shakes her head. "I'm not going to do anything, James. I swear. Sometimes I just get really down. I feel really low, and I've wondered what it would be like to not be here. But I'd never want to leave you or Zahara. I'm just coping with the depression I feel. That's all."

I pull her against my chest and bury my face in her hair, thanking God that I still have this angel I don't deserve. She breaks down her walls for me, and I hold her while she releases her emotions. I keep my voice soft and calm while I whisper in her ear. "I know what it's like to feel that way,

Gen. To not want to be around. But I swear to you, that you make this world a better place. I would die without you in it, sweetheart. I would literally fall over and die."

She wraps her arms around me. "I would die without you too."

I squeeze her and shut my eyes to ward off my tears. "No. You'd recover. You'd survive. Not me. I'm not nearly as strong as you. You are my life, Genevieve. If you ever feel like things are too much, tell me. Please tell me before they get worse. I would never forgive myself if anything happened to you. And neither would anyone we know."

She smiles through her tears, and it helps settle my stomach. "What did you have to do today? You were gone for a while."

My stomach drops again, and I feel lightheaded. "Something terrible."

She frowns. "How terrible?"

I keep my hands wrapped tightly around her. "I had to kill someone."

She gulps. "Who? Is it someone we know?"

I open my mouth and my throat closes up. My head throbs, and my heart hurts. I can't say. I can't tell her. As soon as I do, she's going to freak out and curse me out. She's going to get upset all over again, run upstairs, and tell Mom. And then my mother is going to have a nervous breakdown or kill me. I can't deal with any of that happening.

I look into her shiny eyes. "Please don't make me tell you."

She tenses. "James. Tell me now."

"Genevieve—"

"James!" Her voice shakes and she stares at me fearfully.

"Genevieve, I don't want to fucking talk about it right now. That's all I'm going to say about it. Do you understand me?"

Her eyes go wide and she glares at me. "Fine. I understand." Before I can stop her, she stands up and heads for the elevator.

I get up and kick myself for pissing her off once again. I'm supposed to be making her life better. Not worse. I hate who I'm becoming. I feel just as shitty as my father was.

"Genevieve, wait."

She ignores me and presses the button to go up.

"Genevieve, I have a lot I'm dealing with right now. I need you to understand that."

She takes a breath and turns to face me when the doors open. "I do understand. I understand that more than anyone, James. Believe me. But I have a lot that I'm dealing with right now too."

I don't get another word out before she turns away and the doors close. I unbutton my shirt and go to our office where I lock the door behind me. Feeling the weight of the day crash down on me, I grab the bottle of vodka I've been avoiding, pour two shots, and toss them back.

This is what it is to be damned. I'm a slave to an organization I never wanted to be a part of. The love of my life sees me as a villain, and I am one. And I lose a piece of my soul every day to the mistakes I've made.

I'm so broken that I can't even cry. I cried in front of Gen the day I told her I loved her, and I think I expelled all the remaining tears in my body. That's how I know I'm fucked up. Because I can't even express my emotions properly. After telling myself I'm a piece of shit over and over, I have one more shot and lean back in my chair, avoiding the rest of my responsibilities of the day.

Chapter Seventeen

GENEVIEVE

Three weeks pass in a blink. I can't believe it's already October. Meredith came over yesterday, and I'm now cleared for exercise. And sex. As soon as Meredith said that last part, I glanced at James and he looked at me like he wanted to eat me. Not fuck me. But literally eat me. Like he was a man forced to live off vegetables for a year and I was a juicy piece of steak.

However, when she left the room, I did too, and he knew anything physical was off the table. I won't deprive him forever, but I'm not ready to be intimate with him again yet.

I'm outside in the backyard, not too far from the farm, trying to do some yoga. I used to do it every day, and I forgot how much I missed it. I've lost some of my flexibility, but I know I'll slowly start gaining it back. I also want to do more cardio, so once I'm done with my yoga, I'm going to go back inside and try out my new mini stepper Odette bought me last week.

I truly am starting to feel like myself again, and my mood has been better because of it. My stomach swelling has gone down tremendously, and apart from a few extra stretch marks, it almost looks like it did before I got pregnant. I've graduated from leggings and sweatpants and can wear jeans again as well as my old tops. The only things that don't fit are my bras, but I'm not upset about that. And my incision has stopped bothering me.

We still bottle-feed Zahara. I tried to get her to breastfeed a few more times, but she still won't latch. James offered to have a lactation consultant come over, but I declined. I don't want to try something that might not work when we have a system that's working just fine. Plus, it's one thing to be rejected alone and entirely different with a stranger observing. It's something I don't want to experience.

I feel closer to Zahara now than I did when she was born, but I still feel slightly disconnected. Like something's missing. But I also still feel depressed, and I think it might just be that.

However, she's the happiest baby I've ever seen, and I hope she stays that way. I pray she never loses her joy.

Things have been tense the last few weeks with James. We haven't spoken much since our fight in the den about what he did. I'm not surprised he killed someone. In fact, I expected that that's what they were going to ask him to do. What bothers me is that he wouldn't tell me about it.

That's not how we are. We tell each other everything. We don't keep secrets from each other. I've tried to bring it up again, and it only results in an argument. I can't tell if I want to be furious at him for hiding it from me or terrified that he can't say it. I think I feel a combination of both.

I still get my nightly massages, but there hasn't been any flirting. Despite that, the sexual tension has still been there, and as angry as I am at him, I can't deny that I miss having him inside me. Just the thought of the orgasms he gives me makes my pussy throb. And seeing him get possessive always drives me wild.

Things in the society are still as strange as ever. We've still been barred from holding meetings, and everyone is extremely antsy to know what's going on. Draco has been helping James hold things down and I know he's grateful for it, but he hasn't been allowed back over since he was last here, and it's probably for the best. He's a nice enough guy, but I am not comfortable with him trying to cross any boundaries, and I hope he never tries. And, as much as I like my husband's jealous side, I don't want to see him kill anyone over it.

After spending twenty minutes stretching, I go say hi to my girls, Olive and Faith, head inside to do fifteen minutes on my mini stepper, and finish up with a protein shake and a shower.

When I come out of the bathroom, I'm startled by James sitting on the bed in a pair of gray sweats holding our baby.

He wets his plump pink lips. Those lips that I miss having on my—

"Hi, Genevieve."

I tuck my towel tightly so that it doesn't slip off while I rummage through my dresser drawers. "Hi, James."

He leans back against his pillow, his eyes following me as I grab a black lace maternity bra and matching panties. "I want to apologize to you."

I toss my undergarments on the bed and cross my arms. "Apologize? What for?"

He sighs. "For being a dick the past few weeks. I should've apologized to you immediately after our fight. I didn't and I fucked up. I'm sorry. Please don't be mad at me, baby."

A lock of his black hair falls between his warm brown eyes. I love him so much. All I want to do is crawl into his lap and forgive him. But I'm still pretty angry.

I sit at the edge of the bed, out of his reach. "Thank you."

He frowns and rocks Zahara softly. "Are you still mad at me?"

I sit for a moment to really think about it before answering. "Yeah."

"I figured you would be. So I'm getting you out of the house tonight for a change of scenery. We're going to dinner."

This is the first date James has asked me on since brunch, and I can't deny how giddy it makes me feel. "All of us?"

He smirks. "No. Just Mommy and Daddy. Zahara's staying home with her grandmother. What do you say?"

Yes. A million times yes. Of course, I want to go out with him as just us. "I don't know."

His eyes widen. "Please let me make it up to you. I want a chance to earn your forgiveness."

I'd give it to him instantly, but I love the idea of him working for it. I think about what I want and make my first request. "Are we going to have a discussion about what happened?"

He closes his eyes and takes a breath. "Yeah. We'll talk about it."

That was easier than I thought it'd be. "Okay. I'll go out with you."

He stares back at me and shows me his perfect white smile. "Good. I have a few errands to run, but as soon as I get back, we'll head out."

I stand up off the bed. "That sounds good. What should I wear?"

"Something fancy." He stands up and puts Zahara in her crib. "And I won't be too long, so start getting ready now."

After James tosses on a T-shirt and sneakers, he leaves the house. I pick up my phone and call Odette. "Hey."

Her chipper voice flows through and makes me smile. "Hey, baby! What's up?"

"Can you come upstairs? I need help picking something to wear."

Odette sits on the bed holding Zahara while I stand wearing a white robe in a pile of dresses on our plush white bedroom carpet.

"I have no idea what to wear."

She looks at my top picks on the bed. "I know. All four of them look great on you." Her eyes wander around the room. "At least we narrowed it down from the twenty we started with."

I sit on the bed and we both laugh.

She picks up the black semi-sheer one. "This one is *hot*, but it definitely screams, do me. So if you want him to keep his grabby hands to himself, maybe pick something else."

I look at the other three. "Odette, these all scream *do me*."

She sighs. "True. Maybe you should wear the black one. I want more grandbabies."

"Odette!"

She smirks. "I'm just being honest."

We lock eyes and laugh more.

I grab the fire engine red one and toss it on the floor. "This one is a little too attention-grabbing."

"I agree."

Next up is a dark brown one. "I look practically naked when I wear this. The color is too similar to my skin."

She nods her head. "Yes. You definitely look naked in that."

Last up is a baby blue sleeveless leather dress that I bought before I moved in with James. It has a high neckline, so it'll keep my boobs from spilling out, but it's extremely short, so it'll show off my legs and give James a view he'll enjoy. I pick it up and Zahara pulls Odette's waist-length hair and squeals.

She kisses Zahara's cheeks and holds her close. "I think we have a winner."

I pick up the garment and have a look, making sure I can actually squeeze into this thing. Once I give it a few tugs and confirm I can, I toss my bra and panties sitting on the bed onto the ground. "I don't have anything to go with this dress. Do you?"

She shakes her head. "No, baby." I feel my cheeks heat when she winks. "Looks like you're going to have to go commando."

Once Odette helps me find shoes to go with my dress, baby blue leather pointed stilettos, I pump, get dressed, and smooth my curls back into a low bun. I swap my signature diamond studs I always wear for silver hoops, and I complete my look with a blue leather choker.

I complement my vanilla soap smell with my classic perfume I can't get enough of, and head downstairs to wait on James.

He comes through the front door not even five minutes after I come down, and he stops in his tracks when he sees me. "Jesus Christ, Gen. You are unreal."

I press my lips together to fight back a grin. "Thank you."

He runs a hand through his hair. "Give me twenty minutes, and then we can go."

"See you in twenty."

I play on my phone while I wait for James to come downstairs, looking at the latest pieces from Orchid Oblivion and feeling left out of the action. I'm pulled out of my daze when I feel two strong hands on my shoulders and warm lips on my neck. "Time to go, Mrs. Barlow."

Turning around, I stare into my husband's lustful eyes. His black hair is smoothed back, and I see the cutest single gray hair near his ear. He wears a black suit with a dress shirt underneath that matches my dress, no tie, and matching shoes. I place my hand in his and scream inside, excited and nervous for the night ahead.

Chapter Eighteen

JAMES

I'm taking Rebecca out for dinner tonight at a new French restaurant in town. I'd prefer to eat at home and have her cook for me, but I screwed up and am trying to make things right.

My wife was not a fan of the mock Vows of Submission Ceremony. She didn't want to agree to the vows, and she was mortified when I told her I was going to fuck her in front of everyone. Usually, she likes being tied up, but that part didn't go over well either. And since she's with child, I've decided to be patient with her and give her a chance to correct her actions.

It's my wife's duty to submit to me both as her husband but also as her Head Father. She should obey my every wish, command, and desire, but my wife grew up spoiled, so I am still working on correcting her ways.

And as much as I'd like Rebecca to behave and give herself over to me, I know she'll respond better if I show her some kindness and build her trust. If you have a woman's trust, you can get her to do anything. That's part of the reason for this dinner tonight. To build my wife's trust.

I watch her slide into her black silk dress and toss her soft brown hair over her shoulders. All I want to do is wrap it around my fist and lead her around the house while she crawls on her hands and knees, but I know that's just going to tick her off more than she already is.

Instead, I get dressed and try to think of ways to make her swoon for me. I need her to forgive me. I need her to let me back in.

Flowers. I'll start with flowers. What woman doesn't like flowers?

-From the Diary of Jude Barlow, 1933

When I open the car door for Genevieve, her jaw drops.

"James, how did you do this?" She picks up the bouquet of blue peonies—her favorite flower. I remember when I first told her they weren't technically real and I was only able to grow them through genetic modification, she was devastated. But she instantly perked up when she realized that I went through so much trouble to make them real for her.

I help her into her seat and secure her seatbelt across her small waist. "I had Paul cut them from the garden. He met me halfway here a little while ago."

She grins from ear to ear, and I pat myself on the back for starting the evening off so well. "They're gorgeous, James. Thank you so much. Can we put them inside? I don't want them to wilt while we're out."

"Of course." I take the blooms from her and run inside to get them in a fresh vase of water. Once they're set up, I go back out to the car, get in on the driver's side, and head off to our destination.

I have to fight myself to keep my eyes on the road and not stare at Genevieve. She's an absolute bombshell. Her ass fills out her dress so perfectly, and I know she's not wearing a bra with the way her nipples poke through the leather. If I'm lucky, she's not wearing any panties either. My cock has been aching for weeks without her tight little cunt wrapped around it, and I am desperate to be inside of her again. After some good food and a little seduction, I'm confident I can make my wish come true tonight.

She fidgets with the hem of her insanely short dress. "So. Where are we headed?"

I breathe in her sweet perfume that fills the car. It's my favorite smell in the world mixed with her body chemistry, and it's what home smells like to me. "It's a surprise."

She rolls her pretty eyes and smirks. "It's always a surprise."

I drive at a steady speed down the road. "It is. But you love my surprises."

She pokes out her lips, and I have to refrain from stopping the car and hiking up her dress right here. "You're right—I do."

She relaxes in the passenger's seat, and my heart soars. This is the happiest she's been since giving birth, and I feel like we're finally on the up and up. Eventually, we make it to our destination in the city, and her eyes sparkle.

We pull up to a jazz club in the city and I help Gen out of the car before leaving it with the valet. She marvels at the art deco-style entrance with its geometric columns, vibrant green door with diamond-shaped glass, and tiger statues on either side of the entrance.

I hold her small hand tightly as we walk in, and my senses are overpowered by everything in the room. Loud but good music plays, waiters rush around with plates of rich food, and my body temperature warms up quickly under the lights.

"Stay with me." I keep her close while we squeeze past dancing people and lead her off to a corner with a private table that I reserved for us. It has a view of the stage, but it's secure with curtains on either side, and a comfortable teal velvet loveseat is positioned behind it.

Genevieve leans into me when we sit down. "This place is lovely. Thank you for bringing me here."

I wrap my arm around her and slide closer, basking in how good it feels to have her body pressed up against mine. The past few weeks have been hard, with minimal cuddles and kisses. I hate being shut out by Gen and I'll do whatever it takes to get her heart back. Her eyelashes flutter when I whisper in her ear.

"Thank you for going out with me."

Her sky-blue eyes stare up at me. "I could never say no to you."

Great. I haven't even been here five minutes, and I already have a hard-on. I do not deserve this woman. I'm not worthy of her. Her kindness. Her loyalty. But I'll treasure her and everything she gives me as long as she'll let me.

Our waiter comes by and brings us water and menus, and I pick mine up to peruse. When I open my mouth to ask Gen what appetizer she wants, she catches me off guard, and my pulse skyrockets.

Her voice comes out low and controlled as she stares at me with a neutral expression. "What did you do, James?"

I forgot that when Gen agreed to go to dinner with me, I promised her that I'd tell her about my first assignment from The Caledonia Council. I guess I'd hoped that she'd be too distracted by everything going on to remember.

I'm an idiot for thinking she could ever forget. My wife remembers everything, and it's one of my favorite things about her.

I put down my menu and scoot closer to her. With our private seating and the loud music and conversations around us, I have no concern that anyone will hear us.

"Genevieve, I think we should wait until after dinner to discuss this. What do you say?"

She shows me her perfect smile. "I say, you should tell me right now, or I'm going to get a cab home."

Shit. I don't want to start our evening out like this. I know as soon as I tell her, she's going to get upset, and things will likely go downhill from there. But I know if I don't tell her now when I've already made her wait so long, I'm just going to piss her off more.

I rub small circles on her shoulder while I keep her in my grasp. "Fine. I'll tell you. But you have to swear that you will not cause a scene or get up from this table to run to the bathroom or outside."

"I'll think about it."

"No thinking about it, Gen. You'll stay right here and you'll behave. You'll eat dinner, finish this date with me, and if you are still pissed by the time we're done, we can go home and I'll give you as much space as you need until you're no longer angry. Have I made myself clear?"

She glares at me. "Yes."

"Good."

"Go on then."

Okay. I can do this. Breathe.

I keep my arm wrapped around her and slide my other through my hair, trying to soothe myself. Pressing my lips to her ear, I let go of the weight I've been holding.

"I killed Shane."

She gasps and immediately tenses under me, and I slide my hand from her shoulder to wrap around her waist. "Calm down."

She lowers her voice and seethes. "James, please tell me you're kidding."

I keep her close, ignoring the way she recoils at my touch. "It's true. He was still alive. They wanted him dead, and they made me do it."

Her eyes water. "Did he deserve it?"

This is the part I hoped she wouldn't ask me. My throat catches. "I don't know."

I feel her try and pull away, and I keep her locked in place. "Genevieve Barlow, I swear to God—"

Her eyes go wide. "What are you going to do, James? If I get up, are you going to kill me too?"

My eyes burn. "Baby, you know I would never. You didn't mean that, did you?"

She stares at me for far too long and sighs. "No. I didn't. But I do want to go home. I don't want to be around you right now. I'm so angry with you. God, James, I'm so upset with you. I can't be around you right now."

My heart feels like it's about to disintegrate. Genevieve has never looked at me with such disgust, and I feel despicable. I can't let her push me away. I can't lose her.

"Genevieve, please. Please give me a chance. Give me tonight to make it up to you. I swear I will make you happy by the end of the night."

She grits her teeth. "I'll give you tonight, James. I don't think you can do it, but we'll see."

I kiss her knuckles. "Thank you."

Her next words chill my entire body. "And if I'm not happy by the end of the night, I don't want you sleeping in my bed anymore."

Chapter Nineteen

GENEVIEVE

I don't know why I said that. I'd never kick James out of our bed. But I'm so pissed right now, and I want him to understand how upset I am.

He squeezes my hands. "You're on."

My eyes widen on their own. "Do you think this is a game?"

He trails his hand up my thigh, and I bite my tongue to stifle my moan.

"Yes, and I'll be damned if I don't win." He picks up his menu like everything's fine and keeps his hand on my leg. I let him keep it there while I look at mine, enjoying the way his fingers massage me.

I've been eating mostly healthy since I gave birth, and I'm looking forward to indulging tonight.

Our waiter returns with a smile on his face. "What can I get started for you both?"

James looks over at me. "Whatever my wife wants."

Tom, our server, grins. "A man with the right answer. What would you like, ma'am?"

"We'll have the fried pickles and oysters." That should keep James from trying to seduce me tonight.

"Those are my favorites. I'll have them out to you shortly." He turns on his heel and walks away.

James slides his hand up my back and massages my neck. "Gen, I know you better than you know yourself. And if you think eating greasy seafood is going to keep me off of you tonight, you are sadly mistaken."

My body warms up and I cross my legs. The music quiets down, and the sounds from the piano calm my nerves.

I look out into the crowd at couples slow dancing. "I have no idea what you're talking about."

James scoffs. "Yeah. And I'm the Pope."

I roll my eyes and he stands up.

"Where are you going?"

He holds out his hand to me. "Come on. We're going to dance."

James and I don't dance often, but I always have an incredible time when we do.

"I'm not feeling up to it."

He clenches his jaw. "Don't embarrass me, Gen. Be a good girl and come dance with me or I will bring you to your knees and show everyone who you belong to."

My jaw drops and he smirks, and I can't help but place my hand in his. "One dance."

He brushes his thumb over my wedding band. "I'll have as many as I want."

I bite my lip and fight back a smile as I follow him onto the floor. Looking back at our table, I see our food hasn't arrived, so I guess we can spare a few minutes on the dance floor.

Wrapping one arm around his shoulder, I lean in and let him take my other hand in his. His rich amber and musk cologne commands me to stay close to him. I look around the room while we dance, noticing nearly everyone else swaying along to the music with a loved one or on their own.

My high heels bring the top of my head to James' nose, and he brushes it against my hair while his hand that holds me slowly slides lower down. "Eyes on me, Gen."

Like a puppy in training, I obey and chastise myself silently for fawning over him like he's a celebrity. He smiles softly and I can't help but smile back.

"See, Gen—you're already happy and the night has only begun."

I step on his toe making him glare at me. "Don't get cocky. A smile means nothing."

He lets go of my hand and wraps both arms around me. "Your smile means everything to me."

How does he say things like that? It's such a simple statement, but it makes my body tingle.

"Kind words and flattery won't get me to drop my dress for you."

He keeps an arm wrapped around me, holding me close, and slides the other up the front of my thigh. "I don't need you to drop your dress for me to have access to your cunt." I try to think of a sassy comeback but don't get one out before I feel one of his fingers slide into my wet pussy.

"Such a needy whore for Daddy. I knew you'd be wet."

I hold my breath and start to get lightheaded. I forgot how weak he makes me. Looking around, I see no one's interested in what we're doing. Everyone's drunk in their own little worlds.

I stare into his eyes while he pumps in and out of me inconspicuously and strokes my clit with his thumb. "All I get is one lousy finger?"

He chuckles. "If you want more, all you have to do is ask, pretty girl."

Without warning, he shoves two more in, and I lock my knees to prevent them from buckling. "James." My heart hammers in my chest and I start to see stars. I haven't had an orgasm in weeks, and I already feel on the verge of tipping over.

He buries his head in my neck. "I think you meant to say, 'Yes, Daddy. More, Daddy.'"

I take deep breaths and try to slow down my building pleasure. "If you don't stop, I'm going to come right here."

He pulls out one of his fingers and slides the other two in slowly, going as deep as possible before drawing them nearly all the way out and then repeating, over and over while his thumb works my clit. "Come then."

He stares into my eyes and my entire body burns. "Actually, I'm not sure you should come yet."

I open my mouth and he slides his fingers out, sucking them without anyone noticing. I follow his eyes that wander over to our table.

He takes my hand in his. "Our appetizers have arrived. Let's go eat and decide what we want for our main course."

I follow him on shaky legs back to the table, ignoring the slickness that sticks my thighs together.

Once I get seated, I feel even more self-conscious. The leather of my dress traps my heat, making it more noticeable than if I had on a regular dress with underwear.

I whisper low. "James, I'm soaked."

He takes off his blazer. "Good."

"I need to clean myself up."

He pulls his handkerchief out of his jacket. "Spread your legs."

I look around the room, nervous to show my crotch to anyone. "James!"

"Just open them a little."

I follow his command, and he slides the cloth between my thighs slowly, wiping up my obvious display of desire. I shudder when he rubs it over my clit and dips the fabric into my slit, making me spill even more.

Once he's dried me as best as possible, he tucks the cloth in his pocket. I reach for one of the appetizer plates, and he pulls it away from me. I follow his hand that picks up a fried pickle, and he stares at my lips.

"Open your mouth, Gen."

What has gotten into him tonight?! "James, I can feed myself."

He licks his lips. "Daddy's going to feed you."

I open my mouth, and when he slides the morsel in, I bite the tip of his finger before he can pull away.

He smirks and licks his teeth. "I like it when you bite me, baby. But if you do it again, I'm going to bend you over this table and spank your ass until you cry."

I lean into the couch and cross my legs. "Maybe I want you to."

He stands and draws the curtains closed. "Is that so?"

My heart pounds in my chest, and I can't tell if I want to challenge him more or behave like the good girl he wants me to be.

I give him a genuine smile. "I'll let you feed me."

"Good girl." He leans down to kiss my lips and I pull away.

"I said feed me. Not kiss me."

His nostrils flare. "I *will* be kissing you before the night is over."

I stare at the curtains. "Fine. Can you resume feeding me? I'm starving."

He opens back up our view and sits back down, getting ready to feed me a fried oyster. "When my hand reaches your lips, I want your mouth open and ready."

I feel myself falling into step, enjoying the moment. "Yes, Daddy."

He feeds me and takes bites for himself in between, and I feel overcome with joy from the food alone. Everything is so decadent, and I want to try it all. Once we finish our appetizers, we decide on a pasta carbonara big enough to share, and I lean into him without realizing it when the waiter leaves to put our order in.

James leans his head up against mine. "I know I'm a bad person. But I hope you'll continue to love me regardless."

The little bit of joy I was feeling is ripped out of me at his self-deprecation. "I'll never stop loving you, James."

He breathes slowly in and out. "I know you're upset, and I know I've let you down, but I swear, I'm just trying to protect our family and keep us safe. That's my duty as a husband and a father, Gen. To keep my family safe. And I have done something disgusting and horrible. I'm not sure if it was right or wrong, but I'm hoping it was right. Because I'd do it again in a heartbeat if it meant keeping you and Zahara safe. I don't care what happens to me. I just want to keep my girls safe."

My eyes water and I blink a few times to prevent myself from crying.

How can I be mad at him?

He's a killer, but he kills to protect his family. Our family. Everyone he's terminated has been an enemy. Everyone apart from Shane. I don't know whether he deserved death or not. I know Odette said he wasn't a good man, but she didn't share why.

Oh, Odette.

My heart aches. Odette will be devastated when she finds out. And when she finds out it was James, I don't know how she'll react.

His voice shakes. "Don't give up on me, Gen. I don't know what else I have to do, but there are four more levels of it, and I can only complete them with you by my side. I'm just trying to get us to the other side. Then we can live in peace. And raise our kids in a normal fucking environment. I don't want them to live the life that I did. And I don't want their lives taken from them before they've even had a chance to begin."

I wrap my arms around him tightly and bury my face into his shirt collar, thankful that we're away from the crowd in our own space. "I will never leave your side, James. I want to do this life with you. My world is complete with you in it." He kisses my head and I look up at him. "Even if I hate you sometimes."

He captures my gaze and kisses my nose. "That means everything to me." His lips travel lower, almost dusting mine, but I pull away when the waiter returns with our food.

"Dinner for two. Enjoy! If you need anything else, let me know."

James scowls. "Thank you. We'll be sure to."

When we're left alone, he tries to slip his hand back between my thighs, but I clamp them shut, preventing him from getting access.

"Dinner, James."

He pulls the plate toward him and twirls noodles on a fork to feed me. When he shoves the utensil in my mouth, he bites his lip. "Fine. Dinner. But after, I *will* be having dessert."

I stay quiet while James feeds me and himself. He slides the fork in and out of my mouth patiently and carefully, and I love the special treatment. Once our plate is clean, he flags down the waiter and pays the check.

I cross my arms and glare at him. "You promised me you'd make me happy by the end of the night. I'm feeling pretty neutral."

He takes my hand and helps me off the couch. "The night isn't over yet."

I wear James' blazer as panic courses throughout my body.

I don't know if I can do this.

He holds my hand as we walk through the gate. "Have you really never been on a Ferris wheel?"

I trip in my stilettos. I should've worn something completely different tonight. "Yeah. I've never been interested. I'm not interested now."

He pays the fare and helps me into the gondola. "You'll love it. Trust me."

My heart slams against my rib cage rapidly. "I thought I was going to finish this date with a smile on my face. Not tears."

He grips my thigh. "I plan on you finishing this date with both."

My stomach flips when the contraption starts moving, and my eyes dart all around. James pops my ass. "Come sit on me. Everything's okay."

I lift my butt for a split second to climb onto him like a scared little kid. I wrap my arms around his neck and lean into his chest.

At least we're in a closed gondola. I start to calm down when his fingers trail up and down my spine. I look around out the window and don't see any kids. In fact, I don't see anyone else on this thing but us. I start to panic again.

"Do you think Zahara's alright?"

James grins. "I'm sure she's fine."

"What if she needs me?"

He stares at me for nearly a minute before speaking. "If we're needed, Mom will let us know. But I'm glad you care about her so much. You're a good mommy."

My nipples brush against my dress, and I feel something terrible about to happen.

"James."

He kisses my neck. "Yes, baby?"

"I'm going to start leaking."

He frowns. "I thought you pumped before we left the house."

"I did. But I need to do it again."

Panic washes over him but then he masks it with a smile. "I'll handle it."

"How?"

He slides the blazer off of my arms and drapes it over my shoulders. "Unzip your dress."

"What?"

He growls. "Straddle me and unzip your dress."

I peer out of our window. The only person I see is the Ferris wheel attendant playing on her phone. "I can't do it."

I feel his hands slide up my back. "I'm going to unzip your dress, then I'm going to empty you out, okay?"

I can't believe he's suggesting what he's suggesting.

Is he really about to drink my milk? I've never been more self-conscious in my life, but his help would make me feel better. Looking at the girl operating the Ferris Wheel, I can see she's still distracted. And James' blazer gives me a lot of coverage. No one would see.

But Zahara. Shouldn't I save this for her? I guess she does have plenty at home. I overproduce sometimes. Maybe I should wait still.

I straddle him for my own enjoyment and look into his eyes. "Maybe I should just try and wait until we get home."

His brown eyes look pitch-black under the moonlight. "Gen, we're not going home tonight."

He grabs my zipper and pulls it down slowly as my resolve crumbles.

"James, this is weird."

He puts his hands on the top of my shoulders. "I'm your husband. There's nothing weird about it."

Breathe. Don't be a fucking chicken. It will be over before you know it.

"Okay."

He smiles and his teeth sparkle in the darkness. "Okay?"

"Yes."

I hold my breath while he pulls the leather down my body, exposing my breasts and leaving the material bunched around my waist. I half-expect him to ask for instructions on what to do, but he doesn't. Instead, he holds my heavy tits up like he's done this a million times before, pushes my nipples together, and wraps his lips around them.

Fuck. I forgot how much I loved having his mouth on my tits. I feel a slight pull as he sucks, and it feels good to get relief. I sink my hands into his hair while he sucks me and drinks me like I'm his source of life.

After a few minutes, he pulls back a second for air. "Gen, you taste so fucking good."

I laugh before he puts his mouth back on me, drawing more milk from my wells. He gently nips at my nipples, and I have to stop myself from grinding on him.

I rest my chin on the top of his head. "I've missed you so much, James."

Once he's sucked every drop, he pulls back and zips my dress back up. For a second, I think I see a tear in his eye, but I blink, and it's gone.

He wraps his arms around me and sniffles. "I've missed you more."

Chapter Twenty

JAMES

I have never experienced something so intoxicating in my entire life. It hasn't even been ten minutes since I had my wife's tits in my mouth, and I already want back on them.

I have been denied those tits for weeks. *Weeks.* I have thought about them day and night and how I would make it up to them once we were finally reunited. The moment we had a few minutes ago was just the beginning.

Had anyone told me that my wife's breast milk would have the flavor of melted ice cream, I would've been after a taste on day one. When I offered to help her empty out,

I genuinely did want to make her feel better, but I had no idea how good it would make me feel too.

Our encounter at the club was fun, but what we did on the Ferris wheel was spiritual. Connecting with Gen in such an intimate way gave me a renewed appreciation for her as a mother, and I feel closer to her than ever before.

I was hard as hell while enjoying her nourishment. My mind wandered to all the fun I plan on having with her milk and how she's going to love everything I introduce her to. Then she told me she missed me, and I was snapped out of my daze. Those simple words nearly made me have a breakdown. I have missed my girl so fucking much, and I think she's finally letting me back in.

However, I know she's still recovering emotionally, so I don't want to expect too much of her for the future. Though we're having a great time now, she could be feeling completely different in the morning. I'm no stranger to her mood swings due to her hormones, and I understand that she can't control them nor do I want her to. I just want to show her how much I love her and have an amazing time with her right now.

With my hand gripping Gen's smooth thigh, I pull up to a luxury hotel in the city not too far from where we ate dinner. I barely register leaving the car with the valet, getting the overnight bag I packed for both of us from the trunk, and carrying Gen inside. The colors of the walls and carpet don't matter to me, nor do I remember the name of the person who checks us in at the front desk or if the lobby was empty or full. All I know is that I've got my favorite person in the universe in my arms, and I am determined to end the evening as a hero in her eyes.

Once we get to our room, Gen unlocks the door with her phone, and I shut it behind us with my foot. My entire body is vibrating with energy, and I don't know how I'm going to be slow or romantic right now. To be honest, I don't have any intention of being either of those things tonight. I am a starving man who has been freed from his shackles, and before him is a feast for a king from God himself.

I sit Gen down on her feet, and she stands in front of me in our presidential penthouse suite. There's an office, a bathroom with a glass shower and soaking tub, and a lounge area in addition to the California king bed. The city lights illuminate the space with our floor-to-ceiling large window view. But there's only one thing on my mind right now, and it has nothing to do with the features of this room.

My hands tear at my dress shirt, and I rip it off, grateful that I packed a spare to wear home. I slide out of my pants and socks and stand in my underwear towering over her.

She crosses her arms but her eyes are wide with wonder. "I'm still upset with you, James."

I turn her around and take her hair out of her bun. "What for?"

Her breath catches when I unzip the back of her dress. "I don't know."

I peel the material down and slide it to the floor, helping her step out of it. Her plump ass sits in my view, and all I want to do is shove my face in it.

"Well, I don't care. I'm still going to fuck you."

She turns around to face me and I take my underwear off, standing completely naked in front of her. All she has on is her shoes, and she'll be keeping those on.

Her nipples harden and she stares at my cock. "Are you going to be gentle with me?"

I step closer to her and cup her cheeks, brushing my thumbs across her jaw. "No."

She grins. "Good."

My cock is so hard that it hurts. My balls literally ache. Shamelessly dripping precum, I squeeze her huge tits and drag my hands down her hourglass frame. "Go stand facing the window."

Her eyes go wide. "There are no curtains, babe."

I stroke myself subconsciously. "I'm aware."

Nervousness surges through me with the fear that she might be offended and get dressed. But she holds her shoulders back and heads to the window. I hear her slickness with each step she takes, and I feel myself smile when I go to stand behind her.

She looks down and across the street at an office with the lights on inside. "What if someone sees us?"

I grip her hips. "Then they'll get a great show. Hands on the glass."

Gen obeys, pressing her hands against it, and I tease her slit with my dick, sliding back and forth against her opening while she moans. I slide my hands in front of her, pulling her pussy open and using my hips to press her body flush against the glass with her tits and clit up against it. She turns her face to the side so she can breathe, and I position my tip at her soaked entrance.

Moving her soft hair to the side, I slide my tongue up her neck, tasting her salty skin and sweet perfume before whispering in her ear. "I'm not stopping until there are tears streaming down your face."

She licks her pretty pout. "I wouldn't want it any other way."

I move my hands to the outside of hers on the glass and drive into her in one swift stroke. She screams out, and I slam my hips into hers, over and over while her legs shake in her pretty blue high heels. My body is on fire imagining how gorgeous she looks from the other side, and I grab her hip with one hand while I use the other to squish her face into the glass, fucking her harder and faster.

Her breath shudders and she whimpers while I pump in and out.

"Daddy's little whore missed being used, didn't she?"

She squeezes her eyes shut. "Yes."

I yank her hair, pulling her face off the glass. "I am going to fuck this needy little cunt of yours so many times tonight that you are going to have to be carried out of this hotel tomorrow."

She pants and gasps for air. "I want you to use me like I'm a whore you paid for."

I slap the side of her tit. "I'm going to use you for way more than whores I've paid for."

Tears stream down her pretty face as she gets closer.

God, I'm right there. I can't wait any longer. Without warning, I spill into her and groan in her ear. When I pull out, she turns around and glares at me with a smirk.

Knowing exactly what's on her mind, I ease her concern. "You'll come. When I say you can."

She puts her hands on her hips and watching my seed spill down her pretty thighs keeps me hard. I hope to God I get her pregnant again tonight.

Her bright blue eyes shimmer. "Was that everything you dreamed it would be?"

I pull her close. "Yes. And more. How long until you can go again?"

She nibbles her lip. "Ten minutes."

I give her a quick peck. "Get on the bed on your hands and knees. Shoes stay on."

I watch her while she crawls onto the center of the plush black duvet. When I promised to make her happy before the night was over, I meant it. And although I don't plan on going easy on my wife tonight, I do plan on worshiping every inch of her body and showing her how incredible and sexy I think she is.

I kneel on the bed behind her and run my hands up and down her thighs. "Do you trust me, Gen?"

I feel her tense. "Yes. Of course, I do."

I slip my thumb between her cheeks and rub her tight hole just how she likes. "And you know I would never hurt you right?"

"Yes."

Why am I nervous all of the sudden? I have done this before. I know what I'm doing. But I've never done this to a woman who was brand new at it.

I pull her cheeks open, letting the cool air hit her asshole. "Do you really want me to fuck you back here?"

She pauses and the room goes silent for nearly a minute. "Yes."

I fight back my smile at her nervousness. "Well, I'm going to tonight. But before I do, I promise I'll get you ready first. Okay?"

She peers over her shoulder at me. "Don't hurt me, James."

I squeeze her firm ass. "I won't. I swear. I'm still going to be rough, but you're going to love it. I promise."

"Okay."

I lower my face and hold her ass open, slowly dragging my tongue up and down her seam. She shows me gratitude immediately by pressing her ass into my face and letting me slide my tongue in circles around her rim. My heart swells with pride at her trust in me. I value it more than anything in the world next to her love and kindness.

I poke my lips out and give her soft, wet kisses on her rosebud. She hums softly and my confidence grows, giving me encouragement to keep going. She yelps when I bite her cheek. I lift my head and rest my chin on her backside. "I can't wait to feel this pretty ass squeezing my cock."

I hear her sniffle while she cries softly. "I'm so wet."

I look between her legs and see her dripping for me, the remnants of my cum mixed with her arousal. Dragging my tongue between her thighs, I lap up her juice, keeping it in my mouth, and spill it between her ass cheeks.

Her legs shake while I work her wetness in and out of her tight hole with my tongue. When I can tell she's ready for more, I use my fingers to drag her wetness between her cheeks and gently finger her hole with one digit.

She closes her thighs together, probably looking to ease the blooming tension between her legs. "That feels so good."

I rub her legs with my unoccupied hand. "Good. I want you to press back slowly against my finger, okay, pretty girl?"

"How much?"

"As much as you can."

She lets out a breath and slides back slowly, past my first two joints and then farther than we've gone before. When she hits the resistance of my hand, I take a breath to calm myself so I don't come on her ass.

"You're doing so good, baby. Are you still feeling good?"

"Yes."

"Perfect." I slowly spin my finger inside her tight channel as her hips rock back and forth. She's so warm and comforting. But she's so fucking tight. Once I can tell she's gotten comfortable, I pull my finger out and open up one of the nightstand drawers I had stocked before we arrived.

"Stay right there."

Gen glances at me with a smile, and I'm glad to know she's having a good time. I grab a bottle of lube and get back in position behind her.

Squeezing the cool gel between her cheeks, I speak to her softly. "I'm going to go back in with two fingers for a little bit. After that, I'll use my dick. Tell me if anything feels bad."

Her soft voice washes over me. "I'll let you know."

I circle her rim a few times with my thumb, and when her pussy starts to drip again, I slowly slide my index and middle fingers into her ass. Her breath catches, but she doesn't stop me.

My heart races while I move my fingers in and out slowly, not wanting to hurt her. I tease her hole for a few minutes, enjoying the sound of her heavy breathing. "Does it feel better or worse with two fingers?"

She moans. "Better."

"Great. We're nearly ready to get started. Do you feel ready, sweetheart?"

Her back arches. "Yeah."

"Good girl."

I slide my fingers out of her ass and coat my cock with lube. Once I'm ready, I hover over her and kiss her face and neck, slowly moving my lips down her spine until I reach her seam.

Grabbing her hips, I line myself up while she pants with need. She'll finish the night with her pussy milking my cock, but she's going to come this way first.

"Breathe in, and breathe out slowly when you feel me slide in, baby."

She takes a deep breath, and I gently breach her opening.

My legs shake while I will myself not to drive into her like a savage. "Christ, baby."

She whimpers when I get halfway.

I rub her back softly, easing her tension. "Everything's okay. Just relax, and let me in. Give yourself over to me completely."

She takes another breath, and I feel room to push in further. I squeeze myself in slowly until I'm fully sheathed, and I count to ten to slow myself down.

Sliding my hands back to her hips, I rub and squeeze them softly. "Does my cock feel good in your ass, Darling?"

"Yes. Holy shit, James. I'm so close already."

Fuck me. "That makes me so happy. I'm going to start fucking you now, and you're going to come for me like the sweet girl you are."

I grip her hips tightly and pump in and out of her at a steady pace, not going slow, but not giving her full power quite yet.

We grunt like animals while we fuck each other.

Seeing her handle my cock makes me prouder than I anticipated. I pick up my speed and intensity, making her entire body tremble. "I can't believe you're letting me deflower your pretty virgin ass, Gen."

Her mouth hangs open, and the only things that come out of it are incoherent mumblings.

I can't help but smile. "You look so pretty, baby. I love having you wide open for me like this. Willing to let me fuck and use every part of your perfect body."

I hear her start to cry again.

"James." Her tits shake with every thrust, making me feel possessed. Everything about this is so raw and primal, and I can't believe we waited so long to try this.

I slap her ass. "It's Daddy."

"Fuck, Daddy."

I yank her back by her hair with one hand and use the other to play with her clit. "Tell me you're going to be a good girl and come for Daddy."

Her back arches further as her chest sinks into the mattress. "I'm going to be a good girl and come for you, Daddy."

I rub her clit slower and with more pressure. "This is where you get to make Daddy proud." I drive my hips into her as hard as possible making her scream out.

"Oh, God."

"Gen, you are squeezing me so damn hard. Your ass is going to suck the cum out of my body."

She sobs into the mattress while her body shudders, and her ass pulses, letting me know she's coming undone. I come into her ass without effort while her muscles clench around me. Pulling out slowly, I send a thank you to heaven that I didn't make her bleed.

I lie her down on her back and slip off her heels. "Are you alright?"

She smiles through her tears. "Yeah."

"I'll be right back."

I leave her to rest and head to the bathroom to clean off and get something to clean her up. After I've got us situated, she snuggles against one of the pillows and closes her eyes. But they spring back open when I grab her ankles and pull them apart.

"What are you doing?"

I kiss her thighs and toss her legs over my shoulders. "What does it look like I'm doing?"

Her eyes widen. "I don't know if I can go again."

I kiss her clit. "I know you've got a few more in you. I'll prove it to you."

She bats her eyelashes and shakes her head. "If you say so."

Dipping my head between her legs, I slide my tongue inside her and lick softly and slowly, tasting her like she's a piece of forbidden fruit.

"I've missed tasting this pretty pussy."

She shoves my head down. "I've missed it more."

I ignore my need to breathe and bury my nose inside her, while I suck her soft inner pink flesh with my lips. I'm rewarded with her sweet murmurs and whimpers, and I rock my hips into the mattress, already needing to be back inside her.

Her eyes stay closed while I kiss and nibble her, and I allow her a brief moment of rest. When I slide two fingers into her and suck her clit, her eyes spring open and she starts to shake.

"I'm getting close. I don't think I'll have another one in me after this."

"Are you sure?"

She nods her head. "Yeah. I'm exhausted."

I hold my tongue flat against her clit, and she grinds her cunt on my mouth desperate for release.

When she's about to come, I pull back and sit her up straight.

Laying on my back, I hold out my cock. "Come ride."

She pouts. "I don't get to finish on your tongue?"

I smile at her. "No. Whores earn their orgasms."

She grins and slides on top of me. As much as I love being inside her ass and look forward to being in it again, I'll never get enough of being inside her pussy.

Red tinges the corners of her eyes, and I can tell she's getting tired.

I grab her hips and stare at her pretty tits. "Give me all you've got, and I'll take over when you're tapped out."

She bites her lip. "You're going to be taking over very soon."

Placing her soft hands on my chest, she inadvertently pushes her tits in my face, and she huffs while she bounces up and down, using every bit of energy she has left. Her curls are everywhere, hanging over her tits and down her back. I use one of my hands to brush them out of her face so I can see her eyes.

"Such a gorgeous girl."

She presses her clit up against me, out of breath, and I know it's my turn.

I grip her hips tightly and slam into her over and over while she slumps on top of me. Half-asleep, she comes harder and louder than she has the entire evening, and it takes me seconds to follow behind her.

I ease her off me and lie her on her back. She opens her mouth slightly, and I kiss her slowly, tasting her and showing her through my gentle pecks and nibbles how much I love her. She wraps her arms around me, deepening our kiss, and I climb on top of her, keeping our lips locked while she rests under me.

When we come up for air, I pull her into my arms and rub circles on her back, whispering softly in her ear while I prepare to ask her for one more round. But when I fix my lips to make my request, my phone buzzes.

Gen looks up at me with wide eyes. "Do you think it's Odette?"

"I don't know. Let me check."

Getting out of bed, I rummage through our clothes on the floor to find my phone.

Shit. Where did I put this damn thing?

I step on something hard, and when I pull my phone from under my foot, I thank my lucky stars that I didn't crush it.

But my brief moment of joy is replaced with fear when I see the message on my screen from an unknown number.

> Tomorrow at noon. Level two.

Chapter Twenty-One
GENEVIEVE

"Shit." James tosses his phone on the ground and paces around the room.

Part of me is concerned with the message he just received and the other part of me is focused on his perfectly sculpted body. My entire body aches, but I already want those strong hips slamming into me again. I can't believe this gorgeous man is mine.

I try to pull the buttery soft blanket over me, but James grabs it and tears it away from my grasp.

"I want to see you."

He sits down on the bed next to me and attempts to smooth back his sex-disheveled hair. "I guess I need to get used to getting those texts."

He draws his brows together, and the mood in the room shifts slightly. I turn on my side, facing him. "Do we need to go home?"

"No. Tonight is all about you, and I intend to finish what I started."

I roll onto my back as he climbs over me, suddenly aware of my tender ass.

I really let my husband fuck my ass.

As much as I want more, I don't know if it's possible. "I might've reached my limit, love."

He presses his lips against mine softly and strokes my incision above my pelvis gently. "I just want to kiss you."

I cup his face and rub circles on his cheeks with my thumbs. "So you're not going to try and fuck me again?"

His laughter makes my body shake. "I'm going to try that too, but I still want to kiss you."

We press our mouths together, and he strokes my tongue with his, sharing our taste with me. I could never get tired of kissing him. He tastes me softly and patiently, like I'm a delicate flower he doesn't want to destroy. He destroyed me, but now he's trying to put me back together.

It doesn't take me long to get wet again. The realization that I'm not on any birth control washes over me, and it's very possible that I might be pregnant after tonight. I'm not sure how I feel about that, but I don't want to worry about it right now. I already know it would make James very happy, and that thought alone excites me slightly. Not to mention, we've never used protection together before, and I have no intention of starting now.

He nips my lips and plants kisses all over my jaw and neck. "I'm going to fuck you now."

My lips move on their own, already knowing what I want. "I'm ready."

It takes two seconds for him to pull my thighs open and hold them down with his strong hands, leaving me completely exposed. The cool air hits my center, but I warm up immediately when he slides into me slowly, making my toes curl and my stomach tighten.

I stare into his eyes while he pumps in and out, enchanted and mesmerized. "You're beautiful."

He blushes under the bright moonlight that illuminates the room. "I'm not nearly as beautiful as you."

I rub small circles slowly on my clit with my middle finger, and he smiles as he picks up his pace. "I love watching you play with yourself. I want to watch you do it more."

My nipples tighten and I apply more pressure to myself, loving how he fills me while I do it. "What do you want to see me do?"

He groans and rolls his eyes back. "I want you to show me every single way that you make yourself come."

"I'd love to."

We fuck silently, just our noises and the sounds of our bodies connecting filling the room until I'm on the very edge.

I close my eyes and try to catch my breath. "I'm so close, baby."

James wraps my legs around his waist and pumps deeper. "Come for me, Gen."

I cling to his shoulders and open my mouth while I rush over, and he seals his lips over mine, swallowing my screams. My entire body shakes, and he fills me up, further proving his intent to expand our family.

When he pulls out, he lies on his back, pulling me into his arms and draping the covers over us. No matter what's going on around us, this is where I always feel safe. In the arms of the one person who understands me and accepts me more than anyone else.

James rubs circles on my back and I start to cry softly. He kisses my hair and buries his face in my neck, his body tensing as he does so. "Please don't cry, Gen. Tell me what I need to do to make you happy. I'll do *anything*."

I pull away to look into his eyes, smiling through my tears. "You don't need to do anything. I already am."

⋕

James and I get up at seven a.m. to head home before his task this afternoon. He helped me relieve myself again in the night which led to one more round that I didn't know I had in me, but we'll be back just in time for me to pump, so my supply will go to our baby next.

I hold his hand in the car as he drives us home. I'm thankful that he packed my glasses and my favorite tracksuit to wear today so I can be comfortable. Plus, I'd also rather not leave the hotel looking like a call girl regardless of if I was acting like one.

He plays with my fingers while he keeps his eyes on the road. "Will you be with me when I tell Mom?"

Last night before James and I went to bed, we had a detailed discussion about what he did to Shane. It was hard to hear, but I'm glad he finally told me. I'm definitely on edge about what else they'll require him to do, and I hate that he didn't have more time to talk to Shane beforehand, but we both agreed that it's time he tells his mother.

I don't know how she'll react, but I hope it doesn't drive them further apart. I know James also feels so guilty for killing him without knowing if it was justified or not, and maybe Odette can help him get closure as well as herself.

My heart hurts at the thought of her being crushed. She's so sweet and pure and I hate that things didn't work out between her and Shane. Zahara has kept her in good spirits, but I don't know if my baby will be enough to keep a smile on her face after the news she receives.

My baby. I miss my girl so much. It was so weird not having her beside me last night, and I had a horrible dream that she was taken from me. When I woke up and realized everything was okay, I cried in James' arms and he held me until I felt better. I feel so blessed to have him by my side.

I squeeze his hand reassuringly. "Of course, I'll be right beside you."

He swallows hard. "Good. What if she stops speaking to me, Gen?"

Regardless of the issues James has had with his mother, I know he loves her deep down. He tries to pretend that she only cares about me, but I know she would die if anything happened to him.

"She won't stop talking to you. Don't stress about it right now. Just tell her the truth, and see what she has to say."

His jaw clenches. "I know she won't be happy."

"I know. But she won't be alone. I'll be home with her today, and I'm feeling better than I have in a while. Maybe I can convince her to go out."

He tenses. "If you go out, don't go far from home. I need to know where you are, especially on days when I'm doing dirty work for The Caledonia Council."

"We won't go far. And I'll let you know where we're going before we go."

"Good." He pauses. "And I'll keep Draco in the loop."

I fight back a laugh. "So he can babysit me?"

"No. So he can shoot to kill. If a threat arises."

I shiver at his sharpness. "Do you really think someone would come after us while we're out to lunch or at the mall?"

He sighs. "I can't take any chances. I won't take any chances. Not when it comes to my wife and child."

A fear plagues my mind, and I'm scared to share it out loud. James squeezes my hand while I stare out the window. "What's wrong?"

Don't say it.

"Do you think Shane was right?"

The car slows down as we approach a traffic light. "Right about what?"

There's been one thing on my mind on a loop, over and over since James told me about that day. The day he killed Shane.

I grip his hand tightly while I use the other to play with my jacket zipper. "Do you think he was right about The Caledonia Council—that they'll never let us go?"

He lets go of my hand and grips the wheel. "I don't know. But I don't want to believe it. I can't believe it because believing it means there's no hope."

"We have to have hope, James. We can't live our lives like this forever. I want to be with you without this society looming over us. We have to have a future without them. I don't know how I can survive if we don't."

His hand pulls mine into his lap. "Whether what he said was true or not, I will get us out of this. One way or another. If I have to take them down one by one and dismantle the entire thing myself, I'll do it."

"That'll be a lot of bloodshed. The brands will be affected and things will need to be restructured if they're to stay open. Everyone's lives will be disrupted."

"Maybe that's what needs to be done."

"And what will everyone do?"

He bites his lip. "They'll have the option to leave and get the inheritance that belongs to them, and we can all go our merry ways and never speak to each other again. Or if they want to continue the bullshit, they can do it without us. I'm not going to let anyone stand in my way."

My heart starts to race. "Okay. Let's hope it doesn't turn into a war. For now, let's focus on the most important thing we have to do which is talk to Mom."

#

As soon as we get home, Odette pulls me into a hug and I have to suppress my inner turmoil and put on a fake smile for her.

"Did you two have a good time together?" She grins and links her arm in mine.

My body gets hot remembering the events of the evening. "Yeah. It was really nice. Thanks for looking after Zahara."

She kisses my cheek before picking my baby up out of her bassinet to hand to me. "She's such a good baby. I love her so much. I'll watch her whenever you two need." She winks and kisses Zahara's head before hugging James.

He immediately tenses under her touch. "Hi, Mom."

She frowns. "You should be smiling from ear to ear right now after the night I'm sure you had. What's wrong?"

He looks at me and my heart stops.

Odette turns to face me with a worried look in her eyes. "Genevieve?"

I cradle Zahara and bounce her gently. "We all need to sit down and talk."

Her eyebrows draw together. "Talk about what?"

James runs a hand through his disheveled hair. "Gen needs a moment, and when she's done, we can talk."

Without letting her say another word, James and I take the elevator upstairs, and he helps me pump in our bedroom.

"James, she's probably downstairs freaking out right now."

He helps me with Zahara's bottles and starts feeding her. "I know."

"We should've just told her right then. No need to make her suffer any longer."

Light pink tinges his cheeks. "I froze up. How do you tell your mother you killed her boyfriend?"

We finish upstairs, and James holds Zahara while we take the elevator back down.

"We just need to rip the Band-Aid off. You'll tell her, and I'll hold her hand while you do it."

"Okay."

Once we get back to the first level, Odette's eyes lock on us. "I need you two to tell me what's going on right now."

I take her hand while James holds our baby. "Let's go to the living room."

We all head there together, and I pull Odette down on the couch beside me while James passes Zahara to me to kneel in front of Odette in his white dress shirt and black pants.

His brown eyes shine while he stares at her. "I have bad news."

Her breath shakes. "Go on. Just drop the bomb on me already."

He sucks in a breath. "Shane is dead."

She scoffs, but her eyes water. "Yeah. I figured."

He stares at her before he clenches his eyes shut.

She grips my hand tightly. "What? What else is there?"

James sucks in a breath. "I know how he died."

Odette freezes and her jaw drops. "How, James?"

He looks at her and frowns deeply. "I did it, Mom."

She grits her teeth. "You did *what* exactly?"

He shakes his head. "A few weeks ago—when I went out on my task—I killed him. He was still alive. He had been tortured and they had him in a trunk. That's what they made me do. They made me kill him."

Tears stream down her face and her voice quivers. "Oh, God."

He presses his lips together and takes a breath. "Mom, I—"

Her small hand cuts across his cheek with a slap that fills the room. Without another word, she pulls her hand out of mine and stands up.

I start to panic. "Odette."

She ignores me and runs up the stairs, crying hysterically.

James gives me a halfhearted laugh. "That went well." He smiles, but I can see that his eyes are full of sadness and pain.

I look down at my phone. "You need to get ready to go soon. Let's take a shower, then we'll eat before you head out."

I stand up, holding Zahara, and give him my hand to take, ignoring the way it shakes as we head back upstairs.

#

My shower with James was not nearly as fun as it usually is, and he looked as if he was on the verge of tears the entire time. He won't cry, but I know he'd feel so much better if he did. But he puts on this brave face for everyone, and I don't know how to show him that he's safe expressing himself that way in front of me. That there will be no judgment or fire. Only love.

After we got dressed, we went downstairs, and I made him an omelette. He now sits in the kitchen with me at eleven a.m. looking at his phone.

He puts on his black suit jacket. "They never told me where to go."

I take off my powder blue velvet jacket, leaving me in a white tank top and my matching blue velvet pants. "You still have an hour. Just give it a few minutes."

His big brown eyes stare at me. "I'm really stressed, Gen."

Zahara sleeps softly in her bassinet beside the island while I go up to James and hold his hands. "Do you want me to come with you?"

He grunts. "Hell no. My family was offered to come to that first meeting with Annabelle. Not anything else."

I think back to that first meeting he had with her. "Do you think they still want to meet me and Zahara?"

The tension radiating off his body courses through mine. "I don't want you anywhere near those people, Gen."

I pull his head against my chest and rub his hair. "You went to the meeting and you were fine. They didn't do anything to you. They're not going to do anything to me."

He wraps his arms around me tightly as he pulls me between his legs. "I don't want to talk or think about that right now."

I kiss his head, feeling him start to relax when his phone chimes. He keeps an arm wrapped around me while he picks it up for us to look at.

> Get in the car.

Goosebumps coat my bare arms. "Are they outside?"

He stands up and heads for the windows. "Wait right here."

I watch while he peeks outside and shakes his head. He mumbles something under his breath before he turns to me.

"Take Zahara and go upstairs."

"James, what's going on?"

He grabs his things off the counter. "There's a car outside waiting for me. I need to get in and go. I don't want you two down here."

"But—"

"You can watch me upstairs."

I stand there staring at him, and he growls.

"Now, Gen."

"Alright." I pick up our growing girl and hold her tightly while I go up to him. "Can I have a kiss before you go?"

"Of course you can." His lips seal mine, and he kisses me deeply before breaking away. His pinch on my ass lets me know he's tired of me dilly-dallying. "If you go anywhere today, text me beforehand. And if you try to reach me and I'm unavailable, call Draco. Keep your gun on you."

I head away from him toward the elevator. "I will. I love you."

He gives me a soft smile before turning away. "I love you too."

Chapter Twenty-Two

JAMES

*D*erek leads me through a large empty warehouse with white walls. "This will be the new location for meat processing."

I look around the spacious area, eager for it to be filled with machines and butchered animals. I met Derek through Bill, and he oversees our meat department within the society. He's also a meat inspector, so he's helping facilitate expansion while approving the product we produce.

"This is great, Derek. I'm happy to be moving forward with this location. I want our meat sold throughout the country. I want it to be of the best quality and flavor. I want to take over the world."

He smoothes back his platinum-blonde hair and pats me on the back. "I like you, Jude. You're going to do great things. All of us are going to do great things together."

I haven't spent much time with Derek yet, but I like him too. He's to the point, bold, and he's got a mind like mine. I wish he was my brother or cousin. He should be one of us—a Wild White Orchid. But this is a family thing only, so he'll have to remain as just a friend.

He catches me off guard when his voice lowers. "So, Jude, I've been speaking to Bill about that elixir."

Bill hasn't finished creating the elixir we've been discussing, but I have hope he will finish it soon. I wonder what Derek knows about it. While I'd like to discuss big topics like this as a group, I don't mind hearing what Derek has to say since he already seems to be in the loop.

"What about it?"

He beams. "Well, I think we may be able to use it in the meat too. If you wanted."

Use it in the meat? A chemical that's going in our perfume.

I scratch my chin. "Is it safe?"

He nods his head reassuringly. "Most definitely. It's addictive, for sure, but it's edible. And it'll be odorless and tasteless, so it'll be like it's not even there. This is going to help you stand out from the crowd."

I ponder the idea of having the elixir in the meat. It wasn't what I originally planned, but I like the sound of it. And it's safe. I want my family to be set up for success for years to come.

Tucking my hands in my black suit pockets, I give Derek a smile. "How fast can we get it ready?"

He laughs deeply. "For you? I think we can have it ready by tonight."

-Jude Barlow, 1933

The luxury black car before me looks like one out of a movie. My palms sweat, and I avoid checking for my guns and knife, knowing I brought them with me before I left the house.

I instinctively want to turn my head up to the window to see if I can spot Gen watching, but I refrain, not wanting to draw attention to her.

What if The Caledonia Council really tries to meet my family? I don't want my girls anywhere near this mess, but I fear that it may be a step toward our end goal. And having them with me is probably safer than leaving them on their own. But having them away from me provides safety too.

God, I don't know what to do. I'm so tempted to ask for help. To send a prayer up above. But I'm scared that He might smite me for my sins. And if He's going to smite me, I'd rather He not do it where my wife and child can see, so I decide to save my prayer attempt for when I'm not standing in my driveway.

The windows are tinted, and the door to the back is open. I can't see who the driver is, but I know there is one.

Confidently, I stride toward the vehicle and get inside carefully. Once I shut the door, the bald man in sunglasses takes off.

I stare straight ahead, watching him as well as our route, trying to memorize it. Gen has my location, but I'll likely lose my signal today like I conveniently have in the past.

The man doesn't speak to me, and I don't speak to him. Everything in me tells me that he's just a cog. He's my driver, and he's nothing more.

Part of that realization comforts me. I don't know how long this journey is to my destination, but I try to relax on the way. If I'm going to be dropped off at some other unknown location for a murder, I might as well try to ease my nerves before I have to get myself riled up again.

We drive for a while until we pass my old neighborhood, and I tense immediately. I've gotten so used to being away from the society and having meetings postponed that I was almost able to convince myself that none of this is real. But it's very real, and it still exists, even though I don't have to see it every day. I wonder what's going through everyone's heads and how they'll react when we get back in the swing of things. But hopefully, I'll be out of this mess before then.

We drive further away from my home to another rich neighborhood, and after fifteen minutes of driving in it, we make it to a secluded mansion in the back. It looks like something owned by a drug lord. Flashy, over the top, and hideous. My cousin Draco would love it.

The driver pulls up to the front glass door and parks, waiting for me to exit the vehicle. I pat my jacket and look around the car, making sure I don't leave anything behind.

When I open the door, and plant my feet on the ground, I hear his low voice from inside the vehicle.

"Good luck, sir."

"Thank you." I step out, shut the door behind me, and walk up the pink marble steps to the glass entrance.

I half-expect the door to open on its own, but it doesn't. I press the opal gemstone doorbell, and after a moment, a man in a blood-red suit opens the door. He has my height, build, and complexion, and he's got dark brown hair. But with the wrinkles on his face and creases in his skin, I can tell he's at least fifteen years older than me.

"James, welcome. I'm Jack." He shows me a wide smile full of veneers and holds the door open for me to enter.

"Hello."

He chuckles softly. "You Barlow and Burke men sure are tense. Follow me—we'll chat more in my office."

I already despise this prick. My dress shoes clack on the tile floor while we walk through his gaudy mansion. He wears slippers with his suit, and it's fucking ridiculous.

Tense is not a word I would use to describe myself or the men in my family. The word I would use is ominous. Or barbaric. Despicable would work too.

Eventually, we make it to his evil lair. He has a desk just like Annabelle, but the floors are wood, and there's a massive fish tank behind his desk chair with a small shark in it.

He sits in his seat and gestures for me to park it across from him. "Get comfortable, James. You can relax."

I have no intention of relaxing, but I sit across from him anyway.

He pulls out two glasses from under his desk and a bottle of whiskey. "Would you like a drink?"

Absolutely the fuck not. "No, thanks."

After he pours enough booze for two in one glass, he starts to sip his drink. "Thank you for meeting with me today, son. You're always on time. I admire you for that."

I nod my head. "Thanks."

His blue eyes observe me carefully as if he's trying to read me. "You're probably wondering who I am, where you are, and what you have to do."

Letting my intrusive thoughts win, I blurt out a response. "No shit, Sherlock."

He laughs loudly. "Annabelle told me you were funny. I thought she was lying. Strong, powerful, smart, good-looking, and with a great personality. You're the full package, James."

I give him a tight smile and wait for him to go on.

"Well, I won't keep you in suspense forever. Let's start with who I am. I'm one of the sector leaders, and I manage the society's meat products. I do a lot more than that, but that's my area of expertise. And in regards to hierarchy, Annabelle was over Shane, and I was over Annabelle."

He *was* over Annabelle. As in, he's not anymore.

I feel myself smirk. "What happened, Jack? Did you get demoted?" Annabelle was small, but she was tough and didn't take any shit. Maybe when she took over for Shane, she got moved up on the ladder.

He frowns. "No. I'm exactly where I've always been. Annabelle's not around anymore."

I remember the excited look Annabelle had on her face when she told me that she was celebrating fifteen years with The Caledonia Council. She seemed like this was a permanent thing for her.

"Did she leave?"

He chugs his drink until it's half-full. "Well, she didn't leave willingly. I didn't want to see her go. But I had to get rid of her."

My stomach lurches. "So, you killed her then."

He sighs. "Yeah. And I know you're no stranger to killing, James, so don't act all offended when you barely knew the bitch."

I flinch at his choice of words. "What did she do?"

He rolls his eyes. "It's your fault, James."

"Me? And what the fuck did I do?"

"You didn't follow instructions."

My skin crawls as I'm flooded with irritation. "All I've been doing is following instructions."

He shakes his head. "No. Everything was almost done correctly during level one, but there was something you did wrong. Do you remember what it was?"

Leaning back in my chair, I go over that day in my mind. I arrived on time, I went to the correct location, and I did what was asked of me.

"I don't know, Jack. You're going to need to enlighten me."

He grins. "You're smarter than that, James. You were told to do something, or not to, and you did it anyway. What was it?"

I did it anyway.

I did it anyway.

My stomach drops when I finally remember. It was the tape. I took the tape off of Shane's mouth. I was supposed to just kill him, but I removed the tape first.

I sit up straight in my chair, trying to prevent my voice from shaking. "He didn't tell me anything."

Jack scratches his jaw. "It doesn't matter. You still didn't listen. Annabelle was supposed to control the situation. But she failed because you ignored her. So, she had to die."

My head throbs, and I clench my fists.

Jack finishes his drink. "No point in worrying about it now. If it makes you feel any better, she had a closet full of skeletons. Much like Shane. They deserved it, son. I can see the guilt eating you up."

I feel my throat tighten and lie through my teeth. "I don't feel guilty."

He smiles softly. "Yes, you do. That's why you want to get you and your family out of this. Because you still have a soul. Anyway, the most inconvenient thing about Annabelle's death is that she's ruined my freezer. I'm hoping I can get her out of there soon to bury her properly."

My eyes widen on their own and he licks his teeth.

"Don't worry, James. I'm not going to make you see her. I'm not sure you could stomach it. Next up, let's discuss where you are."

He stands up out of his chair, and my eyes follow him as he walks around the room. The walls are burgundy, and much like my office, there's a bookshelf and windows with views.

His slippers slide across the shiny floor. "This is my office, of course, but this mansion is my home. I don't typically do business at home, but you're a special case."

I play with my wristwatch. "Cool. So I know who you are, and where I am. What do I have to do?"

Jack stares out the window. "There's a lot you have to do, James. However, there's nothing you're going to have to do today."

I feel a rush of relief followed by a wave of panic. Part of me is thrilled that I don't have to do anything today. I was riding the high of making love to my wife for hours after being restricted from touching her for weeks, and my mood came crashing down when I broke my mother's heart. I don't consider myself to be a very sensitive person, but seeing her get upset bothered me more than I anticipated. And getting slapped by her made me feel like shit.

However, I was looking forward to letting off a little steam and causing some destruction. A little bit of violence to take my mind off of things. So as relieved as I am for the break, I'm also anxious that I have to wait longer to do what I need to do.

He returns to his desk and sits across from me. "Do you have any questions for me?"

Questions? Let's see. Why the fuck are you so deranged? Do you sell drugs?

I take a breath before speaking. "What's next?"

He smiles. "What's next? Well, a lot of things. First, you and I are going to get a lot more acquainted with each other. With Annabelle and Shane gone, we have to redistribute some of the workload on The Caledonia Council, so you'll be completing levels two and three under me. When you pass and go onto level four, you'll get to meet Eric. But I don't want to get ahead of myself."

Eric. One of the other individuals on the lease. I wonder who the last person is. I'm sure with a little digging, I could try and figure it out.

Jack slides out of his blazer. "Today, I'll give you the details for level two. Due to your aversion to wrongdoing, you may not be pleased with it, but you should thank me."

I scoff without thinking. "Thank *you*? For what?"

"For showing you mercy, James. I don't know what Eric has in store for you, but it'll certainly push you out of your comfort zone. And there's no telling what you'll face at the end." He grimaces. "But I fought for you, son. They wanted me to go harder on you, but I got to pick this next challenge for you, and I did it to offer you a reprieve as things are only going to get harder from here."

A reprieve? I've only just begun this journey. Can't I save my reprieve for later on?

My skin crawls at the thought of things getting worse. Sure, I figured things would get worse as I advance in each level, but it's not nice hearing that said aloud. And I hate when people expect thank yous. It's not a true gift if you expect something in return.

I glance at my watch, eager to get home to my wife and baby. Gen had a hard time being away from Zahara last night, but I did too. My little girl has already carved a big place in my heart, and I don't like being away from her for too long. Plus, she's already over a month old and I'm already mourning her baby days. I don't want her to grow up.

"What's my next challenge?"

Jack puts on a pair of red glasses and pulls out a little black book from his desk. "Level two will be a society-related mission composed of multiple parts. I'll send you my phone number in a little while so you can update me once everything is complete. I'll need to check behind you to make sure things were done properly, but I won't be present while they occur."

"Let me guess. I have to burn someone at the stake?"

He chuckles. "You're so smart, James. I knew you'd figure it out before I could tell you. Yes, there will be a death by fire, but that's only part of it."

Heat travels throughout my body at the thought of another death on the Exit Ceremony field. My father was the first and last person I ever thought I'd have to kill that way. I don't know if I can stomach it again. I don't know if Gen can, and even if she could, it's not fair in the slightest to ask her to. And I'll be damned if I bring my daughter to something like that.

"Who do I have to kill?"

He holds up his hand. "I'll get there. Don't you want to know the full details first?"

I weigh out the options in my head. I want to know what all he expects me to do right now, but I need to know who I have to kill. While I'm not fond of the men in my family, there's no one currently who I'm itching to take out. I'll take out Draco if he gets too close to my wife, but I won't have the patience to wait for him to burn. I'll have to take him out immediately.

Taking a moment to be patient and get out the details, I nod my head for him to give me the full explanation of my tasks.

He grins. "For one, societal operations will need to resume. I know you want out of this thing, but until you're gone, you've still got to be the Head Father of this place. Everyone's had a nice little break, but the men on the council are getting way too antsy, and we don't need an uprising. Given that it's the first week of October, this weekend is perfect timing for the next community meeting. You'll need to resume council meetings as well."

I expected that meetings would resume eventually, so I'm not surprised. Hearing that that's one of the things I have to do calms me down a bit as those are simple duties that I'm very familiar with.

"Council meetings and community meetings. Check. I can do that."

"Perfect. I like the way this is going already." He checks something off in his notebook. "Next, I need you to plan a New Birth Ceremony for Zahara."

My entire body locks up.

Jack shakes his head. "Don't give me that look, James. I said plan one. Again, this is a part of your expectations as Head Father. If it is to take place, I'll let you know, and you can choose the date. But you must at least plan it."

I try to slow my racing heart. "Fine. What else?"

He drags his pen down his page. "There are two more things. And they both involve punishment. We need to talk about Damion and Jessamine."

Damion and Jessamine. The two society adulterers. That I'm aware of at least.

I try to act nonchalant. "What about them?"

"You failed to punish them. So I'm giving you a chance to rectify that."

I try to get ahead of him. "I'll think about what I can do for them."

He shakes his head. "No, no, no. You already know that's not how we do things. Jessamine must be punished by the instructions laid out in the Guiding Mother's Text. Genevieve will carry that out."

My need to protect overtakes me. "This is my challenge. What does Genevieve have to do with this?"

"Correct. This is your challenge. But this punishment must be carried out by the Guiding Mother. You'll oversee her. You guys can handle it."

I hate being told what I can handle, and I hate people making assumptions about my wife. He doesn't know the first thing about her, and I'm anxious about what she'll have to do.

"I'd rather she not be involved at all."

He clenches his fist. "That's not an option, James." His eyes search mine and he relaxes. "Are you aware of the guidelines and what she has to do?"

I think back to my Head Father's Text and can't remember anything about punishment for infidelity for wives. I know it's in Gen's book, but I haven't had much time to go through it. Embarrassed, I tell him the truth.

"No. I don't know."

His smile makes my skin crawl. "You have nothing to be worried about, James. It's not that bad—I promise. As long as Jessamine cooperates, it should go over smoothly. What comes after is what you won't like."

"And what comes after?"

He sighs. "Damion's punishment."

Damion. My cousin who's been nothing but a friend to me. *Damion's punishment.* Fire. He's the one I have to kill.

I grip the armrests of my chair. "I won't do it. I won't kill Damion."

A frown stretches across his worn face. "That won't do, James."

"Give me something else. Another task."

"This is the task, James. Resume meetings, plan the New Birth Ceremony for Zahara and all future daughters born, punish Jessamine, and punish Damion. If you complete those jobs, you will advance to level three. This is the best I can do for you. I swear."

Fuck. I can't kill Damion. There's got to be another way. A way out of this. A way to fake it and let him go.

"Fine. I'll get those things done and let you know as soon as I've completed everything."

Jack extends his hand to shake, and I give him mine, thankful to seal our deal without blood. He stands up, and I do too.

"I'd like to hear from you by the middle of next week, James. End of the week at the latest."

End of next week at the latest? That gives me less than two weeks to get all of this shit done. I don't know how I'm going to manage it.

"I'll handle it."

He stares at me with a neutral expression. "You're going to follow all of my instructions correctly, right, James?"

Probably not. "Of course."

As if he can sense my dishonesty, he frowns. "I caution you, James. Please do this the right way. If you deviate from the plan, something terrible will happen. Something that will tear you apart."

Another threat. That's the number one thing this council is good at. Intimidation and threats. But Annabelle threatened me, and nothing happened. Well, nothing happened to me. She was killed on the other hand. I'm sure Jack is just scared about what'll happen to him if things go south. The way they keep picking each other off, there won't be anyone to give me instructions soon enough.

I put on my best poker face and tell him the opposite of what I feel inside. "I have no intention to deviate from the plan, Jack. I will follow your instructions to a T, and I'll advance to level three."

Whether he believes me or not, he grins from ear to ear and claps his hands. "I like you, James. I can tell everything will go off without a hitch."

Chapter Twenty-Three
GENEVIEVE

I lie on the bed with Zahara on my chest. She stares at me with a big grin on her face, and my heart swells. Tears prick my eyes, but like last night, they're not sad ones.

I love her so much. I have a baby. A real baby. She's so sweet and small and loving, and I can't believe she's mine. Every time I look at her, I see James, and I can't believe my life is real. Things are very bad right now, but they're really good too. I'm head over heels in love with my husband, and I'm suddenly obsessed with my little girl. I already want to give her a sister.

Rubbing her back, she coos against my chest, and I feel so content with her in my arms. I'm worried about James and what he has to do today, but my baby feels like a security blanket.

I want to take her out to the farm to meet Olive and Faith.

But I can't do that right now. Maybe later. Right now, I need to do something more important. I need to speak with Odette.

My heart wrenches in my chest. I hate that Shane had to die. I've heard nothing but how he's helped us, and it hurts that he wasn't rewarded for his kindness. I also know how much Odette loved him, and now she'll never get to speak to him or see him again. She deserves so much better than that.

And as much as I love my husband, I'm still not happy that he killed Shane. Shane's death is our fault, and I don't know if I can ever forgive myself for the part I played in it. I'm not sure James will ever forgive himself for it either. And I'm worried about what engaging in too much violence will do to James.

I know violence has been a way for him to cope with his past, but it's not the best way. I just worry that an unhealthy habit will develop if he has to hurt anyone else.

James has shown me his dark side before, and it's terrifying. I don't want him to get lost in it.

Both of us could use therapy, but there's no time for that right now. We're far too busy, and who would we even talk to anyway? The demons we carry are not fit for any regular therapist. We'll have to deal with our trauma another way.

I scoop my giddy girl up and stand off the bed. I'll never stop being amazed by how happy my baby is. She's always thrilled, and she's a beacon of light in our home. Her joy is infectious, and I think she's been healing me slowly these past few weeks. Hopefully, some time with Odette will help her feel better too.

Zahara grips my jacket while I walk into the hall. Normally she likes to pull my hair, much like her father, but I have it in a bun so she can't reach it right now. I'd love to have it braided, but I still don't have the energy. And the one person I trust to do it hasn't returned any of my calls.

I kiss Zahara's forehead and hold her hand while we take the elevator down. Her curly hair gets thicker each day, and I can't get over how soft it is. Once we get to the second level, I take a few deep breaths before stepping into the hall. Not to my surprise, Odette's door is closed. It's usually open, but I know she wants to be left alone.

Regardless, we need to talk, and I know she'll feel better after a hug. And she'd never turn down a chance to hold her granddaughter.

Once I muster up the courage to do what I have to, I use my arm that's not holding my baby to knock on her door.

"Odette, it's me. Can I come in?"

I'm met with silence. I knock again, but a little harder this time in case she's in the bathroom or something.

"Odette! Can we talk please?"

Again, nothing.

I hate to barge in unannounced, but I don't feel comfortable going back upstairs without seeing her first. If she wants me to leave, that's fine, but I need to at least make sure she's okay physically.

Twisting the nob, I pray that her door is unlocked.

Thank God.

I push it in slowly and feel myself relax when I hear noise coming from her bathroom.

What am I going to say? I don't want her to be sad or angry. I know she's probably still processing the news, but I can't just spend all day avoiding her. I don't want to. I won't feel good until we clear the air.

I place Zahara in her crib beside Odette's bed and sit down on the plush mattress trying to get comfortable. I try to cross my legs underneath me, and I instantly regret it. My vagina feels like it's on fire after the night I had. I'm used to going multiple rounds with James, but I think we hit a new record last night in quantity and intensity.

And my ass. My ass is so tender. But everything we did was so worth it.

I should just apologize to her. That's what she deserves. An apology. She's been nothing but good to me, and I'm part of the reason why someone she loves is dead. And after I found out, I kept it from her. Granted, I only found out last night, but still. I hugged her this morning like everything was fine, and I feel so guilty about it.

My eyes wander around her large room. The walls are light beige, and she has the softest baby blue rug on the tan carpet. The walls are covered with tapestries and seashells, and she has a small white bookshelf next to her window with classics.

The bathroom door handle jangles and I freeze at the sight of her. Tears stream down her face, and she wears a navy blue robe with her hair in a messy bun.

Her eyes meet mine, and she sobs harder. I feel my eyes start to well up, and I stand up off the bed. When her body slumps, I skip over to her, ignoring the soreness between my legs. I pull her into my arms and wrap my arms around her tightly, tucking her head into my neck and holding her shaking body still.

She doesn't hold me back, but I don't care. I cry softly, trying to quell myself to keep her strong. I know what it feels like to feel broken. To have your entire world turned upside down and feel like there's no hope. Sometimes it almost feels like it's too much to bear.

Once her cries quiet down, I take her hand in mine and pull her to the bed to sit down.

I can barely look her in the eyes, but I need to. Talking through this will make us both feel better. Hopefully.

I wipe away her tears and take a deep breath in and out. "Odette, I'm so sorry."

She finally wraps her arms around me and buries her head in my neck. Zahara is fast asleep, and I'm grateful that she's calm. I'm not sure what I'd do if both of them were crying right now.

I don't know how long she cries, but eventually her tears slow. Her voice comes out barely above a whisper. "I can't believe he's really gone, Genevieve."

My heart physically hurts. I kiss her cheek. "I'm so sorry."

She pulls away and wipes the tears I forgot were falling. "You haven't done anything wrong, Genevieve."

I sit back and hold her hands. "Are you kidding? I'm the reason that this happened."

She rolls her eyes. "No. My idiot son is the reason that it happened."

I flinch at her response. I know she's upset with James, but I know he was doing what he thought was best. I'm also very protective of him and don't like anyone saying anything bad about him.

As if she can sense how I feel, she sighs and frowns. "I'm sorry. He's not an idiot. I just—I can't believe he killed him. Not only is he gone, but my own son?" Her voice shakes. "How could James just walk past me the past three weeks knowing that he did what he did? I just don't understand."

I rub her palms. "I don't know what to say. I just hate that it happened. I know you probably don't want to hear this right now, but he feels really bad about what he did. It's been eating him up, and I don't think he'll ever forgive himself."

She sniffles. "Are you just saying that to make me feel better?"

I squeeze her shoulders. "No. He really does feel guilty. I swear. He's worried that he took an innocent life. That he killed someone who didn't deserve it and that he's damned."

Odette cries softly and looks toward the ground. "He was so good to me, Genevieve. Incredible. I can't explain it. No one ever treated me the way he did. I don't think I'll meet anyone like him ever again."

I start to cry again. She wipes away my tears and frowns. "You can tell James he has nothing to worry about."

"What do you mean?"

Her hands squeeze my thighs. "Shane did deserve it, baby."

I let out the breath that I'd been holding in. "What did he do?"

She leans back on her pillow and stares at the ceiling. "How long you got?"

Ignoring my natural urge to let out a nervous laugh, I lean back on the pillow next to her. "As long as you need."

Odette grabs my hand and sniffles. "You are a gift from God, Genevieve. I've never been as close to anyone as I am with you." She glances over at me. "I don't even know all of the bad that Shane did. But I know enough."

"Do you want to talk about it?"

She shakes her head. "Not really. But I need to tell you. That way my son can quit kicking himself. Shane ruined a lot of people's lives."

I cozy up on my side, facing her, trying to relieve my ass. My pussy throbs, but the pain makes me think of James, and I'm already wanting him back home so he can make me feel better. With his dick.

"What did he do?"

"Shane has killed more men than we have on the council. Some deserved it. Some didn't. He's intimidated people and made them quit their jobs. He's lied and stolen. And he's never had any remorse for anything."

"Oh."

She frowns. "Yeah. And he may have treated his wife the same way that Bryson treated me."

I think back to everything I know about Bryson and Odette's relationship, and it shocks me that she'd get with someone like him. But it also feels wrong to judge.

I readjust my bun. "Why did you want to be with him, Odette?"

"I know. It makes no sense when I was with someone just like him. But as terrible as he was, he made me feel special. And loved. He never said he loved me, but it felt like he did. And I knew we could never be together, but when I saw him every weekend, it was like I could escape from my life and pretend I was someone else. And I pretended he was someone else too."

Her voice shakes. "I feel so bad, Genevieve. I loved him even though he was evil. I'm horrible, aren't I?"

I rub my aching head. "No. You're not horrible. You didn't choose your life, and we've all done things we're not proud of. I'm not proud that I'm encouraging James to hurt others to protect us."

She shakes her head violently. "You're not doing that. He made that deal without you, and he didn't really have a choice. Even if you asked him not to, he would've done it anyway. My son loves you and Zahara more than anything, and I know he'd do anything to protect you two. Don't be upset with him for it."

I feel myself smile. "I won't be upset with him if you won't."

She laughs and wipes her eyes. "Deal."

I sit up on the bed. "Do you want to go out? We could go to the mall or see a movie?"

My phone pings with a message from James.

> I'll be home soon.

Odette bites her lip. "I'm fine, baby. You can spend time with James."

"Are you sure? He's just telling me he's on his way back."

She gets up and goes over to Zahara's crib. "I'm sure. I know he'll want to see you as soon as he gets back. Plus, I need some girl time with my grandbaby."

My baby squeals, eager for the attention.

I cozy back up on the bed to text James while Odette picks up Zahara. He wasn't gone as long as I expected, and that makes me excited but nervous. I hope everything is alright. I think of what to say, trying to get more information from him.

> Be safe. How did today go?

> Good and bad. I didn't have to do anything, but I will soon. I'll fill you in later.

> That's good. I guess.

> It is. But I'm stressed.

> Is there anything I can do to make you feel better?

> Yeah. But I don't know if you're up for it.

> I am. Tell me.

> When I get home, I want you in the office. On your knees with your head down wearing something red. Heels too.

> I'll let you know what we're going to do, and if you agree, we'll have some fun.

> And what if I don't agree?

> Then we can curl up in the den, watch movies, and forget about the whole thing.

> I'm teasing. I'll agree.

> That's my good girl. Don't forget. Head down, and on your knees.

> You got it. See you soon, Daddy.

Chapter Twenty-Four

JAMES

The driver who picked me up this morning is the same one who drives me home. He doesn't say a word to me and I don't say anything to him. I'm just grateful I didn't have to take another life, and if I have my way, I won't be killing anyone else for the remainder of these challenges.

Eventually, I return home, and my heart races when I step out and go up to the front door. On one hand, I'm terrified to enter my home because my mother is there. Things did not go over well this morning, and I'd be lying if I said I didn't care that things are tense between us again. I've gotten so used to not having a good relationship with my parents that I convinced myself it wasn't something I needed. Then I started letting my mother back in, and I've really been enjoying having her back in my life. But it feels like a wall is back up between us, and I feel like the neglected little boy I used to be.

At the same time, my heart races because I know my wife is waiting for me in our office, and I'm eager to spend some quality time with her. I've been so needy the past few weeks missing her, and now that I can have her again, I don't know how to act. And tonight I'm looking forward to doing something with her that we've done before, but I fucked it up last time. This time will be better.

I need to speak with my mother, but I need my wife more right now. I open the door and relax when I don't see my mother in the kitchen holding a knife. I couldn't shake this fear that she'd be waiting for me when I got home, prepared to take me out for killing her lover. Fortunately, that's not the case, and I can go on in peace.

When I get to my office, I grab the door handle and pause. I want to do this right. I will do this right. I have to. Plus, I'm going with a softer approach tonight, and I feel very confident that we're both going to enjoy ourselves a lot. Once I calm myself down, I open the door and smile at the sight before me.

My beautiful girl is on her knees, just like I told her to be. Her curls are out, and they hang around her tits and the middle of her back. She's wearing a little red silk dress that barely covers her ass with spaghetti straps and lace cups. And she chose a pair of red leather stiletto sandals to go with.

"Fucking perfect."

I go up to her and stroke her hair softly, loving the way her soft strands feel under my hand. "Look up at me, pretty girl."

She stares up at me with her bright blue eyes. I rub my thumb across her cheek. "Here's what we're going to do tonight. I'll be your Dom. You'll be my sub. I have some work to do on the computer, and you're going to stay in here with me while I do it. I'll give you some simple instructions, and you'll follow them. If you want to stop anything, you'll use your safe word. After I'm done with my work, I'm going to make love to you. A lot. Does that work for you?"

She nods her head sweetly and smiles. "Yeah. I'd like that a lot."

I stand behind her and massage her shoulders for a moment, loving the way she always softens under me instantly. "Good. I'm going to go sit at my desk, and you're going to come sit on my lap. But I want you to crawl to me first, okay?"

"Yes, Daddy."

"Good." I leave her on her knees and get seated in my chair, thankful it's sturdy enough for two. Once I get my notebook out and my computer turned on, I glance over at my girl. "Go ahead and crawl to me, sweetheart."

She winks at me, making my dick twitch before she crawls to me slowly. When she reaches me, she crawls between my legs and reaches for my belt.

I pop her hands playfully. "Not right now. I'll let you do that later. I promise. Come sit."

She sits on me, and I wrap an arm around her while I grab my pen and open my notebook.

"What are you working on?"

"I'll tell you later. Right now I just want you to sit here and look pretty."

Her soft lips press against my neck, and she nips my skin. "Alright."

I don't feel like doing what I'm about to do, but I want to get it over with quickly. Though I won't be obeying all of Jack's instructions, I will follow some of them. The first task I'm working on is creating a New Birth Ceremony for girls. I'm keeping it pretty similar to the one we currently do with a few minor modifications.

Genevieve nestles her head in my neck, clearly missing me as much as I missed her. I wrap my arm around her tighter, snaking my hand between her legs and stroking her clit. "I love touching your pretty pussy, Gen. You're so wet for me already."

She arches her back and grinds against my fingers. "I'm so sore, but I need you again already."

I think back to everything we did last night and start to feel a little guilty. I don't regret a single thing and would do it again in a heartbeat, but I should've let her rest and recover more. Her ass is probably killing her, and I've got her downstairs on my lap in high heels. I should be bathing her and then massaging her before putting her to sleep.

Taking a moment to put my selfish desires to the side, I pause to check in on my wife. "I want to take a quick break. Do you need to rest? I know last night was pretty intense, and if you need time to recover instead of doing this, I understand."

She cups my face and kisses my lips softly. "I can rest later."

Fuck me. I push my notebook to the side and keep a hand on her waist while I use my other to caress her sexy little body. I trace the neckline of her cherry silk dress, and she shivers.

"I'll never get over how pretty you are, Gen."

She smiles, and I run my thumb over the lace cups of her dress, softly squeezing her full breasts. Slipping my fingers inside, I roll her nipples between my thumb and forefinger, loving the way she squirms underneath my touch.

"Did you pump before I got home?"

She nods her head, and I slap her tit making her gasp. "Daddy wants some later."

She nibbles her lip. "Yes, Daddy."

Moving my hand away from her body, I pick up my pen and open my notebook back up. She rests her head against my shoulder, still sitting on my leg while I play with her soft curls.

I have no intention of baptizing my daughter in the ways of this society, but I'm still going to plan a nice ceremony nonetheless.

The vows will remain the same, but the location will change. Instead of having the New Birth Ceremony at the meeting hall, we'll have it outside in a garden.

Gen attempts to unbutton my shirt with one hand, but I pull her soft fingers away, trying to focus. She reaches for my belt again. "How long are you going to make me wait?"

I take her hand in mind and give it a gentle squeeze. "Not too much longer, but if you keep being a brat, I'm going to punish you first."

She ignores me by reaching for the buttons on my shirt again, and I realize that I need to give her something to do to keep her busy.

"Straddle my leg, and grind your needy pussy up against it until you feel better."

She stands up for a moment to straddle my right leg, and my balls tighten when her slip lifts and exposes her ass. I use my left hand to keep writing while I stroke the seam of her ass with my right.

In addition to the New Birth Ceremony taking place outside, I want to make an adjustment to the baptism. Instead of plain bath water, I want the tub filled with pink rose petals. Zahara is still really young, but I can already tell my girl's favorite color is pink. So, I want to incorporate that into the ceremony.

Gen grinds against me softly, breathing deeply in and out while she grips my thigh. I feel her cream seeping into my pant leg, and I'm desperate for a taste.

I grip her hip while she moves hers back and forth. "You're doing such a good job, sweetheart. I have a few more things I need to do, and then I'll take care of you."

She looks over her shoulder at me with her pretty mouth hanging open. "I can't wait."

Her massive tits look like they're about to spill out of her dress while she rides. I grab the straps of her silk gown, and pull them down, letting the fabric pool around her waist. She turns away from me, arching her back and playing with her nipples while she rocks her hips back and forth.

I quickly scribble the remainder of my notes for the New Birth Ceremony, setting a mental reminder to text Jack the details later. After pushing my notebook to the side, I wipe the drool that spills from my mouth from watching Gen.

Pulling her closer to me, I wrap my arms around her and rub her clit. "Do you need me to take it easy on you today?"

She pants and twists her nipples. "No. I want it rough and nasty."

I groan and pull on her hair, making her tits lift up higher. "I'll give you what you want. But don't say I didn't warn you."

She smiles and I do too. I caress her shoulders and kiss her cheek. "Get on your knees."

My girl does as I request, and I stand up to grab something I hid behind the bookshelf a while back. A brand new leather riding crop. This one is red, and it matches Gen's pretty outfit. When I get back to my desk, I reach into my drawer and pull out Gen's choker. It doesn't take me long to put it on her, and I stand in front of her with the crop in my left hand.

Her chest rises and falls faster as her breathing picks up. "What now?"

Undoing my pants slowly, I pull out my cock and rub her soft lips with my thumb. "Now, you're going to fuck my cock with that tight, wet mouth of yours, and I'm going to spank you while you do it."

Her blue eyes darken, and she pokes out her lips while she slides them onto me softly. I'm always amazed at how she takes me so easily like it's what she was made to do.

I stand in place while she moves up and down, squeezing her lips and trying to get me as wet as possible.

Looking down at her, I'm completely entranced. She looks like a goddess kneeling before me. I grip the crop in my hand and lift it slightly before giving her a spanking. She moans around my dick, and I spank her other cheek, making her breasts shake.

"Do you like being spanked with Daddy's cock in your mouth?"

She comes up for air and wipes the drool from her cheek. "Yes."

I play with the heart charm on her choker. "Such a good girl. Open wide and spit on my dick."

Gen opens her mouth and cranes her neck so she's hovering over my length. I rub small circles on her ass with the crop while spit pools in her mouth. When she's got enough, she sticks out her pink tongue, letting it spill down my shaft.

My dick twitches from the wet warmth, and my precum mixes with it. I pinch her hard nipples with my unoccupied hand. "Suck."

She opens wide and slides her mouth back on me, making me groan louder than I intended. I hope my mother is still upstairs because if she's on the first level, she definitely heard the noise I just made.

I keep spanking my girl harder and faster, losing count of how many I give her. I almost get carried away with rage, but I look down at her. Keeping my eyes focused on my sweet girl adoring me, I think about how much I love her and cherish her, and she keeps me grounded and in the moment.

Her slurps become sloppier and messier, and her saliva drips all over the hardwood floor, making my balls hurt with need.

I need to taste her. I have to. I look between her legs and see her spilling onto the floor, and I know I can't wait any longer.

Pulling out of her mouth, I turn to my desk and shove my notebooks, keyboard, and desk pad out of the way, clearing space.

"Get on here. On your back."

I help her stand, not wanting her to trip in her stilettos as she climbs on top of my desk and lies down on her back.

I hold her legs open, dragging my tongue back and forth along her thighs, barely grazing her center when I go over the middle. She reaches out for my head, but I hold her down by her neck. "No moving."

She relaxes, and I press soft kisses against her dripping slit, resisting my overwhelming desire to bury my face in her.

I stand in front of her, hovering over her while I pick up the crop. "We're going to do something a little different. If you don't like anything, let me know. Alright?"

She nods her head. "Yes."

"Good." I run my fingers between her folds before pulling them back and licking them. "So fucking delicious. I want your cream dripping down my desk."

I position the crop over her pussy, rubbing small circles on her clit before I pull it back and smack her center.

She flinches, like I expected, but she doesn't say anything. Her wetness pours out of her, dripping down into her exposed ass.

I smack her pussy again a little harder. "How do you like having your creamy cunt slapped?"

She lets out a shaky breath. "I love it."

Smacking her again, I wipe up her spillage with my cock, dragging it along her ass cheeks and then over her slit.

"Good. A pussy this pretty deserves to be punished."

She whimpers and I smack her cunt again, living for the way her body shakes each time I do so.

"I need you inside me so fucking bad."

I smack her cunt again. "Do you?"

A tear streams from her oceanic eyes. "Yes."

Another smack. "Beg me for it. Be a good girl and beg Daddy for his cock, and maybe he'll give it to you."

She cries softly, smirking at me. Gen cries so much during sex, and I adore her for it. It's the sweetest thing ever.

"Please, Daddy. Please give me your cock."

I give her one final smack. "Beg harder."

Her voice shakes. "I'll do anything."

I drop the crop to the side and pull her open, focusing on her pink center. "That's all I wanted to hear."

She doesn't get another word out before I kneel before her, drinking her up and cleaning her with my tongue. She moans loudly, and I relish in her pleasure, feeling myself on the edge of exploding while I eat her out.

I kiss her swollen clit, making her body buck. "What was it you were saying about my cock?"

Her legs wrap around my neck. "Put your mouth back on me, James."

I nip her clit with my teeth. "Be patient and I'll give you what you want."

With shaky legs, she takes slow breaths in and out, waiting while I hover my mouth over her heat.

"Good girls know how to wait patiently, don't they?" I give her another wet kiss on her trembling bud.

"Yes."

She tries to close her thighs together, and I can tell she's ready to burst. I give her a few more licks making her tremble before I position myself over her and drive my hips in.

"GOD! JAMES!"

I hold her hands above her head by her wrists, pounding her into oblivion. "This greedy cunt will be the death of me."

Her tits bounce with every thrust, and she sucks in a breath when I go deeper.

Her baby blue orbs sear into me. "What a worthy way to die."

Goddamn.

I wrap my arms around her and lift her off the desk, keeping myself sheathed and my pants around my ankles while I spin her around and pin her up against the wall. "Are you ready for me to destroy you?"

Her pussy squeezes my dick harder while she keeps her legs locked around my hips with her heels digging into my ass. "I was born ready."

Holding her arms above her head, I drive into her over and over, pressing her back into the wall as I grunt in her ear. I'm so in love with this woman it hurts. My head spins thinking about all of the things we've been through, and my heart beats rapidly with love, lust, and possession. I bite her neck and tits while I fuck her.

"You belong to me, Gen. Don't you ever forget it."

She pants and squeezes her legs around me tighter. "I'm all yours."

I drive into her mindlessly, using her body as I try to permanently etch myself into her soul. "I can't wait to fill you up with another baby."

She smiles, arching her back and letting me have my way. "You just want to keep me pregnant forever, don't you?"

I suck one of her nipples into my mouth, drinking her supply that's already replenishing. "Fuck yes."

She gasps when I suck her other nipple. "Don't take it all. I need some for Zahara."

Against my wishes, I back off her tits. "If I don't get some later, I swear I will have a tantrum."

"I swear there will be enough for you." She quiets down while her breath shudders, and I can tell she's nearing her orgasm.

I kiss her neck and slow my strokes, sliding in and out of her warmth patiently. "There better be. Because if there's not, I'm going to spend all night punishing you. And you might think you want that, but you don't. This tender pussy needs rest."

Her breathy moans make my knees weak. "I promise I'll save some for you, Daddy."

I feel so close, and I know she is too, but I don't want to stop. I know without a doubt I'm going to have to carry her out of this room for fucking her so hard over the last twenty-four hours, but I can't help myself.

Pulling her off the wall, I carry her back to my desk and slide out of her, setting her on her feet. "Bend over, sweetheart."

On shaky legs, she gives me her back and bends over. I pull her slip down her legs and keep it wrapped around her ankles as I position myself at her entrance.

She holds her hands behind her, and we link our fingers together. I stroke her palms softly with my thumbs and plunge into her, pumping quickly while she grinds her clit against my desk.

Our sweat mixes along with our arousal, filling the room with our sweet scent.

I keep my pace steady, giving her what she likes and what makes me feel so fucking good. "Are you getting close, baby?"

She takes a moment to speak, already letting me know the answer. "Yeah. You're gonna make me come, baby."

I release her hands and grab her hips which allows me to pull her back on my dick while I drive into her. "I'm so close too, sweetheart. Let me know when you're about to."

She breathes faster and faster while I control her, and before I know it, she's gasping for air. "I'm right there."

I slide my hands under her stomach, reaching forward and squeezing her tits while I give her everything I have. "Come with me, sweetheart."

She cries out and shudders while her entire body tenses, and I spill inside of her, feeling her pulse around me over and over while I do.

"Jesus, Gen."

"I love you so much, James."

I continue fucking her until I've given her every drop, and then once she's stopped shaking, I pull out and scoop her up, sitting her on the desk facing me.

"I love you so much, Gen."

She wraps her arms around my waist, and I lean down to meet her for a kiss.

After I get my pants back on, I take off Genevieve's heels and choker. She sits on the couch in the office bundled up in a blanket, wrapped in my arms. I want to carry her upstairs and pamper her the way she deserves, but before I can do that, I need to clue her in on my meeting with Jack and hopefully clear the air between me and my mother.

She tucks her head under my chin and beats me to the punch. "Tell me about today."

I massage her scalp. "Well, it went exactly as I would've expected, but it was completely different too." I fill her in on everything from my ride to the house, the weird exterior and interior, my calm but creepy meeting with Jack, and what I'm expected to do.

Gen groans and closes her eyes. "Is that what you were working on at your desk?"

"Yeah. The New Birth Ceremony. That's all I was able to get done before you seduced me." I try to pull her blanket down, but she swats my hand away.

"It was *you* who asked *me* to be on my knees when you got home. And I take it you don't plan on killing Damion, right?"

My cousin Damion. A good friend, but a little incompetent. As much as he annoys me at times, he's dependable overall, and he's not the worst person in the world.

"No. I have absolutely no intention of killing Damion."

She shivers. "What do you plan on doing then?"

I came up with my plan for Damion on the way home, and I can't tell if it's genius or the dumbest thing I've ever thought of. However, I'm an innovator, so I'm willing to give it a try with the small caveat that it might blow up in my face. I don't know if Gen will be convinced, but I'm hoping I get her to support me anyway.

"Well, I was going to speak with him about running away."

She tenses. "James, do you not remember what happened with Deacon?"

"Of course, I remember."

"So what made you think that we should try something like that again?"

I get up to sit on the other end of the couch to massage Gen's feet. "Well, we got caught with Deacon because Shane was by the house watching. And we gave him a lot of money. I don't plan on giving Damion any money, but I'm still giving him a chance to escape."

She moans when I pick up her right foot and dig my thumbs into her sole. "There's no way he's going to just leave Theresa."

"He's already cheating on her."

She rests her head on the pillow behind her and closes her eyes. "Still. You're asking him to just up and leave her without warning. He's not going to do it. Plus, I don't know if the best solution to avoid the wrath of The Caledonia Council is running."

I move my hands down to her heel, squeezing and kneading. "I agree. Which is why this is just a temporary fix. I'm not saying Damion has to go away forever. Just until I can get this mess sorted with The Caledonia Council. I want to do some digging and get Draco to help me—maybe we can find out who's at the top of this thing."

"What then?"

"We offer them an ultimatum. Disband our society and the councils, and let everyone go."

"And if they don't?"

"Then I'll do everything in my power to do it myself."

Chapter Twenty-Five
GENEVIEVE

I close my eyes, trying to enjoy the foot massage James is giving me while I process his idea. The thought of dismantling the society is really exciting, whether it's possible or not.

"I like the idea, but I don't know how we're going to do it."

He switches feet, giving my left foot attention. "I just need to find a way to get to whoever's at the top. Shane was over societal operations, Annabelle managed fashion, and Jack's over meat. That leaves someone who's over our other food products and home products, and someone who manages perfumes.

"Who do you think is at the very top?"

He bites his lip. "Perfumes. It has to be. It was our first business."

I pull the soft green blanket up, trying to keep my naked body covered. "Maybe we have the information we need right here."

"Come again?"

"The sector leaders, James. Maybe we have their contact information here."

His brown eyes go wide. "Gen. Don't you think if that were the case, we would've found it already? I'm sure the information is not buried in the walls or floorboards."

I roll my eyes and pull my foot away. "I don't expect the information to be in the walls or floorboards. I'm talking about the stuff Mom gave us. You know? That big velvet box of shit. We never did go through it. There could very well be a way to contact them there."

He pulls my foot back in his lap, resting it on his bulge. "I don't know. I looked through it, and it was just crap. Old trinkets, receipts, journals. Nothing special."

Journals. "Maybe there's an address book. We should go through it again. If we don't find anything, whatever. But I have a feeling *something* in that box could help us. Why would the Head Fathers and Guiding Mothers keep all that shit if it didn't have a purpose?"

He pauses. "True. Alright. I'm willing to give it a go."

I sit up. "Good. Where's the box?"

He stands and straightens out his clothes. "In the library. I'll go grab it."

I sit up and cross my aching legs. "Bring me a shirt too. And pain medicine."

I sit on the office floor on a butt pillow with an ice pack while James sits across from me digging in the box of artifacts. He pulls out old necklaces, pocket watches, jewelry boxes, receipts, family trees, and maps. At the bottom of all the clutter is a pile of twenty or so books. He pulls out the leather journals, and we start to flip through them, trying to figure out what they all are.

He picks up a black one and opens it up, flipping through the pages quickly. "This is a fucking recipe book."

I laugh and readjust my position on my pillow, making my pussy sting. "You really wrecked me, babe. I don't think I'm going to be able to have sex for a week."

"I'll give you the night to rest. You'll feel fine after that. I promise."

I ignore him and grab the next notebook. This looks like a personal journal. Dark purple leather with a silk ribbon.

Opening it up, I confirm my assumptions. "This one is a diary. Rebecca Barlow?"

James freezes. "Yeah. My great-grandmother. That's her diary?"

I turn through a few of the pages. "Yes. She talks about Jude in some of this."

"You hold onto that one. Whatever sick shit my great-granddad did to her, I don't want to know."

We laugh and he picks up the one below it. It's a black leather notebook.

He opens it up, staying silent as he slowly flips through. His brows dip, and he turns the pages rapidly, looking as if he's trying to absorb everything all at once. "This is his journal, Gen."

"Whose journal?"

He sighs. "My great-grandfather's. The eldest founder and the first Head Father. Jude Barlow."

I watch him as he closes it, gripping it tightly in his hands. "Are you sure you can handle looking through that? I can if you need me to."

He frowns. "I need to look through it. I'd rather not, but I have no idea what this is going to have in it. I don't want you to read something terrible. I'm sure Rebecca's has something terrible, but hopefully not as bad."

I run my fingers over the journal in my hand, wondering what kind of life Rebecca lived. Did she love Jude? Did she marry him willingly? I get a chill, fearful of what I might read going through these pages. Part of me feels disgusted going through them. This is someone's personal diary. A private safe place that they never intended to share. And now I'm going to be digging through it.

We dig through the rest of the notebooks and don't find anything else of importance.

I look up at James who runs a hand through his messy black hair. "When do you want to start going through these?"

He stands up. "Let's do it tonight. First, I want to have a chat with Mom if she'll let me. Then we'll get Zee and bring her in here with us to eat and sleep while we work. After that, I want to plan out the next council and community meetings. I'll call Damion for a chat beforehand to get him caught up to speed, and then I'll call Draco. I think he has some family journals and things at his house that he can look through."

I take his outstretched hand and stand. "Okay. And are we still giving Jessamine her punishment?"

He frowns. "I don't know. Do you know what it is?"

One day when I was flipping through my Guiding Mother's Text, I saw a section on punishments for women in the society for various things. I glanced through it, not too concerned as I knew I wouldn't break any of the rules.

One of the infractions was infidelity, and I do remember what the punishment was for it. It's not a nice thing at all, but it could definitely be worse.

"Yeah, I know what it is."

He grimaces. "Is it something we can handle?"

"I don't think it will be a problem. Unless she declines."

He nods to my desk. "Have a seat and get started. I'll talk to Mom and you can catch me up as soon as I get back."

"Deal."

He groans. "And if I'm not back in fifteen minutes, send help."

#

It doesn't take James long to speak with Odette, and when he returns, he looks relieved. He has Zahara swaddled against his chest with her baby bag in his arm, and she wriggles underneath the cloth, eager to get loose.

I adjust my butt pillow in my desk chair. "How did it go?"

He brings Zahara's bag over to me, putting it on my desk and unpacking it.

After getting the pump set up, I take my shirt back off and get started while he tells me about his conversation.

"She started crying as soon as she opened her door, but after I hugged her and apologized, she apologized for slapping me and told me what she told you about him."

"Do you feel any better?"

He rubs Zahara's back while he keeps his eyes trained on my chest. "I don't feel great, but it is nice knowing he was a piece of shit."

Once I've emptied out, James helps me clean everything up and bottle feeds Zahara before putting her in her crib beside his desk.

After putting my shirt back on, I open up my Guiding Mother's Text and curl my finger at James to come stand beside me.

He looks over my shoulder while I explain to him what I learned. "It's changed a bit throughout the years, and there are variations depending on the circumstances, but the current punishment for unfaithful widowed wives is as follows—a ceremony is held with the Head Father, Guiding Mother, the woman in question, and her next male relative. She then has to get on her knees and beg forgiveness. If it's granted, the Guiding Mother shaves her head, and she must live in her next male relative's house under his supervision for the following year. She isn't permitted to be with anyone else during that time."

James nods his head and rubs my shoulders. "Okay. Super weird but doable. And the end goal is to end all of this shit, so I'm sure Jessamine can handle living with Simon and his wife for a few months. And her hair will grow back."

"Yeah. But it's still pretty demeaning and degrading."

He squeezes me harder. "Yeah. But it's that or death right now so she can deal."

"When do we want to handle all of this?"

He goes to his desk to grab his chair and pulls up next to me at mine. "This Saturday, I want to have the council meeting. Sunday will be the community meeting. We'll schedule the Exit Ceremony for Wednesday. Damion will be held in the basement at the meeting hall after I announce his infraction at the council meeting. Draco will help me stage an escape for Damion on Tuesday night. Wednesday, I'll tell Jack that everything is handled apart from the Exit Ceremony due to Damion's escape, and I'll advance to level three."

He makes it sound so easy. Way easier than it'll be. I don't know where Damion plans on hiding or how they plan on staging an escape. And I don't think this Jack guy will be happy to be crossed.

"I don't know if he'll believe you, James. He'll assume you had something to do with it."

"He might. But he won't have any evidence. He'll have no choice but to accept what I tell him."

Anxiety courses through me. "And what happens when you piss him off? He'll surely retaliate. Look at what happened to Annabelle. What do you think he'll do? Are you prepared?"

"I am." He shifts in his seat.

"And what do you plan to do?"

He sighs. "After I tell him everything's done, I'm sure he'll want to meet. I don't like that they know where our house is. They had to have followed us home from the hospital after Zahara was born. Anyway, we're not moving again, but we're going to stay somewhere else for a while. When Jack asks me to meet again, you, Zahara, and Mom will go to our new location while I'm out, and then I'll meet you guys there after. Once I'm sure I'm not being followed. We'll stay here in the meantime so we don't draw attention."

Leaving our home? We're going in hiding? I don't know what I expected him to come up with, but it wasn't that.

"And where are we going, James?"

He smiles softly. "The cabin."

My body heats up at the thought of the cabin. James and I haven't been there in nearly a year, and I'm eager to go back. It's a little out of the way from civilization but is absolutely gorgeous. We had an amazing time when we went, and it'll be fun to go as a family.

"I could be okay with that."

He grins. "I knew you would be. I'll call Samuel—he'll give you guys a ride. He's the only person I trust who's not in the society to get you guys there without anyone following. If you're okay with it, he and his grandson can stay a night or two with us before they drive back."

I think back to when James told me Samuel was going to be a grandfather. His little grandson is nearly a year old now, and we haven't had a chance to meet him yet. "Of course that's alright. It'll be nice to see them."

James kisses my forehead and takes my hands in his. "And I know you were supposed to have a baby shower before you gave birth, but we weren't able to. I was hoping to get a little something planned for early next week after I speak with everyone at the community meeting. Only our close friends of course—Mai, Paul, Ella, Mom, Samuel, and a maybe few others. What do you say?"

Before I had Zahara, I was looking forward to having a baby shower. The girls were so excited to plan one, but I went into early labor and we had to cancel. I forgot about the whole thing until just now, but it would be nice to get together with everyone and catch up. I know they'd all love to meet Zee too.

"I think that would be really nice. Are you okay with everyone coming over here or will we meet somewhere else?"

He opens my notebook and starts making a shopping list. "We'll have it over here. I'm not inviting anyone who I see as a threat. Plus, I'll be prepared regardless. I think it'll be a really good time."

I feel myself getting excited about the event. It'll be nice to do something fun with how crazy everything's been. And a house this grand deserves to be enjoyed by friends and family. Maybe we can have more gatherings down the line.

I wrap my arms around James' neck, giving him a kiss. He slides his hand up my shirt, gently stroking my naked body underneath while I rest my head on his shoulder.

"Thank you. Thank you so much, babe."

He kisses my hair and squeezes my thighs. "What for?"

"For always making me feel special. I know a baby shower is a small thing, but it's a really big thing to me. Thanks for always remembering what's important to me and going out of your way to do special things for us."

He tucks his hands under my thighs, hoisting me out of my chair and pulling me into his lap. His soft fingers trail up and down my back while he stares at me like I'm the most perfect thing in the world. He's got a look on his face like he wouldn't rather be anywhere else but here.

My heart flutters when he kisses my lips softly and caresses my cheek.

"You don't have to thank me for anything, Gen. And I love doing special things for you. I'll never stop doing special things for you. I've only just begun."

After James and I finish up in the office, he brings Zahara back to Odette's room for some more one-on-one time, and he scoops me up to carry me back to our room. I keep my arms wrapped around his neck while he holds me bridal style.

I snuggle my head against his chest in my oversized navy tee while he presses the elevator button to head up. "You don't have to do this. I can walk."

He steps into the spacious box, pressing the button to our floor as the doors close behind us. "Gen, baby, you were literally limping. I know you are aching from head to toe. Let me take care of you."

No matter how hard I try, I can't resist James. He's the perfect balance of stern and gentle, and I love it when he takes control. He takes control most of the time, but I really don't have a problem with it.

I glance out the window over his shoulder, trying to get a glimpse of the farm. I miss my girl, Olive, and I want to make sure to spend some time with her tomorrow.

"Well, I'm limping because you obliterated me, James. I have never been fucked so many times in a twenty-four hour period."

His laugh shakes my body in his arms. "Neither have I. But I don't have any regrets nor do I feel bad about it because you loved it."

I stare at his sharp jaw while he steps into the hall. "Hmmm. It was okay. *You* loved it though. I was just doing it for you."

His mouth flies open. "Did you forget how you were begging me for my cock in the middle of the night?"

My neck heats as I remember exactly what he's talking about. "No recollection of such a thing."

He opens our bedroom door and uses his firm ass to shut it behind us. "No, I think you remember. It was when I was sucking your big milky tits and you were grinding your greedy little pussy against my thigh saying, 'I need you so badly, James.' Does that ring any bells?"

I fight off my laughter, surprised that he remembered exactly what I said. "I literally don't know what you're talking about."

He sits me down on the bed and starts undressing. "Bullshit. You were humping me, saying, 'Suck me harder, baby. Oh, God. Fuck me, please, Daddy.'"

I laugh out loud, unable to continue the charade any longer. "Fine. You win. I remember every moment. How could I forget?"

He grabs my ankles and pulls them open, making my shirt lift and exposing my bare pussy. "I know you remember, you filthy little whore."

I try to close my legs while he resists, keeping me open. "I can't go again right now."

He kneels before me, kissing my thighs. "I need you, Gen. Are you going to deny Daddy?"

I feel myself starting to get wet with his tender touches. He strokes my legs softly, running his fingers up and down my skin. "You told me you'd give me the night to rest."

He looks up at me with darkened eyes. "Maybe I lied."

I wrangle my legs away from him and shut them, ignoring the throbbing between my legs and the wetness on my thighs. "I am not letting you fuck me right now, James."

He grips my thighs, still on his knees before me. "I thought you wanted me to take it from you, Gen."

I let out a gasp making him laugh loudly. "I still want that. But not right now. I want to rest first."

Standing up off the floor, he sits on the bed and pulls me into his lap. I straddle him, resting my hands on his chest while his erection sits against my stomach.

"Okay. I'll let you rest."

I kiss his nose. "Thank you."

He stares at me and strokes my hips softly. "Will you elaborate on what you meant?"

"What I meant regarding what?"

He blushes. "When you said you wanted me to take it from you. I need to know what you meant by that."

I try to look away but he grips my chin, keeping my eyes on him. My mind wanders back to our brunch date. I felt flirty for the first time in a while, and the words just slipped out of my mouth. I surprised myself, but I didn't regret saying them. And when I thought about it, I thought it might be fun.

I stroke his strong arms. "What I meant was, I would like you to *playfully* take it from me. Like how we do with the Dom/sub stuff, we plan a day and time to do it."

He nods his head. "Okay. Keep going. Tell me what happens when we do this."

"It would be like a game. Like tag or something. You'd chase me around, and when you caught me, you would fuck me however you want. Maybe I'd resist a little, but you'd... do it anyway. You'd *do me* anyway." I tear my chin away and look away from him.

Out of the corner of my eye, I see him smirk. "If that's what you want, it's nothing to be ashamed of or embarrassed about. And I'll do it gladly. As long as you agree to use your safe word if you need."

I look back at him. "I promise."

He grips my hips. "And I'd hate to ruin the moment, but I might check in on you in the middle, just to make sure we're still okay."

"That's fine."

He smiles. "Good. And how do you want it? Soft or rough?"

"Both."

His eyes glitter. "Both. I can do that. Do you want me to stop if you start to cry?"

I shake my head. "No. I swear I will use my safe word if I need to, James."

He nods his head. "I believe you. I just have to ask you these questions anyway. It's important."

I brush my curls out of my face and pull them into a bun with the scrunchie on James' nightstand. "I understand."

He pulls me closer and kisses my cheeks. "And when you do want to do this, sweetheart?"

I close my eyes, trying to think of a good time for our new activity. "Maybe this weekend?"

He flips us over, pinning me on my back. "This weekend works. When I get home from the council meeting?"

I spread my legs wider, allowing him to grind his cock against my clit. "That's perfect."

He kisses my neck and whispers in my ear. "We're on then. This Saturday when I get home. Make sure Zee's with Mom."

I moan while he nibbles my neck. "I will."

He lifts my shirt, exposing my breasts. "Is there anything off the table?" His lips close around one of my tits.

Writhing underneath him, I try to answer his question. "Anything we've done together before is allowed."

He bites my peak. "Perfect. God, you're so naughty, Gen. I can't wait."

Spreading my legs wider, he slides his cock back and forth across my slick center. "Do you want me to fuck you, Gen?"

Yes. *Yes.* God, yes. "No. I want you to give me a bath."

He groans before he pulls away, standing up off the bed. "Absolutely. I'll get it ready and come back for you in a second."

As he turns away, I pull off my top, wincing at the soreness between my legs, and try to focus on anything other than fucking him senseless.

Chapter Twenty-Six
JAMES

I stand in the bedroom getting ready for the first council meeting in weeks. I'm filled with anxiety as I grab a pair of black boxers to wear under my suit. Gen lies in bed naked while Zee sleeps in her crib, snoring softly. I still can't believe my little baby is nearly seven weeks old. It's nearly the second week of October, and she's so much bigger than she was the day we brought her home. Gen cried yesterday, feeling bad for being so distant with her during her early days and feeling depressed because she can't get those times back, and I nearly cried too. My girl has the best mommy in the world and I don't know what I did to deserve either of these angels in my life.

I slide into my underwear slowly, trying not to wake Gen. She rustles in bed and turns over to face me, ogling my figure.

"Come back to bed, James."

My dick twitches with need, and I adjust myself, trying to stay focused on what I'm supposed to be doing. "I can't, baby."

She reaches out for me with her classic French nails. "Please. Just for a few minutes." Her eyelashes flutter.

I haven't touched her for the past few days in an effort to help her recover from the marathon I put her through, and she's been going crazy. I have too, but my self-control is a little stronger than hers.

"Gen, baby, if I don't leave in the next fifteen minutes, I'm going to be late."

She licks her plump pout. "Give me ten and you can have five to get dressed."

Good God.

I count to ten, trying to get my boner to go down. "I promise I will take care of you later, sweetheart. We're going to have a lot of fun trying that new thing you requested we do."

She sits up in bed, letting the blanket fall at her waist with her tits on display. "I know. But I want you right now too."

I close my eyes, trying to ignore the heavenly sight before me. "Gen, no. Please cover yourself."

I hear her rustling, and when I open my eyes, she's lying on her stomach, giving me an excellent view of her firm ass.

"Jesus, Gen. I am going to be late. Don't do this, baby. Please."

She looks over her shoulder at me with hooded eyes. "Five minutes, James. Please."

My cock drips as my resolve crumbles. "Spread your legs, you little slut. You get five minutes, then I'm out the door."

She grins and spreads them. "That's all I need."

I climb behind her, still wearing my underwear, and lower myself to her pussy. I take a moment just to smell her. Her scent drives me mad. She's my source of life. My oxygen. I'm overcome by the need to breathe her in, and I slide my tongue between her shaved lips.

She murmurs into her pillow, letting me know how much she loves my touch. I kiss her all over before sliding my tongue further forward and flicking her clit. I smile when she tries to press herself against me, eager for more. I slap her ass before I go in for another taste, dipping my tongue inside her and sliding it back and forth slowly.

"Oh, James."

I pull her pussy open and spit inside her. "It's Daddy."

She whimpers. "More, Daddy."

I pull her ass cheeks open and spit on her hole before I drag my tongue from her pussy to her asshole and swirl my tongue around her rim. My balls ache remembering how good it felt to be buried in her tight, warm ass, and it takes everything in me not to pull my underwear down and drive into her.

Feeling myself getting weaker, I pull away and drape the blanket back over her. Her head whips around when I step off the bed and start putting my pants on.

She frowns. "What are you doing?"

I look at my watch. "Believe it or not, your five minutes are up, sweetheart. I've got to go."

Her blue eyes glitter. "And when do you plan on us doing our thing?"

I slide into my black silk shirt and grab my blazer. "As soon as I get home, we can start. So do whatever you need to do before then and be ready when I get back. I'll let you know as soon as I'm on my way home."

She sits up but keeps the blanket covering her. "Okay. Do you have your gun?"

I open up my nightstand drawer and pull out my knife. "Of course I do. Both are in the car."

"Be safe, James. Please don't start any fights with anyone."

I kiss her lips and squeeze her hair. "I will be safe. No one is going to do anything. I swear. I'm prepared."

She leans against her pillow, sinking into it as she starts to relax. "Okay. Tell me everything that happens."

I slide into my boots and grab my cloak. "I promise, I will. Get some rest before I get back, and let me know if you need anything."

She pulls me close for another kiss. "I will. I love you."

I squeeze her tits through the blanket making her squeal. "I love you too."

###

I turn on the radio on my way to the meeting hall listening to a playlist Gen made for me, but I keep it low. The music comforts me, especially since my favorite person compiled it for me, but I need to also keep my head clear which is why I can't have it too loud.

Today is a very big day. Never in our society's history, as far as I know, have we gone this long without a council meeting. It's just unheard of. For a moment, I almost wanted to thank The Caledonia Council for disrupting my life for the sheer fact that they postponed these fucking meetings. But then I remembered that they're trying to ruin my life, so my gratitude dissipated as soon as it appeared.

A small part of me is relieved to resume meetings as this is a part of my current challenge. A stepping stone to get to where I really want to be. And since my first task was so horrendous, it's nice to be doing something a little more simple. I'm not sure how things will go over with Damion and the escape plan, but I hope it all works out.

I called him last night before Gen and I went to bed to clue him in. I hope I'm not shooting myself in the foot telling another person about this council that only I'm supposed to know exists. But I didn't know what else to do. At first, he was upset and didn't want to run, but when he considered the alternative, he realized that I'm doing him a favor.

I also clued in Draco as he'll be helping me secure Damion in the basement and aid in his escape. Plus, he already knows about the council, and he's offered to help me in whatever ways I need. My main concern now is how everyone else will take it.

Most of the council will probably be unfazed. The men in my family are not normal by any means, and most of them like violence. We've all witnessed Exit Ceremonies, and they know the repercussions of breaking tenets.

However, some of the men in my family still have a soul, and they'll probably be affected. Especially Simon.

Simon is Damion's older brother, and I'm not sure whether he knows about the affair. Even if he does, he doesn't know about Jessamine's punishment and how he'll have to take her in afterward. I'm still trying to decide how much I want to fill him in on or if I want to leave him in the dark completely. While I do need support to make sure everything goes smoothly, I can't let everyone in on my secret or it will surely backfire.

I also hate to have such a dramatic start to our first council meeting back, but I can't postpone the news about Damion's transgression and his punishment. I need to have all tasks within level two completed by the middle of next week, or I will be fucked. I was reminded of this last night when Jack texted me informing me to contact him by noon on Wednesday.

That gives me barely any time to execute everything, but I'll have to make do. I'm killing two birds with one stone by announcing Jessamine's punishment at the council meeting, and I'll schedule Jessamine's punishment for Monday morning and Damion's Exit Ceremony for Tuesday. I'm also planning for Genevieve's baby shower to take place on Monday afternoon, and I hope I'm not overbooking myself.

Jessamine's punishment is not open to the society as a whole, so I won't announce it at the community meeting tomorrow. I will be announcing the Exit Ceremony, and I'm still trying to figure out how to manage everyone's concerns when Damion goes *missing*.

I turn up the music, deciding to give myself a rest from thinking so much. I think about all of the possible outcomes of what I plan on doing, and I can't tell if I want to laugh hysterically or cry. I know without a doubt that I'm going to piss Jack off, but I can't kill Damion. I won't do it. I'm already being forced to do enough shit against my will by The Caledonia Council, but I won't do this. I'm going to put my foot down, and they're going to see who they're dealing with.

Draco is also coming over to the house after the community meeting tomorrow with the artifacts from his house, and I pray he can help me find something to contact the sector leader over perfumes. The sooner I can climb to the top of this ladder, the faster I can get out of this bullshit and sail to freedom. I'm hoping this plan will be easier done than said because my backup plan is to kill Jack and anyone standing in my way until I get what I want. And while I don't want to take any more lives, I'm willing to do so if it's for my family.

Eventually, I pull up to the library and park my car out back. Looking around, I don't see any vehicles I recognize, and I cross my fingers, hoping that I was the first to arrive.

The sky was cloudy for my entire drive here, and it didn't help improve my mood. However, I know rain can be a symbol of goodness, so I'm hoping I get some showers as a sign from heaven.

Not wanting anyone to show up before me, I exit my car quickly and head to our meeting room. Even in my cloak, I get a chill when I step inside. Today's a cooler day, and the room clearly has not been entered since we've met here. There's dust on the podium, and the chairs are in the exact formation they were last time. No one's even fucking vacuumed in here.

I pace around the room, going over my notes in my head. Though I've done this before and all of these men are family (unfortunately), I've still got a little bit of stage fright.

The door creaks open, and I whip my head up with my hand on my blade. I don't have a silencer, and I'd rather not shoot anyone in the library if I don't have to. But I'm very quick with my knife and can make do with it if necessary.

I immediately relax when I see Draco standing in front of me.

He grins. "Hey, Father."

"Hey, Draco. Are you ready for today?"

He slides his hand over his midnight hair that's styled exactly like mine. "I am. Don't be stressed. I've got your back." He winks, and all I want to do is slap him silly.

Instead of telling him I'm not stressed, because I'm not, I just give him a tight smile. "Thanks."

He heads to his seat and gets comfortable, adjusting his crimson cloak so it doesn't bunch up under him. "How are the girls doing?"

My girls. My Gen and Zahara. My sweet angels. "They're great. Thank you for asking."

"Good! I'm glad to hear it. Genevieve was so upset the last time I saw her. I take it Mommy's feeling better now?"

Mommy. That's what this fucker just called my wife. Only I get to call her that. I grip my knife, getting ready to take off his ear when Damion walks in.

He looks tense but tries to appear calm. "Gentlemen."

I pull him in for a hug. "Hey, Damion. Are you ready for today?"

He sighs. "As ready as I can be. Theresa's not happy about it and my sons will be shocked finding out today, but I'm not sure how much they like me anyway, so they'll get used to the idea of me being gone."

Theresa. I didn't even think about how all of this is affecting her. How it's *truly* affecting her. Not only does she have to play a part in pretending that Damion's run away, but she just found out that he's been cheating on her.

Draco plays on his phone while I continue speaking with Damion. "How is Theresa holding up?"

He frowns. "Not good. She was devastated."

I lean against the podium. "I can imagine. You really fucked up. Why did you do it?"

His jaw clenches. "I'm not sure I ever really loved Theresa. I liked her, yeah, but you know I didn't have a choice on whether I wanted to marry or not. I did, but no one in our family wants to die. So I convinced her to marry me, and the rest was history. I know her feelings for me are deep, or they were, but when I met Jess, I was blown away. And my brother was so bad to her that I convinced myself I was doing her a favor. I saved her."

I think back to when Damion got married. It was a very long time ago, and he wasn't too close to his thirty-second birthday. "Damion, you had time to find someone else. Why didn't you spend more time with her first or try to find the one if she wasn't it?"

He frowns. "Because she was a safety net, James. Why hold out for the one when I could've had security then? And she wasn't that hard to convince."

"Well, we'll get everything squared away as best as we can. Do you not want to try and patch things up with her?"

"I don't know. Jess and I are done at this point, and Theresa is a decent wife, all things considered. And even if I don't love her, she's still a good lay." He smirks, and my stomach curls. "I thought I'd try and patch things up, but I'm really on the fence after last night."

I straighten up. "What happened last night?"

He groans. "When I told her about Jess, she got so upset. She cried hysterically. I couldn't take it. I begged her to stop. To shut up. She really went in on me. Told me I was a bastard. She just said vile things to me. And I snapped."

My blood turns cold. I don't like where this is going at all, but I have to know more. What he tells me has the power to change everything about today whether he's aware or not. "Explain."

He scoffs. "It's like the bitch forgot about our Vows of Submission Ceremony. She made vows to me, and she forgot them by disrespecting me last night. So I reminded her."

My heart pounds as I start to get agitated. I try to keep my voice calm while Draco turns his attention toward us. "How did you remind her, Damion?"

His brown eyes go black. "I did what any man in our family would do. I cleaned her clock. Knocked her out cold. Took her a few hours to come to. For a minute, I thought I'd killed her. To be honest, I wanted to. And if I did, I know you boys would have my back."

I clench my sweating fists under my cloak, having heard everything I needed to make a big decision today. I hear the rain start to pour outside, giving me the confirmation I need. "Did she behave after that?"

He nods his head. "Yeah. She shaped up. But I'll do whatever it takes to put her in check again if need be."

I glance at Draco who's eyes nearly pop out of his head. "Thank you, Damion. I'm glad you've got the situation handled. Have a seat."

He smiles. "Thank you, Father."

Fucking piece of shit prick.

Everyone else slowly starts to file in, and I take a glance around the room to make sure we're all in attendance. I get tense when I look into the crowd and don't see Hades, and then the most magical and depressing day of my life plays over and over in my head. I still can't believe he's gone.

I make eye contact with Draco who has worry etched all over his face. He frowns when I smile, and I know that he knows what I'm about to do.

"Welcome, Wild White Orchids."

All of the men answer me like we haven't had any time off. "It's time to bloom."

I walk around to stand in front of the podium, still wearing my cloak. "It's been a long time, and I appreciate all of your patience and understanding during our break. However, we're back in action, and we have a lot of big things to discuss today."

My confidence grows when no one questions or challenges me. Jace's sons have given me the most grief in the past, but with Bram already supporting me and convincing the twins to stand by my side, the other brothers have calmed down, even if they still hate my guts. And with their father and grandfather gone, the next best person for them to trust and look to is honestly me. The only motherfucker I trust in this room fully is myself.

I straighten my spine, looking out into the crowd. "First things first, we have a community meeting tomorrow. At some point, we'll have a New Birth Ceremony for my little girl." We won't, but they don't need to know that. "And the biggest topic we need to discuss today is our next Exit Ceremony. It'll take place on Tuesday."

The crowd stirs and I clap my hands. "Everyone stay quiet and let me get through this, then we can all go the fuck home. This Exit Ceremony is for a member of the council who has broken a tenet. The tenet he broke is tenet number six. This man was unfaithful to his wife, and that man is Damion."

Everyone remains quiet. Damion scowls, like I told him to. Simon closes his eyes and sighs. Draco shuffles in his seat.

"Damion will remain in the basement of the meeting hall until the Exit Ceremony. Draco, please restrain him."

Damion sits still while Draco cuffs him, completely unaware of his true fate.

"Damion will be escorted by Draco, and Obsidian and Orion will stand guard, giving Damion his meals."

Damion's brows draw together, and I think he may slowly be starting to catch on. It's for the best. That'll save me the time of trying to break it down to him.

Draco nods his head and obeys. "Absolutely, Father."

I smile. "Thank you. After that, things will be pretty quiet for the next few weeks. We'll have our council meetings and community meetings, but nothing big for a while."

Bram speaks up. "Father?"

"Yes."

"When will we have our next Council Entry Ceremonies?"

The Council Entry Ceremonies. How could I forget? We need to replace Jace, Hades, and now Damion.

"I'm still deciding. But we don't have any upcoming votes, so we should be fine. When it's time, I'll let everyone know."

Everyone stares back at me with blank expressions.

I dust off my cloak, ready to be done with this to fill Draco in, and then get home to my family. "Thank you men for showing up today. We'll convene tomorrow at the meeting hall. You're all dismissed."

As soon as I leave the meeting, I send Gen a quick message that I'm heading home. I had initially planned on calling her on the way home to rile her up by saying naughty things in her ear while she touched herself, but I need to calm myself down before I get home to her. I made her a promise we'd try something new, and I can't do it filled with rage. I won't do it. So I need to get myself together.

How fucking dare he? I cannot believe Damion right now. The fact that he put his hands on Theresa makes my fucking blood boil. Now he has to die.

I was totally prepared to let him off the hook. I felt like his escape plan would definitely blow up in my face, but I was willing to give it a try anyway. Not anymore. Not when he nearly killed her and basically stated he would if he felt like it. Piece of shit. I'm doing her a favor. At least that's what I'm trying to convince myself of as I plan her husband's death.

I'm so tired of killing. I don't want to do it anymore, but this feels warranted. And if I don't, he's going to die anyway. The Caledonia Council has proven that if I won't do their dirty work, they'll get it done and still find a way to punish me for it. Jack seemed nice enough, but he had a woman stashed in his freezer. The same woman who told me that if I don't do what I'm told, my wife and child will be obliterated. And my mother. There's no way in fuck I'm allowing that to happen.

While I still plan on finding a cheat code to the top of this fucked up game, I have to play by the rules until I do. I still plan on taking my girls away to the cabin, but I'm still in level two of this thing. I don't want them cooped up in that cabin away from civilization for too long, so I'd like to wait to put them there until I feel it's absolutely necessary.

Bile rises in my throat thinking about Damion's Exit Ceremony. I know I can stomach it, but it makes me sick to put Gen through it again. But she has to be there. And, I feel more comfortable when I'm with her than when we're apart lately. That's another reason I want Samuel to drive them to the cabin. So I can know for sure that no one will find it. I plan on renting a car for when I go there myself just to make sure a tracker won't be placed on me.

And the baby shower. How am I going to convince my wife to have a baby shower when the Exit Ceremony is the day after?

She is going to be pissed. But I'll make it up to her. I've been thinking of ways to show her how much she means to me since Draco's wedding day. She looked so upset at the ceremony, and it nearly broke me. I tried to make our wedding as special as I could, but I know it could've been better. For one, I could've been more of a gentleman and let her know how special she was to me then. But I didn't, and it's one of my biggest regrets.

I should've told her how she made my days better. How she was the first thing I thought about when I got up and the face I saw in my mind when I went to sleep. How I was addicted to her laugh and smile and personality and would've waited a thousand lifetimes for her until she was ready to give me a chance. I hate that I didn't say that to her. However, I've been thinking about it long and hard, and I've come up with something even better to do for her.

Before I get home, I stop by a flower shop and get Gen two dozen red roses. I know she loves her peonies, but she loves these classic blooms too. And although I'm going to ravage her like a savage as soon as I see her, I still want to be romantic. I can't help myself. It's what she deserves. So I also go to a nearby bakery and get her a slice of her favorite German chocolate cake too.

By the time I show up at home, I've calmed down, and I'm ready to get into character. My mom's car is gone, so I know she's out enjoying her girl time with Zahara. While I've preferred to send my mother and Gen out with a tail lately for safety, I'm not too worried today as I've been following the rules. Plus, The Caledonia Council knows me well enough by now to know that if they do anything to my little girl, I will refuse to complete the rest of their challenges.

The rain pours softly outside and I feel myself smile. I hope Gen's ready to get wet. I grab my things as well as her flowers and dessert, exit my car, and head inside.

The house is completely silent apart from the sound of the heater. I wipe off my shoes on the doormat but leave them on, preparing to head back outside very soon. Excitement courses through me, and I'm looking forward to treating my girl to a brand-new experience. I've done things similar to what she's asked before, but not on the level that I'm going to today. Regardless, I feel a lot more prepared than I did when we went into the blue room at our old house as we went over everything in detail a few days ago, and I'm not going to push either one of us beyond our limits.

If she followed my instructions, she should be in the bedroom waiting for me. I let her pick out her outfit, and I'm beyond eager to see what she's wearing. Since I wasn't fully sure of where we'll be, I sent our farmhand out for an early and long lunch. Can't have him seeing anything crazy and thinking my wife needs saving.

Grabbing a vase from one of our cabinets, I trim the stems and put Gen's flowers in it with fresh water. I can't wait to see the look on her face when she sees them. It reminds me of the time I sent her some on Valentine's Day when we worked together.

I store her cake in the fridge, chastising myself for not getting a piece for me too. But my girl is so sweet that I know she'll give me a bite or two if I ask.

I take the elevator up to our floor, wanting to save my energy for later. I don't know how long we'll be, but I don't plan on rushing things with her. Everyone should be out of the house for a while, and I want to take my time to enjoy this slowly. To enjoy her slowly and fully immerse myself in this moment.

The rain picks up a little, as I stare out the elevator window, and my excitement expands. This is going to get dirty and nasty and I can't wait. I step out of the elevator once I get to the top, and my pulse races, eager to get my girl filthier than she's ever been before.

Still wearing my suit and cloak, I go to the opposite end of the hall by the other staircase. Pulling out my phone, I open my messages and send Gen a text.

> Daddy's home. Come out into the hall Darling.

Chapter Twenty-Seven

GENEVIEVE

> Daddy's home. Come out into the hall Darling.

I nearly drop my phone in the bathroom sink when James' text comes through.

Fuck. My period had to come right fucking now.

I feel like I'm about to cry. There's no way James is going to want to do this on my period. We had sex while I was on it once before, but he probably just did it to be nice. I was pretty horny, and he would never turn me down. But I doubt he enjoyed being covered in my blood after.

And my outfit is so cute too. I'm wearing this white long-sleeve crop top with no bra, and a red tartan mini skirt. My look is completed with a pair of black knee-high boots.

And my period means I'm not pregnant. It's not like we were actively trying right now, but I still hoped that I might be. I don't know what to do.

I pull my curls to my back and splash cold water on my face, trying to calm myself down.

I guess I should just go ahead and tell him.

> I'm on my period.

I lean against the sink, waiting for his reply to come through. He's probably going to tell me to get changed so he can give me a massage.

> Daddy's not scared of blood. Get out here. Now. I'm tired of waiting.

I feel myself smirk.

This is going to be messy.

I leave the bathroom and go to put my phone on the dresser when it buzzes again.

> Take your cup out. No panties either.

What?! Is he serious? I cannot go out into the hall free bleeding.

> I cannot just free bleed throughout the house.

> Gen, I will give you five minutes. If you're not out here by then, I'm coming in and I will take it out myself.

Shit. He's not kidding.

Dammit.

I run back into the bathroom, do the unthinkable, and take my cup out. Fortunately, I have a few minutes after emptying it before the flow gets going again. Thank God because our carpet is bright white, and I don't know how we're going to clean it if I get red all over it.

I can't believe I'm about to do this. Do people do this? Is this normal? I can't stay in those thoughts too long or I'll psych myself out of this. And I don't even want to know what James is going to do if I'm not out in that hall in the next thirty seconds.

Not wasting any time, I run out of the bedroom, and I freeze when I see the sight before me. The hall is dark, only lit by the natural light illuminating through the windows which isn't much as it's cloudy and raining outside.

The heater cuts off, and the house is dead silent. I'm standing by the elevator near one of the staircases, and at the other end of the hall by the other staircase, I see a figure. He's wearing his black cloak with the hood pulled over his head, and I can barely make out his face with it half-covered in the dark.

There's movement and I see light reflecting, and I gasp when I see he's holding his knife. The one he's used to kill.

He lifts his head and shows me his bright white smile while he chuckles low. "You better run, Gen."

In a second, he is charging after me at full speed, and I turn to run down the stairs instantly. My heart pounds in my chest, and when I get to the second level of the house, he's already there, waiting for me. He must've turned around and ran the other way, beating me with those long legs of his.

We stand, staring each other down while he twirls his knife. I get a fear that he's going to stab me, but then I calm myself down.

He's my husband. Of course, he's not going to stab me. Right?

He stands in the middle of the hall, but I know that if I try to go down to the bottom floor, I'll run right into his clutches. Instead, I run back up to our floor, trying to catch him off guard.

Do I take the elevator down?

No, Gen. That's stupid. Ugh, fuck. My only option is to run back downstairs, but I can't go the way I just came as I can hear him coming up slowly now.

I run to the opposite end of the hall, standing where he was when we began, and I start running down.

His pace picks up as he reenters the hall and follows closely behind me. "I can't wait to catch you, you little whore."

I don't think about the soreness in my calves from running in my boots or the blood that's starting to drip down my thigh. I just run until I'm at the very bottom.

Panic courses through me as I try to quickly come up with a strategy. There's no hiding down here. Anywhere to hide is just a trap. I run behind the kitchen island and lean up against it, trying to catch my breath. I'm still getting back into fitness after giving birth, and I'm fucking winded.

The familiar sound of his shoes clacks through the house, and I shiver as he gets closer.

His deep voice booms in our empty home. "Gen, I know exactly where you are, and I can't wait to wrap my hands around that pretty little neck of yours."

He steps closer, and I see the corner of his cloak dust the edge of the island. "And I'm going to have so much fun with this knife."

I stare into his pitch-black eyes, and he grins. I stand and turn to run, but he grabs the hem of my skirt. His grip slips, and I'm headed for the back door, outside.

My hands shake as I try to unlock it, and I barely get it open before he's on my heels. He grips it, not giving me a chance to shut it as I run outside.

Rain pours softly outside, wetting my curls and making my white top see-through. My thighs ache while I run, and I don't even have to look back to know that James is getting closer.

He's going to catch me. I'm not fast enough. I can't outrun him.

Glancing over my shoulder, all I see is his cloak, and I whip my head facing front again, amazed at how far we've gone away from the house.

We catch up to the farm, and I'm tempted to run in the barn, but I don't want to get dirtier than I already am. I don't even get the chance before James' strong arms wrap around me and lift me off the ground.

I kick and scream as I actively remind myself that I'm not really being kidnapped or attacked.

His hot tongue slides up my neck, and he whispers in my ear. "Your thighs look so pretty with blood all over them."

My mouth moves without thinking. "I'm scared."

He keeps an arm wrapped tightly around me, and his hand grips his knife while he drags his other hand between my legs. "You should be."

Using his strength, he pins me to the ground and hovers over me.

"My pretty little slut. Dressed like a naughty schoolgirl." He slowly hovers his knife over my abdomen. "Did you do this for Daddy?"

My body shakes, cooling down from my sprint and adjusting to the low temperature outside. "I did it for me."

He growls. "Wrong fucking answer."

Instinctively, I try to wiggle away from him, but he puts his knife away and pulls out black rope. It takes him no time at all to grab my hands and tie them behind my back by my wrists.

My breathing picks up faster than it has this entire time, and James presses his lips against my neck and whispers in my ear. "Gen, baby, are you alright?"

A tear streams down my face. "Yes. Don't stop."

He kisses my lips softly. "Good girl."

I don't get another word out before he's tucking the knife in my waistband and tearing my skirt off me.

"Look at this sexy little body. All mine." He lowers his face between my legs, and I feel my eyes widen.

"James?"

He runs his hands over my soaked top, squeezing my tits. "Shhh." My mouth hangs open while he spreads my thighs, doing something I've never heard of anyone doing before.

I can't stifle the scream that I let out when he sucks my clit into his mouth. My wrists ache, positioned under my lower back, but his warm, wet tongue feels so good that I don't care.

My body tingles as the rain continues to drizzle over me, and I don't even care that I'm sopping wet and on the ground.

He lifts his head with red lips, and he licks them clean. "Do you like having your bloody cunt licked?"

The rain mixes with the tears on my cheeks. "Yes."

He grabs his knife and cuts my top down the middle, leaving it hanging off my shoulders while I lie there fully exposed in just my knee-high socks and boots.

"Good. Now it's time for your bloody cunt to get fucked."

He flips me over, and I rest my cheek on the grass followed by my shoulders with my arms still tucked behind my back. I hear his belt come undone and then his pants zipper, and I am desperate to feel him inside me.

He wastes no time driving into me. "God. Holy hell."

I whimper while he grips my wrists tightly, slamming his hips into mine over and over. He pounds into me fast and hard, and I wouldn't want it any other way.

He doesn't say anything else to me while he fucks me, and I don't either. We just grunt and moan while he slides in and out, the sounds of our bodies connecting filling the space.

My knees ache, but my thighs shake with pleasure as I get closer. He takes one of his hands and rubs my clit slowly and softly before pinching it and flicking it.

His warm cloak brushes over my back as he hovers over me. "Daddy's little whore likes a little bit of pain, doesn't she?"

My tears pool around me mixed with rainwater and dirt. "Yes."

He slaps my tit before pinching my nipples and sliding both of his hands between my legs, rubbing my thighs with one and teasing my clit with the other.

He picks up his pace, somehow going deeper as he does so. "Tell me how good it feels, and maybe I'll let you come."

My entire body warms as I enjoy every single thing he does. "It feels so good, Daddy."

He plays with my tits with one hand and keeps rubbing my clit with the other. "Convince me."

I cry harder. "Your cock feels so fucking good. I never want you to stop fucking me. I want you to fill me up over and over until I'm leaking your cum for days."

He grunts and presses in on my clit harder in the best way, and I come undone, unable to contain myself any longer. Once I've slumped, he grabs my hips and keeps fucking me until I feel his hot liquid hit my cervix.

As soon as he pulls out, I want him back in. I expect him to flip me over and untie me, but he slips his fingers in my soaked pussy, coating them, and drags them up to my ass cheeks, sliding our mixture over my hole.

I feel his hard length slip between my cheeks, sliding his cock back and forth over my rim.

"Do you want more, sweetheart?"

Desperate to come again, I take deep breaths and try to ignore my throbbing clit. "Yes. I need more."

He slides a finger into my ass, teasing it slowly while I press up against him. I remember the first time he touched me like this, I was terrified, and now I fucking crave it.

I feel him slide his cock back into my pussy, wetting it a little more before he pulls out. When he removes his finger from my hole, he positions himself at my entrance and pierces me without warning.

I take a breath, and I let it out while he slides into me slowly. He didn't warm me up as much beforehand like he did the first time we tried this, so the invasion is a little more intense, but I still feel lubricated enough to keep going. He keeps his hips still, buried inside me while he unties my hands.

"Hands on the ground in front of you."

I get into a comfortable position on all fours, and he grips my hips while he fucks me. His pace is quick but not as aggressive as it was the first time we had sex like this.

He moans over and over, making me whimper. I love the sounds he makes while he fucks me, and it makes me so happy to know I can make him feel so good.

His hand smacks my ass, and he slides in and out faster. "I love fucking all of your needy holes, Gen."

"I love having you inside me, James."

He grabs my sopping, dirt-covered curls and pulls my head back. "I know you do. Such a good, greedy girl. So ready and willing to be used. I'm so proud of you. I promise to take good care of you later."

His sweet words wrap around me like a blanket, and before I know it, I'm coming again, and he's spilling inside me.

As soon as he pulls out, the rain picks up, and the blood and cum are washed from my body effortlessly.

James quickly stands up, and he holds out his hand for me to take. Getting up on wobbly legs, I fall into his chest, and he slides off his cloak before wrapping it around me. He sweeps me off my feet, and I bask in the comfort of the warm fabric as we head back inside.

#

When we get upstairs, James doesn't say a word to me as he places me on the bed on top of his cloak after taking off my torn top and my dirty socks and shoes. He goes into the bathroom, and I start to drift off when I hear the water running. I glance at him when he reenters our bedroom, and he strips off his damp clothes, standing before me naked.

I smile at him, and he shows me his beautiful smile as he comes up to me and scoops me off the bed.

I feel so happy and content that I don't know what to do with myself. Everything feels so good and right, and I almost forget about everything else we have going on.

James stands me up in front of our bathroom sinks and bends me over one to rinse my hair. The cool water makes me shiver but feels refreshing against my scalp.

Feeling his dick against me, I press my hips into him making him laugh.

"Bath first. More sex later."

I rest my hands on the counter beneath me. "Fine."

After he gets all the dirt out of my strands, he squeezes my hair out before standing me up and leading me to the tub.

I groan loudly when I step in and the hot water wraps around my legs. I didn't realize how cold it was outside until I got back in our house and into the warm bath. My body aches, and James brings me a small glass of water and painkillers before I can even ask.

I glance out of our bathroom window, inhaling the yummy scent of the vanilla bubble bath while I enjoy the soft light that pours in illuminating the room along with the few candles James lit.

He slides into the tub behind me, and I lean against his chest with my damp hair clinging to his skin. He wraps his strong arms around me, and I feel so safe and loved that I can barely speak. His soft lips keep me warm as he trails kisses up and down my neck. "Did you enjoy everything?"

I turn my cheek to kiss his lips and nibble on his lower one. "Yeah. It was great. Thank you."

He runs his thumb up and down my neck. "Good." My eyes start to close again when he starts rubbing my shoulders, digging his thumbs into my skin before he moves them down and rubs the rest of my body.

I'm half-asleep when I feel him washing me with a plush cloth, taking his time cleaning every inch of me. He rubs the fabric in circles around my nipples, and I feel his hardness press up against me.

When he moves down between my thighs, I grind against his hand while he teases my clit with the cloth tenderly, making me hungry for him all over again.

My breath shudders. "What did I do to deserve this special treatment?"

He keeps rubbing me while he rubs himself against me. "You married me. You deserve it for putting up with my bullshit."

I feel myself smile while he squeezes my breasts, making my mind turn to mush. He slips two fingers inside me, and he circles his thumb over my clit until I'm a whimpering mess, biting my lip and coming all around him.

I turn around and straddle him, grinding my hips against his dick while we give each other soft pecks. "You're in such a good mood today."

"Mmmhmm." He nuzzles his nose in my neck.

I sink my fingers into his hair. "I take it the meeting went well?"

He freezes, and my stomach drops. "It went . . . as expected."

I stop grinding and massaging. "Just tell me what went wrong."

He sighs. "Baby, nothing went wrong. Please—let's just have a good time and we can talk more about it later." He wraps his lips around one of my nipples trying to distract me, but I reluctantly pull away.

"Conversation now, fun later."

"Gen, sweetheart, please. Can't you just enjoy what I'm doing for you right now?" He rocks his hips against mine slowly, making the water move around us.

"I want to enjoy what you're doing for me. I really do. And I can get back to enjoying it as soon as we talk. Just tell me what happened. The faster you get it over with, the faster we can have more fun."

He frowns. "I'm worried that you're not going to want to have more fun with me after what I tell you."

Now I'm really concerned.

"James, I promise. I will not let whatever you tell me ruin the day."

He pokes out his plush lips. "Do you pinky swear?" He pulls my hand in his, wrapping his pinky around mine.

I can't help but laugh at the sweet gesture. "I pinky swear, James. Go on. Don't keep me in suspense any longer."

Nearly a minute passes while he takes deep breaths in and out. I'm about to yell at him when he finally opens up and recaps me on what happened at the meeting. Apparently, Draco said something that pissed him off and put him in a bad mood, but the icing on the cake was the revelation from Damion about what he did to Theresa.

My chest tightens as he tells me everything he was told, and I'm overcome with a million different emotions as I try to process what happened and what James is going to do as a result.

God, I hope Theresa's okay. I never imagined Damion doing something like that to her. I should call her.

He draws his brows together. "Are you upset that I'm going through with Damion's Exit Ceremony?"

I play with the hair at the nape of his neck. I hoped that Bryson's Exit Ceremony was the last one I'd have to witness. And I certainly didn't imagine that we'd ever have one for Damion.

Is this my fault? I'm the one who pointed out Damion's affair in the first place. I feel sick to my stomach.

But he is evil. And the only person I told was James which means that The Caledonia Council already knew about it.

James cups my cheeks, regaining my attention. "Talk to me, Gen."

I shut my eyes while I try to get my thoughts together. "I don't know how I feel. On the one hand, I feel really bad about it. But on the other hand, I don't feel anything at all. Maybe Theresa's better off." I feel guilty as soon as the words leave my lips.

James kisses my nose. "You don't have to feel bad. I think he should die too. I don't feel bad at all."

I lean into his chest and tuck my head into his neck while he strokes my wet curls. "Okay. I don't feel bad for him. But I don't feel great either. Is it really our call to make?"

He wraps his wet arms around me. "Gen, as the Head Father of this society, I'm the judge, jury, and executioner. So, it is our call to make. Because I can go through with this, and we can get closer to where we want to be, or I can say no and put multiple lives in danger as a result. It's a no-brainer—Damion has to go. And he's made things easier for me as he's garbage. I won't lose any sleep over it."

I think back to my night with James after our experience in the blue room. How he told me about his past and his relationship with violence. I understand wanting Damion to die, but he's a lot more relaxed about it than I would expect. Like it doesn't bother him in the slightest to kill someone who was a friend to us, and who we had no hard feelings against just hours ago.

"I'm worried, James."

He kisses my nose. "Worried about what, Gen?"

"Worried about you, love."

He frowns. "What about me?"

"Worried about what this is doing to you. Doing The Caledonia Council's dirty work. I'm just concerned about how this is going to affect you over time."

His brown eyes soften and he pulls my fingers up to his lips to kiss. "Genevieve Barlow, don't be scared. I promise that I will not lose who I am. And if I seem unfazed by some of this, it's because I have to be. That's the only way I'm going to get through this. If I overanalyze everything and try to think too hard about whether it's right or wrong, I'm going to fail. And I can't afford to fail. I'm not doing these horrible things because I want to. I'm doing them because I have to. And if I find therapy in doing these things, then so be it. After I handle this society shit, there's only three more levels."

I put my forehead up against his. "Three more levels of what exactly? You have no idea what the rest of this journey is going to be."

He rubs my back softly as the water starts to chill. "I don't know what the rest of this journey will be. But the end result is a happy life with my girls, and that's what I'm after. Nothing's going to stand in my way."

After we finish up in the bathroom, I slide into a pair of period panties and James pulls me into bed beside him. Odette will be home soon with Zahara, but we're staying upstairs until she gets back.

He nuzzles his head in my hair that he just finished blow drying. "What's wrong, Gen?"

I lie on my back while his hand rests on my stomach. "Nothing."

He chuckles. "Don't lie. You've been tense for the past hour. Don't you want to have some more fun before Mom gets home?"

I am upset, but I'm embarrassed to talk about it right now. It seems like such a small thing with everything that's going on. Like my one little problem doesn't matter in the grand scheme of things. I just feel like I'm running out of my allowed time to be depressed. Like if I stay depressed for too long, people will stop caring and start to shame me for it especially when I have so much to be grateful for.

When I open my mouth, nothing comes out, and James strokes my belly softly. "You can tell me, baby. I won't get upset. I promise."

I open my mouth again, taking a breath this time. "I just thought, I'm just a little sad. But it's really nothing. It's silly."

He sits up, leaning over me. "Nothing about how you feel is silly. What are you sad about?"

"I just thought—I hoped that—I thought I might be pregnant again. Then my period came, and I realized I wasn't. It just made me upset. Like how I used to feel in the past when it happened. I know you—we—want more kids, and I thought it would happen again right away. I'm just a little disappointed, but I'll be fine." I finish quickly, hoping he doesn't hear the way my voice shakes.

James hovers over me, trapping me underneath him. "I know. I thought you would be too. But I'm not upset that you're not, and I love you just the same."

I wipe my tears from my eyes. "I know."

He smiles softly and gives me a peck. "Good. You've already made me the happiest man in the world, Gen. I couldn't ask you for anything more."

He reaches for my panties and starts to pull them down slowly. "I already have all the babies I need, but we still have all the time in the world to make more."

I clench my legs together when he pulls the fabric past my ankles and tosses it to the side. "James, our bedsheets are white."

Spreading my legs open with his, he brushes his hard cock up against my slit. "I know they are. And I'm glad.

That way I can see the pretty mess that I'm going to make of you."

His lips lower to one of my nipples, sucking my peak into his mouth and drinking my supply.

"Don't take too much, James."

He kisses the center of my chest before moving to my other breast. "Don't worry. She'll have enough. Your body knows how to make more." His tongue swirls around my other one, instinctively making me wrap my legs around his hips as I try to draw him in closer.

"Don't make me wait any longer."

I feel his teeth bite me before he pulls his lips away. At the same time, he drives his hips into mine and sinks himself into my heat.

"I'll never get enough of how needy you are for me, Gen. You're so fucking pretty when you beg for Daddy's dick."

I wrap my arms around him, resting my cheek against his and enjoying his warm body over mine. "You love making me beg."

He kisses my neck softly. "I do. It's because you're so good at it."

My mind wanders until he grips my chin, forcing me to look at him.

"I'm going to put another baby in you, Genevieve. Lots of them. I swear. Just relax, and enjoy the feeling of my cock inside your pretty pussy. It's going to be a lot harder for us to fuck with a bunch of kids running around, so I want to enjoy you as much as I can now."

"God, James. I want to have so many babies with you."

He pumps in and out of me faster. "You will, baby. Your belly is going to be round with my babies for years to come. You're so gorgeous pregnant, Gen. I can't believe you gave me a little baby. You're so fucking amazing."

He seals his lips over mine, kissing me while tears stream down my face. My heart is so full and I can't believe that this man is mine. I really do have everything I need and want.

My tears slow with every kiss he gives me that I feel travel straight to my heart. I slide my hands down his back, digging my nails into his ass which makes him slam into me harder. I lift my hips, rubbing my clit against him chasing my release.

He digs his hands in my hair while he stares into my eyes. "Be a good girl and come for Daddy."

I come around his cock on command, and he spills into me, filling me up like he does every time.

I nearly forgot I was bleeding when he pulls out and I see the mess below us on the bed.

I cover my mouth while my cheeks get hot. "Oh, God."

He kisses my lips, then my nose. "Don't worry about that."

"The sheets are ruined, babe."

His laughter makes me relax. "We have extras. I love getting our sheets dirty. It means I'm doing a good job."

Chapter Twenty-Eight

JAMES

I'm sitting on the bed waiting for Rebecca to get out of the bathroom so we can go to our monthly community meeting. I created the monthly community meetings for us to gather as a society and go over important events, announcements, and changes. It's still a small group with just my brothers and cousins along with our wives and sons, but I'm excited for our meetings to grow over time with our children's spouses and their children.

The community meetings take place at the meeting hall, and I bought it with some of the inheritance that I got from my father. The money he got from my mother to be specific.

It's a beautiful historic building, and it has plenty of space for some of our rites.

My favorite thing about the community meetings is that I'm able to assert my dominance. Everyone knows that I'm the Head Father, but it's important for them to see me in action. To know that I take my role seriously and that our society matters to me. And it allows me to keep everyone in line as well.

I hear Rebecca throwing up in the bathroom and my stomach curls. Hearing her vomit always makes me want to vomit. Her pregnancy symptoms overwhelm me sometimes, and I really don't think I can go through this again. But knowing me, we'll probably end up having another. And I'll probably regret it like I do this one that's not even here yet.

Eventually, she cleans herself up and makes her way back to the bedroom. She looks so damn beautiful, and I'm suddenly reminded of why I'm a father of two. I just can't keep my hands off the girl.

-From the Diary of Jude Barlow, 1933

I sit in bed, holding my great-grandfather's journal in my hands. He was such a piece of shit. I can't believe I came from such a horrible line of men.

My dad was a piece of shit too. I don't know if my grandfather Maxwell was, but he was sick for most of my upbringing, and I didn't get to see him a lot. I'm probably the fucked up bastard that I am because it runs in my blood. I didn't have a chance to be a normal guy.

Today is the first community meeting back, and I'm not looking forward to it in the slightest. I hated attending community meetings when I was just the society's Mortality Manager, and I hate community meetings even more now that I'm the Head Father. They're a waste of everyone's time, and they remind everyone that I'm the current leader of this cult that I fucking hate.

But I'm trying to get over my feelings and look on the bright side. I've come up with a New Birth Ceremony for Zahara, I've held our first council meeting back, and after this community meeting, I'll only have two more tasks to complete for Jack before I get to move onto level three. I'm exactly where I need to be, and that in itself helps me sleep easier at night. Not to mention, this meeting will help me make my wife happy.

Another good thing about this community meeting is that it'll allow me to meet with our old companions, and I can invite those closest to us over for a baby shower. I hate that Gen didn't get to have one before giving birth, but I'm still going to give her one anyway. And I can't wait to share with her the other surprise I've been working on.

I just hope our friends won't be too pissed at me not to come. Genevieve is closest with Mai and Ella, so we can't have a baby shower without them. However, I played a part in the deaths of their husbands, and while I've smoothed things over with Mai, I haven't had a chance to speak with Ella. I don't even know how I'm going to look her in the eye with all that's happened. I mean, I killed her fucking son for Christ's sake. She'll never forgive me for that. However, I'm hoping she'll tolerate being in my presence at my home for Genevieve. She might hate me, but I know she doesn't hate my girls.

In addition to Mai and Ella, I plan on having Paul attend as well. I like the fact that he looks up to me, and he's a good kid. It'll be nice to catch up with him and see how he's doing with the house and what he'd like to do with his future. I feel like I'm responsible for him in a way since I killed his father. It's like I'm his unofficial big brother.

I don't want Draco present, but I know Gen will have a fit if I don't invite him and Raven. They'll get an invite. I'll just send a prayer to heaven that they won't show up. I really don't want either one of them at my home let alone holding my daughter.

Apart from that crowd, I plan on inviting Obsidian and Orion, mainly for extra security, and of course, Samuel and his family. I think it'll be a good time for everyone involved.

Gen comes out of the bathroom wearing a fitted black sweater dress that hits mid-calf. I can't believe it's been seven weeks since she gave birth. She looks just like she used to before, except her breasts are still twice the size they used to be. She's a freaking goddess. She slides into a pair of black stilettos, and I help her into her cloak.

It doesn't take me long to dress in my classic suit and coat, and after I grab my weapons, I pick my baby girl out of her crib and hand her to her mama. Gen rocks Zahara back and forth, and my baby stays asleep in my wife's arms. I give both of my girls kisses and then we take the elevator downstairs to meet with Mom.

At first, I wasn't sure how I'd feel about my mother living with us, but it's really nice having her around. She's a major help with Zee, and our house is so big that it never feels like she's crowding our space. I know Gen loves getting to see her whenever she wants, and I don't want my mom alone in her big house right now. I hope she enjoys living with us as much as we do with her because I'm not ready for her to move out anytime soon.

Once we all get seated in the car, I turn on the radio to some classical music Gen likes to play for Zee and head to the meeting hall.

When we arrive, my mom and Gen walk side by side, and we head into the building together. Like I intended, we're the first to arrive, but it doesn't take long for everyone to start filing in. My nerves slowly calm when mingling begins, and the focus doesn't appear to be on me. Mai goes up to Genevieve but keeps her distance, not crowding my baby.

Ella comes in by herself, and she makes her way to the back. I make eye contact with her, and she looks past me. Like she can't even see me. Like I'm dead to her. I ignore the pang of guilt I feel in my chest, making a mental note to try and catch her after before she heads back home.

Looking out into the crowd, I see my beautiful wife, and I feel grounded enough to start the meeting.

"Welcome, Wild White Orchids."

Everyone answers back. "It's time to bloom."

"Thank you all for gathering here today. It's been a while since we've met as a group, and I appreciate you all for attending.

"Today's meeting will be brief, but I ask that you wait a few minutes after I dismiss you as there are a few of you I need to speak to. To start, I want to address the situation with our council."

I clear my throat and stare straight ahead, trying not to make eye contact with anyone in particular. "As you all know, it's been difficult keeping our council at our perfect number of thirty members. We've lost a few of our men recently, but to give everyone time to mourn properly, we won't be replacing them for the next few months."

Everyone murmurs but I clap my hands to regain their attention. "This won't be an issue as we don't have any votes coming up, so we'll do fine with the current number we have. Our next topic of discussion is an Exit Ceremony."

Everyone quiets down, allowing me to continue. "This Exit Ceremony will be for a member of the council who broke tenet six. That person is Damion, and he will remain in the basement until Tuesday when we will conduct his Exit Ceremony. Council members and their wives will be required to attend. It's optional for everyone else. Are there any questions?"

No one answers, and I decide to go on. "The last topic of discussion is a New Birth Ceremony for girls. In honor of my daughter, we will have a New Birth Ceremony that I created for her in the coming months. There is no date set yet, but it will be the ceremony we do going forward for all daughters born in the society."

I glance into the crowd and catch Draco winking at me. "The only other note I have is that council and community meetings will resume at their regular schedule. If there are any births or weddings to be had, I need to be notified beforehand. Thank you all again for your attendance. You're all dismissed."

The chatter resumes, and the first thing I do is go up to my girls and give them hugs. Gen gives me a soft kiss, easing my stress. "You did great, baby."

I pull her close and kiss her hair. "Thank you, sweetheart. Wait outside with Mom a sec while I chat with a few people."

She frowns. "Okay. Is everything alright?"

"Yes. Everything's perfect. I'll be right out."

Once my mother leads Gen to the patio, I make my rounds.

The first person I see is Draco. He wraps his arms around me and gives me a hug before pulling away.

"Father. How are you today?"

I glance at his outfit and instantly think of Hades when I stare at Draco's deep red suit and matching cloak. "Good. Are you still coming over this afternoon?"

He grins. "You bet. I need to stop by my place for the artifacts and then I'll be over afterward."

"Perfect. What are you doing tomorrow?"

His green eyes widen. "Nothing. Why? Is everything alright?"

"Yeah. I'm just putting together a last-minute baby shower for Gen. Belated baby shower. And I wanted to know if you and Raven would attend." I regret the words as soon as they leave my mouth.

He beams. "A baby shower for Genevieve? Of course, I'll fucking be there. Are you kidding?" He scratches his chin. "And Raven . . . she has to work, but I'll still come."

Of course, he will. Fucking prick. I give him my best fake smile. "Thanks. I need to speak to a few others and get out of here. I'll see you later."

He pats my back. "See ya, man."

My next targets are Mai and Paul who are fortunately together. Mai gives me a quick hug. "James. It's so great to see you again. Where's Genevieve?"

"It's great to see you too. She's right outside. But before you speak to her, I wanted to ask you something."

She nods her head. "Of course. Is everything alright?"

I catch Mai and Paul up on the surprise baby shower, and they both grin from ear to ear.

Mai squeezes my arm. "Of course we'll be there. Text me something Genevieve wants so I can pick it up today."

Paul pats my back, and I can't believe he's as tall as me. "I can't wait to meet the society's first baby girl."

My heart swells with emotion and I can't help but gush about her. "She's the sweetest baby in the world, I swear. I can't wait for you to meet her."

Paul looks at Mai. "Mom, you get something for Genevieve, and I'll get something for the baby."

I pat them both on the shoulder. "Thanks, guys. Gotta go, but I'll text you later and see you Monday."

It takes me two seconds to speak to Obsidian and Orion, and of course, they agree to come to the shower.

My last society guest nearly gets away from me, but I catch her arm before she gets outside.

"Ella."

She freezes under my touch, and I pull back when she turns to stare at me. I wait for her to speak, to scowl at me, or to yell, but she just stares at me.

I grab her hands and pull them in mine, and I take it as a good sign when she doesn't pull away. "Ella, I'm so fucking sorry."

Her eyes water, and she frowns. I don't give her the chance to pull away from me or yell. I just pull her into my arms, and she sobs while everyone stays in their own worlds chatting.

My heart feels like it's literally crumbling while she cries against my chest. I hate that I hurt her. Ella's been nothing but good to me my entire life, and all I've done is bring her family pain. Everyone starts to file out, and I decide it's as good a moment as any to try and speak with her.

I place my hands on her shoulders, steadying her. She wears a crimson dress and Hades' cloak. Unlike Mai, I won't take Ella's from her. I can't picture any man other than Hades in it. It wouldn't be right.

"Ella, I don't expect you to ever forgive me, but I hope you'll still allow me to be in your life. Or if not me, Gen. Gen, and our daughter. We love you, and I want you to know that I don't want you to feel alone. We're here for you, and I'll never forgive myself for what I've done."

She wipes her tears and sighs. "James Barlow, I've forgiven you. I forgave you a while ago, but I'm still angry with you. And I don't know when I won't be angry with you."

I squeeze her arms, trying to soothe myself. "Thank you. I don't deserve your forgiveness. But I understand why you're angry with me. Stay angry with me as long as you'd like."

To my surprise, she smirks at me. "I will. You don't have to tell me."

She tries to break away, but I grab one of her hands.

"I know I'm in no position, but I wanted to ask you for a favor."

She lifts a brow and huffs before tossing her braids over her shoulder. "No, son. You are in no position whatsoever to ask for favors. But I'll hear you out anyway."

I smile softly and catch her up to speed. "I'm having a small get-together tomorrow afternoon for Gen. Since she never got the baby shower she wanted. I want you to come over and celebrate with us. If you're willing."

Ella gives my hand a light squeeze and grins. "Of course. I'll be there. I've been avoiding her for weeks in an effort to avoid you, and I need to apologize. I told her I'd always be there for her, and I did exactly the opposite of that by shutting her out."

I place my hand on her back as we head out of the room. "Thank you. I know she's not mad at you, but she misses you like crazy and will be thrilled to see you. And Zee will too."

She places her hand over her heart. "I can't believe Genevieve has a baby. She's going to be an incredible mother. I'm sure she already is. I can't wait to meet the society's new little princess."

I refrain from correcting her. Zahara's not the society's princess. She's my princess. But there's no need to get into a debate about it right now.

"Thank you, Ella. If you need anything at all, let me know. See you tomorrow afternoon."

She smiles and gives my hand another squeeze. "See you tomorrow."

\#

As soon as I get home, I pull my mother to the side and inform her of Genevieve's surprise baby shower details. It's not fully a surprise as I did tell Gen that I'd throw something together for her, but she didn't see me invite everyone, so I think she'll still be shocked.

I take a few minutes to call Samuel, and he agrees to show up with his grandson which makes me more excited than anything. It'll be like it's Zee's first play date, and I'm excited to see how she interacts around other babies especially when Gen and I are going to make more.

Once I wrap up my duties, I leave Gen upstairs with Zee to relax while I wait for Draco in the office. Gen wanted to be present to look through the artifacts, but I could tell she was tired, and I want her to rest. I also don't want Draco getting distracted by my gorgeous wife and adorable baby when he needs to help me try and figure out who the other two members are on The Caledonia Council, so keeping my girls upstairs is the best option.

I pour two glasses of water while I wait for him to arrive, setting the precedent that he won't be drinking in my home. I rarely drink these days, and he acts a fool when he's drunk, so he won't ever have access to liquor at my house.

With my office door open, I hear a knock on the front door, letting me know he's arrived, and I go to the front of the house to greet him.

When I open the door, I'm both thrilled and overwhelmed by what I see in front of him. He has four boxes of shit, and I'm confused about how he has more society material than I do when I'm literally the leader. I push my ego down and let him inside, reminding myself that his access to more things is a good thing for me as I have a better chance of digging up the information I need.

He follows behind me while I lead him to my lair and shut the door behind us. There's nothing I plan to hide from Gen, but I have no idea what he'll say while we're in here, and I would like to protect everyone's ears from his potential crassness. When he dumps his boxes on the floor, he tucks his hands in his pockets and looks around.

"This house is incredible, James."

I sit behind my desk and gesture for him to sit across from me. "I know. So—all this crap you brought over. Do you know what any of it is?"

He glances over at the boxes on the floor. "Not really. It's tons of papers and journals. Crap my dad kept over the years that his dad gave him. I've had it in my place in the city for a while and brought it over to the house when I moved in with Raven. But with all the documents inside, I figured there'd be something important in there."

I take a sip of my water and groan, already regretting this. I'm busy enough as it is by being a husband, taking care of a baby, running a farm, and leading the society, but I know I need to look through what Draco brought over even if I don't want to.

He lets out a breath and stares at me, looking as if he has the same thought in his head. "If we're really going to go through all of this stuff, it's going to take a while. Hours. Are you sure you want to do this?"

I stand up to go grab the first box. "Well, I really don't feel like doing it, but we need to. If the men in our family have kept all this crap throughout the years, I have to have hope that there's a reason for it. And I have nothing else to go on, so I'm counting on you to help me figure something out."

He stands and grabs another box to place on my desk. "I guess we better get started then."

Draco and I spend a full hour sorting through our first two boxes, and we don't find anything useful. After we get the contents put away, he leans back in his chair and shuts his eyes. "You got any booze, man? I don't know if I can do this crap for another hour without a little motivation." He puts his feet, his motherfucking feet, on my desk.

I pull out one of my guns and cock it, making him jolt out of his reprieve. "Is this good enough motivation?"

He freezes and holds his hands up. "Jesus, James. A simple, 'I don't have any booze' would've sufficed."

The devil on my shoulder tells me to smack him upside the head with my pistol, but I put it away, and focus on the task at hand.

"We have two more boxes to go through. I'm only asking for one more hour of your time. Then you can get the hell out of my house and leave me alone until tomorrow when you return for the baby shower. And be sure to get something pink for Zahara because that's her favorite color."

He shakes his head and smirks. "You're a real jerk."

I grab the other two boxes and bring them over. "Thank you."

He opens up the one I put in front of him and starts pulling things out. "Why am I helping you again?"

Did he forget the encounter we had less than thirty seconds ago?

"Because if you don't help me, I'll kill you."

"Right. I guess I don't have any time to waste then."

I start sifting through the documents in my box. "Correct."

We spend another half hour going through journals, blueprints, family trees, and birth certificates. Draco pulls out something and pauses, immediately grabbing my attention. "This is interesting."

I pour myself another glass of water. "What is it?"

He flips through a few pages. "Barlow and Burke Homewares—in 1933, Jim Sharpe and Jude Barlow opened ten new stores with funds from the Sharpe family. The flagship store was created by our family and is under ownership by Jude's successors, but the other stores aren't ours. Apparently, the current owner of the other stores is Eric Sharpe."

Eric. One of the names on the lease at the building where I met Annabelle. "So Eric manages our homeware products."

He pulls out a few more documents. "That, and all of our food products outside of meat. Cereals, snacks, beverages—they're all under the parent company, Barlow and Burke Bread, owned and managed by Eric Sharpe."

I knew that we had partners and distributors helping us with our brands, but I didn't know to what extent. I assumed the sector leaders were just present to help manage everything. I didn't know they owned so much.

"So we are owned by Eric Sharpe, Jack, and some other geezer. What exactly is our shit?"

He frowns. "I don't know. I thought you had all of that information?"

I quickly grab the box that my mother gave me and start flipping through. "Yes, I do have that information." I try to keep the irritation out of my voice. "Not that you need to know, but I own the cabin, and this house and my farm." I grab his documents and flip through them. "I also own the first Barlow and Burke Homewares store, the flagship Orchid Oblivion store, and the original perfume store. As the Head Father, I own all of the homes within the society." Taking a look through my stack of papers, my jaw drops at what I see. "Apparently, my old mansion was also my grandfather's, so it's mine too. Jace's sons own the original meat factory, and that's about it. All of our other stores aren't ours."

He frowns. "And even though the originals mostly belong to you, we don't own the businesses."

I drop the papers on my desk. "That's correct."

He huffs. "So what the fuck does that mean? These people basically own us? All we have is our fucking homes?"

"All *I* have is our homes. The only place that belongs to you is your apartment in the city. But yeah. They really own us."

He chuckles. "I guess you don't want to leave anymore. These are billion-dollar businesses, James. I mean, taking what you have and doing your own thing leaves you with some millions, but nothing on the scale of what we have under The Caledonia Council."

I flip through the rest of our current boxes and start to pack things away when I don't find anything else of use. "Unlike you, Draco, money isn't the most important thing in the world to me."

He sighs. "I get it. You're a lovesick fool. But it doesn't matter how you look at it. Money is the most important thing in the world. I see it every day with my job. People kill for money. You can't do anything without money. It is the source of everything. There's no way you can deny that."

I've lived a very privileged life, and I've never had to struggle for anything. And although money is important, I can't say I agree with him completely.

"The most important thing in the world to me is my family. My wife, and my little girl. They are what's most important to me. Money is not more important than them because they are priceless. I would die one hundred times over for them. I'd walk through fire, drown, and suffocate for them. I wouldn't kill for money. But I'll kill for them any day of the week. I can make my girls happy without money. And money isn't the source of my happiness. My happiness comes from the woman that I live and breathe for. The one that literally created life with me. *That* is what I can't deny."

He stares at me, and I don't have a clue what he's thinking. I expect him to say something else stupid to piss me off or make me kick him out. But what he says scares me more than anything else ever has.

"I envy you, James. Your love for your girls is real and true. I don't think I'll ever have something as beautiful as you do with your family. I don't have that kind of passion in me." He frowns. "But I am terrified for you, man. I'm scared to my fucking core. Your love for your family is very apparent, and it does not go unnoticed. We are dealing with some very serious people here, and I'm worried. You're a risk taker, and you're a rule breaker. That doesn't change the fact that the shit we're dealing with is way bigger than us, and if you don't play ball, it's very possible that they will take away what you love most without warning. And there's not going to be a thing you can do to stop it from happening."

Chapter Twenty-Nine
GENEVIEVE

James and I wake up at seven a.m. to get ready for Jessamine's punishment. After feeding Zahara, we change into matching black suits, and I pull my hair into a sleek ponytail before grabbing my cloak.

As soon as we get in the car and start driving down the road, I feel myself start to get emotional. I've been getting more attached to Zahara each day, and I hate being away from her. Odette says she's started crying more when she's not with me and James, and I hate upsetting my baby.

I'm still adjusting to my new body, and my period is different as well. I mainly had spotting yesterday, and today my flow is back, but it's lighter than normal. I texted

Meredith to get her opinion, and she told me not to worry. That my period may be different and irregular for the next few months, and it's something I'm not looking forward to.

James holds my hand while he drives, but I'm a little ticked off at him. The other day he said we would have a baby shower this afternoon, but he hasn't mentioned it since. It's not a big deal, and I could simply ask him about it, but I wish he would just bring it up. I'm not going to, so if he doesn't, I'll probably pout about it for the rest of the day until he figures out why I'm upset.

Jessamine's punishment will take place at Simon's house. As that will be her new home and it's not an event open to the society as a whole, we agreed that it'd be best to do it there.

Eventually, we make it to Simon's house, and James types a code into the gate before driving down the cobblestone path. The home is so beautiful and grand that I almost forget the reason why we're here.

We park in one of the three driveways, and James comes over to my side to help me out of the car like he always does. It's so hard to stay mad at him when he's so romantic and sweet. As if he can tell I'm swooning, he pulls my hood from over my head and cups my cheeks before giving me a devastating kiss. I nibble his bottom lip, and he gives my breasts a quick squeeze before pulling away and taking my hand in his. "Are you ready?"

I try to remind myself that I'm supposed to be angry with him. "Yeah. Let's get this over with so we can go home."

He chuckles and laces his fingers through mine as we go up to the door.

When we knock, Simon greets us with a solemn look on his face. He wears a deep navy blue suit with a white shirt, and his dark hair is slicked back. "Hello, Father, Mother."

James smiles and places his hand on my lower back as we walk inside. "Where's Annie?"

Simon's wife Annie is home, but she isn't in the foyer.

He bites his lip. "She doesn't want to witness the event. She's furious with Jessamine and Damion, and she is not happy about the adulteress living with us. This is a major inconvenience, Father."

James grips my hand tightly. "I'm sure it is an inconvenience for you. It's an inconvenience for us as well. Fortunately, you live in a big ass house, so I'm sure you'll hardly see her."

He grunts. "I sure hope that's the case."

A few minutes later, we hear another knock at the door, and Simon groans when he looks at his phone. "The harlot is here."

He opens the door, and Jessamine steps inside, wearing her pink cloak with a white, long-sleeve dress underneath. Her look is completed with white boots, and her long brunette hair is braided down her back and falls at her waist.

She frowns at me with tears in her eyes. "Hello, Mother and Father."

James rubs circles on my back. "Hello, Jessamine." He turns to Simon. "Are we ready to begin?"

He groans. "As ready as I'll ever be."

We all follow him down a long hallway into a spare bedroom. There's a king-sized bed, with a white duvet and pillows, white walls and curtains, and gray tile flooring.

There's a chair in the middle of the room, and clippers near it, plugged into the wall and ready to go.

James stands beside me, and we stand off to the side while Simon and Jessamine face each other. She starts to cry softly, and James ignores her by beginning the event.

"We are gathered here today for the punishment of Jessamine Rodgers. She has sinned by engaging in carnal relations with her brother-in-law, Damion Barlow. She will beg forgiveness today at the mercy of Simon Barlow, and if forgiveness is granted, this home and room will be her new dwelling for the next twelve months. Should she decline to ask forgiveness or be denied, she will be killed alongside Damion in his Exit Ceremony tomorrow. Let's begin."

Jess's shoulders shake while she lowers her head. "I won't do it."

James tenses. "Jessamine, please don't do this."

She shakes her head and sobs. "I won't do it, Father. Kill me. I want to go with Damion. I love him."

Simon rolls his eyes and sighs. "For the love of God, Jess. Just get on your knees and beg." He cringes. "Not like that, but you know what I mean."

She wipes her face. "I can't. I can't do it."

James clenches his fists and chuckles low. "Jessamine, you will make your apologies now, or I'll slit your throat right here. We don't have all day."

She curses under her breath and gets on her knees before Simon. "Forgive me, brother, for my sins. I beg of you."

Simon draws his eyebrows together and crosses his arms. "I don't forgive you."

James mutters something and lets go of my hand. "Simon, you have one more chance. I need you both to cooperate. Please. This isn't that hard."

Simon closes his eyes and rubs his jaw. "Fine. You have my forgiveness, and you may find refuge in my dwelling."

Jessamine covers her face and sobs on her hands and knees until I step forward and pat her shoulder.

"Jess, it's time."

Jessamine stands up, eyeing my ponytail that falls down my back and reaches my waist. I instinctively grab it, feeling shitty for what I'm about to do to her. She shakes as she sits down in the chair, and I glance over at James, trying not to frown before he nods his head at me to keep going.

I unbraid Jess's long hair, and I whisper in her ear that it'll be alright, and to my surprise, she starts to relax. Simon and James stand watching as I shave Jess's head, leaving her bald in her cloak and dress.

She tries to pull me in for a hug, but James grabs my wrist and pulls me to him before saying his closing statements.

"The punishment is complete. We'll see you both at the Exit Ceremony tomorrow."

#

James and I don't speak the entire ride home, and I can't read his emotions. I feel frustration, but it doesn't seem directed at me. I don't feel like speaking to him right now, but I'm still upset that he won't strike up a conversation.

Not able to bear the silence any longer, I turn to face him. "What do you have planned for the rest of the day?"

He quirks a brow before smirking. "Nothing. Maybe we could watch a movie?"

A movie? Is he serious right now?

I cross my arms. "Oh. I don't know. Maybe."

His smile widens. "Okay. With Damion's Exit Ceremony tomorrow, I just want to relax until then. You don't mind, do you?"

I turn away from him. "No. Why would I mind?"

He laughs softly. "Is there something upsetting you, sweetheart?"

I roll my eyes and shrug off my cloak. "Nope. Nothing at all."

He laughs loudly for nearly five minutes before we ride the rest of the way home in silence. When we get back, he opens my car door and kisses my nose. "There's a brand new pink dress in the closet upstairs. Put it on with the matching shoes, and come downstairs in thirty minutes."

I scrunch my nose and try to hold back the smile that's forming. "So, you remembered?"

He pulls me out of the car and into his arms. "Of course, I remembered. When have I ever forgotten to do something I promised you?"

I look up into his warm brown eyes that make my insides turn to jelly. "Never."

He grins. "That's right. I always come through on my promises, Gen. Don't ever forget that."

I stand up on my tiptoes and kiss his plush lips. "I promise, I'll never forget."

We head up to the door, and he pats my ass as he unlocks and opens it, gesturing me to get inside and hurry up. He stays downstairs while I take the elevator to our room, and excitement courses through me when I run into our space to get dressed.

It takes me no time at all to shrug off my cloak and suit, and I stand in my white lace bra and thong while I dig through our closet to find my outfit. When I spot the pink dress, I grab it and smile, immediately knowing it was made by Odette. I grab the baby pink, fit-and-flare, knee-length ribbed sweater dress and slide it on. The hem has pearls sewn around it, and there's a thigh-high slit that allows me to show off a bit of leg. It has a V that gives a peek of my cleavage, but it keeps me secure without the fear of spilling out.

I slide into the matching baby pink leather heels, bump the ends of my straightened hair, and put on a little lip gloss and extra perfume before heading downstairs.

I take the elevator down, and when the doors open, I gasp at the sight before me. Our kitchen is filled with people who shout, "Surprise!", and I feel like it's my birthday.

Taking a look around the room, I see so many smiling faces. Next to my handsome husband is Paul who wears one of James' old royal blue suits, and matching him is his mother and my close friend, Mai. Standing next to Mai is Draco who winks at me, and my eyes shoot straight to James who definitely noticed and scowls. Next to Draco is Samuel and his daughter, and my heart swells at the sight of her little baby who smiles back at me. Next to his daughter is Mom who holds my baby girl, and next to Mom is someone I didn't imagine would be here, but I'm so glad she is: Ella.

Tears spring from my eyes as James runs up to me and everyone smiles and claps.

He wipes my tears and kisses my cheeks. "Surprise, sweetheart. I hope this is okay."

I kiss him and wrap my arms around him for a tight hug. "Of course. This is perfect. Thank you."

The first person who comes up to me is Mai, and she pulls me into her tight and cozy grasp. "It's so good to see you, Genevieve. I've missed you so much."

I take her hands in mine and smile. "Thank you so much for coming. It really has been too long." I glance at Paul. "Did you guys have a good drive over?"

Paul smiles and pulls me into a hug. "We did. You look amazing. Thanks for having us over."

I pat his back and can't believe how tall and grown-up he is. "Thanks for being here."

We meander to our formal living room, and Samuel comes up to me next with his daughter.

He slides his hand over his bald head. "I miss seeing you and James at the school. You both are so cute together. I'm glad you're doing well."

"Thanks, Sam. It really means a lot. We miss you too."

His grandson, Theo, wiggles in his mother's arms, and he waves at Zahara who's being carried by Odette.

I smile at Kate who scratches Theo's platinum blonde hair. "If you ever need a sitter, Theo's welcome over here any time."

She gives me the biggest smile and sighs. "I would love that. It's so great to finally meet you." She glances at Samuel. "Dad has only said good things about you."

I squeeze her shoulder and make my way to my party guests who I haven't greeted yet. Ella gives me a small smile and grabs my hands. "Genevieve, I'm so sorry."

I wrap my arms around her and pull her in for a tight hug. "I'm sorry, Ella."

We both hug and cry until James gets everyone's attention and starts a game. We stand off to the side while everyone mingles, and Odette puts the babies in a playpen that she sets up with toys.

James wraps his arms around me and nuzzles his head in my hair. "You look so pretty, Gen."

I sink into his chest and breathe in his familiar scent. "Thanks. You look pretty good too."

He nibbles my neck, making the hairs on my arms stand up while his soft breath dusts over me. "How about we sneak upstairs and have some fun?"

I pull away from his wandering hands and draw my attention away from the heat building between my legs. "James, we are having a party with our closest friends. Now is not the time."

He gropes my ass and pulls me into the hall, pressing me up against the wall by my neck. "It's always a good time."

I feel myself crumbling, eager to be reckless with him when I hear crying. It's crying that I know far too well. My baby's crying.

He lets go, and I bolt back into the room, wanting to know what happened in two seconds. Everyone keeps chatting while Paul scoops Zahara out of the playpen and Odette grabs Theo. Zahara stops crying as soon as he starts rocking her, and I'm impressed at how quickly he is able to soothe her.

I go up to him and pet her soft curls. "What happened?"

He pats Zahara's back. "The babies were doing okay, but Zahara was playing with a toy and Theo took it from her. She started crying, and then Theo did too."

I glance between the two babies who are now dozing off like nothing happened, and I smile at the thought of Zahara having little brothers and sisters.

Am I going to be able to handle multiple babies at once?

After we wrap up games, we all eat from the buffet that Odette prepared, and then we crowd around the kitchen island that's covered in gifts. I sit on a white stool while James stands behind me with his hands on my shoulders.

Looking around at everyone here celebrating with us, I feel so grateful and full of love. Odette hands me my first gift from Mai, and I open it delicately when all I want to do is tear it open.

I expect to see something for Zahara, but I'm completely shocked when I see it's a pale green designer handbag. I look up at her, and she smiles, pointing at James. "This one said that you've been wanting this bag for a long time, but you've refused to get it for yourself. So I decided to be a good friend and get it for you."

Everyone laughs loudly and my cheeks hurt from smiling while I look over my new accessory.

I squeeze her hand from across the way. "It's perfect, Mai. Thank you."

She smiles, and Paul hands me the next gift. "This is from me, for Zee."

I untie the light pink silk ribbon and peel back the hot pink wrapping paper, impressed at the effort put into this gift. When I open the lid to the pale pink box, my eyes water. Inside is the softest blush baby blanket with a pink ladybug attached to it, and *Zahara James Barlow* is embroidered on the fabric.

James squeezes my shoulder and touches the soft blanket. "This is really nice, Paul. Thank you."

He smiles, and Kate steps forward and drags a present I didn't see from behind the island. "Theo had one of these during his first few months, and it was a lifesaver."

I get off my seat and kneel to tear open the massive box before me, and I'm in disbelief when I see what's inside.

A self rocking bassinet? I take a look at the contraption and can't believe how high-tech it is. "Kate, this is too much. You didn't have to do this."

She waves me off and smiles. "It's nothing. Dad insisted." I glance at Samuel who nods his head in approval.

Ella comes forward and places a tiny box in my hand. "For the little princess."

I pull open the box and marvel at the delicate piece of jewelry before me. It's a tiny gold bracelet with beads that spell Zahara's name. It's adorable. "Thank you so much, Ella."

I go through the remainder of the gifts, and by the time I've opened everything, our kitchen is covered in baby clothes, toys, bottles, blankets, and gifts for me as well.

Once I've given everyone hugs and got a kiss on the cheek from Kate's little charmer, Theo, James kicks everyone out and helps me feed Zahara. We both change into matching sweatsuits, and he swaddles Zahara against his chest while I lie beside him on our bed.

I stroke Zahara's soft curls while James strokes my ponytail with my cheek pressed up against his. I feel so happy and content, and I can't believe how blessed I am to have these loves in my life.

James picks up one of Zahara's tiny hands, and she wraps her fingers around his thumb. "That was really sweet of you to offer to babysit for Kate."

I rub Zahara's back while she coos against her daddy's chest. "Thank you. You know me—I love kids, and Theo's such a cutie. It's hard being a new mom, and I want to support our friends however I can."

James' chest rises and falls slowly as he breathes in and out. "You're a new mom, but you're a pro at it. You're so good at everything you do, Gen."

I trace his jaw. "I try."

We lie there in blissful silence until he picks up Zahara and puts her in her crib. Once she's asleep, he climbs on top of me and plants a soft kiss on my nose.

"Are you ready for tomorrow?"

Tomorrow?

Fuck. How could I forget? Tomorrow is Damion's Exit Ceremony.

I'm completely unprepared for tomorrow. I don't know how one gets fully prepared for an Exit Ceremony. But the more I think about it, the better I feel about the whole thing. Damion is garbage, and his absence means he won't be able to hurt Theresa anymore. And, James can move onto the third level of The Caledonia Council bullshit.

I sink my fingers into his dark hair and massage his scalp. "I don't know if I would say I'm ready, but I'm looking forward to getting it over with."

He drags his nose across my jaw. "That's good enough. It's not going to be pleasant, but it'll be over before you know it."

My mind goes back to Sebastian's ceremony which was nearly a year ago, and I shudder. James plays with the hem of my sweatshirt. "We're nearly halfway there, Gen. Just a little longer, and we'll be free of this mess."

I want to believe him, but it's hard to imagine. This society is so grand that I can't fathom being away from it.

I slide my hands down his body, feeling his chiseled chest below his hoodie. "Do you promise?"

He freezes and stares at me, and I think he's going to say no. But he kisses my forehead and wraps me up in his arms while he rests on top of me. I start to relax when he whispers in my ear. "I promise, Gen. You have my word. I will get us away from all of this, and we will cut ties with this society forever."

I wrap my arms around his waist, trying to forget all of my fears and stay present in the moment. He grips me tighter, and before I know it, he's grinding his hips against mine and moaning in my ear. "Is Mommy going to relax and have some fun with Daddy?"

Even when I want to resist James, I can't. He draws me in effortlessly, and I want to give him everything whenever he asks for it.

I start to pull my top off. "As long as Daddy promises to show Mommy a really good time."

He growls and tears my top over my head, leaving me exposed from the waist up. In seconds, he's stripped every inch of clothing off the both of us, and he lies on his back on his pillow.

"Come ride, sweetheart."

I climb on top of him and get ready to lower myself on his hips when he shakes his head.

"Not my cock. My mouth."

I stop and stare at him, unsure of what to do next. We've never done that before. I mean, he's eaten me out a million times over, but I've never been on him like *that*.

"Are you sure?"

He grins. "I would never joke about something like this. Get up here. Don't be shy."

I slide closer while he grips my hips, and I stop when my clit reaches his chin and stare down at him. "Are you one hundred percent sure? Will you still be able to breathe?"

He tucks his hands under my thighs and pulls me forward, breathing on my opening while my thighs shake.

"Genevieve, the last thing I care about is breathing while my tongue is shoved deep inside you."

I open my mouth in protest, but he pulls me down by my thighs and sucks my clit into his mouth. I remember I'm still bleeding when I see light red staining his lips, but it's faint, so I know my flow isn't heavy and I'm probably still spotting. I hover over him, moaning his name over and over again while he tastes me until he pulls away and licks his lips.

"I said ride, sweetheart."

Gripping the headboard, I seat myself back over his mouth and rock my hips back and forth on his face like he's a mechanical bull.

He slides his hands up my chest, pinching my nipples, and I can't help but cry out.

"Jesus, James. You make me feel so fucking good."

He slides his hands up and down my body slowly, massaging me as he does so. I let myself get lost in the moment, feeling adored by his touches until I'm on the very edge.

I sink my hands in his hair, using his head to support me. "I'm so close."

He pops my ass, and I ride harder until I reach my release.

When I come down from my high, I slide off of his face and lie on my back. I start to drift off when he smacks my pussy.

"Don't fall asleep yet. You're going to ride my cock first."

I sit back up, tired but still horny, and climb on top of him.

He smiles and shakes his head at me. "Turn around."

Giving him my back, I slide on top of him while he sits up and tugs on my hair. His soft voice soothes me, making me feel at ease while I bounce up and down softly. "You're so gorgeous when you ride Daddy's face."

Panting softly, I whisper back to him. "I love seeing my blood on your lips."

He groans and pulls my head harder, making me stare up at the ceiling while he grips my hip with his other hand.

"Such a dirty girl. I love fucking your bloody little pussy. It's mine to fuck and use and play with however I want."

I move my hips faster, rubbing my thighs against his while I ride. "It's all yours, Daddy."

He slaps my tit, bucking his strong hips underneath me and hitting my core over and over. "Say it again."

"My pussy is all yours, Daddy. Fucking use me."

He moans in my ear and grips my hips tightly, fucking me harder than I'm capable of fucking him until we both come together.

After he's emptied himself in me, he wraps his arms around me and holds me close while he plants soft kisses on my cheek. "I will love you until the day I die, Genevieve Barlow. And even after that. Promise me that you'll never forget that."

I don't even realize I've started crying until he wipes my cheeks, still holding me close. "I promise. I couldn't forget that even if I tried."

Chapter Thirty

JAMES

It's Wednesday morning, the second week of October, and nearly eight weeks since my little girl was born. Damion's Exit Ceremony was yesterday, and it went better than I expected. The crowd was small, and he died quickly, so it didn't drag on for too long. Simon and Jessamine didn't say a word to me, but I didn't care because I didn't want to speak to them anyway.

Gen is out on the farm with Zahara introducing her to Olive. I have no idea what it is about that cow that draws my wife in, but they have a beautiful relationship. Gen doesn't know this, but I went out to see Olive one day and gave her some blueberries. I know it's her favorite snack, and even though I don't want her eating them too much, I wanted to thank her. I wanted to thank her for being there for Gen during the darkest time in her life. For comforting her in ways that I couldn't. And for never leaving her side.

Now I'm getting ready to do something that I enjoy and something that I don't feel like doing. In a few minutes, I'm going to work out, and I love working out because it's good for my body, it helps clear my head, and it boosts my confidence. I also love that I catch my wife spying on me sometimes, and I work a little harder to show off for her. My favorite times are when she makes her presence known and I take a break to have a little fun with her. But before I get to do any of that, I have to talk to someone I don't feel like talking to. I have to speak to Jack.

At first, I was dreading my next encounter with Jack. I had planned on going off the rails, and I honestly didn't know how it'd pan out. But shocking myself, I followed all of his instructions correctly. While this excites me, it also makes me nervous. It excites me because I know he's not going to make me suffer for breaking the rules. But it makes me nervous because I don't want him to think I'm a bitch who's just going to do whatever I'm told.

Pulling out my phone, I find his contact to send him a message. Part of me wonders how he'll know I did everything correctly, but then I remember that these people seem to have eyes everywhere.

Well, here goes nothing.

> It's me. Everything is done.

It takes him less than a minute to respond.

> Atta boy. Call me.

I'm not his fucking boy.

Not wanting this to waste any more of my precious time, I pick up my phone and dial him.

"Hey, Jack."

I can practically hear his smile. "James. I can't tell you how happy I am right now."

"That makes one of us."

He laughs so loudly that I have to pull my phone back from my ear. "God, James. You are a riot! I'm gonna miss you."

Miss me? "Are you going somewhere, Jack?"

He pauses. "Not exactly. But our time together is through."

When I met with Jack, he said I'd do the next two levels with him. If he's not doing level three with me, who the hell am I going to be dealing with?

"What about level three?"

He chuckles. "Yeah. About that. You know, James, me and the guys thought you'd fuck up level two. I'd hoped you didn't, but I was the only one who had faith in you. So, we made a little bet. Don't get mad at me though."

"Go on."

"Well, I proposed that if you didn't veer off the path, we'd give you a break. Help you out a bit. Give you a reward, so to speak."

What a saint. "What did I win?"

"Well, James, there is no level three. Not anymore at least. You get to skip right on to level four."

My knees buckle, and I lean against the wall to steady myself.

Level four. Only two more rounds of this bullshit. I'm nearly there.

I try to put on a pleasant tone. "Thanks, Jack."

"Of course, James. Now, I bet you're wondering what happens next."

I can't keep the sarcasm out of my voice this time. "You know me so well."

He laughs so hard that he starts wheezing, and eventually, he continues. "Well, you're going to meet Eric next." His tone goes cold. "But I warn you, James, Eric is nothing like me."

I close the bedroom door and lean against it, keeping myself inside. "What's that supposed to mean?"

He sighs. "It means that there's no crossing Eric, James. I like you, kid. Do as he says, and don't disobey. I swear to you, you will regret it if you do."

I get a chill and take a breath to calm myself. I already hate this Eric prick. "And what do I have to do?"

He pauses and sucks in a breath. "That's for Eric to tell you. And I know you're not going to want to do this part, but you've got to bring Genevieve and Zahara with you. A car will pick you guys up the first of November, three weeks from now."

My tone turns cold. "And what the fuck does he need to see my girls for?"

"Nothing sinister, James. They will be fine. I promise. I have a wife and daughter myself, so I understand where you're coming from. Just follow the rules. Don't fuck up right before the end."

"And level five?"

He clears his throat. "Level four is a little different. You'll be . . . graded, so to speak. And if Eric passes you, you'll move onto level five."

"And if he fails me?"

"You'll repeat the level until you pass."

Fuck this. "So I'm just supposed to sit and wait until then?"

"That's right, son. Enjoy the break, and get ready to work when you get back."

I don't get another word out before he ends the call, and I'm left wondering what the hell just happened.

I will get to level five, and I will finish this. But there's no way in hell that I'm going to wait for Eric's approval to do it.

#

After I got off the phone with Jack yesterday, I spent an hour in the gym trying to destress, and when I was done, I spent another hour destressing with Gen in the shower.

Now, I'm doing something not as fun but thrilling nonetheless. I'm returning a call from my cousin, Draco.

Normally I hate speaking with my cousin Draco, but I'm looking forward to it today as he left me a message early this morning that he had information I'd be excited to learn. That can only mean one thing—he has information on The Caledonia Council that we didn't have previously, and it'll hopefully help me speed my way to the top of the pyramid.

I don't want to clue Gen in until I've got a solid plan, so I'm taking the call privately in the office. Normally she'd be in here with me listening in, but she's upstairs with Ella who came over to braid her hair, so I can work privately.

Taking off my black blazer, I sit in my chair and dial his number. He picks up on the third ring.

"James. I think I've found Eric."

Eric. The bastard who I'm supposed to meet with in a few weeks. If he's found Eric, that's a great thing because I can speed up our meeting and convince him to tell me who his superior is.

I try to keep my excitement down as I wait for more information. "Eric. Are you sure it's him? How did you find him and where?"

He speaks quickly, and I hold the phone close to my ear, trying not to miss anything. "We found him at that building you met with Annabelle at. I asked a buddy to keep an eye on it for me, and no one has been to the building for weeks. Then the past two days at noon, he saw some bald guy with glasses go in, and he found his car in the parking garage. A little license plate lookup, and we found out that it was indeed Eric Sharpe."

"So he was there yesterday and the day before at noon?"

"Yes."

"By himself?"

"That's what it looks like."

I take a look at my watch and see it's a quarter past twelve. "Is he there now?"

He pauses. "I'm texting my guy now, and if so, I'll let you know. Have you spoken with that Jack guy yet?"

I catch Draco up to speed and let him know how my conversation went with Jack and what I'm expected to do next.

He sighs. "Well, I guess you just wait for Eric to pick you up then."

"No. No fucking way. I want to meet with him before then. Tomorrow."

The line goes silent for nearly a minute. "Tomorrow?"

"Yes, Draco. Tomorrow. You're coming with me."

He sucks in a breath. "What for?"

I lower my voice, just in case any of the ladies come downstairs. "Look. I'm tired of fucking around. I'm ready to end this."

"End this how, James?"

I know to get to the end of these trials, I have to meet with the head honcho. The one who's in charge of our perfume business. And my new friend Eric is going to help me meet him sooner rather than later.

I take a breath and feel adrenaline course through my veins, giving me the fuel to do what I'm planning to do tomorrow. Keeping my voice barely above a whisper, I decide to run him through my plan. "Do you have a gun, Draco?"

He groans. "No. But I can get one tonight."

"Great. You're going to need it."

I sit behind the island while Genevieve cooks dinner. Zahara sits in her bassinet nearby, trying to keep her eyes on her mommy the entire time.

While I want to have a peaceful dinner with my family, I need to give Gen an overview of my next moves. I didn't have a chance to catch her up on my conversation with Jack, and I need to inform her of what I'll be doing tomorrow afternoon, and how she'll be affected too.

She tosses her long braids over her shoulder, and I have to fight the urge to reach out and grab them.

Instead, I focus on her ass in her pink velvet track pants as she moves throughout the kitchen. "How do you feel about going up to the cabin tomorrow?"

She drains a pot of pasta and looks over her shoulder at me. "It's very short notice, but I'm open to it. Why?" She smiles, but it quickly falls when I don't return it.

Setting the pot back on the stove, she puts her hands on her hips. "What did you do?"

I stand up and go over to her, playing with the zipper on her matching jacket. "Nothing yet. But I called Sam, and he's going to take you, Mom, and Zee there tomorrow morning."

She frowns. "And where will you be?"

I put my hands on her shoulders, trying not to squeeze too tightly. "I'll be right behind you guys. But I need to go somewhere first."

"Where, James?"

I take over cooking, seeing as she's distracted, and tell her everything I learned from Jack and Draco. Then I tell her what I plan on doing tomorrow in the city at noon.

She shakes her head and shuts her eyes. "I don't like this, James."

"Are you asking me not to do it?"

Her big blue eyes meet mine. "I'm not asking you not to do it. But I don't love that you're doing it. How do you know it will even work?"

I plate the pasta. "I don't know. I just hope it will. I'm not taking you or Zee to meet him, and I'm tired of this bullshit. I'm ready to be done with it all."

She wraps her arms around me and buries her head in my chest. "Promise me you won't get hurt."

I kiss the top of her head. "I promise. Don't worry. Everything's going to work out fine.

I barely slept last night, and I woke up exhausted. Doubt invades my mind when I think about my plan, but I'm not willing to back out now. Sam will be here in an hour to get the girls, and then I'll be heading out to do what I have to do.

While my plan isn't solid, it's worth it. Kill the queen and the entire hive dies. I want freedom for my family, but in an ideal world, I'd free my relatives too. Not that they deserve it, but it's time to close the chapter on our society.

I'm sending the girls to the cabin because I know I'm going to piss off a worker bee known as Eric Sharpe, and I don't want him to retaliate by harming those closest to me. At the cabin, they'll be safe, and I won't have to worry about them. Plus, I'm planning on surprising Gen soon, and the cabin is where I want to do it.

After Gen gets up and feeds Zahara, I help her get their bags packed. I packed mine up last night and plan on bringing it later. Once they're ready, we all meet downstairs with Mom waiting for Sam to arrive. We're all wearing black, and it comforts me, making me feel like we have a strong unit.

I grip Gen's hand tightly. "Let me know as soon as you guys arrive. I'll call you as soon as I can and let you know when I'm headed there."

She squeezes my hand, and I hear a car pulling up outside, letting me know Sam has arrived.

My mother frowns with watery eyes. "Please be safe, James."

I wrap my arms around Gen and my mother, ushering them toward the door. "I will. Don't worry."

When I open the door, Sam is stepping out and has his car doors and trunk open. I see baby Theo in the car, and I smile thinking about Zahara having more siblings. It takes no time at all to get everything packed inside the vehicle, and I kiss Gen far too many times before getting her seated. "Call me if you need anything."

She nods her head, and I turn to Sam. "Thank you again for doing this."

He pats my back. "No problem at all. Are you sure everything's alright?"

Sam's a good friend. A great one. He's reliable and trustworthy, and he doesn't care that I'm hiding a million secrets from him. I squeeze his shoulder. "Everything's fine. Let me know when you guys arrive."

He smiles and sits behind the wheel. "Of course."

I wave them off as they drive away, and I start to sweat waiting for Draco to arrive.

Half an hour later, Draco pulls up wearing all black, and I hop in the car beside him.

"Are you willing to do whatever it takes?"

He looks straight ahead and takes off. "Absolutely."

The drive to the city is smooth and quiet, and eventually, we make it to the gray office building where my quest began. It takes a few hundred dollars to pay off the valet, and in no time, we're heading up the elevator to the floor where I met Annabelle.

Looking at my watch, we have about fifteen minutes until Eric arrives, and I start to panic, realizing we have no idea which office is his. Does he use Annabelle's? Or does he use one of the many others on this floor?

Draco looks back and forth down the hall and rubs his hands together to stay warm. "Where should we wait?"

I step away from him and start opening doors. "We need to be inside his office."

He follows behind me and pulls a black beanie over his head. "Which one is it?"

"I have no fucking idea. Try and find something with his name on it."

We spend the next ten minutes going through each room, and they all look exactly the same. Sweat drips down my spine under the cool air, and I start to panic.

Think, James. There's got to be something in one of these rooms to indicate it's his. I check all the trash bins and drawers for wrappers or anything personal and find nothing. It's when I recheck the office at the other end of the hall that I notice something different. The desk chair has an imprint on it, and it's the only one apart from Annabelle's that doesn't look brand new.

"This is the one."

With two minutes to spare, we close all the doors and step inside the room, Draco on one side of the door and me on the other.

We wait for a few minutes, and eventually, we hear the elevator doors open to the floor. I'm so overwhelmed and I can't tell if I want to scream or piss. I hope this goes over as smoothly as I planned it in my head.

The door creaks and light pours in as someone steps inside. I hear a gasp, and he tries to back away, but Draco grabs him first and drags him over to his desk chair before tossing him in. I don't even need to say anything before he's got his gun pointed at Eric's head.

"Don't move."

I go to stand beside Draco and point my gun between Eric's legs. "Do you know who I am?"

The portly sweaty man scoffs and pushes his glasses back up. "Of course I know who you are, you fucking idiot."

My wrist twitches, and I remind myself that I need information. I can shoot him after I get it.

I'm here to make an offer.

He starts hyperventilating. "You're dead, kid. So fucking dead."

I feel my patience waning, but I try to remain calm. "The offer is this. You'll get your boss, the final leader on the phone for me, and if our call goes well, I'll let you go. If you refuse, I'll kill you. If you agree and I don't like the way the call goes, I'll kill you. How does that sound?"

He rolls his eyes. "That sounds like a crock of bullshit." He reaches for his desk, but he stops when Draco steps closer, holding the barrel to his head. "Don't fucking move."

Eric stares back at me while rage courses through me. "Look, Eric. You do what I say, or today is your last fucking day. If you know me so well, then you already know I'm a killer, and I won't feel a thing taking you out."

His eyes start to water. "James, I can't call him. I will be in serious shit if I do. He will fucking kill me and make me suffer. Go ahead and shoot me."

Shit. I didn't think the poor bastard would just give up. I can't let him give up, because his giving up means I don't get what I want. If I kill him, I'm back to square one. I can't lose.

I try to keep the panic out of my voice while I keep my hand steady, hoping he doesn't feel the desperation leaking off of me. "Look, Eric. You help me, and I will kill you quickly and painlessly. There will be no suffering. But if you don't help me, I will torture you until there's nothing left of you. So, you're going to die either way, but it's up to you to choose how it happens."

I see Draco gulp out of the corner of my eye, but he keeps his gun and eyes trained on Eric.

Eric starts to sob, and I start to get impatient. "Eric, I'll give you to the count of ten, and then I'll choose for you. And I brought my favorite knife with me, so I'm prepared to have a lot of fun."

His eyes spring open and he stares at me with snot running down his face. "Fine. I'll call him. But it's your funeral."

The room stops while he slowly picks his phone up off his desk and dials a number. I start to get nervous, hoping that he won't try and screw me when he puts the phone on speaker.

Eric wipes his face and lowers his head. "You're on speaker, Michael."

Michael.

The man holding my key to freedom is named Michael.

The line goes silent, and for a second I have a fear that we're going to be ambushed by law enforcement, but then I push that worry to the side. The Wild White Orchids don't adhere to the law. They never have, and they never will.

The man on the other line clears his throat, and his low and gravelly voice filters through. "James Bryson Barlow. Are you there?"

I hate being addressed by my full name unless my wife's the one who's doing it. Holding my ground, I stand tall and keep my weapon steady. "I'm here."

Another pause. "So I hear you want to speak with me."

I can't tell if his calmness relaxes me or worries me.

"Yeah. I'm tired of playing this game, Michael. I want my family's freedom, and I know you have the power to give it to me. I want you to let us go."

Nearly a minute passes before he replies. "I'll be honest, James. I am sick and tired of you, and it would be a relief to let you and your family go."

My heart races with excitement. "I'm glad you and I are in agreement."

He chuckles. "I'll give you what you want. Gladly. But I'm going to make you work for it."

There's the fucking catch. "I've already been doing the work. What other work is there?"

He sighs. "You've managed to outwit my subordinates faster than you can say whippersnapper, so I'm going to put you through the final test. Complete it, and you're free. I'll send you an address later, and you'll meet me tomorrow morning to discuss the details."

Draco shakes his head, but I agree. "Deal."

Michael responds. "Good. I'll see you then." Eric goes to end the call, but Michael's voice filters through before he can. "And, James?"

"Yes?"

"I want to remind you, that there's a price for everything."

The line goes dead, and my stomach drops.

Draco looks my way, and I gesture him to pocket his weapon.

Eric's eyes go wide. "Don't leave me here."

My head pounds, knowing what he wants me to do. And I want to do it too, but I don't at the same time.

"I can't kill you, Eric."

He starts to cry again. "Please, James. Don't let him get me. You have no idea what he'll put me through. And you promised me. You promised that if I'd help you, you'd kill me."

I promised. I promised him. Draco glares at me. "James, let's go."

I position my gun at Eric's head. "Step out into the hall."

Draco frowns. "You don't have to do this."

I bark at him. "It's my fucking conscience. Not yours. Go out to the fucking hall, and I will see you in a second."

He turns away from me and does as ordered.

I let my body feel the fire flowing through me. "Goodbye, Eric."

He smiles and closes his eyes. "Thank you, James."

I fire, and he falls out of his chair while I secure my gun. I hear Draco curse in the hall, and I meet him outside to leave.

I pull out my phone while he drives me to a car rental facility and start to panic. Gen called me three times, but I didn't have any service in the building. I dial her back and try to quell my pounding heart.

She picks up on the first ring, giving me an instant rush of peace. "James, where are you?"

"I'm on my way to get a car. Is everything alright?"

Her breath quickens. "We just got here, but, Odette's not here."

"What do you mean she's not there?"

She pauses. "We were on our way, and then she said she needed to get something from her house. Samuel dropped her back off at our home, and she insisted that she'd meet us here later. But she's not answering her phone."

Fuck. "Hold on, sweetheart." I turn to Draco. "Head to my mom's house, now."

Gen starts to cry. "What if something happened to her, James?"

Michael's words play back in my mind.

I want to remind you, that there's a price for everything.

I ignore my shaking voice. "Everything's fine. Don't worry."

I know what's coming next, and I can't handle it. Gen's going to ask me to promise her, and I can't do that. I can't promise her that Mom's going to be alright. Because I honestly don't know.

Before Gen can ask me, I steal the space. "I'm going to find out what's going on right now, and I'll call you after. I love you."

She sniffles. "I love you too."

I hang up the phone and take deep breaths, trying to prevent my throat from closing up. I dial my mother, and my hands start to shake with each call that goes to voicemail.

What do I do? What the fuck do I do?

I can't lose her. I can't lose my fucking mom. I pick up my phone and call the only other person I can think of to help. He picks up on the first ring.

"Father?"

"Hey, Paul. Something's wrong. I need you to go to my mother's house right now."

"I'm on my way."

I hang up the phone while the minutes drag on, praying my nightmare doesn't come true.

Eventually, we pull up to my childhood home, and my heart stops when I see an ambulance.

She's gone. She's fucking gone.

I see the gurney being rolled out through the front door, and I let out a breath when I see an oxygen mask over my mother's face.

Draco stops the car and I run out, going up to Paul and a medic.

"What happened?"

Paul runs his hands through his black hair, breathing heavily. "I came over as fast as I could. The door was unlocked, and she was bleeding out. Someone stabbed her and left her here to die."

I shut my eyes, refusing to let Paul see the way they're shining, and when I get myself together, I look back at the medic. Everything becomes a blur as I get back in Draco's car and we follow my mother to the hospital.

I call Gen and tell her what's going on while my mother is in emergency surgery. It feels like hours before they let me see her. Eventually, I'm called in by a nurse, and my mother looks like a ghost with her eyes half-closed staring back at me. Draco and Paul follow behind me.

My mother reaches out one of her small hands. "Baby."

I grip it tightly and smooth out her hair. "Hey, Mom."

I try to get her to tell me what happened, but she didn't see anyone and doesn't have any details for me to go on. I say a prayer, thanking God for saving her.

She squeezes my hand. "Where are my other babies?"

"They're at the cabin."

She coughs. "Go to them. I'll be alright."

I kneel beside her. "I can't leave you."

She shakes her head. "They need you more than me right now. I'll see you guys when they let me out of here."

Paul grabs my shoulder. "I'll stay with her, James."

Draco steps beside my mother. "I will too. Take my car. Raven can come pick me up."

I look between them, grateful for them more than ever. "Please call me if anything changes."

They agree, and I give my mother a kiss on the cheek before heading out the door.

Chapter Thirty-One
GENEVIEVE

I pace around our bedroom at the cabin holding Zahara while I wait for James to come home. Zahara has been crying for the past hour because I've been crying for the past hour, and I haven't done anything to help her relax.

I should've never let Odette get out of the car. I can't shake the feeling that I'm responsible somehow for her injury. When James told me she was stabbed, I nearly collapsed. I've been thinking the worst, but I pray deep down that she'll recover and that she'll recover soon.

Adding fuel to the fire is the news that James gave me regarding Eric and Michael. I should be ecstatic that this is almost over, but I'm the most scared I've ever been. I barely know what's right and wrong anymore and I'm not even sure I care. All I know is that I don't want to lose James, and I'd do anything to keep him safe.

Sam and Theo are in their guest bedroom down the hall, and I'm grateful to not be in this big house all alone. I wish we could just hide away in the cabin forever, but I know we can't. The council may not know where we are currently, but I'm sure they could figure it out rather quickly. And even if they didn't, I don't want to be stuck here forever. I want us to be able to live freely and enjoy each day without worrying about being destroyed or punished. Which is why as much as I don't want James to meet with Michael tomorrow, I know it's our next best move.

Eventually, I get my girl calmed down with some milk, and when she starts to doze off to sleep, I put her in her crib James had sent here a few months ago. As soon as she's down, I hear the front door opening, and I put her in her carrier to bring downstairs, knowing exactly who it is.

As soon as I make it downstairs and see James, he pulls me into his arms and squeezes me tighter than he ever has before. I set down Zahara's carrier, and his hold gets even stronger while he grips me like I might disappear if he lets go. Once we both settle down, he pulls away and kisses me before gripping my face.

"Mom's okay. We'll be able to get her home soon."

I give him another kiss and grip his muscular arms to steady myself. "Are you alright?"

He stares at me, and for a moment I think he might break, but he shows me his classic white smile and nods his head. "I'm fine. Don't worry about me. Everything is alright."

Picking up Zahara's carrier with one hand, he holds mine with his other, and we head upstairs to our room.

James takes off my shoes and socks, leaving me in my black turtleneck and matching skinny jeans. After he changes into a pair of black sweatpants and a matching tee, he comes to bed and starts massaging my feet. I lie down on my back and stare at the mirror on our ceiling, and I don't even remember drifting off. All I know is that I feel him shake my shoulders gently to wake me, and he sets takeout containers on the bed while I start to wake up.

Looking at my phone, it's nearly seven p.m., and I wonder how I slept for so long.

He hands me a glass of water, and I glance over at Zahara who sleeps in her crib. "How's Mom?"

He opens up a container of soup and hands it to me. "She's alright. Paul and Draco are still with her. There's still no news on who stabbed her, but I'm sure Michael had something to do with it."

I shiver at the mention of Michael. "Where are you meeting with him tomorrow?"

He opens up another bowl of soup and lets it cool. "I'm meeting with him near the Orchid Oblivion factory you went to. It's close to the original perfume factory. Apparently, he works there sometimes."

I start to eat my soup slowly. "What's your plan?"

He frowns. "I plan on doing whatever he says. I want our freedom, but I want him to let the other members of the society have their freedom too."

I think about everyone in our society and how much money we all bring in by working together and working for The Caledonia Council. To ask for so many people to be free of this rule is a hefty request.

"That's going to be a big price to pay even if he agrees."

He swallows a spoonful of soup. "I know. But no one's ever had a chance like this. I figure if I'm meeting with him, it's worth a try."

"You're the most admirable man I know, James."

He smirks. "I know. And I want it to stay that way. Which is why I need to do this. I've done so many bad things in my life that I need to try and make things right for all of us. I don't want anyone else to have to suffer if I can stop it."

I take his hand and lace my fingers through his. "You have my support."

He lifts my wrist to his lips and kisses it. "I am eternally grateful for you."

We enjoy the rest of our food in silence, and I eat far too much bread. After we've cleaned everything up, James straps Zahara to his chest, and we head outside to walk around the property.

I remember the first time we came here, everything was covered in snow, and it was way too cold to be outside. The weather is chilly, but the only things covering the ground are dead leaves, so we're able to take a walk and look around.

I look from left to right, in disbelief at how much land there is. "All of this is ours?"

James rests his hand on my back while we walk. "Yeah. It's all ours."

I glance up at the tall trees surrounding our massive space. "I can't decide if I like staying at the cabin or our house better. I want to live there, but I want to live here too."

He turns me to face him. "We can live in both."

"What do you mean?"

He plays with my braids, and Zahara grabs a piece to play with too. "I mean when we're out of all of this society mess. We can spend most of our time at the house and then spend a few months up here at the cabin. Would you like that?"

I close my eyes, thinking about summers at the house and winters at the cabin, having Christmas here with our kids. "I'd love that, James. That would be really special."

He grins. "Good. Speaking of special things, I have a surprise planned for you tomorrow afternoon after my meeting."

I lean into his shoulder while we walk further through the trees. "What surprise?"

His hand slides down and squeezes my ass. "It wouldn't be a surprise if I told you. But you should wear a dress. A white one."

A white dress. It's like I'm getting married again.

"Alright. I'll be here waiting for you wearing a white dress. Will we have guests?"

He shakes his head. "No. Sam's heading home in the morning. It'll just be us."

Things are scarier than they've ever been, but I can't deny how much I love surprises. And James' surprises never disappoint. Taking a moment to focus on the positive, I get excited imagining what he has planned.

"Just us. Sounds like a blast. I can't wait."

Chapter Thirty-Two

JAMES

I wake up at five a.m. Friday morning to meet with Michael. Gen and Zahara are sleeping peacefully, and I hate that I have to leave my girls on this cold October morning.

My mother's still in the hospital, but she's not alone. I dreamt the worst last night, so to wake up and find out that everything's still alright was a major relief. I can't put into words how ready I am for this nonsense to be over. Gen was sick last night, and I think she's just so stressed and overwhelmed by everything. I'm looking forward to my meeting with Michael purely for the reason of getting his request over with and never having to speak to him again.

Part of me's shocked that he's been so close to me the entire time, but the other part of me isn't. I've seen the original perfume factory in photos and videos, but I've never been inside. Even if I had, it's unbelievably massive, and there's no way I'd be able to find him in that large building with nothing to go on especially when he's not there every day.

I pull open the dresser and dress myself slowly. My girls are light sleepers, and if I make too much noise, I'll wake them both, and they'll both get upset about me leaving.

To meet with Jack, I'm wearing my classic black suit with a white shirt and a black tie. I'm also wearing my burgundy wingtip oxfords which are Gen's favorite and a black wool coat. I've got my guns and knife on me, but I'm hoping I won't need them. Once I've gathered all my things, I head downstairs for a quick cup of coffee where Sam is having one as well before he heads out.

I go up to Theo and ruffle his blonde hair. He really is adorable. Not as cute as my baby, but still precious.

Sam finishes the last of his beverage and puts on his coat. "Thank you again for letting us stay the night. It's a beautiful home."

Leaning against the counter, I sip my beverage slowly, trying to ease into the morning. "It's no problem at all.

You're welcome anytime. Thanks for driving my family here."

He smiles. "Of course. And you're sure everything's alright?" He raises a brow with a concerned look on his face.

Lying through my teeth, I pat his back. "It is. Don't worry."

Favoring ignorance, he smiles again and gathers his things. "Kate was sorry she couldn't make it but said to tell you guys if you ever need a sitter for Zahara, the offer is open on her end as well."

"Thanks, Sam. Tell her we appreciate it."

He gives me a pat on the back before getting his things out to the car and grabbing Theo.

Once they've left, I get in my car, not needing to waste any more time and head off to my destination.

My ride to the perfume factory is smooth and almost serene. When I get to the massive building, I start to panic, realizing I have no idea where to park, what door to go in, or who I'm looking for.

My phone pings, and I check the message from the unknown number.

> Park out back. Enter door number ten. My assistant will be waiting for you, and she'll bring you to me.

Of course, the bastard doesn't have the balls to meet me himself. He's probably worried that I'd try to kill him. That's probably what would happen, so I understand.

Once I find a spot, I park, get out, and make my way to door number ten. I turn the knob and enter, and a short woman with short brown hair wearing black glasses and a white lab coat greets me.

"Hello, Mr. Barlow. Follow me."

She doesn't wait for my greeting, and I'm glad because I don't feel like talking to her anyway. We walk down this skinny long hallway that I didn't know was in the building, and after a few minutes, we enter a door to one of the many break rooms.

She claps her hands at the three individuals in the room. "Everybody out."

They stand up and rush out immediately, making me instinctively reach for my knife. The woman ignores my panic and goes up to the vending machine.

Is she really about to get a fucking snack right now?

After pressing a few buttons like she's typing in some hidden code, she takes a step back, and the vending machine lowers into the ground. Behind it is a door, and she pulls a key out of her waistband to unlock it. When she opens it, she points to a stairwell.

"Go up to the third floor." Without another word, she turns on her heel and exits the break room.

I keep my hand on my weapon as I head inside, and the door shuts on its own behind me. Ignoring the chill in the air, I swiftly make my way to the third floor, and the only door on the floor opens.

A man with my height and build steps out of the room. He's got brown eyes like me, a similar facial shape and smile, but his hair is white.

"James Barlow. Come on in."

I follow behind him cautiously and enter his office.

Taking a look around the room, it appears far more normal than I anticipated. There's a single window with a view of the courtyard, a small oak desk with a single floor-to-ceiling bookshelf behind it, and a couch across from the desk with pillows. If I didn't know any better, I'd think that he was a therapist.

He gestures to the couch for me to sit, and I do so reluctantly.

"I'm Michael." He stays seated behind the desk, and I'm glad for the space.

I try to keep the bitterness out of my voice. "I'm aware."

He smiles. "James, you have really fucked up my shit."

I can't stop the corner of my mouth from lifting, feeling satisfaction from upsetting this strange man. "How so?"

Shaking his head, he pours a glass of water. I decline when he holds it out for me, and he starts to drink it slowly. "I'm not sure if you're aware, but The Caledonia Council was created by your great-grandfather."

I never thought about it that hard, but I assumed this was Jude's doing. Only he could think of something so fucked up. I still cannot believe I'm related to that bastard. I haven't been back in his journal since the last time I flipped through it. I saw a photo of him that I swore was me for a split second. I look just like him.

Trying to act more prepared than I am, I sit up straight and look into his eyes. "Yes. I'm aware. Though I can't imagine why he'd give up control to let a group of men tell him what to do."

He grins. "That's where you're wrong. Jude didn't answer to them. They answered to Jude."

I lean back against the cushions, wanting to get comfortable if I'm going to be here for God knows how long. "What changed?"

He strokes his shaved chin. "Well, Jude didn't think anyone could be better at his job than he was. So he arranged for the council to take over privately after his death. And every Head Father under him would have to report to us."

So fucking typical. Why would my great-grandfather want to make things better for his lineage? "How fucking thoughtful of him."

Michael grins. "I'd be upset if I were you too. But hey. It worked for generations. That was until you came along."

I look at Michael's desk and bookshelf, trying to get a read on the bastard. He's got my fashion sense dressed exactly like me but with white shoes instead of burgundy. Other than that, I can't pick up anything.

"Look, Michael. I never wanted any of this. I never wanted to be Head Father."

He nods his head. "I know. That's why you have completely disrupted everything." He stands and faces his window, giving me his side profile. "We've been watching you this entire time. Due to your quick decision-making and natural leadership, we assumed you'd be just like your great-grandfather. I was rather impressed with you. That is until you tried that bullshit with Deacon."

He clenches his fists. "I knew something was wrong then. Honestly, son, I was ready to take you out right after that. But I have my own rules too. Everyone has a boss, James. And I was instructed to keep an eye on you.

"So I had Shane watch you. Only, I didn't know about what he had going on with your mother. Of course, he grew attached, and he grew weak. I had you kill him as a test of your loyalty. I thought maybe we'd still be able to keep you on."

He grabs his glass of water and sips it slowly. "But you just couldn't follow the damn rules. And then I realized that I needed to restructure my own council." His eyes meet mine. "So I had my meat man take out Annabelle. And he had fun chopping her into bits. Jack was a hitman before we met. A great one too. But then you made him look like an ass when you tried that shit with Eric, and I had to get rid of Jack myself. My pigs sure ate up his scraps quick."

He laughs, making my skin crawl. "You made things easy for me by taking out Eric."

I count them off in my head and smile at my discovery. "So, that just leaves you then. You're all that's left."

He sets his glass down on his desk and sighs. "Yeah. Me. Me and my family. I have a family just like you do, James. Except mine's bigger. You're not the only secret society we own."

My eye twitches, realizing that I'm in way over my head. "Then what do you need us for?"

He scoffs. "Money. Labor. What else is there? However, your society is on the brink of collapse."

I answer a little too eagerly. "So, you're willing to let us go?"

He shakes his head. "No. I'll let your immediate family go. But not the others. I don't need you, but they can still serve me. However, I am willing to . . . restructure."

"In what way?"

He goes to sit back behind his desk. "I'm willing to end all murders. I'll restructure the tenets, and everyone born from this day forward will have the choice to be initiated. And all current members under thirty-two will be permitted to request their freedom. And it will be granted if they pass a test. Admission will be open to the public, should they pass initiation of course, and the society will go on."

It's not exactly what I was hoping for, but it's better than nothing.

He frowns. "But, like I said, James. Everything has a price. So if I'm to make those changes, you're going to pay for them."

Payment. Everyone's always got their damn hand out. "And what's the payment?"

Michel pulls out a bottle of bourbon and pours a glass, sipping it slowly. "You have two paths, James. You leave here today with what you own, and you and your wife and mother never speak to anyone in the society ever again. You move out of the state, and you don't set foot in New York for the rest of your lives. That's payment. That's your ticket to freedom."

We can't leave New York. This is our home. My wife grew up here. So did I. And we're raising our kids here. In our houses.

I shake my head. "And my other path?"

His grin stretches across his face. "You get to keep everything you own. You get to stay in the state. And I make all of the changes I mentioned earlier."

"And at what price?"

He taps his nail on the side of his glass. "Three days."

"Three days?"

He nods his head. "You give me three days of your time where you will meet my family. You will explain your reasons for leaving, and then you will participate in an exit ritual. After the trip, you're free to move on with your life. What do you choose, James?"

I look at the clock above his desk, waiting for him to give me a countdown, but he doesn't.

What do I choose. What do I choose?

For the first time in this entire journey, I've been given a real choice. He stares at me patiently, and my skin tingles while my mind races.

I could walk out of here today. I could take my girls and my mom, and we could be free of this. We can have a fresh start and leave this behind us.

Or I can think beyond myself and potentially save the lives of my relatives. I can give the younger guys a fresh start, and no more children will have to be born into this.

I think about my wife and my little girl, and I know that if I were to ask them, they'd tell me to do what I'm about to do.

Standing up to stretch my legs, I face Michael and make my decision. "I'll give you three days of my time. We have a deal."

He stands and extends his hand for me to shake, and I do, grateful that we're not spilling blood. He nods his head when he pulls away. "We have a deal. Meet me here, tomorrow at noon."

###

I leave Michael's office feeling a sense of relief. I think. I'm relieved, but I'm nervous as hell. I just agreed to go on a trip with Michael to meet his "family" in God knows where to do God knows what, and I'm hoping I don't regret it.

But I'm almost at the finish line. I'm doing this to give my girls a normal life. A happy life.

Shit. I'm going to be away from Gen and Zahara for three fucking days. I don't know if I can handle being away from them for that long. I might actually die.

I know Gen's not going to want to be away from me. Especially not knowing where I'm going. But I'll be damned if they take my phone away from me, and I'll still be able to contact her. I just hope she'll be alright while I'm gone.

And my mother. What if my mother needs me while I'm away? And Sam just went home, so Gen and Zee are going to be at the cabin all alone. I can't tell if that's a good or bad thing.

I get a new rental car on the way to the cabin and take a different route, just to be sure I'm not being tailed. The closer I get to home, the more panicked I get.

What if they try to torture me? Lock me in a room? Maim me?

I have to put my hope in my Lord and Savior and hope he has the slightest ounce of love left for me to not let me be destroyed.

The closer I get to home, the more anxious I get. Today was supposed to be serene. Peaceful. And romantic. I had the most special surprise planned for Gen today, but now it's going to be overshadowed by the events of my morning. But I'm still going to go through with it as there's no way I'm leaving my wife for three days without doing what I had planned.

On the way home, I stop by my favorite jewelry store. I put in my order weeks ago, and they told me it'd be ready today. My mood picks up when I see that it is, and I tuck the green velvet box into my coat pocket to head to my next destination.

While there are far more original flowers than roses, I'll never get over the way Gen's face lights up when I give her these classic blooms, so I ordered twelve dozen that all need to fit in my trunk.

By the grace of God, the florist helps me get them all in my vehicle without crushing any of them, and I make my last stop at the local market near the cabin to get what I need to make dinner. I also grab their most expensive bottle of white wine because I'm not a cheap bastard. After I grab the cake I ordered from the bakery, I stuff everything in the back seat and head to our winter home.

By the time I get back, it's nearly one p.m., so I know Gen is up. I pull out my phone to send her a quick message to give me time to get everything set up.

> Stay upstairs until I tell you you can come down. Be dressed and ready.

Chapter Thirty-Three

GENEVIEVE

My phone pings while I style my hair.

> Stay upstairs until I tell you you can come down. Be dressed and ready.

I'm eager to know how James' meeting went, but I'm even more excited to see what surprise he has planned for me. I plan on surprising him myself. He said to wear a white dress, so I'm sure he'll be shocked when he sees me wearing my wedding dress that I'm surprised I can still fit.

I style my braids in the low chignon that Ella did for my wedding day. I don't really wear makeup these days, so after showering and washing my face, I put on a little moisturizer and lipgloss.

Zahara sleeps in her crib while I take my dress out of our closet. We had our wedding outfits brought here months ago when our closet became too packed with my new clothing.

Although Mai and Ella helped me dress for my wedding day, this is a style that I'm able to get into on my own. My boobs are too big to fit a bra in as well, so I'm going without and opting for a white spandex thong for underwear. I grab my veil to tuck into my hair, and then I finish my look with my spring fling/wedding shoes.

I avoid looking in the mirror after I get dressed. I want to see how I look, but I also don't want to compare myself to how I looked on that day. It's a new day, and I'm not the woman I used to be. I've grown and evolved, and I'm someone new. Better and happier.

Zahara starts to wake up, and I see her grinning at me, giving me all the confidence I need to know I look good.

My phone pings again, and I grab it, checking my messages.

> Come downstairs and meet me out back.

My cheeks hurt from smiling while I scoop up Zahara and hold her close to my chest. She breathes softly, and I run my fingers through her soft curls as I carry her downstairs.

A wave of panic hits me when I reach the bottom.

Am I ridiculous for wearing this dress? If he's completely taken aback and laughs, at least we won't have an audience.

When I open the door to the backyard, I freeze. Unable to speak or move.

There's a pathway of roses. More roses than I've ever seen in my life.

At the end of the path is my knight in shining armor, dressed in a black suit with a white shirt and my favorite shoes. I look into his big brown eyes, and he blushes while his eyes water.

He shuts them closed and calls out to me. "Jesus Christ, Gen. Come here."

I walk up to him, and he opens his eyes after suppressing his tears. I still catch the way his lip wobbles when he opens his mouth and sucks in a breath.

"Give me your hand, Gen."

I extend my left hand out to his to take while I keep Zahara tucked in my right arm.

His hand trembles while he looks down at me. "The first time I realized I loved you was a week after I met you."

I feel tears stream down my cheeks, and he smiles back at me. "You were out sick, and I had the worst day at school without you." He pauses and takes a breath. "I thought about you the entire day and all I could focus on was how my chair smelled like your perfume. I texted you that night, asking you some bullshit question about homework assignments because I just wanted to talk to you."

Zahara nuzzles against my chest, and my breath catches. "James."

He wipes my tears and wraps his arms around my waist, staring into my eyes. "If I could go back in time, I'd tell you how you were my first thought in the morning, and thinking of you kept me up at night. I'd tell you how I'd wear certain things to impress you or practiced jokes to make you laugh. I'd tell you how you were the most beautiful woman I'd ever laid eyes on. I'd tell you how I was truly obsessed with you."

He strokes my chin with his thumbs. "How I could love you better than any man on this planet was capable of doing. How I'd live for you and die for you."

His soft fingers cup my cheeks while his eyes darken. "How I wanted to tie you down to my bed and fill your belly with our babies over and over."

I hold Zahara close to me while I sob.

Kneeling before me, he takes my hand again and kisses my knuckles. "I would've asked you out on a date the day we met even though you were with someone else. I would've begged you to move in with me that first week. I would've convinced you that I was the one within the first month. And in our first month together, I would've got down on one knee and asked you to marry me."

He pulls a pale green velvet box out of his pocket and opens it up. "But I can't go back in time and do those things. I just need you to know, Genevieve Barlow, that you're the love of my life, and I will choose you every single day in this life, the next, and the one after that. I choose you for eternity. And I want to know, sweetheart, will you choose me too?"

My entire body shakes while I cry, and eventually, I open my mouth to answer. "Yes. Yes, I choose you, James. Every day. Forever."

His lip wobbles while he pulls the green diamond eternity band out of the box and slips it on my finger. My hand is blinding with my engagement ring, wedding band, and my new piece. Standing up, he wraps an arm around my waist and cups Zahara's head with the other while he captures my lips in a bruising kiss.

When he pulls away, he kisses my nose and my cheeks. "I love you."

I run a hand through his soft hair making him sink into me. "I love you too."

When we get back inside, I feed Zahara and get her situated in the playpen that James set up for her in the living room. I don't even register him starting a fire in the fireplace until he's pulling me away from our baby and into his arms.

I sink into him immediately, letting him run his hands all over my chest. He unlaces the back of my dress, slipping it off my shoulders, and tracing my collarbones as he does. "I would've fucked you so hard on our wedding night."

My thighs clench together, and I put my hands on his shoulders to steady myself while he tosses my veil to the side and slides my dress down to the floor. "You can make up for it by fucking me hard right now."

He tears off his blazer and shirt, sending buttons flying everywhere. I laugh until he slides his pants and boxers down and kicks off his shoes.

His eyes rake over my body. "On your back on the couch. Now."

I keep my shoes on while I saunter over to the large leather sofa, lying down on my back and spreading my legs.

James wastes no time coming over to me and slides my thong down my legs, leaving it trapped around my ankles. Hovering over me, he positions himself at my entrance and plunges in, making me scream out into our empty house.

I'm not as wet as I normally am when we start, but I don't care. I want him so bad that the pain doesn't bother me.

I wrap my arms around him and dig my nails into his back while he fucks me like he paid for me. I don't even need to tell him what I want. He hits my center at the perfect speed and intensity, making my legs shake. His lips cover mine, sucking down every scream and moan I let out like he's trying to devour every part of me.

My heels dig into his hard ass, and he grips my thighs, slamming into me deeper and with more force. The couch creaks as if it might break if he pounds me any harder.

His sweat mixes with my slickness, and our scent fills the air. Dipping his face to my chest, he licks my nipples with his warm, wet tongue, and I slide my fingers between us to rub my aching clit. His loud moans make me squeeze him involuntarily. My orgasm sneaks up on me without warning, and I shudder under him while he comes inside me, the familiar feel of his throbbing cock in my pussy making me feel warm all over.

I keep my legs wrapped around him while he stays buried inside me, grinding his hips into mine like he'll never be satisfied. I feel his cum slide out of me and between my cheeks as he pumps in and out steadily, getting me worked up again. Eventually, he pulls out, and I barely register what happens when he scoops me up and lays me down on my back on a blanket next to the fireplace.

He kisses my lips softly and tastes me for what feels like forever, sucking and nipping my mouth until my lips are sore. He kisses his way down my body until his head is buried between my legs, feasting on me while I cry. I look down at his shiny black hair and massage his head while he pleases me, wanting him to feel just as loved as he makes me feel. He moans against my clit while I do so, making me grind against his face while he holds me down.

Usually, we're both a lot more vocal during sex, but we're so in sync that there's no need right now. The flames from the fire keep my upper body warm while his mouth comforts my lower half, and after I come on his tongue, he gives me wet kisses all over my thighs and calves before he flips me over on my stomach.

He can't get enough and I can't either. Knowing exactly what he wants, I get on my hands and knees and look over my shoulder into his dark eyes. He smirks at me before he grabs my hips and lines himself up. I slide my ass back, and he buries himself into my pussy, rocking his hips steadily while he fucks me. We moan and grunt together, and he softly presses my face down into the floor so he can go deeper and harder.

The sound of my soaking wet pussy fills the room along with the sounds of the crackling fire. In minutes, he's emptying himself in me once again while I tremble around his dick.

When he eventually pulls out, he lies down on his back and pulls me into his arms, stroking my shoulders, breasts, and stomach, telling me how beautiful, sexy, and perfect I am. At some point, I fall asleep as I wake up to him handing me one of his shirts and telling me it's time to pump and feed our baby while he gets dinner started.

Standing up on shaky legs, I complete my motherly tasks and carry Zahara to the kitchen while James puts something into the oven and cooks food on the stove. When he spots me in his white button-down, he comes up to me and gives me a kiss and kisses Zahara on her head too.

My eyes focus on his sweats that hang off his hips while he grabs glasses out of the cabinets. "Are you hungry?"

My stomach rumbles, making Zahara giggle. "I'm starved." I bounce her gently, and he opens up a bottle of white wine. I start to feel sick when he pours it in two glasses and the smell hits my nostrils. "I can't have any. I'm still not feeling one hundred percent."

He frowns and tosses the booze into the sink. "I won't have any either then."

I feel at peace looking around the cozy kitchen and start thinking of all the photos and decorations I want to bring from our main house to display here.

James takes whatever he was making on the stove and puts it in the oven. "I need to talk to you about my meeting this morning." His expression is neutral which makes me nervous, and my heart drops.

Today has been such an amazing day, and I don't want it to end. He comes up to me, leaning over the island while he takes one of my hands. "I have to go for a few days, and I have to leave in the morning."

"What do you mean?"

He tells me everything that happened in the meeting, and I'm excited and horrified. "It's only for three days, and when I get home, we'll go away and do something fun."

I take deep breaths to try and remain calm. "Will I be able to contact you?"

"Yes. I might be delayed responding, but if you need me, you will be able to reach me. I promise."

I rub Zahara's back softly to soothe myself. "What are they going to do to you?"

He frowns. "I don't know. But I'll be alright. Don't worry."

I feel myself frown. "I don't want you to go, James. Don't leave us."

He squeezes my hand. "I'm not leaving you guys. I'm coming back home as soon as I can. I swear."

He comes behind me and rubs my shoulders while I cry. "Do you trust me, Gen?"

I sniffle and look up at him. "You know I do."

He grabs my chin. "Then trust that I know what I'm doing. That in a few days, we will be done with this society and its nonsense forever."

I stare into his eyes, and I know what he's telling me is true. I hate that he's leaving, and I don't know what I'm going to do for three days without him, but I feel in my core that everything will be alright.

I wrap an arm around his waist and press my cheek against him. "Okay. I trust you."

Chapter Thirty-Four

JAMES

I wake up early to head to the perfume factory for my trip. It takes me a few minutes to get dressed in my classic attire, and I pack a bag of things I'll need for my stay. The last thing I want to do is leave my girls this morning. When I last fed Zee, I spent an hour holding her afterward not because she couldn't sleep but because I wanted to. My baby girl is still so small and I feel like a bad father for leaving her. I'm so used to seeing her pretty little mismatched eyes staring back at me all day. I don't know how I'm going to survive without her.

And Gen. When I wasn't feeding our baby and snuggling her, I had my arms wrapped around my gorgeous wife. And when my arms weren't wrapped around her, they were pinning her down by her wrists while I was balls-deep in her cunt. It's fair to say that neither one of us really slept last night, but it was worth it.

I don't know what I'm going to do without her for three days. I honestly might have a nervous breakdown. I literally feel weak when I'm away from her. She's my life source.

While I normally try not to wake my girls, I have to do so this morning. There's no way in hell I'm leaving them for seventy-two hours without their hugs and kisses.

I know Gen needs me more, so I start with my little girl because I know our interaction will be quicker. As soon as Zee's little eyes spot me, she wiggles like a worm, and I scoop up my little tot and squeeze her as much as her little body allows. I have to whisper softly to her to quiet her down so she doesn't wake Gen with her giggles. After ten minutes of giving her kisses and tickling her tummy, I put her back down and wake my favorite girl.

"Gen, baby, wake up." I stroke her bare shoulder softly as she slowly opens her tired eyes.

Immediately remembering what I have to go do, she starts to cry, and I pull her up and into my lap while I hold her, keeping the blanket wrapped around her so she stays warm.

She chokes out her words while she clings to me. "I don't want you to go."

Squeezing her as tight as I can, I bury my face into her neck. "I don't want to go. But it's only for three days. I will be back before you know it."

I hold her until she stops crying, and when she does, I spend twenty minutes kissing and touching her until I'm hovering over her in just my dress pants, and I have to end the moment to get my clothes back on.

Caressing her cheeks while she lies on her back, I kiss her lips one more time before I head off. "I love you so much. I will call you when I can."

She bites her lip, trying not to cry. "I love you too."

###

When I show up to the perfume factory, I'm greeted by Michael who holds open the door to a black limo. The driver steps out and tosses my suitcase in the back.

Michael gestures me in the car, and I step inside.

My eyes focus on the bottle of champagne in a bucket of ice, and I use every ounce of energy I have to not roll my eyes. "What did I do to deserve such special treatment?"

Michael pours two glasses and hands me one. "Nothing. This is all for me. You just get to enjoy it too." He chuckles and tosses back his drink like it's water.

I hand mine back to him. "No, thanks."

He takes my glass and sips it slowly. "You don't drink?"

I think back to the night before with Gen where she didn't get to enjoy the expensive bubbles I bought her. "Not without my wife, I don't."

He smirks. "You don't make many decisions without your wife, do you James?"

"No. I don't."

He pauses. "Do you want to go home and get them? We can bring them with us."

My mind instantly goes to Gen and Zahara, and I know without a doubt she'd want to come too. But I don't know who is going to be on this trip or what they have planned, and I'll be damned if I put my wife and baby in harm's way. I would rather fall on a sword.

I come up with a half-truth, not wanting to offend the bastard any more than I already have. "I can't. Genevieve hasn't been feeling well the past few days."

He frowns. "Oh, that's a shame. I hope she recovers quickly." His tone is so genuine that I almost forget he's forcing me to be here against my will.

"Thanks."

We ride the rest of the way in silence until we get to a private jet. When we step out, Michael answers my question before I can even ask it. "Colorado. I have a house there. It's where we'll be staying the next few days until you go back home."

I silently step into the black jet and get cozy in a seat across from Michael. "So, this is my challenge then? Luxury in the mountains for three days?"

He pulls out his phone and scrolls. "It can if you want it to be."

If I want it to be. Basically insinuating that this trip will probably be more than just a luxury getaway in the mountains.

We spend another journey in silence. Instead of scrolling on my phone, I conserve my power as I realized I left my power cord in my suitcase which is out of my reach. After five hours, we land, and the first thing I do is text Gen where I am.

Part of me expects Michael to lunge over and grab my phone or for some large men to try and handcuff me and lock me away, but none of that happens. Which makes me even more concerned than I already was. This feels too *easy*. Far more simple than it should be.

I follow him up to a massive mansion that reminds me of the one Genevieve and I used to live in. She really would love it here.

The driver carries my bag into the house, and when I step in, I try and take in all of my surroundings at once. But before I can, Michael holds out his hands. "I need your weapons, James."

Just like I thought. This seemed too easy. I'm not surprised he wants my weapons, but does he really expect me to just give them over?

I tuck my hands in my pockets. "No thanks. I'll pass."

He frowns. "It wasn't a question, James."

"Listen here—"

I hear a click, and I whip my head around to see the driver, the fucking driver, has a gun trained on me.

"You will give me your weapons, now, or my staff will be mopping you up off the floor later."

Patting my pants to make sure I didn't piss myself, I take out my guns and hand them to Michael.

He grits his teeth. "I want that pretty knife too."

My knife. He wants me to hand over my knife. The knife I've had for over ten years. I've never let anyone else hold this knife apart from my wife. It's fucking sacred.

I place my hand over it, gripping it tightly.

Michael stomps his foot. "Give me the goddamn knife, James!"

Fuck. I pry my blade out of my hands and hand it to the evil man before me.

He smiles tightly. "Good. That wasn't so hard, was it?"

I grit my teeth. "Not at all."

He curls his lips upward, showing off his obnoxious veneers. "I'm glad to hear it. You'll be meeting with my family for dinner. We don't allow weapons at the table. You may enjoy your room until then."

Out of nowhere, a butler enters the room, his shoes clacking on the marble floors. "This way, sir."

He grabs my bag from the driver, and I follow behind him.

We go up to the second level, and my eyes try and take in all of the fruit paintings on the walls while I drag my feet on the long Persian rug that covers the wood floor. At the end of the hall is my room. It's a massive room with a king bed, a walk-in closet, and a full bath. There's even a mini fridge with snacks. I get so caught up in looking at everything that I don't even realize the butler leaving. All I know is I hear the door close, and when I turn around and go up to it, it's locked.

Chapter Thirty-Five

GENEVIEVE

As soon as James left the cabin this morning, I ran to the bathroom and vomited. I knew him going on this trip would stress me out, but I didn't realize how much.

Once I got myself off the toilet, I cleaned up, fed our baby, and called Draco to see how Odette was doing. She's fine and we can bring her home soon, but I haven't been to visit her as James doesn't want me to leave while he's gone. Draco offered to come over and hang out, but I very quickly declined. Not only am I not comfortable with that idea, but I know James wouldn't be either, and I'd rather my husband not kill his cousin if he doesn't have to.

I don't know what's come over me, but everything disgusts me right now. I took a quick shower and tried to put on some perfume, and I got sick all over again. Part of me is worried I caught a bug. The last thing I need is to get Zahara sick. I know James is feeling fine, so I don't know what's wrong. Part of me wants to call him and talk to him, but I don't want to bother him if I don't really need anything, so I lie down on the bed with our daughter while I wait for him to reach out to me.

My phone chimes, and I open it immediately, hoping it's who I think it is. I can't hide my smile when I look down and see it's from my husband.

> How are you?

> Good. You?

> Could be better. I'm locked in a room.

Locked in a room? I sit up, and my head throbs at the quick rush of blood.

> What do you mean????

I read through his thread of texts informing me that he's locked in his guest room until dinner without his weapons. It hasn't even been a full twenty-four hours, and

I already don't like the way this is going. When I take too long to respond to his messages, he calls me, and I pick up the phone while hovering over the toilet.

"Hey."

He groans. "Jesus, Gen. I thought something happened to you."

I lurch into the toilet and hold the phone away.

His voice goes up an octave. "What's going on?"

"I'm throwing up."

He pauses. "Do you need to see a doctor?"

My stomach gurgles. "No. I'm fine. I swear."

Cursing under his breath, he sighs. "If you're still sick tomorrow, I'm calling Meredith."

Not wanting to argue, I agree. "Fine."

I hear him rustle on the other line. "I'm being summoned for dinner. I'll call you before bed."

"Okay. I love you."

"I love you too."

Chapter Thirty-Six

JAMES

Christ. I haven't even been gone for a day, and I already regret leaving. My girls need me, just like I knew they would.

I can't believe Gen is sick. We've been eating all the same shit. That doesn't make any sense. Unless . . .

I can't even say it out loud. And I certainly won't suggest it to her as a possibility unless she brings it up first. I'm even more eager to call Meredith now and just as desperate to get home. But it's only day one of my trip, and I need to make it through all three.

The butler, Dan, summoned me for dinner ten minutes ago. Fortunately, I'm dressed for the occasion, but I'm having a hard time leaving my room as I have no appetite. I'm also uncomfortable having dinner with a group of strangers without my weapons. Like, who would go to dinner with strangers without weapons?

Dan knocks on my door again, and I know they're waiting for me. Not wanting to drag this out any longer, I pocket my phone and head out to the hall to go downstairs.

When I make it down, all the lights are out, and I hear chattering. I see a soft glow coming from the back of the house, and I follow it cautiously, prepared for a jump scare.

Stepping out into the cool night, I spot Michael at a table with four other guests, all around a circular table with a fire pit in the middle. Not wanting to freeze my nuts off, I go up to it and take my empty seat amongst the strangers.

Michael greets me first. "Hello, James. Did you settle in alright?"

I take a look at the four other individuals staring back at me with blank expressions and decide not to bring up the fact that I was locked in my room. "Yes. Thank you."

Michael sips a glass of wine. "The individuals you see here are my family. With my other council members gone, I've had to bring in some help, and unfortunately, I've been demoted." He laughs loudly.

The woman across from me wearing a white sweater dress takes off her black glasses. She looks nearly identical to how Annabelle did. "My name is Lilith. I'll be taking over the fashion sector."

The man with black hair next to her kisses her cheek and straightens out his burgundy blazer. "I'm Jake. I'm Lilith's husband, and I'll be running meat."

The man to his right scowls. His black eyes match his black suit. "I'm Evan. I'll be taking over everything ran by Eric Sharpe."

The man seated beside me puts his hand on my shoulder and I flinch. He's wearing a white suit that matches his white hair. "I'm Bill. My father was the first sector leader appointed by your great-grandfather. I'm also Michael's father."

I stare at the strangers staring back at me, unsure of what the purpose of this meeting is. "I'm sure you're all aware that I'm James Barlow."

The table erupts in laughter as if I told a joke. The fire keeps me warm under the dropping temperature.

Bill sips his beer. "Would you like something to drink?"

The last thing I want to do is have a beverage from this home, but I'm parched, and I won't survive for three days if I die of thirst. "I'll have a water, please."

A server brings me a chilled water bottle, and I tell myself it hasn't been tampered with as I open it up and bring the liquid to my lips.

Bill snaps his fingers, and the waiter returns with a menu. Michael smiles at me. "What would you like for dinner, James?"

I stare at the menu of two options of five-course meals. One features steak, and the other features chicken. What I'd really prefer is some pizza. "I'm not sure."

Bill leans over, dragging his finger over the page. "Let me help you decide. The first option is more filling. It's rich, heavy, and will leave you feeling satisfied."

I see Jake and Lilith smile at me.

Bill frowns. "But the other option, it's not as good. Not as rich or filling. It'll leave you wanting more."

I sit there for a moment, trying to will myself to decide between steak or chicken, and I have an overwhelming feeling that my choice carries more weight than it seems.

Steak. That's what everyone else seems to be having, and it seems like the choice I'm being pushed to make.

But I hate being like everybody else. "I'll choose chicken."

The corner of Bill's mouth lifts. "Are you sure?"

I glance at Lilith who frowns. Jake looks down. Evan looks like he wants to stab me. And Michael glares.

Staring back at Bill, I put on my best fake smile. "I love chicken. I don't eat steak anymore."

Bill nods his head. "I see. Chicken it is. The kitchen will have it ready for you right away."

The next forty-five minutes become a blur. Everyone tells me things about themselves that I could care less about, and eventually, dinner arrives. I check my phone to see if Gen's reached out, and it comforts me that she hasn't as I know she's alright.

I'm halfway through my dry-ass chicken when I suddenly feel like I'm overheating. I need to go splash some cold water on my face or something. Standing up, I look down at my new associates for the next couple of days. "Is there a bathroom on this level?"

Bill grins. "Welcome to hell."

What the fuck?

I blink my eyes as Bill turns into two people and then turns back into one. Oh no.

I don't get another word out before the world goes black and I feel myself falling.

#

When I wake up, I have no idea what time it is. I'm back in my guest room, and the door is closed. My head pounds every time I blink my eyes, and the bright light from the chandelier makes them burn.

I'm fucked. I see a figure moving out of the corner of my eye, and when I finally focus, I see it's Bill. I try to move my arms, but I'm restrained to the bed like I'm in the psych ward.

Bill paces around the room. "James, you have brought so much shame and embarrassment to The Wild White Orchids. Things will never be the same. And I don't want to let you go. So I'm going to give you a day to think about your decision. Today was day one. Tomorrow, you will remain in here where you can decide if this is what you really want. And if you want to stay, we'll take you back. But if you really want to leave, we'll prepare for your exit the day after."

Gen. I need my wife. I need my daughter. I need to get home.

I open my mouth and cough, trying to fight through the dryness of my throat to speak. "I need to speak to my wife."

He shakes his head. "No. I need you focused, James. You can speak to her in two days when you get home."

I start to really panic. What if Gen needs me? I told her I'd be available. "I need to speak to her. I promised her that she could reach me if she needed me."

He nods his head. "And she can. I had Lilith call her. She's fine. She has Lilith's number, and if she needs you, we'll let you know."

I take deep breaths to prevent myself from shattering. "My wife. I swear if you do anything to my wife or daughter, I will skin you alive."

Bill grins. "I'm sure of it. See you soon, James."

Without another word, he exits the room and turns off the lights, leaving me in total darkness.

I doze in and out of sleep for hours on end. I have nightmares of my family being tortured and my mother being stabbed to death. I wake up and smell piss and have to face the painful realization that it's mine.

I feel nauseous and start to gag, and then I fall back asleep.

When I wake up again, it's because of the butler who peeks in the door. "Genevieve called. Her doctor is going to see her today."

I don't even get my mouth open before he shuts the door, and I'm left in solitude. The room gets darker as the day goes on, and I realize I'm entering my last night in this prison. I don't sleep the entire time and stare at the ceiling.

Eventually, light filters in the room again, and someone comes in the door.

At first glance, I think it's Bill, but it's Michael. He drags something on a metal cart. "Today's the day, James. What have you decided?"

I open my mouth, and words don't come out. Michael brings a small water bottle to my lips and pours slowly.

I choke out my words with a sore throat. "I—I'm going home."

He nods his head. "Yes. You're leaving us today. But will you go home as ours, or as a nobody?"

I cough again, trying to catch my breath. "I'll never be yours, you stupid bitch."

Bill and the rest of the people I met at dinner last night step into the room.

Bill nods to Michael. "Let the exit begin."

I'm staring up at the ceiling when I stop breathing. A cloth is placed over my face, and I'm drenched in ice water. When the flood stops, I suck in a breath, only to be met by more of the same.

I don't know how long it goes on for. All I know is I start to feel like I'm fading, and then the cloth is removed, letting me come up for air.

My entire body shakes, and my wrists and ankles have been rubbed raw from pulling at my restraints for hours on end.

Someone unties me, and I'm hoisted off the bed by Jake and Evan. They drag me down the stairs, and I start to vomit as we go down them.

They drag me through the first level of the house into a bright white room where I'm sat on a stool. Someone tosses a pair of gray twill pants at me, and I'm instructed to change as they all leave the room.

I step off my seat with my legs trembling while I peel off my disgustingly soiled blazer, shirt, pants, underwear, and shoes. There's a mirror on the wall across from me, but I refuse to look at it, horrified of seeing myself in the state I'm in.

Once I have on my new attire, I sit back on the seat before I collapse. I'm fucking starving, and I need a bath.

The men reenter the room, and Michel plugs a pair of clippers into the wall while Bill discards my clothes. I don't even register what's happening before he starts shaving my head.

My hair. They're taking my fucking hair from me. First my clothes, now my hair. I feel like I'm going to have a panic attack. This must be how Jessamine felt when I stripped her of her dignity by taking her hair and making her live with Simon.

I deserve this. I deserve punishment. This punishment isn't punishment enough for the wrongs I've done.

Once my haircut is over, I do look up at myself. I look ridiculous. And dirty and tired. It's sickening.

My baby. My baby's not even going to recognize me. My eyes burn, and I bite my tongue to keep myself together.

I'm hoisted on my feet again, and I'm dragged outside to the fire pit where we had dinner on my first night. One of my dirty socks is shoved in my mouth, and in a blink, someone's sticking a long iron rod into the fire, and then the next minute, I feel my soul leave my body as white-hot heat encompasses me. My right shoulder feels like it's been separated from my body, and when I come to, I realize I've been branded.

I'm not given shoes before I'm taken back out to the front of the house and shoved back on the jet. Michael follows behind me while the rest of the strangers stay in the house.

He pats my buzzed head. "You'll never hear from us again. And you won't speak a word of your experience in the society or in this house to anyone. This was only a taste of the torture you can begin to imagine if you ever betray us."

I'm stuck with a needle, and I blackout again.

#

When I wake, I'm in the back of a cab outside the perfume factory. I check my pockets, and I have my cell phone, but the battery's dead.

The driver calls out to me. "Where to, sir?"

I look out the window and see my rental car is gone. Even if it wasn't, I'm in no state to drive. I muster up enough strength to give him my address, and when I do, he takes off.

I drift off on the ride to the cabin, and I'm woken up by him opening my door. I stand out of the cab and panic when I don't have any fare. He shakes his head. "It's covered, sir. Good day." He gets back in on the driver's side and takes off.

I stand in front of my cabin, and I have to pinch myself to make sure that I'm awake.

I'm free. I'm home and I'm fucking free.

My heart pounds as I step through the leaves and up to the front door. I hope Gen's alright. I hope she doesn't hate me. I hope my baby hugs me.

I dig in my pocket again and find my keys. I try to unlock the front door, but I'm shaking so badly that I can't. I bang on the door, feeling like I might collapse if I don't sit down. My shoulder stings, and I'm in the worst pain I've ever been in.

The door opens, and my wife stands before me in a black cropped tee and black sweatpants with a gun in her hand. She does a double take, and when she focuses her eyes on mine, she sets her weapon to the side on the entryway table.

"James?"

My eyes water, and I lean against the door. "Hi, sweetheart."

She bursts into tears, wrapping her arms around me. "Oh my God. James. I thought—I thought—"

I wrap my arms around her delicate body. "Don't say it."

She pulls away and cups my face, and my tears spill over. She takes my hand and pulls me into the house while I cry, and she pulls me upstairs and into the bathroom.

I sit on the bench by the bathtub, unable to stand anymore. Gen asks me to tell her what happened, and I lean against her chest while she stands, wrapping her arms around me.

"I need to bathe. And eat."

She steps away and exits the room, and when she returns, she's naked and helping me undress to step into the shower.

Gen washes me quickly and tenderly, and I hear her gasp and start to cry when she sees my shoulder. I haven't even had a chance to look at it, and it's the least of my concerns. I'm just so happy to be home.

Once we get out, she helps me dress and puts me in the bed. Twenty minutes later, I'm eating soup and a sandwich she made me, and when I'm finished, she strokes my head until I fall asleep.

Chapter Thirty-Seven
GENEVIEVE

I sit in bed holding Zahara while James sleeps. I've been going crazy the past few days without him. I got a call from that weird Lilith lady, and I had the worst fear that I'd never see James again.

I woke up the day after he left vomiting over and over, and I knew I needed to see Meredith. She came over, and I learned something that I was completely surprised by but that makes sense.

I'm pregnant.

I nearly had a breakdown when I realized I almost had wine the other night, and then I started to panic when I thought I'd have to raise our babies on my own. Then

Draco told me they were moving Odette into the ICU, and everything became too much.

Then Odette was moved out of the ICU and I started to calm down, and before I knew it, James was at our front door.

He woke up an hour ago and told me what happened, and I couldn't believe they treated him the way they did. I never want him out of my sight again.

He stirs next to me, and I rub his shaved head, shocked at how different he looks. He's still as handsome as he's always been, and I love the velvety feel of his head under my hand.

I lean down and kiss his cheek. "Hi, baby."

His eyes water, and he looks up at me. "Hi, Gen."

I wipe away the tear that falls from his eyes. I can't believe I'm seeing him cry again. He tries to sit up, but I keep him on his back and lay Zahara on his chest.

She snuggles up to him like he never left, and he strokes her head with one hand while he squeezes my hand with his other.

"I came back, Genevieve."

I feel myself smile. "I know. And you're never leaving me again."

He chuckles and winces. "I wouldn't dare."

There's probably a far better time to tell him this, but I can't wait any longer. Lying down beside him, I rest my hand on his bicep and press my lips to his ear. "I have some news to share with you."

He sighs. "Please for the love of God, don't tell me something happened to Mom."

"No. She's fine. This is news about me."

He turns his head to face me. "What about you?"

I squeeze his arm and take a breath. "I'm pregnant."

He clutches Zahara while he sobs, and I kiss him softly while he squeezes my fingers.

"I'm so fucking happy. I knew you were."

I wipe my tears that are falling. "How?"

He presses his forehead up against mine. "My soul is intertwined with yours. I could feel it."

GENEVIEVE

Six Months Later

I sit on the bed while James rubs my feet. Zahara is staying with Odette at her house tonight, so James and I are home alone.

Normally I don't like having Zahara away from us, but since Odette lives down the street, I'm not too worried.

After she got home from the hospital from her injury, she stayed with us for a few months until she decided she wanted a fresh start too. The houses that everyone lives in belong to the Barlow and Burke families collectively, so James divvied up the homes, and outside of our new house and the cabin, we only kept our old house that Paul lives in currently.

The society still exists and it still has the same name, but it's already changed drastically since we left. I've gotten my news from Mai and Ella, but apparently, Bill is the current Head Father and things are a lot more strict. A few of the tenets have been amended and joining is now voluntary, but there's still some harsh form of punishment for breaking the rules.

What surprises me most is that no one's requested to leave yet. It's like they're all fine with being trapped. But I have far more important things to worry about like my belly that's twice as big as it was when I was pregnant with Zahara.

James slowly inches his hands higher up my legs. "Do you think the twins will want to share a room?"

I rub my stomach as I wonder how I'm going to handle two newborns at once. "I'm sure the girls will want to share a room when they're younger, but when they get older they'll probably want their own space."

He grips my ankles and pulls my legs apart. "I love being a girl Dad. Do you think we'll ever have any boys?"

I try and shut my legs. "I don't know, but I need to give birth to these two before you try and put any more in me."

He keeps my legs open while a lock of black hair falls between his eyes. "I know. I just want to practice."

His fingers dig into my thighs while he tickles me, and I try to squirm away from him while my cheeks hurt from laughing. "I don't think we need practice. We seem to know what we're doing."

He stands up off the bed and pulls off his white shorts and shirt, standing in his black underwear. "I need you."

My pussy twitches. "And I need sleep. I'm tired."

He frowns. "You can sleep later."

I pull my curls into a bun. "Or I could sleep now."

He shakes his head. "You told me I could have whatever I wanted for my birthday."

I explode with laughter. "Your birthday was last month, James!"

He smirks and runs a hand through his hair. "So?"

I let my eyes wander over his chiseled body, toned arms, and firm legs. Even though I'm exhausted, I still want him. "Fine. But make it quick."

He grins and strips off the last bit of fabric attached to his body and lies down beside me. "I want you on top."

A groan escapes me. "James."

"Gen."

"James Barlow, no. I want you to be in control."

He leans over, helping me peel off my tank top. "Okay. I'll be in control. Either you get over here and ride me, or you'll get on your knees and do whatever I say."

"But I'm pregnant!"

He raises a brow. "I'm well aware. What do you pick?"

I slide out of my cotton panties and climb on top of him. "I'll ride."

Holding my hips steady, he helps me slide onto him. "Good girl."

As soon as he's fully sheathed within me, I moan loudly at how good he feels. He smiles while he moves his hips under me, doing all the work. "See? You get to just sit here and look pretty."

I rest my hands on his chest while my thighs rub his sides. "That's my favorite thing to do lately."

He shows me his big, beautiful smile while he fucks me slowly and sweetly. I start to bounce a little when I feel myself getting closer.

James' breath and pace pick up. "That's my girl. Use Daddy's cock until you come."

I move my hips in circles, using him to make myself feel good while he uses one hand to play with my nipples and the other to rub my clit.

My body starts to slump as I feel myself getting tired.

James smacks my tits, jolting me awake. "Don't give up. Be a good girl and make Daddy proud."

His words give me all the encouragement I need, and before I know it, I'm rushing over and coming all around him.

He rolls me on my back and spills into me, bucking his hips until he's given me everything. When he slides out, he pulls me into his arms and kisses my lips softly, extending my euphoric feeling. "Maybe next time we'll have triplets."

My euphoria is quickly disrupted by anxiety, and one of the girls kicks inside me. I kiss his neck while I nuzzle into his shoulder. "If we do, maybe you can give birth to them."

JAMES

Five Years Later

I sit on the couch in the den while Gen rests her head on my lap sleeping. I get déjà vu looking at all of our close friends and family running around our house. Zahara plays tag with Theo and the twins, Zuri and Zenobia, while Paul, Zahara's godfather, supervises.

I can't believe how big my girls are already.

I can't believe I'm going to be forty next year.

Zahara's black curls are long and fluffy like Gen's, and her one brown and one blue eye make me melt every time I look at her. She's just as attached to Gen as she is to me, and she always wants to be up under us.

Zuri, also known as Zuzu, has Gen's blue eyes and is my shadow. Zenobia, or Zen, has hazel eyes and is Gen's little stalker. They both have dark brown hair like their mom and straight hair like me, and they have Gen's nose and my smile.

My mother holds Zoey, or Zo Bear, who is our youngest girl, and she's almost two years old. She's got brown eyes and curly brown hair, and she's just a little doll.

And due to another early birth, we're having another post-birth baby shower for Zack who was born three months ago and is held by Ella. He has my mother's green eyes, and all the girls have tan skin, but Zack has blonde hair and pale skin.

Zahara gets tired and ends the game of tag, and the twins run up to me while Zahara runs to the kitchen dragging Paul and Theo behind her. Zahara and Theo have been having play dates every month since they met, and they stick to each other like glue.

The girls grab onto their mother, and I shoo them away while she wakes up. She hasn't had PPD since her first pregnancy, but she's had the hardest physical recovery with Zack and is just starting to feel like herself again.

She pulls Zuzu into her lap and I take Zen, and her smile makes my heart beat faster. She may be thirty-seven, but she still looks as young and beautiful as she did the first day I met her.

"Hi, baby." She kisses my lips, and the girls howl, "Ew!"

I usher them away to go bother someone else so I can pull Gen into my lap. Her white babydoll dress brushes against my legs in my khaki shorts, and all I want to do is run away from our party and take her to the lake where we had our first date.

I play with her soft curls, twirling them around my fingers while she presses her warm cheek against mine and glances around the room, looking at all of our kids. Her eyes focus on Zack, and I slide my hand up her thigh, pulling her on top of my erection. "Do you want another?"

Her eyes go wide. "I don't know if I can. I thought we said we were stopping after five."

I'm constantly amazed at how incredible of a mother my Gen is. She's always available for everyone's needs including my own, and she always puts herself last which is why I'll never stop putting her first. The kids go crazy when they're away from their mother, and I do too. She makes all of us whole.

After we left the society, I was able to fully immerse myself in managing the farm, and Gen has helped me manage the business side of things while I do most of the manual labor with our employees. I've been able to take some of her responsibilities off of her recently which has given her time to focus on Precious Peonies, the kidswear brand that she's working on with Mom. Most of the clothes the girls wear were created by my mother and Gen, and I'm so grateful to witness and experience their incredible talent. I hope my girls grow up to be just like them.

I rub circles on the inside of Gen's leg while she grazes my calves with her white stiletto heels. "We did say that. But maybe there's room for one more."

She gasps, and her shuddery breath makes my dick twitch. "I don't know. I think we've got our hands full."

I slide my hands up her body, gripping her slender waist. "We do. But if we had one more, they'd all have a buddy." I squeeze her sides, and she squeals, drawing attention to us.

My mother winks and glances over at her new boyfriend, Richard. I'm not a fan of the bald geezer, but he makes my mother happy, so I'm sure I'll get used to him eventually. Mai and Ella whisper quietly while they point at us, and Paul cleans up the juice that the kids spilled all over the kitchen floor.

Looking around, I can't believe that so many people in the world care about me. That I have a home and a job people dream of. That I have the most amazing and gorgeous wife in the world and a bunch of little kids that I adore. I never knew my heart could grow so much, and I love my family more than I could ever explain.

I have no idea what I did to deserve redemption. A second chance at life. But I've realized over the years that this life is worth living, and I'll never take that for granted ever again.

Playlist:

Intentions – Justin Bieber (feat. Quavo)
FUBT - HAIM
Dress - Taylor Swift
How Long - Ellie Goulding
I Would Like - Zara Larsson
Smoke Signals - Phoebe Bridgers
Dream - Bishop Briggs
Water - Bishop Briggs
Best Friend - Conan Gray
I Bruise Easily - Natasha Bedingfield
saftey net – Ariana Grande feat. Ty Dolla $ign
Hrs & Hrs [Remix] – Muni Long feat. Usher
Versace On The Floor – Bruno Mars
Lucky Ones - Lana del Rey